BECOMING
THE
BOOGEYMAN

BECOMING THE BOOGEYMAN

A Novel

RICHARD CHIZMAR

Gallery Books

New York   London   Toronto   Sydney   New Delhi

G

Gallery Books
An Imprint of Simon & Schuster, Inc.
1230 Avenue of the Americas
New York, NY 10020

First Gallery Books hardcover edition October 2023

GALLERY BOOKS and colophon are registered trademarks of Simon & Schuster, Inc.

For information about special discounts for bulk purchases, please contact Simon & Schuster Special Sales at 1-866-506-1949 or business@simonandschuster.com.

The Simon & Schuster Speakers Bureau can bring authors to your live event. For more information or to book an event, contact the Simon & Schuster Speakers Bureau at 1-866-248-3049 or visit our website at www.simonspeakers.com.

Interior design by Erika R. Genova

Manufactured in the United States of America

10 9 8 7 6 5 4 3 2 1

Library of Congress Cataloging-in-Publication Data has been applied for.

ISBN 978-1-6680-0916-1
ISBN 978-1-6680-0918-5 (ebook)

For Billy and Noah

a note to readers

Becoming the Boogeyman is a work of fiction, continuing the homage to my hometown and my ongoing passion for true crime. As with my previous book (*Chasing the Boogeyman*), there are slices of life depicted throughout that are very much inspired by my personal history, but other events and real people and places and media outlets / social media platforms / publications are used fictitiously, and to provide verisimilitude to this crime novel. Other names, characters, settings, and events come directly from my imagination, which remains at times a rather unsettling landscape.

contents

Contents

BECOMING
THE
BOOGEYMAN

BEFORE

The Baltimore Sun (June 3, 1988)

EDGEWOOD GIRL FOUND MURDERED

Shortly after 10 a.m. on Thursday, June 2, members of the Harford County Sheriff's Department discovered the body of 15-year-old Natasha Gallagher in the woods behind her house on Hawthorne Drive.

The teenager was reported missing earlier that morning by her mother, Catherine Gallagher, after she found the girl's bedroom window open, a broken screen on the ground below, and what looked like a smear of blood on the windowsill . . .

———

Harford County Aegis (June 23, 1988)

TWO EDGEWOOD GIRLS DEAD— WAS IT THE BOOGEYMAN?

Just before midnight on Monday, June 20, local police discovered the body of 15-year-old Kacey Robinson at the playground of the Cedar Drive Elementary School. She had been beaten and strangled.

Robinson had disappeared from the vicinity of her home on Cherry Road at approximately 9 p.m. the night before. After a brief search, her father, Bob Robinson, located one of his daughter's tennis shoes in the middle of the street and immediately called 911 . . .

———

Channel 2 News transcript (June 25, 1988)

REPORTER: We're back with Evelyn Robinson, the very brave mother of Kacey Robinson, talking about the "Boogeyman," which is what the local and national media are calling this phantomlike stalker. It's my understanding that the nickname first appeared in a police report filed several weeks before Kacey's disappearance, and that your youngest daughter, Janie, is responsible.

EVELYN ROBINSON: Yes, that's right.

REPORTER: And how old is Janie?

EVELYN ROBINSON: She's seven.

REPORTER: So, walk us through the events. Late one night in May, Janie wakes you up. Can you tell us what happened next?

EVELYN ROBINSON: She came into our room and told me and my husband that the Boogeyman was trying to get into her window and could she please sleep the rest of the night with us.

REPORTER: And how did you respond?

EVELYN ROBINSON: We told her there was no such thing as the Boogeyman and that it was just another nightmare, but she was so upset that we agreed to make an exception just this one time. The next morning, she was back to her normal self, so I didn't think about it again . . . until I heard the news about Natasha Gallagher.

REPORTER: What did you do then?

EVELYN ROBINSON: My husband called the police and told them the whole story. They came out to the house and searched the yard and took fingerprints. But they didn't find anything and told us that most likely we'd been right the first time—that our daughter had probably just had a bad dream.

REPORTER: Did you believe them?

EVELYN ROBINSON: I honestly didn't know what to believe. I still don't. I mean, what if all of us are wrong—and Janie's right? What if someone really did try to break into her window that night?

What if there really is a Boogeyman . . . and he came back and got Kacey?

A Current Affair transcript (August 15, 1988)

MAURY POVICH: Edgewood, Maryland. A small, peaceful working-class town nestled on the shores of the Chesapeake Bay. Little League baseball parades and Fourth of July carnivals. The kind of place where people don't bother to lock their doors at night. [in a deeper voice] Edgewood, Maryland . . . a close-knit community now held hostage in a death grip of terror and paranoia. Three young girls. Savagely beaten and murdered. The killer has been christened the "Boogeyman" because of his ability to strike close to home and vanish without a trace. As one frustrated lawman lamented soon after the discovery of the latest victim: "It's like the guy sliced open a hole in the night and disappeared back into it."

Madeline Wilcox was eighteen years old. Beautiful. Kind. A bright future ahead of her. Her nude body was found under a bridge on Friday morning, August 12, by local fishermen. She'd been brutally beaten, sexually assaulted, and strangled. There were bite marks on her torso, as well as ligature marks on her wrists and ankles. The killer took his time—and tortured her.

I'm here this evening with FBI profiler Robert Neville—a man who has witnessed this type of grisly aftermath before. Welcome, Robert.

ROBERT NEVILLE: Thank you, Maury. I wish I was here under different circumstances.

MAURY POVICH: Three young girls murdered within a period of ten weeks. What can you tell us about the madman who is prowling the dark streets of Edgewood?

ROBERT NEVILLE: We believe he's in his mid to late twenties or thirties. A white male. Likely single or divorced. Average or slightly higher than average intelligence. Good physical condition. He's either unemployed or has a job that allows him to move around freely at night.

MAURY POVICH: And he has a very distinct M.O.

ROBERT NEVILLE: He does, indeed. The victims are young, attractive, popular. They all have long hair. The wounds left on their bodies are nearly identical. Facial injuries. Bite marks. Strangulation. He severed each of the girls' left ears and took them with him. The last two girls were sexually assaulted before they were killed, signifying an acceleration of violence. When he's finished, he poses the bodies.

MAURY POVICH: The murders possess an almost Grand Guignol sense of exhibition, as if the killer views himself as some kind of a performance artist. Do you think this is intentional?

ROBERT NEVILLE: Oh, most certainly. Look at the locations and the manner in which he poses the bodies. He *wants* them to be discovered. He *wants* an audience for his handiwork. Something else interesting, Maury . . . I've recently learned that the killer has left behind cryptic "messages" for the police after each murder. Telltales, of a sort. I have no idea as to what they are, but this pattern demonstrates . . .

Channel 11 News transcript (September 10, 1988)

NEWS ANCHOR: Johnathon Slate is live at Edgewood High School this morning with breaking news. What can you tell us, Johnathon?

JOHNATHON SLATE: Thanks, Jeff. Neighbors here in the Edgewood Meadows community are on high alert. Yesterday evening at around 7:30 p.m., seventeen-year-old Annie Riggs, a senior at Edgewood High School, was walking home after field hockey practice when she was attacked from behind by what she described as "a large man dressed in dark pants and a dark long-sleeved shirt. He was wearing gloves and a crude mask with the eyeholes cut out." After a brief struggle, the teenager was able to use pepper spray on her attacker and flee to a nearby house to call police.

NEWS ANCHOR: What a courageous young lady. Now, it's my understanding that the mask was left behind at the scene . . .

Maryland State Police report
CID#17-C-9304
November 1, 1988

. . . when I noticed flickering lights coming from the grounds of the Edgewood Memorial Gardens off Trimble Road. I parked and immediately began searching the property. A short time later, I discovered the partially clothed body of a young female with long blonde hair. She was positioned in front of a headstone and surrounded by six still-lit jack-o'-lanterns. She appeared to have been beaten and sexually assaulted. I counted over a dozen bite marks on her chest, torso, and legs. Once I confirmed that the female victim was deceased, I radioed for backup . . .

Harford County Aegis (February 23, 1989)

THE FAMILIES MOURN AND REMEMBER

By Carly Albright and Richard Chizmar

WBAL News Radio 1090 AM / 101.5 FM
(April 3, 1989)

DJ: The task force—headed by Detective Sergeant Lyle Harper and composed of members of the Harford County Sheriff's Department, Maryland State Police, and Federal Bureau of Investigation—promised during last night's press conference to continue pursuing active leads and interviewing additional persons of interest. The tip line remains open.

The murders of Natasha Gallagher, Kacey Robinson, Madeline Wilcox, and Cassidy Burch—all residents of Edgewood—remain unsolved.

Harford County Aegis display advertisement
(April 19, 1990)

CAROL'S BOOKSTORE
Come Meet Hometown Author
RICHARD CHIZMAR
author of
THE BOOGEYMAN: A True Story of Small-Town Evil
Get Your Book SIGNED!

Fangoria (May 1990, Issue #92)
Nightmare Library Reviews
The Boogeyman: A True Story of Small-Town Evil
296 pages
ISBN 1587678820
$19.95
Richard Chizmar, editor and publisher of the fledging horror magazine *Cemetery Dance*, has given us a heart-wrenching and terrifying small-town crime narrative that also delivers a satisfying dose of coming-of-age nostalgia . . .

CNN.com (September 7, 2019)
Laurie Wyatt, CNN—Hanover, Pennsylvania
**BREAKING NEWS—
"THE BOOGEYMAN" IN CUSTODY**

. . . to recap this afternoon's breaking news, members of both the Pennsylvania and Maryland State Police executed a search warrant on a residential home in Hanover, Pennsylvania, and took 54-year-old Joshua Gallagher into custody, charging him with the 1988 murders of four Edgewood, Maryland, teenagers, including his younger sister, Natasha Gallagher.

According to a police spokesperson, Gallagher, a longtime employee of Reuter's Machinery, had been under surveillance for an undisclosed amount of time, while police awaited the results of a DNA test . . .

Interview transcript excerpt—Maryland Penitentiary,
Baltimore, MD (December 5, 2019)

RICHARD CHIZMAR: The media came up with a number of nicknames for you. "The Boogeyman" was the one that stuck. Were you pleased with that name or indifferent?

JOSHUA GALLAGHER: I was pleased. [pause] It seemed to fit, and that was the first time I was able to put a name to the bad thing living inside me.

RICHARD CHIZMAR: You actually began to think of that part of yourself as "the Boogeyman"?

JOSHUA GALLAGHER: I did, yes.

RICHARD CHIZMAR: What do you mean when you say the name seemed to fit?

JOSHUA GALLAGHER: On the nights I hunted, I felt . . . different. I felt powerful. Bold. Invincible. At one with the night around me. As if I could fly and pass through walls and make myself invisible.

RICHARD CHIZMAR: You really believed you could do those things?

JOSHUA GALLAGHER: I could. I did. That's why they never caught me.

————————

Vanity Fair feature article (January 2020)

GROWING UP WITH A KILLER:

THE SAGA OF JOSHUA GALLAGHER
& RICHARD CHIZMAR

. . . and in what has become one of the most talked about stories of 2019, we recently learned that Richard Chizmar is the only journalist that confessed serial killer Joshua Gallagher has agreed to speak with. Chizmar and

Gallagher grew up two blocks away from each other in the small Maryland town of Edgewood and attended the same high school. In the late 1980s, Chizmar, a budding horror author at the time, wrote *The Boogeyman: A True Story of Small-Town Evil*, chronicling Gallagher's five-month reign of terror. Gallagher is mentioned several times in the book, but only as the older brother of the first girl who was killed, Natasha Gallagher. Never as a suspect. *The Boogeyman* was released by regional publisher Eastbrook Press in April 1990 and by all accounts sold only a couple of thousand copies. There was no subsequent paperback edition, and it eventually went out of print in 1995. Suffice to say, Chizmar is staring at a much larger payday this time around.

Publishers Marketplace deal report (November 20, 2020)

CHIZMAR'S "BOOGEYMAN" SPOOKS GALLERY

After an exclusive submission, Gallery Books' Ed Schlesinger preempted Richard Chizmar's true crime memoir *Chasing the Boogeyman*. Kristin Nelson at Nelson Literary Agency handled the North American and open market rights agreement. Nelson said the book, which concerns a string of grisly murders in small town suburbia . . .

Channel 13 News transcript (August 17, 2021)

NEWS ANCHOR: I'm here this morning with Richard Chizmar, author of the much anticipated *Chasing the Boogeyman*, a true crime thriller with heaps of advance buzz, as well as a highly publicized movie deal with Paramount Pictures. Today is release day, and Chizmar will be signing copies this evening at 7 p.m. at the Barnes & Noble in Bel Air. Richard, good morning and welcome. How does it feel to be a hometown hero?

RICHARD CHIZMAR: [laughs] I wouldn't go that far . . . but it's all very exciting. I'm looking forward to hearing what people think of the book and hopefully meeting a lot of new readers.

Goodreads—Community Ratings and Reviews

Chasing the Boogeyman by Richard Chizmar
(Simon & Schuster/Gallery Books)

megs_bookshelf rated it. ☆☆☆☆☆
One of the best true crime books I've ever read. As much about the victims and the promising lives they once led as the unraveling of the mystery behind the killer. Told with an underlying sense of humanity and dignity, Chasing the Boogeyman is a triumph.

Alex rated it ☆☆
As I was reading Chasing the Boogeyman I couldn't help but think about the families of the victims. It's a decent story but at what cost and what purpose? When I turned the last page, I felt like I needed a shower.

Justin rated it ☆☆☆☆☆
Tense. Thought provoking. Heartbreaking. A must read for all true crime fans.

destiny rated it ☆
Sensationalistic crap. Don't see what all the fuss is about and I wish I could get my money back. Not recommended.

Harford County Aegis—Letters to the Editor
(November 4, 2021)

. . . and that's precisely my point in writing today. As a lifelong resident and community leader in Edgewood, I would like to address the recent publication and rampant celebration of Richard Chizmar's *Chasing the Boogeyman*. While many misinformed and miseducated individuals are claiming that Mr. Chizmar has "put Edgewood on the map," I feel strongly that he has done nothing more than add to Edgewood's longstanding reputation of ill repute. Upon reading no further than the introductory matter of *Chasing the Boogeyman*, it became painfully clear that Mr. Chizmar should have titled his book *Chasing the Great American Dollar*. To make matters worse, the only thing worse than Chizmar's ghastly subject matter is his sophomoric purple prose. Both are worthy of the internet tabloids . . .

Variety (April 11, 2022)

While some critics have accused Chizmar of dipping his pen in a fountain of golden-tinged nostalgia, Martin Blevins from the *Washington Post* described the film version of Chizmar's acclaimed book as "*The Wonder Years* meets *The Silence of the Lambs*" and an unqualified success. After making its debut earlier this year at Sundance, *The Boogeyman* has gone on to amass surprisingly strong box office returns and looks to perform even stronger via streaming outlets. Based on the *New York Times* and *USA Today* bestselling book by Richard Chizmar, *The Boogeyman* tells the story of one small town's descent . . .

The True Crime Forum message board (April 17, 2022)

Thread: Chasing the Boogeyman

Started: August 17, 2021

SHIRLEY FINCH

(Sunday, April 17, 2022, 7:14pm) We read it last month in our book club and everyone loved it. We always give the books we read grades and the only one ranked higher is I'LL BE GONE IN THE DARK.

NIGHTHAWK

(Sunday, April 17, 2022, 7:16pm) Can you really swab a piece of furniture for DNA or was that made up?

GREG SALLADE

(Sunday, April 17, 2022, 7:23pm) Good book not great but good

KRIS WEBSTER

(Sunday, April 17, 2022, 7:27pm) What about all those rumors that Gallagher isn't human? Back in 88 one woman told a reporter she saw a dark figure, seven feet tall, unfurl wings and fly over her backyard fence. Someone else swore they saw a man with horns protruding from his forehead trying to break into their basement door. Seems like there were a lot of stories going around like that.

THE SPLAT PACK

(Sunday, April 17, 2022, 7:34pm) It's blood money, plain & simple. You see Chizmar's house in that Vanity Fair article? Holy shit! Who the hell has a lake in their side yard?

SEXYLEXI

(Sunday, April 17, 2022, 7:35pm) I thought the same fucking thing . . . the House That The Boogeyman Built!!!

From: Kristin Nelson

To: Richard Chizmar

May 3, 2022 at 10:29 PM

Hodder & Stoughton, Sperling & Kupfer, and Paramount are offering to co-sponsor a European tour to promote the paperback/overseas film releases. Six countries in 15 days. Kara can go with. They'll let us know proposed dates next week. Discuss later this afternoon?

-kn

NOW

Excerpt from phone interview with Peter Atkins, correctional officer at Cumberland Penitentiary, recorded on May 5, 2022:

ATKINS: He's a big reader. Paperback westerns mostly. "Oaters," he calls them. He gets books by the boxload with all the bad parts blacked out. He's not allowed anything too violent or sexual. He also subscribes to a couple different newspapers.

CHIZMAR: Anything else you can think of?

ATKINS: He's a big game player. Chess. Backgammon. Crossword puzzles. And a lot of cards. Hearts. Spades. Bridge. You name it. He's pretty good, from what I hear.

CHIZMAR: Any disturbing or unusual interactions?

ATKINS: Well, I mean Gallagher's a weird dude, for sure. Keeps to himself mostly. He's usually in his cell sleeping or answering mail. God, he gets a ton of mail. He also talks to himself a lot.

CHIZMAR: What does he say when he talks to himself?

ATKINS: Usually just mumbling that I can't understand a lick of . . . although I've heard bits and pieces here and there. One time he said clear as day, "Hair like sunshine, eyes like pennies." Another time it was "I keep trying, but there's no answer."

CHIZMAR: Anything else that you can remember?

ATKINS: [hesitates] There was one time . . . at night . . . I was doing my rounds and I walked by his cell, and Gallagher wasn't there. I swear to Christ he wasn't. His bunk was empty. He wasn't on the toilet. He wasn't anywhere. Right away, I broke out in a cold sweat and unhooked my radio from my belt, but by the time I got it to my mouth and looked up again, he was lying there on his bunk. Curled on his side, facing the wall, snoring.

CHIZMAR: What did you do?

ATKINS: What could I do? Nothing. It was the weirdest thing. I know I didn't imagine it, but what else could it have been? A trick of the light is what Bobby Deakins said when I told him about it the next morning, but come on. I've been working at that shithole for fifteen years now. The light ain't that tricky. Still gives me the heebie-jeebies every time I think about it.

ONE

LIFE AND DEATH

"He wanted to be seen. This was a performance."

1

The morning of Friday, June 3, 2022, dawned cloudy and unseasonably cool. I watched from my bedroom window as wisps of ground fog—a legion of restless ghosts haunting the predawn—drifted slowly across the dark surface of the pond before dissipating in the woods beyond. Even though I was lying snug beneath a blanket, the sight raised gooseflesh on my arms and sent a chill scampering across the back of my neck.

Later, when the memory returned to me in the midst of a nightmare, I realized it had been an omen of what was yet to come.

2

The house I lived in with my wife, Kara, and my sons, Billy and Noah, was actually two houses in one. The original home—built in 1796 by Thomas Moore, a prominent miller and tanner, and soon after christened Mooresland Manor—was constructed of rough blocks of stone taken from a local quarry. A second, much larger section was added by Moore's eldest son, Eli, in 1841. As a result, the house had two foyers, two sets of stairs leading to the upper floors, and two front-facing living rooms. This was how 701 Southampton Road, Bel Air, Maryland (a mere fifteen-minute drive from Edgewood), became known as the House with Two Front Doors.

The surrounding seven-acre property boasted a spring-fed pond, a meandering creek, an orchard, open fields, and woods. Geese, deer, foxes, and raccoons were regular visitors.

A U-shaped driveway and low stone wall fronted the house, with nearly 150 yards of head-high wooden fencing running along the eastern border of the property, shielding the pond and side meadow from passing cars and pedestrians. A narrow strip of grass and a gravel shoulder separated the fence line from Southampton Road.

It was there, leaning against a fire hydrant, that JJ—Billy's nine-month-old Bernese mountain dog—discovered the garbage bag.

3

A lot had changed in my world since the August 2021 publication of *Chasing the Boogeyman*.

Most of it good, but not all of it.

My oldest son, Billy, had recently graduated from Colby College in Maine and was once again living in his third-story attic bedroom, spending his days writing and editing fiction and working on various film projects. He'd listened dutifully to all the well-meaning warnings and lectures regarding how difficult it would be to follow in his old man's footsteps, but in the end, he'd ignored each and every one of them and forged ahead anyway. I was proud of him. He was working hard and had already earned considerably more success than his father had managed at that age.

Billy's younger brother, Noah, had just completed his freshman year at the University of Virginia. He was spending the summer mowing grass at a golf course in Charlottesville and taking a four-credit statistics class. He'd recently moved into an apartment with three of his lacrosse teammates and together they were learning the finer points of cooking, cleaning, and figuring out how to find and hold on to a girlfriend. Kara and I FaceTimed and spoke on the telephone with Noah several times a week, but it wasn't the same as having him home. We missed him terribly.

It didn't help matters that I was feeling homesick myself. The runaway success of *Chasing the Boogeyman* had led to a seemingly endless string of promotional appearances. Due to COVID restrictions, I'd spent most of the late summer and fall of 2021 participating in dozens of virtual book clubs. That hadn't been so bad. Wash my face, throw on a clean shirt, click a Zoom link, and spend an hour or two hawking books from the comfort of my own home. Easy enough.

But then the holiday season arrived—just as COVID constraints were lifted—and the publicity machine shifted into high gear. Instead of lounging in my home office, talking to a computer screen, I was suddenly crisscrossing the country with a revolving cast of barely-old-enough-to-drink publicists assigned by my publicity director. In-person bookstore signings, radio and television interviews, early morning talk shows, bookfairs (never in my life had I ever imagined there were so many blasted bookfairs)—you name it, I did it.

And to the publicists' credit, the hustle seemed to work.

Chasing the Boogeyman stuck around on the hardcover bestseller lists for seventeen consecutive weeks—a rare occurrence these days unless your last name happens to be Grisham, King, or Patterson—and when it finally dropped off in mid-January, it didn't go very far.

Retail sales remained surprisingly strong throughout the early quarter of 2022. The book surged into a fifth and sixth printing. Eventually, I ran out of bookfairs to attend and got to stay home for a couple of months, long enough to welcome a new puppy to the family and put the finishing touches on a manuscript I had started the previous summer. I even managed to regain a few pounds from Kara's home cooking.

And then it felt like I blinked one morning, and the movie version of *Chasing the Boogeyman* hit U.S. theaters and pay-per-view channels—and off I went again. More red-eye flights and hotel rooms, more signings and interviews, and you guessed it, more bookfairs.

In the past six weeks, I'd only been home long enough to sleep a handful of nights in my own bed—and it didn't look like that was going to change any time soon. With the movie scheduled for overseas release in mid-July, I was already preparing for a whirlwind promotional tour spanning much of Europe.

Kara, who had recently purchased a brand-new set of luggage for the trip, was over-the-moon excited and counting down the days until we boarded the plane.

I was not.

I was dog-tired and moody as hell. Most days, shuffling around the house or my hotel room enveloped within a hazy, dark cloud of unshakable melancholy. Or as my dear departed father would have said: "walking around in a serious funk."

Most likely, I was burned-out. I'd always been a loner by nature, and socializing with friends and strangers alike—even the wonderfully supportive group of readers I'd been blessed with—took a lot out of me. Being a writer had normally been such a solitary activity in my life. I sat by myself in an office with no windows and tapped away on my laptop. That was it; that was the job. But the landscape was different now, the stakes higher, and I was the first to admit that all the travel and publicity had worn me down—not only physically, but also mentally.

Or maybe what I was feeling was just part of life, part of growing older and learning how to embrace the future and let go of the past—something I struggled with, even on my best days. All I knew was that despite my recent successes, the world felt somehow heavier. And with the exception of the ongoing horrors of the pandemic, I could honestly think of only one good reason for that.

The previous fall, one of my best friends in the world, Carly Albright, had lost her husband to cancer. On the October morning he'd been diagnosed, Walter Scroggins was in perhaps the best shape of his life. He cycled and jogged several times a week and played eighteen holes of golf (he was a walker, too—no electric carts for Walter) and mixed doubles tennis on the weekends; he and Carly were even learning how to play pickleball and had recently joined a league at their gym. Six weeks later, he was gone. At the time, it'd felt as if a tornado had touched down out of nowhere and ravaged the lives of an amazing woman and her three beautiful daughters, and then up and blown away without a trace into the treetops. The rest of us had been left standing there dazed and confused, staring up at tranquil, baby blue skies, and wondering: *Did that really just happen?*

And when it was over—after all the tears and hugs and Saran-wrapped casseroles; after the final black-clad mourner had shuffled out of the memorial service and into the parking lot and the heavy doors had closed and the lights dimmed, and the world went suddenly still and silent—what then could you possibly say to a woman who meant so much to you, to a woman who had just buried the beating heart of her entire universe?

"I'm so sorry for your loss. I love you dearly and I'm here for you always."

As it turned out, those were the exact same words pretty much every one else had said to Carly Albright on that dark and dreary day—and during all the days that followed.

So tell me then, how in God's name could they have been the *right* words, the best words, I could muster? When it mattered most, how could they have even made the slightest bit of difference?

No wonder it'd felt as if she were so disappointed in me.

When everything was said and done, as autumn passed into winter and winter gave way to the promise of a new year, it felt as though I'd lost the both of them. Kara and I hadn't seen Carly since before the holidays, at a gift exchange dinner at a crowded Baltimore restaurant that had felt forced and hollow from the onset. Carly and I still spoke on the telephone, but only occasionally and rarely at length anymore. She was different now. Harder-edged. Always busy. Always trying to distract or forget. She often used the girls as an excuse for not having any free time, but how could I take issue with that? How could I blame her? The land-scape of our relationship had shifted beneath our feet and we had be-come like strangers to each other. I knew this sort of thing happened all the time, but it made me sad to think about, so most days I tried not to. Most days, I tried not to think of her at all.

Finally, and perhaps weighing most heavily of all upon my shoulders, was the shameful, secret notion that I was walking around every day feeling like an ungrateful prick. There's a scene in one of my favorite movies, *Willy Wonka & the Chocolate Factory*, where Mr. Wonka says to his younger protégé, "But Charlie, don't forget what happened to the man who suddenly got everything he always wanted."

"What happened?" Charlie asks.

Mr. Wonka grins his impish grin and says, "He lived happily ever after."

Happily ever after.

God knows that should have been me.

As a two-time cancer survivor by the time I was thirty, I've always climbed out of bed each morning embracing an overwhelming sense of gratitude—for Kara and the boys; our wonderful families and friends; our pack of dogs and our lovely home; the clean air to breathe and the warmth of sunshine on my face. If there was one thing I'd learned over the years, it was to take absolutely nothing for granted—including, of course, my career as a writer.

From the time I was a boy, I'd always been a dreamer, but I'd never dreamed this big.

Never once had I entertained the thought of cowriting books with Stephen King or hitting international bestseller lists or having my stories adapted into movies and television series. Hell, I'd never even imagined speaking at a bookfair.

Yet it was happening. It was all coming true.

So why then, Mr. Chizmar, all the doom and gloom and bitching and moaning?

That's exactly what I was trying to figure out.

And pretty much the only reason I was up and out the door so early on that chilly June morning, walking JJ on a leash instead of letting him scamper out the doggy door along with the rest of his siblings into the fenced-in backyard. I'd figured a good, strong dose of fresh air and exercise might help to clear my head. It might even help me to sleep better at night.

That was the plan, anyway.

4

It had rained most of the week, and there were puddles scattered along the driveway and the shoulder of the road. The front yard was soggy and the grass needed to be cut. By the time we reached the fence post that marked the border of our property, my shoes and socks were soaked. JJ, of course, paid no mind to any of this. Tail wagging, nose hovering an inch or so above the ground, he dragged me onward along the fence line, stopping every so often to lift his leg and mark his territory. Still half-asleep, I yawned and let him lead the way. I was in no particular hurry, and the only notable thought bouncing around inside my head was a half-hearted debate involving what I was planning to eat for breakfast. A part of me was leaning toward a relatively healthy combination of cereal and fresh fruit. Maybe some yogurt. A much larger part was craving a cholesterol time bomb of bacon and eggs served with a side of biscuits and sausage gravy. And a sixteen-ounce Sprite to wash it all down. It wasn't a tough decision.

I was trying to figure out where I could hide a big pot of sausage gravy from my wife when JJ suddenly skidded to a halt—and started growling.

JJ was a lot of things—sixty-five pounds of fluffy cuteness, hilariously clumsy, endlessly hungry, and annoyingly energetic at bedtime—but a growler wasn't one of them.

"What's wrong, JJ?" I asked, following his intense stare.

There was a shiny black garbage bag leaning against a fire hydrant maybe twenty or thirty yards ahead of us.

JJ growled louder and retreated a few steps.

"C'mon, boy. It's okay. Let's go see." I gave the leash a gentle tug, trying to nudge him forward. He stared at me and refused to budge.

"I'll give you a treat when we get home. C'mon, boy. You want a treat?"

He tilted his head to the side and licked his lips, considering my offer. After a moment, once again betrayed by his stomach, he inched forward until he drew even with me. He whined and nuzzled my leg with his nose. The message was clear: he'd go with me if he had to, but he was no longer interested in leading the way.

"Big chicken," I said, and started walking. "Scared of a bag of trash."

Head hanging in shame, tail tucked between his legs, JJ followed reluctantly behind me.

Southampton Road cut through the heart of Bel Air, and along with the frequent traffic came quite a bit of roadside litter. Kara and I may have felt as though we lived in the middle of nowhere with our little plot of land and our towering two-hundred-year-old trees, all safely hidden behind a tall fence, but in reality, we lived right smack-dab in the middle of town, not even a half mile away from a number of schools and grocery stores, not to mention 7-Eleven, Taco Bell, and Dunkin' Donuts.

I had already picked up a couple of fast-food wrappers and an empty cigarette pack and stuffed them into the back pocket of my jeans to dispose of later. Other days, it might have been discarded beer cans or broken liquor bottles, windswept pieces of junk mail or cardboard pizza boxes, sunglasses with one of the lenses missing or a rain-swollen magazine. Even the occasional orphaned flip-flop or dented hubcap made its way into our yard.

So I wasn't worried about the mysterious black bag that morning. *Probably just a bunch of leaves*, I thought. Most likely fell off the back of someone's truck. No big deal.

Until I got closer—and then I knew better.

The first thing I noticed was the smell. Faint in the crisp morning breeze, but still strong enough to detect from a distance of fifteen or twenty yards. A putrid, sickeningly sweet stench, like a basket of overripe fruit left out too long in the sun. I glanced around, hoping to find a dead squirrel or raccoon sprawled along the shoulder of the road, but there was only loose gravel and a ragged hunk of rubber from a flat tire.

I took another step closer—and saw the flies. Hundreds, maybe thousands of them, covering the black bag like a writhing second skin. I could hear their insistent buzzing, and it was only then that I realized JJ had started growling again. Louder this time, deeper, with the dark fur along the back of his neck raised in a rigid line and his teeth bared.

I could see that it wasn't a normal garbage bag at all, but rather one of those oversized, industrial-strength bags that landscapers used to dispose of prickly brush and tree branches. Heavy-duty material so thick it was almost impossible to tear or puncture. Whatever was inside the bag appeared to be large and oddly shaped, the shiny plastic bulging outward at a myriad of awkward angles. The top of the bag was twisted shut and sealed with a knotted length of what looked like silver duct tape.

At a glance, the bag looked to be airtight, but by this point I was certain that wasn't the case. Standing this close, the smell was like a charnel house. My eyes had begun to water. My stomach was doing jumping jacks. Backing up against the fence, I bent over with my hands on my knees and retched. Whimpering, JJ squeezed in behind me.

When I was finished, I reached down and touched the cell phone in my pants pocket, confirming that it was there. My internal alarm system was blaring loud and clear inside my head, but I was still hesitant to jump the gun. I'd been the victim of stupid pranks before—targeted by either local teenagers bored on a Friday night or actual fans and/or critics who had traveled to my home from God knew where. Homemade burlap masks had been stuffed inside my mailbox and hung from the branches of trees in my front yard. Hopscotch grids had been chalked on the driveway. Handfuls of pennies tossed on the porch. FREE THE BOOGEY-MAN had been spray-painted on the road in front of my house. And in a seeming tribute to my longtime friendship with Stephen King, PENNY-

WISE RULES had once been scrawled in dripping red paint along a section of our fence. All of these incidents were intrusive and annoying, to be sure, but ultimately, they'd proved relatively harmless.

But this time felt different.

It *smelled* different.

I thought about it for a moment longer, the buzzing of hungry flies growing steadily louder in my ears, and then I pulled out my phone and called an old friend.

5

A pair of Maryland state troopers—lights flashing, sirens off—were the first to arrive on the scene, pulling up from opposite directions.

The first officer—the name tag on his uniform read PERKINS— briefly questioned me, scribbling down notes in a small spiral notepad, before donning gloves and carefully examining the black bag. Once he was finished, he immediately instructed the other trooper to block off the road and got on the radio.

I had texted Kara as soon as I'd finished with my phone call, and explained what JJ and I had discovered. She'd quickly gotten dressed, came outside to retrieve the dog, and gated him in the backyard with the others. I could hear a chorus of impatient barking through the trees. Now Kara was back at my side, her tousled long brown hair defining the term "bed head," and looking none too pleased. Neither of us could hear what the trooper was saying into his radio mic, but the tone of his voice sounded urgent and excited.

The news traveled fast after that.

Before long, Southampton Road resembled a parking lot—with members of the Sheriff's Department, Maryland State Police, and Bel Air Police all vying for space. When the crime lab van finally showed up, a little after nine, no fewer than a half dozen cruisers had to be moved to let it through.

Almost the entire length of fence, along with the narrow stretch of grass that ran in front of it, had been ringed with yellow police tape. A series of plastic screens had been erected around the black bag, shielding it from prying eyes, of which there were plenty.

A large crowd had gathered across the street, and it felt as though each and every one of them was staring directly at Kara and me. Several people were holding up cell phones, taking photographs and videos. A young woman dressed in a tailored business suit, her long dark hair still wet from the shower, pointed a manicured finger in our direction. The older lady next to her shook her head with an air of polite disapproval. I could practically feel my wife's skin crawling from where I was standing. If there was one thing she despised, it was being the center of attention. Especially this kind of attention. We hadn't had more than a minute or two to talk in private before the detective showed up and started peppering us with questions, but I could already imagine Kara's angry voice when we got back to the house: "*I told you, Rich. I knew something like this would happen.*"

I scanned the throng of onlookers—several kids on bicycles and skateboards were zipping up and down the sidewalk, a couple of late arrivals standing on the hill behind them dressed in bathrobes and sipping their morning coffee—and recognized some familiar faces. Ken Klein, from across the street, stood off to the side talking to Roy and Carol Spangler, from a few doors down. Not far from them, Penny Schutz— puffing on a cigarette, a neon-pink scarf wrapped around her permed hair—engaged in an animated conversation on her cell phone. I could only imagine what these people were saying about me now.

"*I told you there was something weird about that guy.*"

"*Did you see that detective grilling him? I bet you anything he's the prime suspect.*"

"*Whatever they're hiding behind those shields has to be bad, and it's no coincidence that it showed up in front of their house—*"

Kara nudged me in the arm. I followed her gaze and watched as a Channel 11 news van rounded the bend on Southampton. It braked to a stop behind a line of orange traffic cones and a tall blonde reporter and her cameraman exited the vehicle.

"I'm surprised it took them this long," I said.

Before Kara could respond, a black SUV with the Channel 13 logo on the door pulled up alongside the van.

6

A few minutes later, I heard a familiar voice behind me.

"Make sure you get video of the crowd."

I turned and Lieutenant Clara McClernan was talking to the detective I had spoken with earlier. As the officer in charge of Maryland State Police cold case files in 2019, Lieutenant McClernan was the one who discovered Joshua Gallagher's missing DNA file and started digging into his past. Once she'd gathered enough circumstantial evidence to indicate that Gallagher was her man, she'd immediately placed him under 24/7 surveillance and came up with a plan to attain a new DNA sample. The rest, as they say, was history.

The lieutenant's long auburn hair was tied up in a bun and she was dressed in civilian clothes. In all the years I'd known her, I'd never seen her out of uniform before. For some reason, I found it unsettling. The detective was a short, stocky Hispanic man with eyes as dark as midnight and an unruly mustache straight out of a period western. The entire time he'd questioned me, I couldn't stop staring at it.

"And make sure we have someone stationed at each end of the road, taking down license plates."

The detective gave her a nod and hurried off.

"Sorry it took me so long to get here," McClernan said, looking our way. She gestured to the pantsuit she was wearing. "I've been stuck in court all morning."

"I'm just glad you got my voice mail," I said.

"I tried to phone you, but I was summoned back in by the judge." She glanced at my wife. "How you doing, Kara?"

"I've been better," she said.

The lieutenant made eye contact with one of the crime lab techs. She held up a finger and mouthed: *One minute.*

"Why don't you two go back inside? I'll take a look around and come talk to you when I'm finished."

Kara didn't need to be told twice. She mumbled a half-hearted "Thanks" and started walking toward the house, head down, avoiding the hungry stares of the neighbors across the street.

"She's not happy," I said, watching her go.

"Can't say I blame her."

"I think she's been waiting for something like this to happen."

"You think? She's made it pretty clear that she's not a fan of what we're doing."

"So ... what are the chances that's just a bag of deer trimmings over there? Someone hunting out of season."

McClernan didn't answer. She just looked at me, her expression giving away nothing, something I still hadn't gotten used to over the past several years.

"I mean, I'm going to feel awfully stupid if this is just another prank."

"Let's wait and see," she said, and I could tell that my time was up.

Before she could walk away, I blurted, "What about Gallagher?"

"I checked on my way over. He's locked up tight. Exactly where he's supposed to be."

"I wasn't really worried. I just thought maybe—"

"Go inside, Rich. I'll come talk to you as soon as I can."

And then she was gone.

7

By the time Lieutenant McClernan made good on her promise, it was nearly noon, and we had already entertained a parade of unexpected visitors.

The doorbell rang for the first time around eleven. It was our postman—Ronald or Donald or maybe Dan; he'd told me his name at least a half dozen times, but I could never remember it—with an Amazon package that was too large to fit inside the mailbox. Normally, he'd leave that sort of thing on the front porch, but it quickly became obvious that he'd wanted to talk to us face-to-face and hopefully get the inside scoop on what was happening. Suffice to say, Kara sent him on his way unsatisfied.

Doorbell ring number two was Ken Klein from up the hill on Runnymede. Ken was in charge of the neighborhood book club and an aspiring writer. Divorced, with adult children, he lived alone in a meticulously kept colonial. He made a point of intercepting me outside every couple of weeks to talk. I'd be mowing the lawn or taking the trash cans down to the curb, I'd turn around, and he'd be right there. Ken was a nice enough guy, but it never felt like a normal conversation with him. It always felt like an interview. Today was more of the same. Questions, one after the other. I finally told him that the police had ordered me not to say anything, and that seemed to do the trick.

Our next-door neighbors Mike and Molly Peele—yes, just like the *Mike & Molly* television show, which I'd never actually watched—showed up next. And who could blame them? Minutes earlier, they'd returned home from the grocery store to find a circus in front of their house. The police had even denied them entry to their own driveway. Instead, they'd had to park on the shoulder across the street. The four of us sat at the granite island in the kitchen, and I filled them in the best I could while Kara apologized and fed them brownies still warm from the oven. Kara always baked when she was stressed. After twenty minutes or so, they'd gone home to put away their groceries, and I was left with the distinct impression that they hadn't believed I'd told them everything I knew.

The final surprise visitor of the morning was Juliet McGirk, one of Kara's closet friends. Juliet and her husband, Ian, owned one of the largest working farms in Harford County and it just happened to be located about a mile down the road from us. The McGirks were good, hardworking people, kind and generous to a fault. Our children had gone to school together from kindergarten all the way up through high school, and the families had grown tight over the years. Juliet had heard about what was happening from a mutual friend—the backyard gossip mill already operating in full force—and driven her ATV to the intersection down the road and walked the rest of the way in.

Knowing that Juliet came from a family of experienced hunters, I posed to her the same question I'd asked Lieutenant McClernan a short time earlier regarding the possibility of someone hunting deer out of season. Her answer was typically "McGirk"—which is to say gracefully forthright and devoid of unnecessary treacle.

She'd immediately offered a dismissive shake of her head and said, "Not likely around here. I know you're hoping against hope, Rich, but I gotta tell you: I think that's a big old bag of bad news sitting out there in front of your house."

As it turned out, she was right.

8

"I'm afraid I have some disturbing news."

Lieutenant McClernan crossed her legs, a worn leather portfolio resting on her lap. The detective I'd spoken with earlier—the lieutenant had introduced him as Detective Sergeant Anthony Gonzalez—sat at the opposite end of the sofa. His posture was so uniformly rigid it made me uncomfortable. I wondered if he was doing it on purpose or if, perhaps, he was ex-military. You spend enough time hanging around with cops and you start thinking these things.

"The bag you discovered on your property this morning contained human remains."

Behind me, Kara made a groaning sound. She was sitting in my favorite reading chair by the window. I was perched on the ottoman at her feet.

"We really can't share much more at the present time," McClernan continued. "All the evidence we have is being processed."

I wasn't sure if I could trust my voice to speak. "Any idea when the bag was left there?"

"That's something we're hoping you two can help us with." She gestured to her partner. "Detective Gonzalez spoke with several of your neighbors, but they didn't have much to offer."

"Neither of your neighbors directly across the street have any prior knowledge of the bag," he said, consulting his notepad. "The Stevensons took their dog for a walk last night shortly before nine thirty. They don't believe the bag was present at that time, but it was dark, and they could've missed it. Mr. Stevenson left for work at seven this morning, but his regular route takes him in the opposite direction. Mrs. Stevenson is working from home today."

He flipped to the next page. "Mr. and Mrs. Halliday were both in bed by nine o'clock last night. Their daughters are at the beach, so it's just the two of them. Mr. Halliday is almost positive the bag wasn't there when he arrived home from work yesterday at six fifteen or so. Neither of them left the house this morning until they noticed all the commotion out front."

I listened attentively to every word the detective was saying, but I still couldn't take my eyes off his damn mustache. It was getting ridiculous, and if the topic of our conversation hadn't been so somber, I might've found the whole thing funny. I felt like a middle school kid sitting in the front row of math class, staring at a humongous booger dangling from his teacher's nose. Any minute now I was going to lose it.

"Is your son home?" he asked, rubbing his mustache with the tip of his thumb, and for a moment I was certain he was reading my mind.

"Billy's working at a lacrosse camp. He left early this morning and won't be back until dinner."

"I'll want to talk to him later. Would he have called or texted if he'd seen the bag when he left this morning?"

"Probably not," I said. "But 95's in the opposite direction, so he wouldn't have gone that way."

The detective wrote something in his notebook.

Kara squeezed my shoulder. "What time did you pick up dinner last night?"

"It was pretty late . . . maybe seven thirty, seven forty-five."

"Did you notice anything at all unusual?" Gonzalez asked.

I thought about it for a moment before answering, wanting to be sure. "Nothing I can remember."

He looked at Kara next.

"I spent all day working in the yard. I didn't see a thing."

Consulting his notebook again. "Mr. Chizmar, when we spoke earlier, you mentioned that you and your wife have been the subject of frequent pranks related to Joshua Gallagher. Your wife even filed a complaint with the sheriff's department."

"I wouldn't exactly say frequent, but yes, there have been some incidents."

"Anything recent?"

I turned around and looked at Kara. "Maybe a couple of months ago?"

She shook her head. "Less than that. The mannequins. You were in Texas or Florida."

"Mannequins?" the detective asked.

"There was a chapter in *Chasing the Boogeyman* called 'The House of Mannequins' and—"

"I'm familiar with your book, Mr. Chizmar."

"Oh, okay . . ." Not *I read your book*. Or *I enjoyed your book*. Just *I'm familiar with your book*.

Sensing that I was flustered, Kara swooped in to save me, something she'd been doing for as long as I could remember. "Someone hung a couple of mannequins on the fence in front of the pond. They were naked and splashed with red paint to make it look like blood. Pennies had been glued to their eyes."

The detective scribbled away. When he was finished, he looked up at me. "Any recent threats?"

"Not really. I get a lot of emails and letters from readers. Some are fans. Some not so much. Gallagher's groupies can get a little rough sometimes, but I usually just ignore them."

"How rough?" McClernan asked.

I shrugged. "Mainly just insults and name-calling. 'Your book sucks.' 'Your movie sucks.' 'Your whole family sucks.' That sort of thing. A few months ago, someone accused me of coercing Gallagher to make a false confession. Someone else claimed that I'd helped Gallagher kill the three Edgewood girls and set him up to take the blame."

"You save all the emails?" Detective Gonzalez asked.

"I do. I have a file. The letters, too."

"I'll want to take a look at those."

"The message board detectives and the true crime fanatics are the worst." Kara scooted to the edge of her chair. "I hate to say it but especially the ones who have lost someone."

The detective looked up. "How so?"

"They're pushy and rude and don't take no for an answer. A few of them even showed up at the house."

"When was this?" McClernan asked. I could tell she was surprised I'd never mentioned it.

"Sometime last fall," I said.

"And again right before Christmas," Kara added. "Remember that older couple?"

I nodded. "Most of them have good intentions. They're just a little . . . intense. They've read about how I'm the only person Gallagher's talking to, so they think I have all the answers. They're desperate for answers."

Kara gave me a look. "It doesn't help that the movie makes it appear like you two were best friends growing up."

There was a sudden buzzing sound and—in unison—all four of us checked our cell phones.

"It's Noah," Kara said. "I better take this." She got up and walked out of the room.

Detective Gonzalez looked at me. "Noah's your youngest son?"

"Yes. He's spending the summer in Charlottesville."

The detective glanced over his shoulder into the foyer. "I noticed when we came in that you have security cameras on your porch. Have either you or your wife reviewed the footage from last night?"

"We haven't had time with so many people stopping by." It was the truth, but checking the cameras hadn't even crossed my mind. And it should have. I felt stupid. "Besides, none of the cameras reach the yard in front of the fence. Too far away."

"They still could've picked up something important," Lieutenant McClernan said.

The detective flipped the page of his notepad. "What do you say we take a look and find out?"

9

The digital footage didn't show much of interest. At least, not at first.

At 9:33 p.m., a compact car with a lit-up Domino's Pizza sign attached to the roof slows down in front of the house, almost coming to a complete stop, before accelerating and going on its way.

At 10:59 p.m., Mike and Molly's sheepdog, Leo, wanders by the front porch, sniffing the azalea bushes on either side of the stone walkway. Appearing to look directly into the camera, he lifts his leg and pees on Kara's favorite rosebush before trotting away toward the side yard. Most likely heading for a late-night dip in the pond. Twenty minutes later, he briefly reappears on his way home.

At 1:13 a.m., a chubby raccoon strolls by with not a care in the world.

At 2:37 a.m., a Bel Air police cruiser traveling east on Southampton Road swings into the left-hand entrance of the driveway and quickly reverses back onto the street. The officer behind the wheel—it's impossible to tell if it's a man or a woman—turns on the flashers and speeds off in the direction from which they just came.

Detective Gonzalez noted all of this in his notepad.

There were two moments on the video—11:44 p.m. and 3:24 a.m.—where a pedestrian appeared to walk along the street in front of the house. In both instances, the subjects were too far away and resembled little more than dark, misshapen blobs moving horizontally across the screen. Kara tried several times to zoom in, but that only made it worse.

The problem with most doorbell cameras—because of their tiny lenses and restricted sight lines—was the further away you got from the camera's designated target area, the fewer details you were able to capture. In the foreground of Kara's laptop screen appeared a close-up view of our front porch and the winding stone walkway leading to the driveway. Everything here was captured in sharp definition. We could even glimpse a family of moths fluttering around the porch light. In the center of the screen was the upper portion of our U-shaped driveway and the majority of the lawn and trees—these images appeared in moderate detail, their edges somewhat softened and darkened by shadow. Finally, along the top portion of the screen was both of the driveway's dual entrances, separated by a low stone wall and lit by a pair of decorative lampposts, as well as a forty- or fifty-yard stretch of Southampton Road. The vast majority of this area was obscured in a blurry haze.

"Can we try another camera?" Detective Gonzalez asked, not bothering to hide his impatience.

Kara tapped away at the keyboard and hit Return.

A narrow window opened in the upper right corner of the laptop screen—and most of our backyard appeared in crystal-clear clarity.

"That's 4K right there," Lieutenant McClernan said, clearly impressed.

"I had the security system installed after that business with the mannequins," Kara said. "There's a total of seven cameras. Two in front of the house, two in back, one on each side, and one on the garage." She leaned closer to the screen, biting her lip, something she'd always done when concentrating on a difficult task. "Now let's see if I can remember how to do this."

A moment later, second and third overlapping windows popped up. The side yard by the pond and the front of the garage. A few more taps on the keyboard and all three images merged into one and disappeared. Then, a single large window bloomed at the center of the computer screen—and there was the bottom half of the front yard and Southampton Road beyond. Several uniformed officers stood in a group on the roadside. One was pointing at the house. The footage was so clear I could practically read the name tag on his uniform.

"I should be able to pull up archived footage . . ." She swiped her thumb and a scroll bar appeared at the top of the screen. "What time are we looking for?"

The detective consulted his notebook. "Try 11:44 p.m. first."

Kara worked her magic—and the scene instantly changed from day to night. The time code at the lower left corner of the window read 11:42 p.m. The street was empty. Leaves stirred on a tree branch from a passing breeze. The seconds ticked away. A minute passed. And then another. Suddenly, there came a scraping sound in the distance, slowly gaining in volume, settling into a rhythm. A moment later, a jogger appeared from the right side of the screen. A middle-aged man, bald, dressed in red shorts and a baggy gray sweatshirt, moving slow and steady.

"Recognize him?" McClernan asked.

I shook my head. "No, I don't think so."

"Not me," Kara said.

The man jogged off-screen, and in my mind's eye, I pictured him continuing down the street. Another ten or fifteen seconds and he would pass the fire hydrant where I'd discovered the black bag. *Was it already there waiting for me?*

"Try 3:24 next," the detective said.

Kara pulled down the scroll bar again, typed in some numbers.

The image on the screen jumped ahead to 3:27 a.m.

"Too far."

She typed again.

3:23 a.m.

The road was silent and still. A tiny insect inspected the camera lens and then darted away. We waited.

3:24 a.m.

More insects flitting around. The lonely call of a night bird. A faraway, muffled car engine. Then silence.

3:25 a.m.

A dark figure suddenly appeared.

Kara gasped and backed away from the laptop.

The man walking along the shoulder of Southampton Road was dressed in dark clothing and wearing a burlap mask with the eyeholes cut out. Over his shoulder, he carried the black garbage bag. The man walked at an almost leisurely pace, staring at the house, as if he knew his journey was being recorded.

And then he vanished off-screen.

"I'm going to need a copy of this right away," Detective Gonzalez said, his voice thick with tension. He turned to Lieutenant McClernan. "Why not park by the woods and come in from the other end of the street by the traffic circle? There're no houses that way. No streetlights."

"He wanted to be seen," she said. "This was a performance."

10

The rest of the day was a blur.

Lieutenant McClernan sat inside with us, asking questions, for the better part of an hour. We went over the previous day and that morning's timelines again, and then she took down a detailed list of workers who had been at the house during the past several months. In addition to the security company Kara had hired, there was a home inspector from our insurance company, a roofing contractor, an HVAC man, the pool maintenance folks, and a couple of landscaping crews. I'd learned the hard way that owning an old house was a lot like owning a used speedboat: They're both loads of fun and real pretty to look at on sunny days, but they're also big-time money pits. The work never ends.

While the three of us were talking in the family room, Detective Gonzalez and a pair of techs were busy working on the security camera footage in the kitchen. I could hear most of the conversation—snippets like "fixed analog" and "megapixels" and "digital WDR"—but I'll be damned if I understood a single word of it.

Outside, a state trooper had been stationed at the bottom of the driveway to prevent members of the media and overzealous neighbors from bothering us. I knew it was just a matter of time before news of what was inside the black bag went public—and once that happened, it would be chaos.

Billy arrived home shortly after six and immediately hammered us with questions. Earlier in the afternoon, Kara had left him a voice mail, filling him in on everything that had happened. He'd called both of our cell phones repeatedly during his drive home, but we'd turned off our ringers a couple hours earlier and missed the calls. By the time he walked in the breezeway door he was nearly bursting with anticipation; he reminded me a lot of myself in that regard, and as often was the case, I wrestled with whether that was a good thing. You could see the flush of excitement on his face when I told him that Detective Gonzalez wanted to ask him a couple of questions. As soon as dinner was finished, Billy hurried outside to see if he could track him down, but the detective had already left. A short time later, he went upstairs to take a shower and work on an essay for his Patreon page. We hadn't heard a peep from him since.

The black bag—I could no longer think of it as a garbage bag now that I knew what had been stored inside it—had been taken away hours earlier. The runners of police tape remained in place along the fence and front yard. As dusk approached, there were still a half dozen uniformed officers and plainclothes detectives canvassing the area. The crowd of onlookers from this morning had finally dispersed shortly after noon, once they'd realized there wasn't going to be any kind of a grand reveal, only to be replaced later in the evening by an even larger group—mostly men and teenagers this time. News crews from Channel 45 and Channel 7 (a Washington, D.C., affiliate) remained at the scene, huddled inside their vans and trucks, eating soggy microwave dinners from 7-Eleven and Wawa, cursing their competition, most of whom were already back at the station or drinking cocktails at their favorite Towson watering holes after filing their live reports for the early broadcasts.

As expected, the internet was abuzz with the news. True crime message boards, websites, and blogs—all ran rampant with speculation. Wannabe detectives and cyberspace lookie-loos flooded TikTok, Twitter, and Facebook. The evening news programs aired a number of tantalizing visuals—close-ups of the plastic shields blocking the view of the black bag; stone-faced police officers manning the roadblocks at either end of Southampton Road; and wide-angle, panning shots of the front of our house, which appeared rather ominous in the late afternoon shadows— but very little information of note. In a now viral video clip, Lieutenant McClernan confirmed that a mysterious object had been discovered on the property of a Southampton Road residence and promised "more details as soon as they become available." Stephanie Stevenson, our neighbor across the street, was interviewed live by a Channel 13 reporter and went out of her way to emphasize that "nothing like this has ever happened around here before. This is normally a very peaceful neighborhood."

Surprisingly, our name was never mentioned during the broadcast.

That would change soon enough.

11

Later that night, while Kara took a bath, I sat outside in the backyard with the dogs.

All day long, I'd been waiting for her to get angry—to cry or yell or throw something and to blame me for the man in the mask whose image we'd captured on camera—but so far that hadn't happened. Instead, she seemed almost numb. I couldn't blame her. That's exactly how I was feeling.

Even the dogs sensed that something was wrong. They were particularly skittish and needy, pooling around my ankles, barking at every random sound and movement. Nighttime was a busy time in the pitch-dark fields and woods behind our house. Lots of deer and foxes on the move.

Geese arguing over at the pond. The pups were used to it and normally minded their own business. But not tonight—they were agitated.

JJ, the star of this morning's misadventure, was the youngest and the largest of the pack. His three siblings—Cujo, Ripley, and Odie, in order of seniority—were tiny little things. Doodle-something-or-others. Stuffed animals come to life. If they stood on their hind legs, they could just about nuzzle my kneecap.

Something moved in the darkness down by the springhouse and all four of them charged off in that direction, a cacophony of barking and growling piercing the night. I begrudgingly got up from the lawn chair in which I was sitting and walked closer for a better look. As I approached the far corner of the fenced-in portion of our yard, the growling intensified, and I turned on the flashlight on my cell phone.

The springhouse had been built over two hundred years ago—making it the oldest such structure in all of Harford County—and it was haunted by the restless spirit of an ancient witch. At least, that's what I told the boys after we moved in. They'd never really bought the story, but somewhere along the line, I'd started believing it myself. One of the hazards of my job. Now, I was fairly terrified of the place.

As I shone the flashlight beam at the low-ceilinged doorway and along the stone walls and slanted roof, I caught a glimpse of something pale and round hovering in the shadows. To my tired eyes, it looked a lot like a man's face—or a mask. And it was staring right at me.

For one breathless moment, standing there alone in the darkness, I was reminded of a long-ago night outside the Meyers House in Edgewood, when my friend Jimmy Cavanaugh and I had almost certainly witnessed the Boogeyman fleeing swiftly into the night.

Startled, I jerked backward and immediately tripped over an exposed tree root, fell onto my ass, and dropped my cell phone. By the time I found it in the high grass and stood up again, the face—which I was 90 percent certain I'd imagined—was gone.

"What a dumbass," I whispered to the dogs, grateful they couldn't tattle on me.

I switched off the flashlight and started back toward the house—and that's when my phone rang.

I glanced at the glowing screen: UNKNOWN CALLER.

Probably too late for a reporter, but if it was, I was hanging up.

"Hello?"

There was a loud beep and then a familiar automated voice came on the line. *"I have a collect call from the Cumberland Penitentiary from inmate . . ."*

"Josh Gallagher."

". . . will you accept the charges?"

I stopped walking. Even after all this time, it was always the same. My palms went instantly sweaty. My heart started thumping inside my chest.

"Yes."

Another beep, then: *"I hear you had some trouble at home today."*

"You could say that."

"I want to assure you I had nothing to do with it."

A brief hesitation. "I know that."

"Do you?"

"Yes."

"And how is your lovely wife?"

"My wife is none of your business."

"I don't blame you for being in a foul mood. Today must've been very upsetting for all of you."

"How much do you know?"

"I'd say I know a bit more than what the local news is sharing at this point."

"*How* do you know?"

"C'mon, now, Rich. You know I have my sources."

"I have to go."

"Come see me. We have lots to talk about."

I ended the call and went inside.

12

CRIME TIME MESSAGE BOARD
Thread: Somethin's up in Boogeyman Land!!!
Started: June 3, 2022

luciouslolita
you guys hear the news?? hella cops at chizmar's house today. and I mean alllll day. they found something in his yard

Ricky Thunder
Any guesses on what it was?

Doc Watson
Dead body.

Parker Lowe
murder weapon

MisterBones
Publicity stunt for the movie. Those MFers have no shame.

Serena
I go to summer school with a girl who lives in the neighborhood across the street. One of her friends said it was a bomb. Her little brother says it was a duffel bag.

Martina Roth
Whatever it was, it's gone now. I just drove by his house like ten minutes ago!

13

Kara and I were upstairs getting ready for bed when a "Breaking News" chyron flashed on the television screen, interrupting tonight's episode of *MasterChef Junior*. When the intro music faded and the lead anchor—a heavily Botoxed Harrison Ford lookalike—glanced up from the sheaf of papers he was holding and said, *"Grisly news today for one local Bel Air family. Earlier this morning, human remains were discovered on the Southampton Road property of Richard and Kara Chizmar,"* Kara nearly spit a mouthful of toothpaste all over the TV. Instead, it showered the curtains behind it and slowly dribbled into a puddle on the hardwood floor.

"Richard Chizmar is a New York Times *bestselling true crime author of numerous books focusing on Joshua Gallagher, also known as the Edgewood Boogeyman. Gallagher was responsible for the murders of four young women during the summer and fall of 1988. Thanks to DNA samples recovered from a crime scene, Gallagher was finally arrested in September 2019 and has since admitted to the additional murders of more than . . ."*

"I hate this so much," Kara said, sitting down on the bed. She looked like she wanted to cry.

I sat beside her. "It'll be okay."

"A former neighbor and childhood family friend of Gallagher's, Richard Chizmar remains the only journalist the confessed serial killer has spoken with since his arrest. In a deal struck with detectives from the Maryland State Police, Gallagher agreed to reveal details of additional unknown victims in exchange for exclusive interview sessions with Chizmar. This controversial arrangement sparked an outcry among . . ."

"You keep saying that, but how do you know it'll be okay?" she asked. "You don't."

My pale face suddenly appeared in front of a tangle of microphones on the television screen. There was a small hole in the sleeve of my T-shirt—somewhere in heaven, my poor mother was having a fit—and I looked a little manic with my hair sticking out from underneath my baseball cap and my too-wide eyes blinking in the glare of the camera lights. Over my shoulder, you could see Lieutenant McClernan and Detective Gonzalez standing next to each other at the mouth of the driveway.

Kara used the remote to turn up the volume. *". . . once the investigation is concluded. Until then we have the utmost confidence in local law enforcement authorities."*

A reporter off-screen asked, "*Do you think this morning's incident is connected in any way to the Boogeyman?*"

My facial expression remained unchanged; I'd been expecting the question. "*Joshua Gallagher is locked up in federal prison where he belongs. I don't see how it could be related.*"

"*Mr. Chizmar! Mr. Chizmar! When did you find—*"

"I don't know why you talked to them," Kara said.

"To get ahead of the story." I took her hand in mine. "McClernan thought it was the smart thing to do."

"Did she also tell you to lie to their faces? C'mon, Rich—what we saw on the security footage is most definitely related to Joshua Gallagher. Hell, it might as well have been him."

"McClernan said it's still too early to determine if it's a copycat or—"

"What else could it be?"

I shrugged. "A bad joke. Maybe someone stole a cadaver from a lab somewhere."

"And dressed up as the Boogeyman and delivered it to our front yard in the middle of the night?" She shook her head. "I warned you something like this would happen. You write about this stuff long enough and you go on television and radio and talk about it, and you never know who's watching or listening. It's like you've become a magnet for psychos."

"This is the first time anything like this has happened."

"But it's been building," she said, her voice rising. "All the pranks and the hate mail. The weirdos who show up at your signings and post on all those message boards. Why can't you see that? Why can't you see that you're allowing Joshua Gallagher to control our lives?"

"And how am I doing that?"

"The book . . . the movie . . . the phone calls . . . the goddamn visits to the prison . . . it's like all that darkness is seeping inside of you. You've lost weight. You don't sleep. I'm worried about you—and so are the boys."

"Which is exactly why I took a break to work on *Looking Back*. You know that."

Inspired by the positive feedback I'd received regarding the autobiographical opening chapters of *Chasing the Boogeyman*—in which I reminisced about my idyllic coming of age in an all-American suburb—I'd spent the past six months, most of it in hotel rooms and diners, completing *Edgewood: Looking Back*, a nostalgic memoir focusing on the innocence and wonder of my childhood years. Both my agent and my publisher had been stridently opposed to the idea and had tried their best to talk me out of it—"No one's going to pay you six figures to write about you and your friends back when you were snot-nosed little kids, not with Joshua Gallagher waiting in the wings"—but in the end I'd held firm. The next Boogeyman book would have to wait. Kara was right; I needed to give my soul a rest from the shadows and spend a little more time basking in the sunshine. Besides, it wasn't as if anyone else was going to beat me to the story.

"Then tell me this: Why do you keep talking to him? You have enough interview transcripts to write a dozen books. Why not make a clean break of it?"

I looked at her. "You know why."

"It's been almost three years and he's given up exactly three bodies. It's not worth it."

"Tell the victims' families that." It was a cheap shot, but I felt cornered.

"I feel for those families, I really do," she said, refusing to take the bait. "But I feel a whole lot more for my own family."

"It won't be like this forever."

"Won't it?" she said, and I could see tears forming in the corners of her eyes. "Do you realize that Joshua Gallagher has been a part of your life almost as long as I have?"

I raised my hands in the air. "For Chrissakes, it's not a competition."

"I know you, Rich. I know how your brain works. You won't stop trying to understand what happened—trying to understand *him*—

until it's too late. It's almost like you blame some part of yourself for what happened. He's all you've thought about since the day he was arrested."

"That's not true. I couldn't care less if I under—"

"Just be quiet for once in your life and listen to me . . . it's time to get off this crazy ride." Most of the anger had leaked out of her voice. "Someone left fucking body parts in our yard last night. If that doesn't convince you it's time to walk away, then nothing will."

I scooted closer to her on the bed. "Hey. It's going to turn out to be another stupid prank. Just wait and see."

"You know what? I don't even care anymore." She laughed bitterly. "Isn't that terrible? I just want you far away from all of it."

I took the remote control from her hand. "Let's just try to get some sleep. We'll both feel better in the morning."

"I don't need sleep." She leaned over and hugged me tight. "I need *you*, you big dummy. And so do the boys."

"I need you back," I whispered. Both of our faces were wet with tears. "And I hear you. I do. I promise I'll be care—"

The doorbell rang downstairs.

Kara and I held on to each other, both of us holding our breath, afraid to move, unwilling to let the world steal this moment away from us.

The doorbell rang again.

14

When I looked out the peephole and saw Lieutenant McClernan standing on the front porch, my first instinct was to turn around and go back to bed. We'd had enough bad news for one day. Whatever she needed to say could surely wait until tomorrow morning.

Instead, I took a deep breath and opened the door.

"I'm really sorry to bother you so late." She didn't wait for an invitation. Stepping past me, she walked into the foyer. I closed the door behind us.

"What's wrong?" I asked.

"We've identified the body and I wanted you to hear the news from me first."

"Okay." I glanced up the stairs and saw Kara waiting there, listening.

"Do you know what yesterday's date was?"

I thought about it. "Second of June."

"And do you know the significance of that date?"

Nothing came to mind, so I shook my head.

"Yesterday was exactly thirty-four years since Natasha Gallagher was murdered. *To the day.*"

I felt an invisible band tighten around my chest. "Jesus, that's right."

"Someone circled the date on the calendar and spent last night cleaning up Joshua Gallagher's unfinished business. And I don't think they're done yet."

"What do you mean, unfinished business?" I could hear Kara coming down the stairs behind me.

"The remains you found on your property this morning belong to Anne Taylor Riggs, age fifty-one, resident of Willoughby Beach Road in Edgewood. She was reported missing last night by her ..."

The lieutenant was still talking, I could see her lips moving, but I could no longer hear what she was saying. The room had begun to spin. The floor tilted beneath my bare feet.

Anne Taylor Riggs.

Anne Riggs.

Annie Riggs.

I remembered her. Seventeen years old. Long, wavy hair. Freckles.

Annie Riggs.

Edgewood High School class president. Field hockey team captain. The girl with the pepper spray.

And the sole survivor of Joshua's Gallagher's 1988 killing spree.

Annie Riggs.

Unfinished business.

The author's home on Southampton Road *(Photo courtesy of the author)*

The mysterious black bag discovered by the fire hydrant *(Photo courtesy of Maryland State Police)*

Richard Chizmar signing copies of *Chasing the Boogeyman (Photo courtesy of the author)*

Graffiti on the fence at the Chizmar residence *(Photo courtesy of the author)*

Graffiti on the driveway at the Chizmar
residence *(Photo courtesy of the author)*

Lieutenant Clara McClernan, Maryland State Police Department *(Photo courtesy of Clara McClernan)*

Anne Riggs *(Photo courtesy of The Aegis)*

Screenshot of "the man in the mask" from security footage *(Photo courtesy of the author)*

Richard Chizmar

Excerpt from Edgewood: Looking Back, *by Richard Chizmar, pages 33–34:*

"It's hotter out here than a bucket of piss," Brian Anderson complained, taking off his Pirates baseball cap and running a hand through his sweat-soaked hair.

I hated the Pirates with a passion—all the kids in the neighborhood did—but Brian's father had helped to wire a shopping mall in Pittsburgh the previous winter, and he'd come home with all kinds of black-and-gold paraphernalia. Brian's little brother, Craig, had the good sense to leave that stuff at home in his bedroom. Brian did not. He wore that Pirates gear with an annoying sense of pride and his typically flamboyant streak of pigheadedness. If there was a more contrary son of a bitch in this world than twelve-year-old Brian Anderson, I'd yet to meet him.

With all that said, Brian was right this time. It was hotter than a bucket of piss. A few minutes past seven in the evening and the temperature refused to relent, still hovering in the low nineties with a suffocating umbrella of humidity. None of us were wearing shirts.

We sat on the curb at the corner of Tupelo and Cherry. Jimmy popped a scattering of tar bubbles on the road at his feet and hummed the *Bonanza* theme song. Brian picked up a couple of pebbles and flicked them at the spokes of Charlie Emge's bicycle tire as he cruised by. I slid my hand into my shorts pocket, feeling for the quarters I'd stashed there earlier, trying to decide whether I wanted to walk to 7-Eleven and play *Space Invaders* or wait around for the ice cream man. I could hear the melodic jingle coming from the truck's speakers a block or two away, and it was starting to make my mouth water.

I'd made a point of sitting between Brian and Jimmy because they were fighting again. Earlier in the afternoon, Jimmy had beaned Brian square in the back with a taped-up Wiffle ball from point-blank range. It had been completely unnecessary, and Jimmy knew it. A half-hearted scuffle had ensued.

After a seemingly sincere apology from Jimmy and numerous promises to never do it again, the game had continued without incident—until two innings later when Brian tried to score from second on a line drive single to center field. As Brian rounded third at breakneck speed, the red welt in the middle of his back standing out like a bull's-eye on a dartboard, Jimmy pounced from behind and leg-whipped him.

Brian went airborne, twisting and turning in a wild somersault, and landed face-first in the Hathaways' sticker bush.

Sensing that he'd gone too far this time, Jimmy took off running for his house.

Brian, maybe the most athletic of all of us that summer, caught up to Jimmy in the Cavanaughs' front yard, no more than a half dozen strides away from safety. Brian's cheeks, forehead, chest, and arms were crisscrossed with bloody scratches. His upper lip was split and swollen. It looked as if he'd been attacked by a rabid junkyard cat.

The fight was quick and decisive. Brian pinned Jimmy to the ground on his back, used his knees to pry Jimmy's legs open, and slammed him in the balls with his fist. Twice. Jimmy groaned and rolled over, gasping "UNCLE! UNCLE!" and it was over.

Unfortunately, so was the Wiffle ball game.

Jimmy spent the rest of the afternoon stretched out on his back in the shade of my weeping willow tree, nursing his swollen balls and drinking my mom's homemade lemonade while Brian and I played marbles and flipped baseball cards. After a while, a couple of other kids came along, and we all went inside to play penny poker.

TWO

THE BOOGEYMAN

"He's wearing a mask underneath his mask."

1

On September 7, 2019, Joshua Allen Gallagher, age fifty-four, a resident of the 1600 block of Evergreen Way in Hanover, Pennsylvania, was arrested and charged with the 1988 murders of four Edgewood, Maryland, teenagers: his younger sister, Natasha Gallagher; Kacey Robinson; Madeline Wilcox; and Cassidy Burch.

Shortly after his arrest, Joshua Gallagher confessed to the four murders of which he was accused. He also admitted to killing three additional young women: seventeen-year-old Louise Rutherford of Hagerstown, Maryland, in 2001; nineteen-year-old Colette Bowden in 2006; and seventeen-year-old Erin Brown in 2018. Both Bowden and Brown were from Juniata County, Pennsylvania.

Between December 2019 and March 2022, I conducted a total of nineteen in-person interviews with Joshua Gallagher in a secure interrogation room located at the Cumberland Penitentiary in western Maryland. In addition, I spoke with him on the telephone approximately thirty times. As a result, I amassed more than seventy hours of recorded conversation.

These discussions were arranged by detectives from the Maryland State Police Department, who brokered a deal with Joshua Gallagher's public defense attorney in which Gallagher agreed to provide details of additional unknown victims in exchange for my exclusive access.

In his only public statement, released via his attorney, Gallagher claimed, "Richard Chizmar and I share an incontrovertible bond. We grew up a block away from each other in the same small town and our families were friends. Chizmar is a well-respected author and member of the Edgewood community—and the only person I trust to tell my story."

To date, I remain the only journalist Joshua Gallagher has spoken with.

2

Joshua Allen Gallagher was adopted in 1966 by Russell and Catherine Gallagher.

The Gallaghers were in their midtwenties and had always wanted to have children, but for a number of years they'd been unable to achieve a natural pregnancy. In 1965, after Mr. Gallagher was promoted at the Havre de Grace insurance office where he worked, they decided to pursue adoption. They filled out the necessary paperwork, paid the assorted fees, and waited. In early November, they received the news they'd been praying for, and just after Thanksgiving, they brought home Joshua—named after a paternal grandfather—from a Russian orphanage in Mordovia. He'd just turned eighteen months old.

Early life was good for the Gallagher family—Russell prospered at work and Catherine positively bloomed as a young mother and homemaker—and it got even better in 1972 when Natasha was born. The Gallaghers had never given up trying to conceive, and their prayers had finally been answered. At long last, they felt like a complete family.

The Gallaghers had decided early on not to tell Joshua that he'd been adopted, and now that he had a baby sister, they felt certain that they'd made the correct decision. The last thing they wanted was for the boy to feel like some kind of an outsider within his own family.

Shortly after Natasha was born, the Gallaghers moved from the Harford Square townhouse in which they'd been living to a roomy split-level on Hawthorne Drive. There was a detached garage, a fenced-in yard, and a big bay window at the front of the house where the Gallaghers set up their Christmas tree every Thanksgiving as soon as the dinner table was cleared and the dishes were washed. Later, once it was dark outside, the four of them gathered in the front yard—dressed in their favorite holiday sweaters, their mittened hands cradling steaming cups of hot cocoa—to admire the blinking lights and decorations.

As the years passed, many fond memories were made on Hawthorne Drive. Mr. Gallagher built a tree house for the kids in the backyard. Mrs. Gallagher started a vegetable garden and grew prize-winning roses along the side of the house. Joshua and Natasha made friends in the neighborhood and did well at school. There were birthday parties and sleepovers. Movie and game nights. The hill out front was perfect for sledding in the winter and Slip 'N Slides in the summer. Eventually, Joshua grew up to be a star wrestler on the high school varsity team and earned a scholarship to Penn State University. Natasha was named captain of the cheerleading squad and won so many gymnastics medals that her father built a custom wood showcase with ornate glass doors for her to display them in.

The house on Hawthorne Drive would remain Catherine Gallagher's home until shortly after her son's arrest in 2019.

3

The most significant requirements—other than sufficient safety measures—for my cooperation with both the Maryland State Police and Joshua Gallagher were that no topic would be considered off-limits and all conversations would be deemed officially on the record. Of course, I knew going in that some of the information we discussed would be extremely sensitive and would have to be sat on for a period of time in order to allow for authorities to safely do their job, but as long as eventual across-the-board access was mine and mine alone, I was all in.

As of March 2022, only a handful of topics remained untouched.

Despite numerous inquiries, Gallagher had yet to reveal the significance of the various telltales he'd left behind at the Edgewood crime scenes: the hopscotch grid, missing-dog sign, pennies, and pumpkins, as well as the numerology involved. All remained a mystery.

He'd also rebuffed my repeated attempts to further discuss details of the night and circumstances of his father's death.

4

On the morning of Joshua Gallagher's arrest, he didn't look like a monster.

He was wearing jeans and a blue-and-gray flannel shirt. Perhaps ten or fifteen pounds overweight, with dark circles beneath his eyes and disheveled short brown hair, he resembled the type of nondescript, middle-aged man you might see in a checkout line at the grocery store or pumping gas at the corner Texaco station. He walked slowly, with just a hint of a limp. If you ran into him on a dark and isolated street, you wouldn't necessarily feel in any danger; you probably wouldn't even bother crossing the street to avoid him.

More than anything else—and yes, I've read and listened to the myriad of colorful accounts describing how evil and reptilian-like his eyes appear in his mug shot—he'd looked tired and defeated and perhaps even a little sad.

I wished that hadn't been the case.

I wished he'd looked like a monster—with glowering, coal-red eyes and razor-sharp fangs dripping with blood and mangled bits of human flesh, and gleaming, curved claws instead of fingers.

That would have been more comforting.

That would have made more sense.

Instead, as I sat in my living room, watching the news footage of Joshua Gallagher being escorted into the police station, all I could think was this: *He's wearing a mask underneath his mask.*

5

I wrote those words on a note card:

HE'S WEARING A MASK UNDERNEATH HIS MASK

And on the days that I made the three-hour-plus drive from Bel Air to Cumberland Penitentiary, I taped that note card to the dash of my truck—to help me remember.

6

I was thinking about that note card on the morning of March 8, 2022, when the guards led Joshua Gallagher into Interrogation Room C.

He still doesn't look like a monster.

Gallagher's physical appearance had undergone a number of changes in the two and a half years since his arrest. He'd lost some weight, but it was difficult to tell how much due to the fact that he was always dressed in standard-issue baggy orange overalls. Mainly, you could see it in his face. His double chin was gone, and his cheeks weren't nearly as fleshy as they once were. He now had a discernible jawline. His hair had yet to lose any of its color and was still cut in a crudely short fashion. The puffy dark circles remained beneath his eyes, but I suspected they were there to stay.

There were other subtle differences. For starters, his eyes no longer appeared sad or lost. It sounded strange to say in relation to a confessed serial killer, but Gallagher's eyes seemed to have gained a kind of sparkle over the past year. Indeed, if he'd been a free man working at a regular nine-to-five job and going home to his family every night after quitting time, I would've said that he looked happy to be alive, perhaps even high on life. There was something *renewed* in his gaze, a sense of contentment, maybe. It was hard to put an exact finger on it, but it was there—and it was different. *He* was different. I was sure of it.

Another thing was he didn't limp anymore. During a previous visit, he'd told me that years earlier he'd suffered an accident at work and torn the ligaments in his right ankle. They hadn't healed properly because he'd quit going to his physical therapy appointments, and ever since he'd walked with a slight hobble. But now it was gone. His gait appeared steady and confident. I wasn't sure how that was possible—maybe being stuck in his cell all that time had helped it to heal—but I'd noticed the improvement on more than one occasion.

The biggest change that had occurred since Gallagher's incarceration at the Cumberland Penitentiary was anything but subtle—and it had nothing to do with his physical appearance.

As difficult as it was to comprehend, Joshua Gallagher had become a celebrity of sorts.

I'd recently been shocked to learn that Gallagher received more mail than all the other Cumberland inmates combined. Among the letters and packages that were delivered daily to his cell were marriage proposals (his ex-wife, Samantha, had divorced him two years earlier), drawings and paintings, handwritten poems, inspirational greeting cards, boxes of books, and dozens of Bibles. There were also any number of pleas for information regarding missing persons he was suspected of crossing paths with during his former life, most from immediate family members of the missing. Some of these letter writers promised forgiveness if Gallagher helped them, while others wished nothing more than for Gallagher to "burn in hell where he belonged." Gallagher also received scores of requests from all around the world sent to him by journalists who wanted to interview him; doctors, lawyers, and psychiatrists who wanted to study him; and professors and graduate students who wanted to write research papers about him—all of which he dutifully ignored.

There were a multitude of popular websites and message boards and social media accounts devoted to Gallagher, the majority of them updated daily. Many of his followers were middle-aged women with romantic or maternal aspirations; others were young, frivolous devotees to whichever pop culture icon currently captivated the national spotlight. But there were still others with much darker—and dangerous—interests. An Arizona teenager who frequently participated on one of the more popular Boogeyman message boards had been arrested late last year after compiling a "kill list" of classmates at his high school. The police had found rope, duct tape, ammunition, and a semiautomatic .22 rifle—as well as a homemade burlap mask—hidden in his bedroom closet. There was no telling what might've happened if his ex-girlfriend hadn't turned him in.

The Boogeyman Lives, one of the highest-rated—and most heavily trafficked—true crime podcasts of 2021, was sponsored by heavyweights Monster Energy drink and Trojan condoms. Cohosts Robin Frank and Gerald Whitty were Boston College graduate students who had originally started the podcast as a class project and were now earning six-figure annual salaries. Every Friday night, listeners of *The Boogeyman Lives* podcast heard a live panel of "experts" discuss the murders, Joshua Gallagher's background, and other Boogeyman-related topics of interest. The last half hour of each ninety-minute show was devoted to taking audience calls, most of which involved rampant speculation about Gallagher's involvement in a number of unsolved crimes. There was also a biannual contest, where the grand prize winner (and a guest) was awarded an all-expenses-paid weekend trip to Edgewood, Maryland. A limousine picked up the lucky pair at BWI Marshall Airport, and after dinner at the Venetian Palace on Route 40 (attended by the show's cohosts), they were given an "extensive midnight tour of the Boogeyman's hometown hunting grounds."

FREE THE BOOGEYMAN T-shirts and bumper stickers and "authentic" burlap Boogeyman masks were brisk online sellers. A recent *People* magazine cover featured the stage-front crowd at a Phoenix music festival mere minutes before the concert turned deadly due to faulty wiring in the pyrotechnics system. Front and center in the now infamous photo was a young, tanned college girl with long bleach-blonde hair riding high above the crowd atop her boyfriend's shoulders. She was smiling and wearing a beer-soaked tank top with THE BOOGEYMAN'S A STUD printed inside a big red heart on the front of it. Online sales of the tank top soared after the issue hit newsstands and the cover photo went viral.

While there certainly existed a long and sordid history involving America's fascination with evil—I'm thinking about cold-blooded killers turned behind-bars lotharios such as Charles Manson, Ted Bundy, Richard Ramirez, and more recently, Christopher Watts—it was nearly impossible to ignore the fact that these men were considerably younger than Joshua Gallagher and, according to many firsthand accounts, charismatic, handsome, and disarmingly charming.

None of which were attributes that could be used to describe Joshua Gallagher.

So, then, why the apparent fascination and adulation?

My theory was twofold.

First, there was the nickname: *the Boogeyman.*

Universally recognized, instantly feared.

From the time we were children, we were taught that the Boogeyman was out there, somewhere, lurking unseen in the shadows, and that if we weren't careful, he would come for us.

The Boogeyman was all of our terrors wrapped up into one shapeless, faceless nightmare.

Did the Boogeyman even resemble a human being or was he a hideously deformed monster brought forth from the depths of our collective imaginations? No one really knew for sure—and in the end, it didn't really matter.

All that mattered was that the Boogeyman was out there, somewhere, watching and waiting.

When the John Carpenter–directed *Halloween* opened to lines-around-the-block audiences in 1978, much of the buzz came from word of mouth. Why? Because, finally, the Boogeyman had been given form and substance. But even then, Carpenter was wise enough to only take it so far. After all, in the shooting script, his masked killing machine is simply referred to as "The Shape."

At the conclusion of the film, a terrified and bloodied Laurie Strode says to the haunted Dr. Loomis, "It *was* the Boogeyman."

He stares out the window at the empty yard below where, just seconds earlier, the killer had been sprawled, and answers, "As a matter of fact, it was."

The low-budget *Halloween* went on to become the highest-earning independent film in box-office history—because audiences came out in droves to see the Boogeyman up close and personal, and when the popcorn and Jujubes were gone and the theater lights blinked back on, they got to go home again to the safety of their own beds.

In the summer of 1988, when Joshua Gallagher began his killing spree on the streets of Edgewood, the local media was quick to dub him "the Boogeyman," attributing the nickname to the ferocious and stealthy nature of his crimes. As summer turned to autumn, the police and FBI struggled to track down a single substantial lead to investigate. A task force was formed. A curfew enforced. Neighborhood watch groups were called into action.

And yet the murders continued unabated.

Rumors soon began to spread throughout the town. The killer wasn't human. He was a shape-shifter and could appear in two places at once. Some residents swore the killer had wings and could fly. There were reports of ghostly apparitions appearing in backyards and alleyways. One hysterical woman insisted that someone had tugged on her hair while she was climbing the stairs to go to bed, yet she lived alone and there was no one else present in the house. There were whispers of devil worshipping and cults and demonic possession. A local pastor told his congregation that he'd awoken in the middle of the night and felt evil's cloying presence there in the room with him. Paralyzed with fear, he'd lain awake until dawn, praying, only to toss back his covers in the rays of morning sunshine slanting through his bedroom window to discover that *something* had bitten him on the chest during the night. He showed his parishioners a Polaroid of the bite mark, and although more than a handful agreed that it looked a great deal like your everyday, garden-variety hickey, most of his followers believed him and were extra generous that Sunday morning when the collection plate was passed.

All of these stories, and dozens more like them, only served to add to the overall mystique and—dare I say—allure of the Boogeyman.

Once again, it was a lot like watching a horror movie unspool in real life.

Looking back, it's clear that it was happening even then.

The public's burgeoning fascination with the human monster lurking in the shadows.

It was the stories within the stories that grew Joshua Gallagher's legend.

The Boogeyman's legend.

He didn't have a proper identity back then.

He was a phantom.

He was "the Shape."

7

Ever since Joshua Gallagher's 2019 arrest and his subsequent confession that he had murdered seven young women, Gallagher had unfailingly intimated that he was responsible for the deaths of as many as a dozen additional victims.

However, as of June 2022, he'd managed to provide police with the identities and locations of only three of those alleged victims. Some prominent public figures, as well as many members of the national media, believed that Gallagher was playing games and stringing along Maryland State Police detectives in an effort to gain special treatment, such as more favorable living conditions, protection from violent inmates, and better food. Depending on election cycles and current television ratings, these people could be very vocal with their assertions.

Lieutenant McClernan admitted privately—and on more than one occasion—that she was unsure if this was the case or not, but offered no signs publicly that she was willing to discontinue accommodating Gallagher. It was the closure she'd been able to provide for the three missing girls' families that inspired this level of patience.

As for me, I was also uncertain. My opinion wavered—sometimes visit to visit, other times day to day—although I never once admitted that to McClernan. Or my wife.

As was the case with Gallagher's previous victims, the three young women he'd named had all been attractive teenagers with long hair—confirming yet again that the bittersweet specter of Anna Garfield, Gallagher's ex–college sweetheart, had continued to haunt Joshua Gallagher long after his 1988 killing spree.

The first of the three girls, Shannon Degnim of Glen Burnie, Maryland, had gone missing in August 1999, the summer she'd turned eighteen years old. Shannon was the only child of a dentist father and an elementary school teacher mother and was headed to Rutgers University in the fall to study psychology. She was a spirited girl—the first in her class to get a tattoo and her nose pierced—who often spent her free time alone in the woods, reading or hiking or photographing nature. She was an avid jogger, and the afternoon she disappeared, she'd been out for a run on the hilly trails surrounding Loch Raven Reservoir. When Shannon failed to return home that evening and none of her friends knew where she was, her concerned parents phoned the police. During an extensive search the next day, a member of the Baltimore County Park Police discovered Shannon's Sony Walkman cassette player and earphones abandoned on a steep trail overlooking a shallow cove near the northwest corner of the reservoir. The cassette player was broken, and smudges of blood were found on the bright yellow plastic case. A countywide search continued for the next several weeks, but Shannon was never found.

Until July 2020, nearly two decades after her initial disappearance, when a team of detectives—using a hand-drawn map provided by Joshua Gallagher—was able to locate Shannon Degnim's skeletal remains buried deep in a heavily wooded area of Loch Raven Reservoir.

"I saw her standing in line at the Royal Farms store on Timonium Road," Gallagher told me not long before her body was discovered. "She was buying a bottle of water and a packet of sunflower seeds. I eavesdropped on her conversation with the cashier. She had a pleasant voice. Very polite and friendly." He closed his eyes, lost in the memory. "I waited in the parking lot and followed her into the woods. And then I stalked her and raped her and strangled her." He opened his eyes and looked at me. "She fought me, but I was too strong. When I was finished, I buried her in a gully and covered her with leaves and brush. I cleaned myself up in the car and drove home to my family."

As soon as the interview was over, I googled Shannon Degnim's name and stared at her photograph on my phone screen. With her long blonde hair, blue eyes, and dimples, she bore a striking resemblance to my childhood girlfriend, Rhonda Biskup.

After that, I had nightmares for weeks.

8

I never knew what to expect on the days I interviewed Gallagher.

Talking to him required patience. He was like a child in that regard. He often didn't fully listen to what I had to say before responding. Conversations took off in a dozen different directions at once. It was difficult to get straight answers from him. He obfuscated and constantly needed to be reined in.

Other times, though, he was contemplative and calculating. He would answer even the simplest questions at length and at least appear to strive for accuracy and diligence. He was intelligent and surprisingly well read, and he liked to ask questions. He was a talented storyteller.

9

When people asked me what Joshua Gallagher was *really* like—and you'd be surprised how often it came up, most commonly at social gatherings where folks had too much to drink—I usually responded with some variation of the same nonanswer: "He's like your least favorite uncle who shows up for Thanksgiving. He doesn't make a big impression either way. He's just kind of *there*."

What I didn't tell them was this: Joshua Gallagher's eyes were the most extraordinary—you could even say beautiful—shade of gray I'd ever seen. They looked like the ocean on a stormy day. They looked like a thunderstorm sweeping over the horizon. Gallagher's eyes were alert and measuring. There were tiny flecks of white and blue in his irises. Sometimes I thought they looked like an artist's rendering.

He also had a curious odor—neither pleasant nor unpleasant—that was difficult to detect (in my opinion, he often slathered on cheap aftershave to mask it) and even more difficult to describe. When detectives questioned Annie Riggs after her run-in with the Boogeyman during the fall of 1988, she told them that her assailant "smelled funny . . . he didn't stink like BO or sweat. Instead, he had an organic, almost earthy smell." While that description didn't ring entirely accurate to me, I struggled to come up with anything better. The best I could offer was that it just wasn't normal, and after you'd smelled it once, it was impossible to forget.

And then there was this: Joshua Gallagher hummed when he remembered. He would often pause in the middle of telling a story—you could practically see the cogs and wheels of his brain turning as he tried to bring forth more details from his memory—and while he was doing so, he would inevitably begin to hum. At first, I'd found this habit to be unsettling, then for a time, annoying. Finally, I'd grown used to it. It became just another subtle mannerism to observe and catalog, no different from the way Gallagher tapped his feet when he was in a good mood or the way his left eye sometimes developed a tic when he didn't get enough sleep.

Interestingly, it was always the same melody that he hummed. The same dozen or so notes over and over again. I'd tried to identify it on more than one occasion but thus far had been unsuccessful. Perhaps he'd made it up himself.

10

Excerpt from in-person interview with Joshua Gallagher, age 55, inmate #AC4311920 at Cumberland Penitentiary, recorded on March 8, 2021:

CHIZMAR: When did you first make contact with Loretta Stamford?

GALLAGHER: It was the summer of 2011. At Rocks State Park.

CHIZMAR: You were living in Hanover at the time.

GALLAGHER: Yes. We were invited to a cookout by some old friends from Edgewood Meadows. I wasn't that keen on going, but Samantha really wanted to. So we went.

CHIZMAR: Your children were with you?

GALLAGHER: Yes.

CHIZMAR: Did Loretta Stamford attend the same cookout?

GALLAGHER: No. She was at the park with friends.

CHIZMAR: Go back in time and tell me what you saw . . . what you felt.

GALLAGHER: I was fishing with my youngest son in Deer Creek—

CHIZMAR: Phillip being your youngest son.

GALLAGHER: Yes.

CHIZMAR: Sorry, go ahead.

GALLAGHER: We were fishing, and Loretta and several of her friends floated by on inner tubes. The other girls didn't pay us any mind—barely even looked in our direction—but Loretta smiled and waved and even joked around with Phillip.

CHIZMAR: Did you know right away that you wanted to kill her?

GALLAGHER: No. I thought she was pretty, and she had a nice smile. But that was it. Nothing else.

CHIZMAR: Had you been struggling with dark thoughts in the days leading up to the cookout?

GALLAGHER: No, not at all. Not since Colette Bowden.

CHIZMAR: So, we're talking almost five years now.

GALLAGHER: That sounds about right. I was feeling good.

CHIZMAR: What happened next?

GALLAGHER: Later in the day, Loretta and her friends arrived at the picnic area and set up their blankets not far from where we were eating. I watched her for a while. I was curious.

CHIZMAR: Just . . . curious?

GALLAGHER: At that point, yes. [yawns]

CHIZMAR: Am I boring you?

GALLAGHER: Not at all. I'm never bored these days. I just didn't sleep much last night. I was awake writing.

CHIZMAR: Writing what?

[no response]

Okay . . . so, you watched her.

GALLAGHER: [nods] Eventually, I followed her to the parking lot.

CHIZMAR: Did you speak to her?

GALLAGHER: No. I watched her take a small cooler from the back of her Jeep. Once she rejoined her friends, I snuck over and found her purse hidden beneath the driver's seat. It's amazing how some people just leave their personal belongings unsecured. I made sure no one was looking and then took a picture of her driver's license with my phone and put it back.

CHIZMAR: So you knew by then? That you were going to kill her?

GALLAGHER: [nods] I knew by then.

CHIZMAR: Okay. I'm just trying to get a sense of the timing here. When *exactly* did you decide you were going to kill her? Right there in the parking lot, looking through her stuff?

GALLAGHER: I would say it was a little earlier. Around the time I decided to follow her. I was eating a hamburger and I got some ketchup on my shirt. I was cleaning myself up. And that's when I saw me with my hands around her neck, clear as day.

CHIZMAR: Was it the ketchup?

GALLAGHER: [laughs] No, no. No silly blood symbolism or anything like that. It could've been a squirt of mustard and I would've experienced the same thing.

CHIZMAR: You're sure of that?

GALLAGHER: I'm positive. It was the same as with the others. I just *saw* it, like a movie playing inside my head, and knew that I was seeing the future. I saw it and I *felt* it.

CHIZMAR: What did it feel like?

GALLAGHER: Like a moment of pure clarity . . . and stimulation.

CHIZMAR: Sexual stimulation?

GALLAGHER: Yes, that too. I was hard in seconds. I had to sit down, take some deep breaths to hide it from my family and the other people around us.

CHIZMAR: [pause] Were you surprised to find out that she lived in Pennsylvania, and not far from you?

GALLAGHER: Not really. I wouldn't say that, despite the convenience. It just felt right. Everything about her did.

CHIZMAR: After that first time at the Rocks, how long was it before you saw her again?

GALLAGHER: [humming quietly] Two days later. I followed her from her house to work.

CHIZMAR: Her parents' house, you mean.

GALLAGHER: Yes.

CHIZMAR: You know, Loretta Stamford was six months short of her seventeenth birthday at the time of her death.

GALLAGHER: [humming] She looked older.

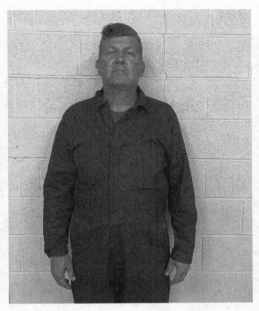

Joshua Gallagher at the Cumberland Penitentiary
(Photo courtesy of Maryland State Police)

Joshua Gallagher at work as a machinist in 2018 *(Photo courtesy of Leonard Forrentina)*

Louise Rutherford in 2001 *(Photo courtesy of* The Baltimore Sun*)*

Erin Brown in 2018 *(Photo courtesy of* The Aegis*)*

Colette Bowden in 2006 *(Photo courtesy of* The Aegis*)*

Loch Raven Reservoir *(Photo courtesy of David Stuart)*

Shannon Degnim burial site at Loch Raven Reservoir *(Photo courtesy of Maryland State Police)*

Excerpt from in-person interview with Joshua Gallagher, age 56, inmate #AC4311920 at Cumberland Penitentiary, recorded on December 7, 2021:

GALLAGER: You want to hear something interesting?

CHIZMAR: Sure.

GALLAGHER: I'm changing.

CHIZMAR: Changing. Changing how?

GALLAGHER: I'm taller. Haven't you noticed?

CHIZMAR: Ummm, no, I can't say I have.

GALLAGHER: Almost two-thirds of an inch. I've been keeping track on the wall in my cell.

CHIZMAR: Why would you do that?

GALLAGHER: [shrugs] I honestly don't know. I started last year. Maybe I knew something was going to happen. Maybe I knew that I was already in the process of changing. I also like peanut butter now. No, that is incorrect—I love it.

CHIZMAR: And . . . you didn't used to like peanut butter?

GALLAGHER: Couldn't stand it. Haaated it. Ever since I was a kid.

CHIZMAR: That is interesting. Anything else?

GALLAGHER: Oh yeah. Lots.

THREE

THE NEXT DAY

"The killer had been sloppy."

1

The state trooper assigned to watch our house overnight gave me a wave as I drove past him in the driveway. When I lifted my hand from the steering wheel to wave back, it felt like I was holding a dumbbell. I was exhausted. After Lieutenant McClernan's late-night visit, I'd only managed to get a couple hours of sleep. Tired of tossing and turning and trying to make my brain behave, I'd finally gotten up shortly after five thirty. It was still dark outside my bedroom window, which immediately made me feel worse. Suffice to say, even on my best days—which this was most certainly not—I wasn't much of a morning person.

Kara woke before her alarm went off and we made breakfast together, neither of us saying much. After we ate maybe half of the ham-and-cheese omelets, wheat toast, and fresh fruit piled on our plates, she went back upstairs to shower and get ready for an eight-thirty appointment with her allergist, and I climbed the steps to my office above the garage hoping to get some work done.

That didn't last long.

No more than a half hour later, I gave up trying to write anything decent and closed my laptop. I turned on the television and switched the channel to CNN. After suffering through commercials for Viagra and some kind of high-blood-pressure wonder pill I couldn't even pronounce,

I watched a feature story about the war in Ukraine. Good people fighting the good fight against overwhelming odds. On any other day, I might've felt inspired.

As soon as they cut away from grainy footage of street fighting in Kyiv, anchorwoman Brianna Keilar—her long blonde hair coifed to such absolute perfection that she resembled a Barbie doll—appeared on-screen, teasing breaking news about a mall shooting in Wichita and the gruesome discovery of human remains at the Maryland home of a best-selling true crime author. Just before they moved to commercial break, she turned and stared directly into the camera and, in her most dramatic voice, asked: "Was it simply a coincidence of the darkest nature . . . or is the Boogeyman really back?"

I cringed and hoped that Kara wasn't watching in the bedroom while she got dressed.

Either way, she'd hear about it soon enough. The news about Annie Riggs had traveled fast—exactly what I'd been afraid of.

I turned off the television and grabbed my truck keys.

2

The press vehicles had been moved further down the street—fifty yards or so beyond the intersection of Runnymede and Southampton, where they'd been parked the day before—and there were quite a bit more of them. As I coasted down the driveway, I spotted the familiar CNN logo on a pair of white vans, as well as MSNBC on the side panel of an SUV with blacked-out windows. Even if I hadn't already caught the teaser on television, it would have been painfully clear: the Annie Riggs story was national news and quickly gaining momentum.

There was a grassy field, maybe two acres, located directly across the street from our house. We had no idea who owned it or if there were any future plans for the lot; all we knew was that county workers came out a couple of times a month during the summer to mow it. That's where the news crews had set up. There were a dozen or so two- and three-person teams camped out there, sharply dressed on-air personalities paired with mobile camera operators, a handful of younger folks—most likely interns—schlepping convenience-store cups of coffee or sitting around holding boom mics.

When they saw my truck roll out of the driveway, they scrambled to their feet en masse and swarmed onto Southampton Road—and started chasing me. I watched incredulously in the rearview mirror as a woman in a short red dress and high heels tripped over another reporter's foot and they both went sprawling to the pavement. Not one person stopped to check on them or help them up; the others just kept on coming, waving their arms and shouting their questions. If the traffic light at the intersection hadn't turned green, they might've caught me.

Instead, I made a right-hand turn onto 543 and headed south toward the Route 40 bypass—and the town of Edgewood just a few miles further down the road. All morning long, it had felt like I was sleepwalking around the house. Now, it felt like I was driving on autopilot, my destination preprogrammed.

But the truth of it was I didn't know where else to go.

As I merged into the morning rush-hour traffic, I rolled down my window and turned the radio off—and listened to Lieutenant McClernan's voice inside my head.

3

There was a lot to unpack from last night.

Lieutenant McClernan had brought with her several glossy photographs of the man in the mask, eight-by-ten stills captured from the security footage. The images were enlarged and remarkably clear, and they'd provided the detectives with a number of invaluable details.

The man was wearing black jeans, a black sweatshirt with no logo or hood, and black or brown lace-up boots. He was also wearing latex gloves on both of his hands. The mask, made from burlap, was tied in the back with a length of twine. It hadn't yet been determined if the mask was of the homemade variety or a mass-produced version of the original Boogeyman mask, which was sold by online retailers all across the country. The man's hair was hidden beneath the mask and not visible in the photos.

Detectives estimated his height at somewhere between six feet and six feet, two inches, his weight between 170 and 190 pounds. There was an ongoing discussion as to whether the man walked with a slight limp or if it was merely his gait. He was most likely right-handed. He was also strong.

The black garbage bag he carried over his right shoulder weighed almost 115 pounds. The bag itself was a ProGrade contractor bag. It was a popular brand, sold everywhere from Amazon and Walmart to Home Depot and Lowe's. Many locally owned hardware stores also stocked it on their shelves. The man had wanted the bag to be found—and quickly. Not only had he left it in a highly trafficked location, but he'd also poked a series of small holes in the bottom of the bag, allowing for bodily fluids to escape into the ground and freeing the highly offensive odor that JJ and I had detected. The police had found no discernible blood trail, indicating the holes were made after the bag was placed in its final resting spot.

Last night, in a daze, I'd asked McClernan if the victim's left ear had been missing. It was at that point that Kara had finally had enough and retreated up the stairs to our bedroom. I couldn't really blame her, and a few seconds later, when the lieutenant answered my question, I was especially grateful she was no longer in the room.

"This is all off the record," McClernan told me, waiting for my nod of agreement before continuing. "We have no idea about her ear. The body was dismembered. The torso, limbs, and internal organs were all present inside the bag . . . but her head was missing."

The floor tilted underneath my feet again. Leaning against the foyer wall to steady myself, I pictured the seventeen-year-old Annie Riggs I remembered so well from the summer of 1988. Big brown eyes. Toothy smile. A scattering of freckles across the bridge of her nose. The quintessential girl next door.

After recovering from the initial shock, I mumbled, "Other than the mask, nothing about this matches Gallagher's M.O."

But I'd spoken too soon.

"There were ligature marks on what was left of her wrists and ankles, and bite marks on both of her legs," the lieutenant continued. "We took impressions, but we didn't have much to work with. The killer was sloppy. Presumably because he was in a hurry."

"What are your profilers saying about the dismemberment?"

"They're working on it. All we know right now is that it's a very rushed timeline. Less than fifteen hours between the last known contact with Anne Riggs and the discovery of her body. He abducted her, took her somewhere and killed her, cut her into pieces, and left her in your front yard—all within a fifteen-hour window. That's not an easy thing to do. It takes time to do that to a human body."

"So he's local to the area . . . or he had someplace nearby waiting to take her."

"We're working on that, too."

The only bit of good news Lieutenant McClernan had to share was that the police already had a lead. Maybe.

A witness had stepped forward. A forty-three-year-old man who lived with his wife and daughter in the neighborhood just past the traffic circle. He worked the late shift as a Baltimore City firefighter and usually got home around four in the morning. He often took the dogs for a walk to help him wind down before going to sleep. Around 4:30 a.m. on June 3, he noticed a pickup truck parked on the shoulder of Southampton not far from where it crossed Route 543. He couldn't remember if the truck had been black or dark blue, but he was fairly positive it'd had Maryland license plates and 100 percent certain that there had been a Grateful Dead bumper sticker on the back window (the round one with the skull and roses). When he'd circled around that way twenty or so minutes later, the truck was gone. Could be something. Could be nothing. The detectives were looking into it.

4

I should have known I'd end up on Willoughby Beach Road that morning.

The road ran parallel to the triumvirate of Edgewood schools (looking left to right: high school, middle, elementary) and provided the only entrance and exit to a number of housing developments in which many of my good friends once lived. I'd spent an awful lot of time on Willoughby. At first, on foot, usually with the rest of the Hanson Road crew by my side; later, once I'd gotten my driver's license, cruising down the twisting back road in my souped-up hot rod—which actually only existed in the secret world of my imagination. My first car had been a dog-crap-brown Toyota Corolla with 150,000 miles on the odometer. My second, a bright orange four-door Datsun. Neither went above fifty miles per hour without shaking so hard on its frame that it made my teeth rattle.

I had particularly fond memories of the waterfront area located at the tail end of Willoughby. Long, lazy summer days spent eating hamburgers and hot dogs and swimming at Flying Point Park; fishing for white perch and carp and catfish from the bulkhead at Trojan Harbor Marina; playing tag and hide-and-seek and riding the miniature train at the playground.

The summer after my sophomore year of high school, Brian Anderson and Jimmy Cavanaugh and I borrowed the keys for Brian's father's boat—which Mr. Fred kept just across the Bush River at Otter Creek Marina. None of us were old enough to drive yet, so we walked the nearly four miles from our houses on Hanson Road, cutting across Edgewood Road and picking up Willoughby until we finally reached Flying Point Park. Once there, we rested for a few minutes before setting off on the lengthy swim across the river. And thus commenced a legendary, hot

July afternoon of boating, swimming, fishing, and chugging warm left-over beers from Mr. Fred's fish cooler. At the end of the day, sunburned and exhausted, we docked the boat, swam back across the river, and walked four miles home in the dark. Our parents were waiting for us—and they weren't pleased.

The whole thing was irresponsible and dangerous and downright foolish. It was also one of the best days of our young lives. None of us had ever forgotten it.

5

Annie Riggs's house was a gated stone contemporary situated right on the water. There was an old basketball hoop attached to the garage out front and a swimming pool with an outdoor kitchen in the backyard. At the rear of the property, a T-shaped pier extended deep into the Bush River, a thirty-foot Bayliner and a pair of bright yellow Jet Skis moored to its pilings. Annie had done well for herself.

An unmarked sedan and a crime lab van were parked in the drive-way, next to a sporty red VW and a late-model Suburban. A group of kids on bikes were gathered on the grassy shoulder across the street. One of them—a tall, lanky, acne-scarred teenager wearing a black Ramones T-shirt and leather wristbands—flashed me the middle finger as I drove by for the third time. Embarrassed, I slouched even lower in the driver's seat.

Thanks to Lieutenant McClernan, I knew that Annie Riggs had worked as a structural engineer at Aberdeen Proving Ground for almost thirty years. After graduating from high school in 1989, she'd attended Virginia Tech on an academic scholarship and finished in the top 5 per-cent of her class. The summer after graduation, she'd accepted a full-time position at APG and had been there ever since—steadily working her way up the ranks until she was put in charge of the entire operation in early 2015.

Annie had married fairly young, had two children—a son and a daughter—and had gotten divorced shortly after her fortieth birthday. There was no drama involved; they'd simply grown apart over the years and fallen out of love. The divorce was, by all accounts, amicable. The ex-husband lived in New Mexico with his second wife and rarely saw the children now that they were older. Detectives from the Las Cruces Police Department were checking him out.

According to family and friends, Annie rarely dated after the divorce. She was an avid reader and boater and enjoyed working in her flower garden. These activities—as well as being a doting grandmother to a brand-new grandson—occupied the majority of her free time and brought her much happiness. She was almost never lonely or bored. Six months ago, as a favor to an old friend, she'd gone on a blind dinner date with a man named Michael Buckley, who was a history professor at nearby Harford Community College. They hit it off immediately and had been seeing each other regularly ever since.

On the evening of June 2, Annie Riggs left her office at the usual time of 4:45 p.m. There was security-system footage of her walking alone across the parking lot, getting inside her car, and driving away. No other vehicles appeared to follow her. Four minutes later, there was additional footage of her exiting the proving ground by way of the main gate on Maryland Boulevard. She called her daughter, Joanne Mather of Carrs Mill Road in Fallston, shortly after from her cell phone. They discussed plans for the weekend and hung up. The call lasted six minutes. That was the last time anyone heard from her.

Joanne thought she remembered her mother saying she needed to stop and pick up groceries on the way home. But she also admitted that she could've been mixed up and the shopping comment might've been part of a previous conversation. She wasn't entirely sure. Just in case, police were interviewing employees and checking security footage at a number of local grocery stores.

Mr. Buckley and Annie Riggs maintained separate residences but often spent the night at each other's homes. That Thursday evening, Mr.

Buckley was expected for dinner. He showed up at the house at the pre-arranged time of 7 p.m. with a bottle of wine and ingredients for a salad he'd picked up at the Abingdon Wegmans. To his surprise, Annie's car was not parked in the driveway and the front door was locked. Mr. Buckley used the key Annie had previously given him to gain entry to the house and, after checking the garage, immediately called and left a voice mail on her cell phone. Fifteen minutes later, when he hadn't heard back, he left a second voice message. Approximately thirty minutes after that, not knowing what else to do, he phoned Annie's daughter, Joanne. She immediately drove to her mother's house. Additional voice mails—from both parties—were left on Annie's phone with no response. At 9:37 p.m., Mr. Buckley, with Joanne at his side, called 911 and reported Annie Riggs missing.

Officer Steven Moore, a fourteen-year veteran with the Harford County Sheriff's Department, arrived at the Riggs residence at 10:05 p.m. and began his initial investigation. After completing a thorough walk-through and confirming with Riggs's daughter that nothing was amiss inside the home, Officer Moore grabbed a flashlight from his squad car and examined the exterior and grounds. What he discovered was troubling. A screen covering one of the ground-level windows facing the backyard had been sliced open and there were what appeared to be pry marks on the window frame. The window—which looked out from Annie Riggs's home office—was securely locked from the inside and the hardwood floor beneath it appeared undisturbed.

"Technicians found only Anne Riggs's fingerprints on both the interior and exterior panes of glass, as well as the windowsills," Lieutenant McClernan told me. "There was, however, significant 'smudging' on the outside of the window, indicating that the prowler had been wearing gloves."

The detectives noted in their initial report that they believed the attempted break-in had occurred recently and almost certainly failed. There was also mention of a pair of broken light bulbs in lampposts located at the rear of the property. By that point in the investigation—going on 2 a.m. Friday morning—detectives were almost certain that Annie Riggs had been abducted from somewhere other than her home, a theory soon supported by statements from her neighbors.

Annie Riggs's next-door neighbors, Todd and Cindy Richardson, spent that Thursday evening in Churchville, watching their son's Little League baseball game, and after a late dinner at Applebee's, they returned home at about 8:45 p.m. As a result they had no idea if Riggs's car had been parked in her driveway at any point that evening. Pam Hershfeld, who lived with her husband and four children in a sprawling rancher directly across the street from Riggs's house, was a different story altogether. She'd spent the entire day at home. In fact, for most of the afternoon and evening, she'd been busy reorganizing the floor-to-ceiling shelves in the family's two-car garage. "I had a perfect view of Anne's house and driveway from where I was working," she told Officer Moore and then promptly walked him over to the mouth of her garage so he could see for himself. "I got started around two thirty or three, and the only person who pulled into that driveway was Mike, her boyfriend. A lot of days, she gets UPS or FedEx deliveries—sometimes both; I tease her about it all the time—but not yesterday. Mike was the only one until her daughter showed up."

Officer Moore and the detectives continued working the case throughout the night and into the next day, speaking with a number of Annie Riggs's family members, friends, neighbors, and coworkers. The police took a particularly close look at Riggs's boyfriend, but at some point the next morning, everything came back clean on Michael Buckley, including his alibi.

On the evening of Friday, June 3—approximately twenty-four hours after Mr. Buckley called 911—a connection was finally made between the Annie Riggs missing-persons case and the unidentified human remains discovered earlier that morning in Bel Air. Later that same night, at 8:55 p.m., Officer Steven Moore and Detective Sergeant Anthony

Gonzalez—using several tattoos as well as a recent surgical scar and an engraved Virginia Tech class ring—made the initial identification of Annie Riggs's body.

6

The kid in the Ramones shirt made me nervous. The last thing I needed was for him to call his parents—or even worse, the cops— and tell them there was a stranger creeping around Annie Riggs's house. There was a good chance I wouldn't be recognized, but with all the recent buzz surrounding *Chasing the Boogeyman*, there was always the possibility that I would be.

If the press got word of it, that could be very bad for me.

Still not ready to head home, I swung into the Flying Point parking lot and braked to a stop at the water's edge. There was a single crabber at the end of the pier. Only a couple of boats out on the river. Despite the sunny skies and narrow channel, the water appeared dark and choppy. *Too much wind,* I thought, reaching for my cell phone. I had turned off the ringer before I'd left the house and I wanted to see if Kara had called after her appointment.

Five voice mails, not one from a number I recognized, and—Jesus, how was that even possible?—196 texts.

I quickly scrolled down the list.

Paul Chizmar: Hey cuz lemme know if you need anything.

Jimmy Cavanaugh: Holeee-shit! Just saw the news. This keeps up and you're gonna get blacklisted from the Wood. From hometown hero to hometown zero. Just kidding! Hahaha. See you in a couple weeks, brother!

Noah Chizmar: Saw you on tv in the clubhouse. Griff says you're kinda ugly for a movie star.

Stephen King: Yikes. Give me a call when you get a chance.

Ken Klein: I saw a movie like this once. Got a question for you when you have a chance.

Nancy Chizmar: Come hide out with us in Tahoe!

And here the mystery of almost two hundred text messages was partially solved. My sister, Nancy, had sent me more than fifty texts all by herself. A record, even for her.

Billy Chizmar: Thought you'd want to see this right away...

He'd attached a photo. Someone had started a makeshift memorial for Annie Riggs next to the fire hydrant in our yard. There wasn't much to it—just a simple wooden cross sticking out of the ground surrounded by a couple of stuffed bears and a framed photograph that was too small to make out—but the sight of it still gave me chills. Instantly reminded of the elaborate memorials family and friends had erected for the four young Edgewood victims, I said a silent prayer that history wouldn't repeat itself. Eager to move on, I continued scrolling.

Kara Chizmar: Grabbing lunch after my appt w/ Juliet. Will call to see if u want anything.

Sam English: Hope you're okay, Mr. Chizmar.

Sam had just finished his sophomore year at Edgewood High School. I'd met him the previous fall at an after-school book club meeting I'd attended as guest speaker. Half the kids who showed up fell asleep—but not Sam. He listened attentively, asked smart questions, and even took advantage of the invitation to email me for additional guidance. Eventually, Sam wanted to go to college to study journalism, but right now, he was most interested in writing fiction. And he was good at it too. His prose was often raw and unfocused, but it was also filled with remarkable insight and an honesty that was impossible to fake. In no time at all, I'd become a sort of mentor to him. We met once a month when our schedules allowed, and he often emailed his stories to me when I was on the road. Passionate, hardworking, and full of dreams, he reminded me a lot of Billy at that age.

Brian Keene: Happy to stand armed guard at Chez Chizmar if you need me...

310-491-5632: The Boogeyman is coming for you next!

443-307-5555: Ya fuckin vulture! U happy now?

Bill Caughron: I told you to steer clear of those weirdos.

302-714-8762: the next time it'll be u in that garbage bag

I put the phone down.

My cell number was unlisted, but it wasn't very difficult to get ahold of. There'd been a time, during the initial success of *Chasing the Boogeyman*, when I'd thought I might have to change it. Every day I was bombarded with calls and texts. Offers for book signings and speaking engagements. Never-ending requests for interviews. Congratulations from friends and classmates I hadn't heard from in years. Invitations to go to lunch or dinner with former neighbors. Flirty messages from old girlfriends. Every teacher I knew asked me to stop in and speak with their students. The Route 40 Business Association asked me to join their advisory board. The Edgewood PTA asked me to speak at graduation. It was a wonderful feeling to experience such hometown love and appreciation, but it quickly became overwhelming. There were never enough hours in the day to respond to everyone.

Then, as time passed and the surge of appreciative messages slowly began to subside, I started to hear from an altogether different group of people.

Not everyone, it seemed, was happy with the book's success.

Antonio Franklin, a well-respected community leader, told a reporter from the *Aegis* that *Chasing the Boogeyman* had done nothing more than add to Edgewood's long-standing bad reputation. He claimed I'd written it solely for the money and added this zinger: "The only thing worse than Chizmar's ghastly subject matter is his sophomoric purple prose. Both are worthy of the tabloids." Franklin's controversial comments sparked a monthslong feud—spearheaded by one of the moderators of my Facebook page—in the letters to the editor section of the *Aegis*.

Several local business owners, upset that I'd turned down their offers to host speaking events, accused me of favoritism, even though I'd politely explained that although my schedule was currently full, I'd be more than happy to set up something at a later date. Before long, I was being called a "sellout" and word was spread around town that I had gotten "a big head and forgotten where I'd come from."

That fall, a public protest by a Harford County anti-violence group was held in front of the Edgewood Library, calling for the swift removal of all copies of *Chasing the Boogeyman*. Several speakers using a bullhorn took turns riling up the modest crowd gathered outside in the parking lot. Ironically, the police had to be summoned after the protest turned violent.

Earlier in the year, a national boycott was called by the Alliance for Adopted Children, a well-funded adoption organization that had accused me of unfairly portraying adoptees in the book's final chapter. The group labeled me a "fearmonger" and petitioned for months to get Walmart and Costco to stop carrying my book. The last I'd heard, they had amassed over 125,000 virtual signatures.

And then there was the religious group based in upstate New York called the Guardians of Angels, who'd named me as one of the fifty most dangerous entertainers in America. Stephen King, Caroline Kepnes, and I were the only writers who made the list, the three of us deemed guilty of "spreading and glorifying the rhetoric of evil in their filthy books and thus inspiring other dark souls to commit similar acts of wickedness."

But none of these folks held a candle to the true crime fanatics and the Joshua Gallagher groupies. There were just so damn many of them, and the vast majority were true believers. These people had purpose and they had intent. And more than anything else, they had the utmost faith that what they believed was the absolute truth.

And that, my friends, is what you call a dangerous combination.

Still, I was stubborn and never did change my phone number.

My film agent once told me, "It doesn't matter how many times you change it. They'll find you eventually. In this day and age, they always find you. It's just a matter of time."

I glanced at the screen of my cell phone.

The Boogeyman is coming for you next!

Karma's a bitch!

I shuddered and started the truck.

7

As I was pulling out of the parking lot onto Willoughby Beach Road, I was forced to slam on my brakes to avoid hitting a couple of kids on bicycles who'd ignored the stop sign and zoomed right through the intersection. One of bikes caught a tire on the loose gravel shoulder and slid sideways, spilling its rider into a muddy culvert that ran alongside the road.

I slowed down to make sure the boy was okay and was only a little surprised to see that it was the Ramones T-shirt kid from down the street. Splashes of mud streaked both of his cheeks and forehead. His hair stood up in filthy spikes.

He scowled at me and spat, "Hey, asshole, why dontcha watch the hell where you're going?"

I smiled down at him—feeling a tickle of satisfaction—and said, "Oh, I *was* watching."

And then I flicked him the bird and took off.

8

The satisfaction didn't last very long.

Not even a mile down the road and I was already feeling guilty for messing with the kid. It had been mean and out of character, and the only excuse I had wasn't a good one. I could hear my father's voice scolding me from the passenger seat: *"Your run of bad luck shouldn't turn into anyone else's."*

Of course, he was right. Dammit.

As I drove past Edgewood High School, I suddenly felt like a stranger in my hometown. The original school had been torn down nearly a decade earlier and replaced by a sprawling state-of-the-art, modern structure. Towering columns of red brick and sun-sparkled glass as far as the eye could see, the new building resembled a metropolitan office park more than it did a suburban high school. I knew I should've been grateful for the progress, even felt a healthy sense of pride—God knows, the students deserved it after so many years of being looked down upon by the rest of the county—but today the sight of the new school just left me feeling sad and lost and longing for simpler times.

Maybe it had been a mistake coming here today.

Maybe Kara was right—and the darkness was everywhere, seeping into my soul.

Usually, driving through my hometown felt like visiting with a long-lost friend. The familiar streets and landmarks brought me a sense of calm and comfort and served as a reminder of the person I'd once been and the hardscrabble path I'd taken to become the person I was today.

But something felt off-kilter.

Something felt different.

The town itself *was* different; I knew that.

It had grown old and tired, just like the rest of us.

Over the years, many of the houses along both sides of Edgewood Meadows had fallen into disrepair, the lawns unkempt and overgrown with weeds and witchgrass. Junked cars and discarded toys littered driveways and sidewalks. Even the roads seemed to hide more potholes. The 7-Eleven on the hill where I'd once bought Slurpees and played video games, where Fred Anderson and the rest of the old-timers used to hang out, gossiping and drinking coffee spiked with bourbon, was nothing more than a memory now. The Santoni's shopping center was gone too. No more Plaza Drugs, where I'd bought my first pack of baseball cards; no more pool hall or laundromat or Discount Liquors with Edgewood's first *Asteroids* machine and the world's best pizza subs.

As I turned left onto Cedar Drive—where, so many years earlier, Kacey Robinson's nude and battered body had been discovered at the bottom of a playground sliding board—I noticed a faded yellow strip of leftover police tape dangling from a telephone phone. According to a series of articles in the *Baltimore Sun*, the hard drug trade—along with the inevitable surge of street violence that accompanied it—had made its way to the streets of Edgewood from Baltimore City (located just twenty-something miles west on Route 40). Every month now, there was news of shootings and stabbings in Harford Square, and it had gotten so bad in the row homes behind what used to be the Giant shopping center that the Harford County Sheriff's Department had recently opened a new substation in a nearby office building.

Unlike the majority of my longtime friends, I often found myself wrestling with the reality of the situation—or as they put it: *ignoring what was right in front of my face*—but deep down inside, I knew the truth. I just didn't want to admit it. Edgewood hadn't merely grown old and tired. It had become mean and rough around the edges. It had grown teeth, and they were sharp. There was no curfew in place—as there had been during the summer of 1988—but folks were afraid to walk around outside after dark. Muggings and beatings were commonplace. Litter was everywhere on the streets. Graffiti marked many of the buildings. There were homeless encampments in the woods bordering Route 40, and this past winter an elderly couple on Trimble Road had frozen to death in their ramshackle home after their heat had been turned off. It was all so frightening and depressing, and I was glad my parents weren't around to see it.

I'd tried on more than one occasion to pinpoint when the decline had first begun. Most people blamed the influx of subsidized housing that occurred in the mid to late 1990s. Others insisted that it was due to the government cutting thousands of civilian jobs in 2001 at Edgewood Arsenal and Aberdeen Proving Ground. Yet I couldn't help but wonder if it had all started even earlier—for instance, sometime during the summer or fall of 1988.

The last time I'd visited Edgewood—it'd been early December, with strings of Christmas lights glowing along the rooftops and snow flurries dancing in the air—I'd found myself parked across the street from the Gallaghers' old house on Hawthorne Drive. I'd sat there alone in my car for almost an hour, the heater blowing warm air on my legs, listening to classic rock on the radio and staring out the snow-streaked windshield, imagining what it had been like for the four of them inside that house. What had they talked about at dinner? What television shows did they watch? What were their favorite board games? Did they ever get in arguments? Did they joke around with each other?

Eventually, a minivan had pulled into the driveway, and a woman and a little boy had gotten out. The little boy had been carrying a knapsack with one hand and holding an ice cream cone with the other. He'd looked cold but happy. I watched him slip and slide across the driveway and wondered if he knew who had lived in the house before him. I wondered if he knew about the body they'd found in the woods in his backyard and if the kids at school ever teased or tried to scare him. *"You live in the Boogeyman's house! What if he breaks out of prison and comes home again?! Like Michael Myers!"*

Before they went inside, his mother looked over her shoulder and held my stare, as if to say, *That's right, we live here now. The past is the past. Time moves on, buddy, so why don't you move on too, and get right the fuck on outta here?*

So that's what I'd done that day, driving away as fast as I could on the snow-slick streets, red-faced and ashamed to my bones, feeling like an imposter.

Feeling very much like I did today.

What if he breaks out of prison and comes home again?

And right there was the hard truth of it:

Edgewood was as much Joshua Gallagher's hometown as it was mine.

And while Gallagher might've burned the town to the ground, I was the one who had thrown gasoline on the fire.

9

I made one final stop before heading home.

I parked across the street from 920 Hanson Road and waited until the traffic passed, and then I rolled down my window and used my cell phone to take a picture. I wasn't exactly sure why I was doing it, but for some reason, it suddenly felt important.

I looked down at the image I'd captured on my phone. Since my last visit, a tall white fence had been erected around the side yards and backyards, giving the house a somewhat lopsided appearance and hiding most of the lawn from view. My father would have hated it. He would've also hated the crooked shutter hanging next to my old bedroom window and the weed-choked tree stump in the front yard. A green minivan with two flat tires sat in the driveway.

As I was parked there, a little boy of maybe nine or ten strolled around the corner of Tupelo and headed up the hill on Hanson Road, where my father and I used to watch the summer storms roll in. The boy stopped in front of what was once Bernie and Norma Gentile's house and bent down to tie his shoe. When he was finished, he stood and abruptly took off at a sprint as if someone were chasing him. I turned and searched the street, but no one was there.

It wasn't until later, after I'd gotten home and was sitting out back with the dogs, that I realized the kid had most likely been running away from me. A stranger wearing a baseball hat pulled low over his eyes, slouched down in a truck across the street. A stranger who was watching him. The boy's parents had probably warned him about men like me. They'd probably told him all about the Boogeyman.

10

Later that night, before I went upstairs to bed, I sat out back and made three phone calls that couldn't wait any longer.

The first was to my oldest sister, Mary. We spoke for fifteen minutes, and after reassuring her that we were all okay and the police were handling the situation, she said she loved me and good night.

The second call was to my other sister Nancy. I knew she was busy at work on the West Coast, but I also knew that if I didn't leave a message, I was likely to wake up to fifty more texts the next morning.

The last phone call went to my agent, Kristin Nelson. She answered on the first ring.

"Hey there, you doing okay?"

"Mostly," I answered. "It's been a long couple of days."

"Have you thought about grabbing a nice hotel room somewhere? Get away from that circus I saw on the news."

"Not yet, but we might have to if it gets any worse."

She cleared her throat. "Listen, not to be insensitive, but I spoke with Ed today. There's never been a better time to nail down a follow-up."

"I'm sorry, I can't even think about that right now."

"I figured you'd say that, but hear me out and I'll be done. With everything that just happened, I think we're looking at high six figures . . . maybe even seven. You hold all the cards here, Rich."

"I don't know . . ."

"Talk to Kara about it. See what she thinks."

Talking to my wife about a new Boogeyman book was the last thing I wanted to do. Besides, there was something I needed to do first.

"Before I do anything else," I told her, "I want to talk to Gallagher. Face-to-face."

The vacant field on Southampton Road where the media set up camp *(Photo courtesy of the author)*

Anne Rigg's boyfriend, Michael Buckley *(Photo courtesy of* The Aegis*)*

Anne Riggs's home on Willoughby Beach Road *(Photo courtesy of* The Aegis*)*

The "new" Edgewood High School *(Photo courtesy of the author)*

Excerpt from Edgewood: Looking Back, *by Richard Chizmar, pages 83–84:*

Spooky Fox Mulder from *The X-Files* would have loved my buddy Bobby Eiring.

When it came to UFOs and extraterrestrials, Bobby was what we called a "true believer." He had stacks of books and piles of photocopied research (the Edgewood Library charged a nickel a page to use the massive photocopier in the lobby) in his pigpen of a basement bedroom, as well as a secret file of what he called "undeniable photographic proof" that the military scientists at Edgewood Arsenal were conducting postmortem research on alien life-forms. We'd all seen the photos and agreed that they presented some interesting questions.

Bobby Eiring was five-three, weighed maybe 110 pounds soaking wet, wore eyeglasses with thick brown frames and Coke-bottle lenses (which were always covered in so much grime that I'm pretty sure he attended all three years of middle school legally blind), once went an entire year without brushing his teeth (not because he'd lost a bet or anything remotely sensible, but simply because he'd grown tired of the process), and was the most fearless backyard tackle football player I'd ever seen.

Bobby also had epilepsy.

As kids, we didn't know much about epilepsy. What we did know was that our weird friend took a ton of pills every day, and from time to time, he had either "episodes" or "seizures."

An episode could be anything from Bobby suddenly going silent midsentence and staring off into space for a minute or two before snapping out of it with a blank look on his face and no memory of what he'd just been talking about, to Bobby zoning out while shuffling the cards during penny poker and flinging them everywhere around the room (which usually led to a rambunctious game of fifty-two-card pickup and the inevitable bloody noses and lips).

And then there were the seizures—where Bobby dropped to the ground and started flopping around and drooling. These seemed to come and go in cycles. I'm sure there was a good reason for this, but as a bunch of twelve-year-olds, we never asked. All we knew was that the seizures were often scary and always entertaining— and when they came, they came without warning. Over time, we learned how to ensure that our friend didn't swallow his tongue and the best way to cushion and protect his head.

We also learned how to imitate his seizures—something we often did at the grocery store or the school cafeteria (I won't even mention Steve Sines's ill-fated attempt during one Sunday morning church service).

I guess the lesson here is that soon enough we got used to having a friend with a serious medical condition. It became part of Bobby's identity, and we did our best to look out for him and even started calling him "Eppy" (did I mention that we were twelve?).

Bobby had his own theory regarding his condition. He swore up and down that an alien life-form had infected him with some kind of interplanetary virus, and each time he experienced a seizure, he was actually communicating with the little green bastards. He even started a glossary of ET terminology in a spiral notebook. Our suspension of disbelief only stretched so far, but it was hard to argue with someone who had his mind made up like that.

As the years passed, Bobby's epilepsy was often at the center of one adventure or another. I once let him drive my moped to 7-Eleven with me on the back. As luck would have it, he zoned out in the middle of Edgewood Road, crossed over two lanes of traffic, and smashed directly into a curb at twenty-five miles per hour. We both went over the handlebars. Another time, in the middle of a game of football, we realized Bobby had gone missing. After calling time-out and searching for ten or fifteen minutes, Carlos Vargas spotted him at least a hundred feet up in one of the trees that overlooked the back field of the Meyers House. Jimmy and I braved the climb to rescue him and found Bobby holding on to a swaying branch with one hand. His other hand was dangling at his side with an absolute death grip on a half-eaten stick of strawberry Laffy Taffy. With storm clouds gathering on the horizon and the wind swirling, we desperately tried to wrestle the candy out of his hand. But he refused to loosen his grip. Suddenly, we were rocking back and forth, the branches beneath us creaking in the sudden gale. The three of us moments away from plunging to our deaths, Bobby finally woke up, looked at Jimmy, looked at me, and as calmly as could be, said, "Stop trying to steal my taffy, Chiz." Then he climbed down to safety. Without our help.

FOUR

RETURN OF THE BOOGEYMAN

"You'd think the guy was Elvis fucking Presley."

1

It only took one phone call the next morning to discover that sitting down with Joshua Gallagher was going to be a whole lot easier said than done.

"It'll be at least a few more days," Lieutenant McClernan told me. "He's a busy boy right about now."

"Busy doing what?"

"Talking to my detectives. Having his belongings searched."

"And how's that going?"

"It's going," she said. "He's a bit agitated, as you can imagine."

"I'll bet."

"My guys aren't exactly thrilled either. Gallagher gets more fan mail than Justin Bieber. They have to sit down and read through all of it."

"You think Gallagher might've communicated with Annie's killer?"

"I think that only happens in Thomas Harris novels, but we have to be sure."

"Is he actually doing much talking?"

"Some." She paused. "Why? You jealous?"

"Why would I be jealous?"

"You know, that whole 'he only talks to me and no one else' shtick. I wouldn't blame you if you were feeling a little . . . territorial."

"I'm not feeling anything. I know he talks to you guys. I'm actually glad he does."

She made a *tsk*ing sound in her throat. I'd heard it before: *C'mon, don't try to bullshit me.*

"I'm being serious. As long as it has nothing to do with his past or how he actually *feels* about anything, he's a regular blabbermouth. And I'm fine with that." I could hear the rumble of the engine as she started her car and the *beep-beep-beep* of her seatbelt alert.

"Speaking of blabbing," she said, "I heard he called *you* a couple nights ago."

"He wanted to reassure me that he had nothing to do with what'd happened."

"I'm a little surprised you didn't mention it."

"I would have . . . eventually. It got a little lost with everything else going on."

She made that *tsk*ing sound again.

"You think I was hiding it from you?"

"Nah. You would never do that."

2

The Sunday, June 5, 2022, edition of the *Baltimore Sun* featured a lengthy article about Annie Riggs's murder. It was written by James Jackson, a veteran newsman who did exemplary work. The headline, which ran in large, bold type just below the front page fold, read:

RETURN OF THE BOOGEYMAN?

Three full-color photographs were positioned side by side, yearbook-style, in the center of the page: what appeared to be a standard federal employee ID shot of Annie Riggs, the author photo from my most recent book, and Joshua Gallagher's mug shot. We made an unlikely trio.

When I was finished reading the article, I tossed the entire News section into the recycling bin. Kara didn't need to see that. There were heartbreaking quotes from both of Riggs's children, as well as her boyfriend, Michael Buckley. A devastated Buckley revealed that he had recently purchased an engagement ring and was planning to ask Annie to marry him at a family cookout during the Fourth of July weekend. Riggs's children had already given him their blessings.

If that wasn't bad enough, someone in law enforcement had leaked information regarding the condition of Annie Riggs's body. The opening paragraphs of the article spared few of the graphic details when it came to describing her dismembered corpse. There was even mention of her missing head. McClernan had been livid when we'd spoken about it and sworn that she was going to find whoever had talked. Frankly, I was surprised that Jackson had chosen to go in that direction, but then I remembered the *Sun*'s plummeting circulation figures and it suddenly made a lot more sense. After all, if it bleeds, it leads. I only hoped that the security footage of the man in the mask would remain under wraps. If the press got ahold of those photos, all hell would break loose.

Speaking of security footage, yesterday afternoon I'd asked Kara to show me how to access the system on my laptop. After a grueling ninety-minute lesson—during which we both developed splitting headaches from butting heads (figuratively, of course; I admit I've never been very good at following directions)—I could now call up digital surveillance from all seven cameras and run a global search by date and time code. Over the past two days, I'd probably watched four or five hours of cumulative footage and seen absolutely nothing of value. Still, it was addictive.

In fact, I had just settled on the back porch with a bottle of water and my laptop on the table in front of me when Billy called to me from outside.

3

"Everything okay?" I asked, climbing the stairs to the breezeway and opening the back gate.

"Can you sign a book real quick?"

Billy was standing next to Carl, our UPS driver, who was at least five or six inches taller than him. There was a package resting on the driveway at their feet. The state trooper on duty that morning was watching us from afar.

"Hey, Mr. Chiz," Carl said. "I hate to bother you, but I promised my wife I'd ask."

I took the book from his hands. It was a brand-new hardcover of *Chasing the Boogeyman*. A Barnes & Noble receipt, dated yesterday, was tucked inside. "What's your wife's name?"

"Cheryl."

He spelled it for me, and I started scribbling.

"Uhhh . . . would you mind making it out to me, too?"

"Already done." I finished and handed it back to him.

He opened the book to the title page. I could see his lips moving as he read what I'd written. "She's gonna be happy as a clam. Thank you so much."

"My pleasure, Carl."

Billy and I watched him walk away, those long legs of his covering some ground in a hurry. Before he climbed into his truck, he turned and waved at us. He was still smiling.

"I didn't know whether you were busy or not," Billy said. "He was so excited."

"It's fine. Carl's a good guy." I turned to my son. "What do you have going on today?"

"Taking the dogs to the MA and PA Trail and then getting some writing done. You?"

"Lieutenant McClernan's stopping by with some papers for me to sign. They want to put tracers on our cell phones."

"Mine, too?" I couldn't tell if he looked hopeful or concerned.

"Just mine and your mom's, for now." I gestured across the street to the press pool, which had nearly doubled in size in the past forty-eight hours. There was a sea of cameras with long, telephoto lenses pointed in our direction. "Be careful pulling out. If anyone tries to follow you, stop and turn around. If you can't do that, circle the block. The police will put a stop to it."

He started to say something, then hesitated.

"What?"

He shook his head. "Nothing."

"Say it."

He took a deep breath. "For a second, I thought someone was following me last night on my way home from Ryan's."

I could feel my jaw tighten. "Why didn't you say anything?"

"Because I wasn't sure."

"Tell me exactly what happened."

"You know how Ryan lives in the middle of nowhere . . ."

It wasn't a question, but I nodded anyway.

"It's a dead-end road and there's never any traffic, especially at night. But pretty much as soon as I turned out of his driveway, there was a truck behind me."

"What kind of truck?"

"No idea."

"Color?"

"Black. Or maybe dark blue."

"Go on."

He shrugged. "It was still behind me when I got to 22. I turned right. They turned right."

My chest was starting to hurt. "Then what?"

"I tried to get a look at the driver at the next stoplight, but I couldn't see in the glare. I think their high beams were on."

"Did they follow you all the way to Southampton?"

"I don't know."

"What do you mean you don't know?" There was an edge to my voice now. Billy was frowning.

"I ran into traffic once I passed the college, where the road turns into two lanes. I didn't notice it after that."

I looked up and saw Lieutenant McClernan's unmarked sedan swing into the driveway. All of a sudden, we heard the frenzied *click-click-click*s of the cameras from across the street.

"Do me a favor . . . before you take the dogs for a walk, tell the lieutenant everything you just told me."

4

"He's probably right that it's nothing," the lieutenant told me later. "But it's good that he's on high alert."

We were sitting on lawn chairs in the backyard, nursing half-empty glasses of iced tea. A neat stack of manila file folders rested on a small table between us.

"I hate that he even has to think about it."

"Can't do anything about that now. You're caught in the middle of this."

I blew out a deep breath. "What else is new . . ."

The lieutenant took a long drink, emptying her glass, and watched the dogs chase each other around the yard. Ripley was the smallest of the four, but also the quickest. The others yipped and whined as she sprinted gleeful circles around them. For just a moment, I saw the tension drain from the lieutenant's eyes—and then it was back again.

Lieutenant McClernan had done her best to bring me up to speed on the investigation thus far, while also reminding me that she wasn't able— nor willing—to share *all* the pertinent details. It had always been like that with her. No matter how much sewage we slogged through together— and in the past three years, we'd wallowed in quite a bit of it—she was always careful to maintain clear-cut boundaries. I admired her for that. Although I'd never admit it out loud—especially to my wife—it was something I wished I'd done a better job with when it came to my relationship with Joshua Gallagher. Too many times, it felt like Gallagher was the one calling the shots instead of me. Too often, as I left our sit-downs or hung up the telephone, I found myself wondering why I'd given so much and received so little in return. I'd crossed the line more times than I could count, and not even the secret shame and guilt I carried with me was enough to put a stop to it. Most days, it felt like I was caught in a whirlpool and it was just a matter of time before I was sucked under.

This is what Lieutenant McClernan told me on that Sunday morning:

No prints, hair fibers, or DNA (not belonging to the victim) had been found on the black garbage bag or the length of silver duct tape used to bind it. The killer had used a pointed tool—most likely an ice pick or an awl—to puncture the bottom of the bag a total of seven times. A trace of canine urine (Leo strikes again) had been discovered on one lower section of the bag.

Annie Riggs's 2019 Honda Accord had been located the previous afternoon in a Target parking lot on Middleton Road in Aberdeen. In-store surveillance footage indicated that Annie had never entered the building. Detectives believed that she'd been abducted immediately upon exiting her vehicle. The car was found unlocked. No sign of her keys, wallet, or cell phone. The exterior security camera in that area of the parking lot was not functioning on the night of Annie Riggs's murder. A repair order had been submitted two weeks earlier but no one had shown up to fix it.

None of Riggs's neighbors had noticed anything unusual in the days leading up to Annie's disappearance. No strangers lurking about. No door-to-door salesmen or water meter readers. No suspicious cars cruising the street. Her children and boyfriend, Michael Buckley, all maintained that Annie's recent mood had been relaxed and cheerful. She hadn't appeared the least bit anxious or uneasy and was looking forward to the long Fourth of July weekend.

Detective Gonzalez was currently interviewing an independent contractor whose company had recently repaved a half dozen driveways along the stretch of Willoughby Beach Road where Annie Riggs resided. The man had a felony record for sexual assault and had served time in prison on two different occasions. "We're taking a good look at him, but don't get your hopes up," McClernan said. "He's been clean for over a decade and appears to have an alibi for the night of June 2. We'll see."

The police were conducting background checks on employees from a number of home improvement companies that had recently done work within a half-mile radius of our home. They were also looking at both of our mailmen, Carl the UPS man, all our Amazon delivery drivers, and various "seeing-distance" neighbors. When I asked which neighbors they were talking to, McClernan shook her head and declined to name them.

So far, detectives had discovered little of interest in Joshua Gallagher's personal correspondence—but they were barely a third of the way finished. Cybertechs were sifting through various Boogeyman websites and messages boards but were running into the same problem. "There's just so damn many of them," McClernan told me. "You'd think the guy was Elvis fucking Presley." No dangerous contraband or weapons were found in Gallagher's cell, but the lieutenant emphasized that they could have been removed prior to the search.

The techs were also taking a good look at Annie Riggs's social media accounts, as well as both her work and personal emails. They'd examined more than ninety days of security footage from Riggs's office building and spotted nothing suspicious. Follow-up interviews with family, friends, neighbors, and coworkers had failed to turn up anything of note.

In the past forty-eight hours, police had received more than thirty anonymous phone calls related to Annie Riggs's murder, many of them naming potential suspects. Each and every person on the list was being looked at with various degrees of attention.

Police were also keeping an eye on the makeshift memorial that had sprung up next to the fire hydrant and had received permission from the Stevensons across the street to install a surveillance camera on their property. Since its initial appearance, sometime yesterday morning, the memorial had grown considerably.

The initial forensics report had come back on Annie Riggs's body. A standard bone saw had been used to sever the various limbs—with the exception of Riggs's hands, both of which appeared to have been chopped off with a handheld axe or hatchet. All the cutting wounds had been caused postmortem, and there was no evidence that a bone-dust vacuum had been used. Annie Riggs had not been sexually assaulted before or after her death. Additional tests were pending.

5

"Too bad the fence was in the way," Kara said as we loaded the dishwasher after dinner. "It would have been funny if it ended up on the news."

"Not really."

"I can see the headlines now: 'Bestselling Author Drives Riding Mower into Pond, Almost Drowns.'"

"That's not what happened."

"Then what happened?" She was trying hard not to smile.

"I told you. The ground gave out beneath me. It's called erosion."

"Are you sure it's not called '"Born to Run" came on your headphones and you lost control'?"

"That happened one time, and I regret ever telling you."

"And what about 'Purple Rain'?" She was grinning now.

"Okay, fine . . . twice."

Giggling, she dried her hands on a towel. "It feels good to laugh."

"Always happy to amuse you."

Wrinkling her nose, she said, "You smell like pond mud. Want to take a swim?"

"Sure."

She gazed out the kitchen window. "We have a pond."

"That's right," I said, giving her a look. "It was there when we moved in."

"And an orchard." Her eyes sparkled like emeralds in the beams of sunlight slanting through the window. Sometimes, with all the tension in our life, I forgot how beautiful she was.

"And a creek," I said. "And a whole mess of trees."

She looked at me then, and in those shimmering green eyes, I saw a sharp-edged glint of anger. "Why do we need anything else?"

"Who said we did?" I could feel the eggshells I was walking on crumbling beneath my bare feet.

"Me. You. Billy. Noah." She glanced down at the dogs sprawled on the kitchen floor. "The pups. This house. We're so blessed, and yet . . ."

I'd heard this speech before. Many times. "I don't know what you want me to say."

A moment of agonizing silence, then: "I want you to wake up." A single tear rolled down her cheek. "Before it's too late."

6

Standing in front of the kitchen window, I listened to her climb the stairs to our bedroom in search of a bathing suit. It was the smallest of victories that she still wanted to go swimming, but I was grateful for it. She had every reason to be pissed at me. As usual, she was right about everything.

I grabbed my cell phone from the island and headed outside.

No missed calls. No texts. No emails. It was a miracle.

The phone suddenly vibrated in my hand.

Startled, I nearly dropped it.

Spoke too soon.

It was a local number—with no name listed.

I'm not sure why I decided to answer.

"Hello?"

Dead air.

"Hello?"

A rustling sound.

"Is anyone there?"

Someone breathing.

"Who is this?"

The breathing grew louder.

"I'm going to hang—"

A loud *click*.

I stood there for a moment and stared at the screen—thinking about the series of creepy hang-ups we'd received at my parents' house that long-ago summer—and then I shoved the phone into my pocket. Joshua Gallagher had later admitted that he was responsible for the calls. He'd been trying to scare us—and it had worked.

Walking to the swimming pool, I gazed around the backyard. The deepening pockets of shadow beneath the magnolia trees suddenly appeared ominous and threatening. For just a moment, I was certain that someone was watching me.

7

Kara and Cujo were having a snoring contest—and I was stuck right smack-dab in the middle of it. It was like being tortured in stereo.

I shifted onto my left side, facing the dog that was stretched out on her back along the edge of the bed. I always worried that she would roll off in the middle of the night and tumble to the floor, but in almost seven years, that had yet to happen. Without really meaning it, I thought: *Tonight would be an ideal time to break that streak.* Cujo tipped the scales at twelve pounds and had a nose the size of a breath mint, so I figured she had to be the lesser of the two snorers with whom I was currently sharing a bed. After several interminable minutes, I decided it was too close to call and gave up trying to fall asleep.

I unplugged my cell phone from the charger on the end table. After checking my Twitter account to see if there were any comments I needed to delete—there was only one, from an anonymous poster, claiming that Joshua Gallagher and I were lovers—I clicked over to the doorbell camera app. I tapped the arrow and watched as the front porch and lawn appeared on my phone screen. I zoomed in for a better look.

The man in the mask was standing at the edge of the driveway.

Gasping, I sat up and kicked the blanket off my feet. I nudged Kara to wake her but she just mumbled and went on snoring.

The man in the mask strode across the driveway and up the stone stairs onto the porch.

I jumped to my feet and searched the room for a weapon.

"Kara!"

She didn't even stir. It had been a long, stressful day, and she was out.

As the man in the mask approached the door, he bent down and examined the camera. Tilting his head, first one way and then the other, as if fascinated by what he was seeing. He reached for the doorknob.

I sprinted out of the bedroom and started down the stairs, fumbling with my phone to call 911. Over the booming drumbeat of my heart, I could hear the doorknob rattling.

The operator answered right away. "Nine-one-one; what's your emergency?"

Switching back so I could watch the video, I whispered, "701 Southampton Road. Hurry. Someone's trying to break in." And hung up.

The man backed up a couple of steps.

He's going to kick it in, I thought, rushing into the foyer. I could see his shadow through the decorative panes of glass bordering the door. He looked impossibly tall.

Instead, the man slowly reached up and removed his mask.

It was Joshua Gallagher.

He smiled, and it was ghastly . . .

8

In the dark of our bedroom, bathed in a sheen of sour sweat and clutching a pillow to my chest, I woke up screaming.

Kara wrestled me into her arms and cradled me against her chest while I caught my breath. A few minutes later, she handed me a bottle of water from the nightstand and went into the laundry room to find me a change of pajamas.

She knew the routine all too well.

A popular Boogeyman message board
(Photo courtesy of the author)

Public warning addressing rumors posted on Facebook by the Harford County Sheriff's Office *(Photo courtesy of the author)*

Police searching the area after the discover of Anne Ric *(Photo courtesy of* The Aegis*)*

Excerpt from in-person interview with Joshua Gallagher, age 55, inmate #AC4311920 at Cumberland Penitentiary, recorded on August 16, 2020:

CHIZMAR: I'd like to talk about Louise Rutherford, Colette Bowden, and Erin Brown.

GALLAGHER: Okay. What about them?

CHIZMAR: Many of the details of their murders are identical to the four girls from Edgewood. These three were sexually assaulted. Cause of death in each case was strangulation. Their ears were taken.

GALLAGHER: We've already discussed this.

CHIZMAR: They were all young and attractive with long hair.

GALLAGHER: You're very persistent today, Richard.

CHIZMAR: Hear me out. There were significant differences. No calling cards were left behind for the police for those three. You disposed of the bodies in isolated rural areas instead of posing them for discovery. Why? Why the change in M.O.?

GALLAGHER: [sighs] I just didn't want anyone to find them.

CHIZMAR: Why not?

GALLAGHER: I didn't want to get caught.

CHIZMAR: Joshua, I'm going to level with you here. An awful lot of people think you're playing games with me and the police. I hate to say it . . . but this is one of those days when I find it difficult to argue with them.

GALLAGHER: I see. So . . . you think I'm playing games with you?

CHIZMAR: I don't know. [pause] Many mass murderers exhibit signs of gamesmanship. It feeds their egos. Ted Bundy used to—

GALLAGHER: I am not Ted Bundy, and I am not many mass murderers. You know that all too well. I'm unlike anyone you or the authorities have ever dealt with before.

CHIZMAR: Don't flatter yourself. FBI profilers have spoken with some pretty bad people. There was a guy down south, Samuel Little. He confessed to killing almost one hundred people between 1970 and 2005.

GALLAGHER: [shakes head] I am not like the others. Do not compare me to them.

CHIZMAR: Okay. How so?

GALLAGHER: No one like me has ever been taken into custody.

CHIZMAR: Maybe I'm not explaining myself properly. You're very unique, I'll give you that, but—

GALLAGHER: There are others like me . . . a handful . . . but they haven't been caught yet . . . maybe they never will be.

CHIZMAR: Who else is out there?

[no response]

CHIZMAR: Josh? Who else is out there?

[no response]

FIVE

BURIED SECRETS

"Can you imagine what these would do to human fingers?"

1

Lagging not far behind that old writing chestnut—"Where do you get your ideas?"—was the second-most commonly asked question I heard from readers (many of them well-meaning and genuinely curious): "What originally sparked your fascination with the dark side?"

And then, of course, there was that other group of literary-minded folks (not quite as well-meaning) who often used a more direct, less politic approach: "Why do you waste your time writing thrillers and horror and true crime when you could be writing something much more pleasant and respectable?"

Whenever I was presented with either of these probing questions, I usually just smiled and shrugged my shoulders and said something like this: "Well, it all started when I was young with *Abbott and Costello Meet Frankenstein* and *The Mummy*, *The Twilight Zone* TV series, and the *Creature Feature* monster movies that used to air every Saturday afternoon. From there, I moved on to *Alfred Hitchcock Presents*, *The Legend of Sleepy Hollow*, Ray Bradbury and Richard Matheson short stories, and finally, the novels of Stephen King.

"By that time, I was probably thirteen or fourteen years old, and the hooks were set pretty deep. Destiny was in motion."

That, dear reader, was my standard response—and every word of it was true.

But there was also something else.

Something so unsettling and disturbing that it'd haunted my dreams ever since.

I'd never told this story to anyone.

Until now.

This is what happened.

2

I spent most of the summer after graduating from Edgewood High School—this was 1983; *Return of the Jedi* was crushing the box office and "Every Breath You Take" by the Police was dominating the airwaves—working as a laborer at the nearby Aberdeen Proving Ground. Mostly, I cut grass and worked a gas-powered Weed Eater from eight to four, with a thirty-minute break for lunch in between. Occasionally, I was pulled off the lawn crew to help out with a variety of other jobs. Sometimes, it was lugging wheelbarrows full of wet cement or helping to lay asphalt; other times, it was pulling up railroad ties or repairing broken playground equipment. I wasn't very handy with a tool, but I was a hard worker and didn't mind getting dirty, so the full-timers were just fine having me around.

Shortly after the Fourth of July weekend, I was "loaned out" to a veteran three-man crew who'd been tasked with clearing a patch of overgrown trees and brush behind the waterfront houses on Officers' Row. There had been a recent change in command on the base, and the new general had put in an immediate request (translation: a direct order) for an improved backyard view of the Gunpowder River.

I knew two of the men, Frankie and Marcus, both in their late forties and friendly enough—a month earlier, I'd helped them install a new swing set next to the softball field—but the third guy was a stranger. He didn't have much to say that first morning, but after we ate lunch together, and he and I partnered up against Frankie and Marcus in a quick game of Uno—a game we won, to his clear delight—the new guy pretty much wouldn't shut up the rest of the afternoon.

He told me his name was Henry, but everyone called him Hank. He'd spent the previous two years working at Edgewood Arsenal before being transferred to Aberdeen in early April. He was still getting used to his new surroundings. Hank was a big man, at least six-three and two hundred plus pounds. His face looked like a shovel—flat and broad. His nose had been broken before, maybe more than once, and the back of his thick neck was sunburned a deep scarlet. He didn't give his age, but I put him at around thirty, perhaps a little older.

By the second day on the job, we had split up into two-man teams, which was just fine with me—Frankie and Marcus were good guys, but they squabbled like an old married couple. Headache inducing. While those two tackled the heavy stuff with an array of government-issued chain saws (which usually meant they didn't work worth a damn), Hank and I used machetes and branch cutters to clear the thicket of chest-high brush that covered the steep hillside rising from the water's edge. It was grueling work—it felt like we spent as much time trying to keep our footing as we did clearing ground—but we made a good team. I had no complaints. At first.

It was midafternoon, a full week into the job, and hot as hell when I noticed Hank staring at me. I'd paused to use my shirtsleeve to wipe sweat off my face and saw him standing there, maybe fifteen or twenty feet away, eyes locked on me, a machete dangling loosely from his hand. He seemed almost in a daze. After a moment, finally realizing that he'd been caught, he flashed me a lopsided grin and returned to work. I didn't think much of it at the time. Just mopped my brow and went back to chopping.

Until the next morning when it happened again. And again.

By the third or fourth time, it was not only starting to make me uncomfortable, it was pissing me off. *What's his deal anyway? It's not like I have snot running out of my nose or my ass crack is showing.*

I thought about saying something to him at lunch but decided not to. *Why rock the boat?* I figured. *Two more days and I'll be back to cutting grass with the rest of the part-timers. He's probably just gassed and catching his breath. Why make him feel bad?* Hell, he might even have epilepsy or something like my old friend Bob Eiring. Maybe he was having some sort of an episode. I hadn't even considered that, and just the thought of it made me feel guilty.

The rest of the afternoon I kept my head down and resisted the urge to check if Hank was watching me. Several times, I *felt* his eyes pressing into the center of my back, but I could've just as easily been imagining it. That was my hope, anyway.

Later, after we'd finished working for the day and I was busy loading the truck, I found Hank sitting in the passenger seat with the door open, cleaning a pair of pruning shears with an old rag. He was really going at it and doing a job on them; it reminded me of the way my mom used to polish her good silverware right before Thanksgiving and Christmas. When he was finally satisfied, he looked up at me with that dreamy expression of his and said, "Can you imagine what these would do to human fingers?"

I stared at him, waiting for the punch line—or at least one of those lopsided grins to show that he was messing with me—but it never came. Instead, as if ensnared in a spell, he went back to polishing those shears like it was the most important thing in the world.

A minute later, Frankie hopped in the driver's seat and Marcus climbed in back with me, and we headed downtown to the old red barn that served as our home base.

3

It was about a twenty-minute drive from Aberdeen Proving Ground to my house on Hanson Road—and thoughts of Hank were swirling around in my head the entire time.

He was a weird dude; that was for sure.

Can you imagine what these would do to human fingers?

What the hell kind of question was that?

And what kind of fingers are there besides human ones?

I'd mostly convinced myself that Hank had been yanking my chain and fishing for a reaction for whatever reason, but between the question itself, the odd expression on his face when he'd asked it, and the whole staring business, the guy was starting to give me a first-class case of the creeps. At the same time, I reminded myself that I would only be working with him for a couple more days, what the hell, and that made me feel a little better.

As I made my way home among the steady flow of Route 40 traffic, I tried to recall the previous conversations we'd shared. Nothing really stood out. He followed the Atlanta Braves and liked to talk baseball. He was a fan of popular detective shows on television; *Magnum, P.I.* and *Hill Street Blues* were his favorites. He read comic books and had taken to calling me "Richie Rich" after the popular 1950s character. He loved beef jerky and knew an awful lot about it—certainly nothing horrifying about that, unless it was secretly of the *Motel Hell* variety. His best friend back in Georgia was a man named Brennan. They used to fish and play horseshoes together on the weekends, and they'd once spent almost two years rebuilding a vintage convertible Mustang in Brennan's garage. Hank lived in an apartment in Havre de Grace and had a pet snake named Ginger. He was thinking about buying an aquarium for tropical fish. Every other Thursday night, he played bingo with the old ladies at the fire hall. A couple of months back, he'd won a $250 coverall. Hank also liked to go to the movies but only if he could get there early enough to sit in the back row. He always ordered a large root beer and a small buttered popcorn from the snack bar, but he snuck in his own candy because it was cheaper that way.

And that was about it. Nothing at all really out of the ordinary. Maybe even a little boring, but then again, I wasn't one to talk—I wasn't exactly Indiana Jones myself.

4

The next day was a Thursday, and it was pouring rain, so there wasn't a lot of talking on the job. Overnight, the hillside had turned into a quagmire of mud and tangled tree roots. It was like trying to work on a tilted ice rink. I lost count of how many times the four of us slipped and fell. It was only by God's grace that no one had slid all the way down the hill into the Gunpowder and been swept away by the fast-moving current. By the time lunch rolled around, the four of us were covered in mud from head to toe and had run out of cusswords to spew.

I had to admit that the crummy conditions did have an upside. Trying to keep my footing had taken all of my focus and concentration, and as a result, I hadn't thought about Hank and his omnipresent, weird-ass question a single time all morning, nor had I felt him staring at me.

A few minutes before our break was over, an olive-green four-door pickup truck—identical to the one the four of us were sitting in (runnels of mud slopping onto the seats and floorboards) with the exception of the government-ID number printed on the side panel—pulled up alongside us. The driver's window slid down. Frankie cursed and rolled his own window down. A muffled conversation took place, in which I heard my name mentioned more than once. I immediately got nervous, although I had no reason to. A minute later, the windows went back up—but the other truck didn't pull away.

"Grab your stuff, Richie Rich," Frankie said, wiping the rain and the smirk off his face. He knew damn well how much I hated my new nickname. "You're going behind the fence to help clear out a warehouse."

"Better you than me, kid," Marcus said around a mouthful of ham sandwich.

"What's that mean?" I asked. "It's got to be better than this."

Marcus shrugged. "Depends on what's inside that warehouse."

I slung my knapsack over my shoulder. "See you, fellas. Try not to go swimming without me." Before anyone could answer, I got out and slammed the door.

After jogging through ankle-deep mud to the waiting truck, I climbed into the passenger seat and immediately apologized for making a mess with my dirty boots and wet clothes. The driver, a tall man I'd never seen before and sporting an impressively thick beard, shrugged and said, "What can ya do? Ain't your fault it's rainin'."

We pulled away, gears grinding. I gave the guys in the other truck a wave. Frankie and Marcus, already back to arguing about God knows what, never even glanced in my direction.

Behind them, in the back seat, Hank's face was pressed up against the window, his eyes following us as we drove away. Rivulets of rainwater trickled down the glass, making it appear as though he were crying.

5

As it turned out, the warehouse was stuffed with cardboard cartons full of 1960s-era paperwork headed for the shredder. There were thousands of them stacked on the concrete floor. Not a single pallet in sight. Doing it by hand was at least a two-week job.

On the drive home that afternoon, my back and shoulders already aching, my thoughts once again turned to Hank, and I decided that I'd probably never see him again after today. And that was a-okay with me.

But I wrong.

6

I spent Sunday afternoon playing golf with friends. None of us scored very well, but the sun was shining, the beer was cold, and the Orioles extended their winning streak to five games in a row (we listened in between shots on Jeff Pruitt's portable radio). We also laughed a lot, and for at least a few hours, it felt like summer might last forever and none of us were going away to college in a little over a month.

On the way home, I stopped off at Santoni's to pick up a bottle of salad dressing and a loaf of French bread for dinner. My mom was making one of my favorites, chicken cacciatore, and my mouth was already watering.

As I crossed the parking lot on the way back to my car, I noticed a man sitting on a bench in front of the library across the street. Even at a distance, I thought it was odd that he was wearing long pants and what appeared to be a letterman's jacket when it was almost ninety degrees outside—and then I realized that the man looked somehow familiar.

I got in the car and put on my sunglasses to take a better look, but even without the sun's harsh glare, I couldn't make out the details of his face. Still, there was something about him.

I turned the key, and the Kinks blared from my cheap PX speakers. The dashboard began to vibrate. I cranked up the volume even louder and swung a right onto Hanson Road, using my thumbs to play a drum solo on the steering wheel. As I cruised past the library, I remembered to glance over at the entrance.

The bench was empty.

I was almost to the traffic light when I suddenly realized who the man in the letterman's jacket had looked like: *Hank*.

7

It was almost 1 a.m. on Tuesday morning, and other than the muffled, rhythmic heartbeat of my father's snoring in the next room, the house was dead silent. The only light in my bedroom was the alien-green glow of the computer screen. Outside my second-story window, the drooping branches of our ancient weeping willow tree swayed in the whisper of a night breeze, casting a spiderweb of dancing shadows across the yard. I found that if I stared at those shadows long enough, they made me sleepy.

I was writing a ghost story about a young girl who had died in a horrible accident on the railroad tracks that ran behind her house. A new family had recently moved into the home and the little boy who had taken over the young girl's bedroom was just beginning to realize that things weren't as they seemed. Sometimes, alone in his room, he caught flickers of movement from the corner of his eye. Other times, he discovered his glasses or the book he was reading or his baseball glove in different places than where he'd left them. And the antique pocket watch his grandfather had given him for his ninth birthday was missing.

In the section I was working on tonight, the boy—his name was Quentin—was sprawled out on his bed doing his math homework when his father called him downstairs for dinner. A short time later, when he was finished eating, he returned to his room to find that someone—or *something*—had scribbled the words *HELP ME* across the top of his worksheet. The pencil he'd been using had been broken in half.

It wasn't exactly Hemingway, but I'd managed to give myself a serious case of the heebie-jeebies. That was usually a good sign that the story was working.

Ready to call it a night, I clicked on save and glanced out the window just in time to see someone duck down behind the azalea bush in the side yard. A single streetlight stood at the corner of Hanson and Tupelo, and its reverse cone of illumination extended right to the edge of the bushes.

I knew what I had seen. I hadn't imagined it. A man dressed in dark clothing had been standing on the sidewalk watching me in the window, and as soon as I'd looked up, he'd darted away.

I stared at the bush, willing the man to reveal himself.

My heart thudded in my chest.

A minute passed, then two.

I turned off my computer, cloaking the bedroom in darkness.

Three minutes.

I tapped on the window with the tips of my fingers. Not too loud. I didn't want to wake my parents.

Four minutes now, then five.

The dark pressed against the glass.

Six minutes . . .

I opened my eyes—and realized with a jolt that I'd fallen asleep.

But for how long?

I glanced at the digital alarm clock by my bed. Twelve minutes had passed since I'd first spotted the man lurking in the bushes. I leaned closer to the window. For all I knew, he was long—

The man made a break for it, head down, sprinting away from the house and across Hanson Road. In a matter of seconds, he was gone. Swallowed by darkness.

But I had seen enough.

Even from the back, I'd recognized him.

I'd watched that same man running across a parking lot in the pouring rain to a work truck waiting to take us to lunch.

It was Hank Metheny.

What the hell is going on here?

8

Two weeks later, on the final weekend of July, Kara and I went to a Saturday afternoon Orioles game at Memorial Stadium. The Texas Rangers were in town for a four-game series and both teams were right smack-dab in the middle of the playoff hunt. It was also Eddie Murray Bobblehead Day and a raucous, sold-out crowd filled the ballpark. Kara and I had upper-deck seats down the third-base line. Not many foul balls came our way during the game, but the hot dogs were plump and delicious, and the Budweiser man never once asked for my ID (the first time that'd ever happened, I realized with a mix of joy and sorrow). By the seventh-inning stretch, the O's were in the lead, I was pleasantly buzzed, and the prettiest girl in the world was sitting next to me. What a day.

And then I saw him.

I was using the binoculars Kara had borrowed from her father's boat to scan the crowd behind the Orioles' dugout. Growing up, my family had strictly belonged to the upper deck and bleachers fan base, and I was curious to see what kind of folks ponied up the big money to sit so close to the field. After checking out row after row of spectators, I was convinced that they didn't look a whole lot different from the fans I was used to sitting with. Maybe a few more collared shirts and dresses, but otherwise pretty much the same.

I was about to switch over to the visiting team's dugout when I noticed a man sitting in an aisle seat looking back in my direction with his own pair of binoculars. Sunlight glinted off the lenses. *I wonder if he sees me,* I thought, smiling. I gave him a wave just in case.

The man lowered his binoculars, and even with the wide-brimmed straw hat he was wearing casting most of his face in shadow, I recognized Hank right away.

Despite the warmth of the sunshine, I felt an icy chill track its way across the back of my neck. "It can't be," I said, not realizing I'd spoken the words out loud.

"What can't be?" Kara said.

Fingering the focus knob to see if I could get a better look, I said, "Do you remember that guy I told you about at work?"

Half a stadium away, Hank lifted his binoculars and stared back at me.

"Which one? You've told me about a lot of different guys."

"The weird one. Hank."

"Oh, yeah, I remember."

I hadn't told her about that night outside my house. I hadn't told anyone. "Well, he's sitting down there behind the Orioles' dugout. And unless I'm drunker than I thought, he's looking right back at us."

"What? Let me see," she said, reaching for the field glasses.

I handed them to her and pointed. "Left side of the dugout. Four rows up. Right on the aisle. Look for the straw hat."

She stared through the lenses. "I don't . . . wait . . . no, that's a little kid."

"Count the rows."

"I did. Fourth-row aisle is empty."

"Can't be. Let me have those back."

She gave me the binoculars. I lifted them to my eyes. Got my bearings. She was right—the seat was empty.

Hank was gone.

9

The last three weeks of work flew by—with no more Hank sightings on or off the base—and before I knew it, August was almost over, and I was preparing to leave for college.

My emotions were all over the place. Lifelong friends were heading off in a dozen different directions, some of them traveling hundreds of miles away to their new homes. I realized that it was only temporary and I would see most of them over the Thanksgiving and Christmas breaks, and then again the following summer, but right at that moment it didn't feel that way. It felt like I was losing them forever. Fall lacrosse practice started in ten days, and I had no clue what to expect from my new teammates and coaches. And while Kara would soon be returning to the familiar confines of Edgewood High School, for the first time in my life, I would be venturing out on my own. I hadn't even left yet, and I already missed her.

Everyone from my sisters to the guidance counselors at school had warned me ahead of time that this transition was going to be both scary and exciting—but I wasn't even a little bit embarrassed to admit that I was mostly just terrified. Anything resembling excitement had yet to make an appearance.

I'd spent that Thursday evening by myself, shopping for jeans and a couple of new dress shirts—the final items on my college list—at White Marsh Mall. Kara had been helping her mother with some kind of real estate event, and the handful of friends who hadn't already left town had been busy with their own families. My mom had offered to go along with me, but I'd politely declined. My head was a mess, and she didn't need to see that. She worried enough about me.

After shopping, I ate two slices of pizza in my car and listened to the ball game on the radio. When I pulled away from the mall parking lot, the streetlights were just coming on and I could see flashes of heat lightning in the distance.

I was halfway home when the car suddenly gave a violent shudder, and then the engine sputtered and coughed and decided to quit working. Lovely timing, as usual. I immediately slipped it out of gear, drifted onto the shoulder of Route 7, and turned on my hazard signals. My 1976 hand-me-down Toyota Corolla was a temperamental old girl, so I was used to the routine.

After letting the car rest for a few minutes—I had no idea if I was supposed to do that or not; all I knew was that it'd worked once or twice in the past—I tried to start it again.

Nothing. The engine wouldn't even turn over. Goddammit.

Which meant only one thing: I was walking.

With a heavy sigh, I double-checked that the car was in park, got out, and locked it. The Dew Drop Inn was a mile or so down the road. They would have a pay phone I could use to call my father. Under the circumstances, he wouldn't be happy to hear from me, but what else could I do? The car had been working just fine earlier in the evening.

It was almost eight thirty when I started off and there was hardly any traffic. Crickets whirred in the tall grass that bordered both sides of the road. Fireflies blinked to life in the encroaching darkness. Some kind of animal stirred in the woods across the street and then went still again. An old panel truck roared past—buffeting the tree branches and almost blowing the hat off my head—before disappearing around the bend, its taillights winking a long goodbye. An angry dog barked somewhere faraway. A moment later, a lonely train whistle answered its cry.

And then the world around me suddenly went to sleep.

Whatever birds were still flying around stopped singing. The fireflies went dark. Even the crickets ceased their nightly chorus. Nothing moved. Not even the hint of a breeze.

The author of the book I was currently reading—a not-very-good British horror novel about a haunted manor—had used a descriptive phrase that I'd never heard before. I liked it quite a bit, and it came to mind now as I was walking along in a cocoon of such utter silence. *Graveyard quiet.*

The road and surrounding countryside had gone just that.

It was at once peaceful and unnerving.

Then, as if on cue, a car crested the hill behind me, it's bass-heavy stereo piercing the night's stillness. I peered over my shoulder and saw with a shiver of unease that its headlights were off—and it was moving fast, weaving all over the road. I inched further onto the shoulder and, while walking backward, started waving my arms above my head. "Slow down," I said, my voice not even loud enough for my own ears to register above the deafening music. I began jumping up and down, trying to get their attention.

And it must've worked because the driver immediately began pumping his brakes and the car swerved onto the shoulder no more than thirty or so yards from where I was standing.

I could hear the deep, throaty rumble of the car's engine as I jogged toward it.

"Hey, thanks for stopping!" I shouted. "I'm good, I don't need a ride!"

A bottle suddenly came hurtling out of the darkness and shattered on the road at my feet, beer spraying everywhere. Drunken laughter erupted from inside the car—a black Trans Am with orange flames painted on the doors—and then the driver laid on the gas, peeling rubber and spraying me with pellets of gravel.

I crossed my arms over my face to shield my eyes, and by the time I lowered them again, the car was gone.

"Asshole," I muttered, and resumed walking. The sooner I got off this road, the better. I brushed the dust off my T-shirt and spit tiny pieces of grit out of my mouth. It felt like a swarm of angry hornets had stung my entire body. My shoes and the bottoms of my jeans were soaked in beer. My mother was going to absolutely love that.

Just as I made it to the bottom of the hill, my feet *squish*ing with every step I took, I heard another vehicle slowing down behind me. I didn't even bother to turn around and look this time. And when the car crept slowly past, washing me in the glare of its headlights before pulling off onto the shoulder, I didn't even bother to quicken my pace. I'd had enough foolishness for one night.

The passenger window slid down.

Here we go again, I thought.

And then I noticed a piece of rebar, maybe fourteen inches long, lying on the asphalt at my feet. I instinctively bent over, picked it up, and pressed it against my leg. *Just in case.*

I called out to the driver. "Thanks, buddy, but I'm good!"

The car waited on the shoulder, engine idling.

As I drew closer, I saw that it was a late model Monte Carlo with a MARYLAND IS FOR LOVERS sticker on the back bumper. Barry Manilow's syrupy smooth voice escaped from the dark interior. I approached the open window. "I appreciate you stopping, but I'm—"

"Hey, Richie Rich, hop on in."

The driver leaned across the seat and smiled at me.

It was Hank.

Stunned, I took an involuntary step backward.

"Hey . . . Hank. What . . . what are you doing here?"

Hank leaned over a little further and pushed open the passenger-side door. He was wearing a red-and-white letterman's jacket. "Get in before someone comes along and runs you over."

My mouth had suddenly gone bone-dry. I said the first thing that popped into my head.

"My father . . . he's waiting for me at the Dew Drop up ahead."

"Then I'll give you a ride there," he said. "Come on. Get in."

I didn't move.

"What's the matter? You coming or what?"

I could hear the impatience rising in his voice. Glancing into the back seat, I half expected to see a pair of shiny gardening shears or perhaps even a gleaming machete, but the seat was empty.

"Is something wrong?" he asked. "I thought you'd be happy to see a friendly face. Especially under the circumstances."

Something else had changed in his voice, and I didn't like it. Bending down for a better look, I wasn't at all surprised to see that he was no longer smiling. His eyes were different too. Glazed and faraway. I'd seen that expression before.

"No . . . no . . . nothing's wrong. I just need to get on my way. Like I said, my father's waiting."

"Well, if you're going to be rude, the least you can do is shut the door for me." He sounded like a petulant child.

Without thinking, I stepped closer and reached for the door—and then I froze in my tracks.

I thought you'd be happy to see a friendly face. Especially under the circumstances.

How did *he* know what the circumstances were?

Unless—

That's when I saw there were no handles on the inside passenger door—and realized I was in big trouble.

It all came to me in a rush: Hank followed me and tampered with my car in the mall parking lot. Then he waited until I was alone on the side of the road. *And now once I get close enough to shut the door, his hand's going to snake out of the darkness, grab my arm, and yank me inside the car. What comes after that I don't even want to think about—*

"C'mon, I don't have all night."

Why does his voice suddenly sound so close?

I shook away the dark images that had formed in my mind and—to my absolute horror—saw that Hank had somehow managed to slide all the way across the Monte Carlo's bench seat and was already halfway out of the car. He was smiling again, but there was nothing sane left on his face.

I backed up, almost tripping over my own feet.

He grunted, like an animal, and lunged for me.

I scrambled around the rear of the car, the whisper of his fingertips brushing against the sleeve of my T-shirt, and blindly swung the piece of rebar. It connected with the side of his head with a meaty *thunk*. Shocked, I dropped it to the ground and sprinted away as fast as I could down the center of the road.

Behind me, I heard an inhuman howl of rage.

I never once looked back to see if he was following me.

10

I didn't call my father that night.

I didn't call the police, either.

Instead, I told Jimmy Cavanaugh that I'd had too much to drink and asked him to pick me up at the Dew Drop Inn parking lot. All of us carried fake IDs back then, and thanks to the assholes in the black Trans Am, I smelled like a brewery, so it was an easy story to believe. I spent the night on a leaky air mattress on the floor of Jimmy's bedroom, one final sleepover for old time's sake. My parents were happy to see me spending time with friends before I left and were none the wiser about the car.

The next morning, I asked Jimmy to take me back to the Dew Drop. I offered him gas money for the hassle, but he refused. He was a good friend. I was going to miss him something awful.

I didn't say much on the drive over. My head was still spinning. I wanted to tell Jimmy what had happened. I wanted to *do* something about it. But I was all locked up inside. I was seventeen years old and about to head off on my own for the first time in my life, but I felt like a frightened little boy.

There were only three cars in the parking lot when we got there, but Jimmy never said a word about my Toyota not being one of them. He'd never been the kind of guy to notice things like that. Instead, he was probably thinking about the game of *Zork* he was going to play on his computer when he got home or reciting the lyrics to an AC/DC song in his head.

Once he was gone, I pulled out a slip of paper from my pants pocket and called the number I'd written on it earlier that morning in the Cavanaughs' kitchen after consulting their copy of the yellow pages. The guy who answered the phone sounded like he was talking with a wadded-up ball of sandpaper stuffed in his mouth. He mumbled a price, which I agreed to right away, and we were in business.

I hung up the pay phone and started walking.

When I reached the bottom of the hill, I stopped and looked around in the bright light of day for signs of proof that the incident with Hank had actually happened as I'd remembered it. The entire previous night felt like some kind of bizarre fever dream, and there was a small part of me that was still hoping that was exactly what it had been. Either that or I'd somehow imagined the whole thing.

When I was seven or eight years old, I'd convinced myself that a witch lived in the miniature wardrobe in the darkest corner of my bedroom. Every night, after my parents went to sleep and the lights were turned off, she came out to torment me. She had awful green skin with warts all over her face and bony, clawlike fingers with black fingernails. Her hair was long and gray and greasy and there were bugs squirming around in it. Her lips were blood red. Every night, I'd hide under the covers, too scared to open my eyes, until it felt like my bladder was going to burst, and then I'd spring out of bed, eyes still squeezed shut, and I'd point at the witch with a trembling finger and order her back to the haunted wardrobe where she belonged. Then I'd run as fast as I could to the bathroom down the hall before I peed in my pajamas. This went on for an entire summer before I finally confided in my father one desperate morning. That night, he slept with me in my bedroom, and for the first time in months, the witch failed to make an appearance. The next night, I slept alone but with the door open, and once again, the witch was a no-show. Another week passed and I started sleeping with the door closed. I never saw her again after that. The imagination is a mighty powerful creature.

I surveyed the shoulder at the bottom of the hill, but I didn't find much. There were a couple of scuff marks in the gravel that could've been made by any number of things—including someone's shoes—and the hint of a skid mark running back onto the road. I looked everywhere, but the piece of rebar was gone. Not far from the white line, I noticed several dark stains—none of them larger than a quarter—that could've been blood. Or oil. Or who knew what. I bent down and rubbed at one of the spots with my fingertips. They came away smudged black and greasy like I'd just been fingerprinted. Nothing like blood.

Maybe it really was a nightmare, I thought, and started walking again.

But a few minutes later, halfway up the hill, I came upon the remains of a broken beer bottle—and I knew better. I kicked the shards of glass into the weeds and kept on going.

It was almost eleven when I arrived at the car.

Remembering Hank's howl of rage I'd heard behind me as I'd fled, I half expected to find my old Toyota in shambles—tires slashed, windows shattered, upholstery sliced and diced—but other than a layer of road dust on the hood and roof, it looked exactly as I'd left it.

The mechanic pulled up a short time later in a tow truck. He introduced himself as Lou and asked if I had the keys. Once I handed them over, he took a toothpick from the pocket of his shirt, clamped it between his front teeth, and got to work. The guy didn't look much older than me, but he damn well knew his stuff.

After a remarkably short time under the hood, he looked up and said, "Coupla loose wires is all."

It started on the first try.

He grinned around his toothpick and only charged me half the quoted price.

I thanked him and drove home.

Three days later, I left for college. And that was that.

11

I don't know why I didn't call the police that night.

I've had almost forty years to think about it, and I still don't have an answer.

At least, not a good one.

For those first eight months—right up until the day I stumbled upon the article in the newspaper—I'd convinced myself that what I was most guilty of was overreacting. After all, I *had* been kind of rude. Hank had every right to be annoyed. Maybe he hadn't actually attacked me at all. Maybe he'd just gotten out of the car to give me a piece of his mind, and I'd imagined the rest under stress. His darkening tone of voice. His fingers grasping at the sleeve of my T-shirt. His howls of utter rage. All of it the product of my usual twisted and overactive imagination. I'd been seriously spooked that night. The road had been dark and desolate—it had been graveyard quiet.

The fact that I never saw or heard from Hank again after the incident only served to reinforce my theory. If he'd really wanted to harm me that night, why hadn't he followed me in his car? Why had he just disappeared and never turned up again?

And then there was the harsh reality that I'd been embarrassed. That and ashamed. If Hank really had come after me, wasn't I supposed to stand up for myself? Hadn't I been taught to never back down from a fair fight? Instead, I'd run away, taken off like a scared rabbit. The last thing I'd wanted to do was share *that* news with the rest of the world. Hell, I hadn't even mustered the courage to tell Kara.

Of course, none of that really mattered—not once I'd read the article. In the end, it all came to down to a single hard truth.

Ever since I was a little boy, my father had tried to instill in me one governing principle with which to live by: *When faced with the choice of doing the right thing or the easy thing, always do the right thing, no matter how difficult it is.*

That August night, on that lonely, dark road, I had done the easy thing. I had fled from danger and warned no one.

And my decision had cost an innocent woman her life.

12

The next time I saw Hank's face, it was staring back at me from the newspaper.

It was eight months later, April 1984, and I was in my dorm room. Whenever my parents visited me on campus, they brought along a brown paper grocery bag stuffed with snacks that my father had picked up at the commissary on Edgewood Arsenal. Pop-Tarts, Oodles of Noodles, Oreos, boxes of cereal, and my all-time favorite, Entenmann's crumb doughnuts. And they almost always tossed in an old issue of *Reader's Digest*, along with the latest edition of the *Aegis*.

I recognized Hank's face as soon as I unfolded the newspaper.

He was front-page news—and for all the wrong reasons.

LOCAL MAN ARRESTED FOR MURDER
Police Hint at Additional Victims

Two photographs accompanied the article. In the first, a smiling Hank was shirtless and wearing a baseball glove on his left hand. The banner hanging on the backstop behind him read: APG SUMMER LEAGUE SOFTBALL. The second image was his mug shot. Hank's eyes looked dazed and faraway, just as they had on the night he'd offered me a ride.

With my heart pounding, I began to read:

Thirty-six-year-old Henry Metheny, a civilian employee at Aberdeen Proving Ground, was taken into custody Wednesday morning at his Havre de Grace apartment and charged with the first-degree murder of Bernadette Palletto.

Palletto, 29, a resident of Joppa, MD, worked as a server at the Musical Inn restaurant on Route 40 in Aberdeen. Her body was discovered Tuesday night in a wooded area behind her townhouse by a neighbor who was talking a walk. She had been stabbed more than a dozen times.

Evidence recovered at the scene, as well as eyewitness testimony, led Maryland State Police to . . .

13

It took three weeks for the rest of the story to come out.

When it finally did, the details were horrifying.

Henry Thomas Metheny was charged with two additional counts of first-degree murder for the stabbing deaths of Patricia Cotter, thirty-one, in August 1982, and Noelle Stockton, twenty-seven, in February 1983. At the time of their deaths, both Cotter and Stockton were employed as exotic dancers at the Doll House in Aberdeen, Maryland. Forensic reports on both women, as well as evidence recovered at Henry Metheny's residence, indicated that Metheny dismembered his victims in a rented storage locker and over a period of several weeks, partially consumed their flesh.

In addition, Metheny was now suspected of the 1978 murders of Brennan Lloyd, twenty-six, a warehouse worker in Macon, Georgia, and Carlton Bowers, twenty-eight, a plumber's assistant in Centerville, Georgia.

Further investigations were pending.

14

I was seventeen years old the summer Henry Metheny attacked me.

I was eighteen when I discovered that he was a monster.

When this book is finally published, I will be fifty-seven.

In all that time, I'd told no one.

The easy thing.

Henry Metheny at home in 1982 *(Photo courtesy of* The Aegis*)*

Henry Metheny in 1983 *(Photo courtesy of* The Baltimore Sun*)*

The Dew Drop Inn *(Photo courtesy of James Lee)*

The main gate at Aberdeen Proving Ground *(Photo courtesy of the author)*

The Route 7 shoulder where Chizmar encountered Henry Metheny
(Photo courtesy of the author)

Bernadette Palletto *(Photo courtesy of* The Aegis*)*

Excerpt from Edgewood: Looking Back, *by Richard Chizmar,*
pages 165–166:

The muddy stretch of Winters Run located at the dead end of Hanson Road and Perry Avenue was one of our holy places.

We spent countless hours there—it didn't matter what season of the year—fishing for crappie and bluegill, shooting at crows with BB guns and Wrist-Rockets, making bonfires with books of matches lifted from gas station cigarette machines, and taking part in any number of other barely legal activities.

I still have a scar on the back of my right shoulder from where Jimmy accidentally snagged me with a Mepps spinner as we were crossing over the creek on a fallen log. Despite his mischievous nature, I actually believed it was an accident this time because Jimmy had long ago proved himself as one of the worst fishermen in the entire universe. He spent more time tangled up in trees, bushes, and other people's lines than he did in the water. To this day, I'm still not sure I've ever seen the guy actually catch a fish.

Much later, when we were in high school, long after a summer storm had swept away the fallen log, workers from the park service built a narrow wooden bridge where the log had once stood. When we'd just begun dating, Kara and I used to go on long hikes in the woods surrounding Winters Run. I remember standing next to her on the bridge looking for crayfish the first time I summoned enough courage to reach over and hold her hand. I even carved our initials into one of the handrails with the Swiss Army pocketknife my uncle Ted gave me.

The first summer I came home from college, Bill Caughron—who'd grown up a couple of blocks away on Perry Avenue—and I went back there to try our luck at fishing. The bridge was in pretty rough shape, despite being only a few years old. A length of the handrail was gone (including the section with RC+KT carved into it), and the main walkway was missing several planks and leaning ominously to one side. From the parking lot, it looked like a big wooden sneer minus a couple of teeth. Bill, who could talk the paint off a wall, was unusually quiet that afternoon, and I could tell he was just as lost in the past as I was.

I reached out with the toe of my boot and nudged the walkway. It swayed perilously back and forth, and then went still again. I looked over at Bill. He was staring back at me. Neither of us said a word. With the bittersweet memories of youth walking beside us, we crossed the bridge and went fishing.

SIX

PEYTON

"When is this going to end?"

1

On Monday, June 6, 2022, Peyton Bair was dropped off at the Willoughby Woods Swim Club on Laburnum Road in Edgewood at 8:40 a.m. by her stepfather, who was on his way to work. She was twenty minutes early for her shift, but as a first-year lifeguard she was responsible for wiping down the tables and setting up the chairs around the main pool. They were tedious tasks, but she didn't really mind. Most mornings, she listened to music on her headphones and planned out how she was going to spend her evening once she got home. She had a lot on her plate these days and liked to stay organized.

As she began unstacking chairs and placing them around the tables, she focused her thinking on road signs and following distance and when you should and shouldn't use your high beams. For the past couple of weeks, it was pretty much *all* she'd been thinking about. In forty-eight hours, she was scheduled to take her driver's test. She was a little nervous, but mostly just excited.

Peyton Bair was two days short of "sweet sixteen and a half," as she'd begun calling it, and couldn't wait to get her license. She'd started saving money to buy her own car the year she'd turned fourteen. While her friends were out spending their allowances on trendy new clothes and Starbucks and Spotify Premium, Peyton was dog-sitting for neighbors and raking leaves and designing highlight videos for her older brothers' lacrosse friends. The bulk of her earnings went into a savings account at the M&T Bank by her house. The last time she'd checked her deposit slip, the balance had been a little over $4,000. Impressive.

Six months ago, Peyton's parents had surprised her with a used Volkswagen convertible for her birthday. It was baby blue—her favorite color—and the car of her dreams. When the garage door opened, revealing her gift (with a big red bow attached to the hood to complete the effect), Peyton dropped to her knees and cried. When her stepfather handed her the registration papers, she cried even harder. A short time later, when the tears finally stopped, her parents explained the deal: as long as Peyton used half of her savings to reimburse them for the down payment and continued to earn good grades in school, they would cover the monthly payments and the cost of her insurance. A sweet deal.

Peyton couldn't agree fast enough. She still couldn't believe her eyes. Jumping up and down on the driveway, spinning in circles with a brand-new VW key chain in her hand, she declared it the best present ever and the happiest day of her life.

It gnawed at her very soul that the car had sat inside the garage gathering dust ever since.

Not for long, Peyton thought as she began wiping down the tables. *Just two more days!*

2

Steve McLaughlin was dead broke.

This was not an unusual circumstance for the thirty-six-year-old Edgewood resident, but it was particularly troubling to him this morning because he wanted to go fishing.

And fishing meant two things: bait and beer. Both of which cost money.

McLaughlin, who'd been unemployed for the past five months thanks to a bum knee and a shitty attitude (this according to his wife), had already collected for donating blood this month, so that initiative was out. He didn't own anything valuable enough to sell. Even his fishing pole was a cheap Zebco purchased from the sale rack at the local Walmart. He owed too many people too much money, so any kind of loan was out of the question. McLaughlin had no real taste for crime—petty or otherwise—so that left him with dwindling options.

Least favorable on the list was doing the work himself. It had rained recently, so he supposed he could catch his own minnows in the creek behind the high school. He had a net in the trunk of his car (which was out of gas) and plenty of old buckets in the backyard. He could also dig up some worms if need be.

Beer, though—*that* was the problem. Even if he skimped and got the cheap stuff, he needed at least a twelve-pack to catch a valid buzz. But still, dead broke was dead broke. Where in the world was he gonna come up with seven or eight bucks?

3

Peyton Bair may have appeared diminutive in stature—standing only five foot three and weighing an even one hundred pounds—but anyone who knew her even in passing was well aware of her reputation for being tough. The starting goalie on Edgewood's varsity lacrosse and soccer teams, she was widely respected for her scrappy style of play and unflappable leadership. She wasn't much of a talker, something she'd learned at an early age from her three older brothers, preferring to let her actions speak for themselves. During her freshman soccer season, she'd taken a cheap shot to the face, gotten thirteen stitches above her left eye immediately after the game, and returned to the practice field the very next day. The following season she was voted captain. Her teammates and coaches revered her because of her tireless work ethic; they adored her because there wasn't an arrogant or unkind bone in her entire body.

Despite her popularity at school—not to mention her natural beauty; she had luxuriously long brown hair, sparkling auburn eyes, and the cutest upturned nose anyone had ever seen—Peyton Bair did not have a boyfriend, nor did she want one. Mature beyond her years, she was focused on her training (she hoped to play lacrosse in college) and her studies (she hoped to one day become an oceanographer). The boys falling all over themselves would just have to wait.

Not that Peyton's life was all work and no play. She was an avid hiker and video game enthusiast and was learning how to water-ski from a classmate that lived by the river. She was addicted to Netflix and Amazon Prime and was known to binge-watch an entire series in a single weekend when her schedule allowed. She liked all kinds of music and loved going to concerts with friends. She'd recently started listening to hip-hop and rap, especially while she was working out. Her mother loathed the R-rated lyrics, so Peyton wore headphones whenever possible to save herself yet another lecture.

Despite her brothers' insistence that Peyton was "the golden child" of the family, Mrs. Bair would be the first to tell you that her teenage daughter could be a handful. On any given day, her bedroom resembled the aftermath of a tornado. She was physically incapable of returning a library book on time. She often talked with her mouth full when she got excited and regularly snuck the family dogs her food at the dinner table. She was competitive to a fault. Most game nights in the Bair household ended in an argument of some sort. Two of Peyton's three brothers refused to play her in gin rummy because they were convinced that she cheated. She also took ridiculously long showers, using all the hot water, and left her dirty, wet towels on the bathroom floor.

In other words, Peyton Bair was a typical teenager.

4

Steve McLaughlin didn't believe in God, but sometimes he had to wonder.

Take today, for example.

All morning long, he'd tried his damnedest to come up with a plan to get some beer money—but nothing had worked. Time and time again, his hopes had been dashed. When noon came around, the only option left in his mind was putting out a hat in front of the gas station, but if his wife found out he'd been panhandling again, she'd whup his ass from one end of town to the other.

Bottom line: he wasn't proud, but he *was* damn well scared.

Dejected and finally coming to terms with the realization that there would be no fishing for him today, he started hoofing it home. As he crossed Edgewood Road in front of the car wash, a semitruck driver high on amphetamines laid on the horn, spit a mouthful of chewing tobacco out the window at McLaughlin, and hollered at him for being a "blind motherfucker"—all while narrowly avoiding running him down. McLaughlin heard the angry shout and felt the warm blast of air as the truck roared past him but he didn't even bother to look up. He was too damn sad.

Head hanging, he cut across a litter-strewn parking lot and took the shortcut through the woods behind the library. Halfway down the path, he spotted a shiny penny lying in the dirt in front of him. He bent down and picked it up, brushed it off, and put it in his pocket. Perhaps this was the beginning of his bad luck starting to turn around.

And then, it did.

Like a saintly whisper sent from the heavens above, the answer he'd been searching for fell right into his lap.

Storm drains.

There were dozens of them scattered around town. And many of them were big enough for a grown man—especially a skinny-bordering-on-emaciated grown man—to crawl into. McLaughlin and his friends had done it all the time when they were kids—usually while playing hide-and-seek or flashlight tag, but sometimes just for fun—and they'd found all sorts of cool stuff down there. Including money.

The follies of youth completely forgotten about until now, when he needed divine intervention the most. *Someone* up there was looking out for him.

The dirt path emptied onto Rosewood Drive, so that's where

McLaughlin decided to try his luck first. Donna Cornett, the prettiest girl in his eighth-grade class, had lived on the corner of Rosewood and Hanson. He'd spent countless summer afternoons skateboarding on the street in front of her house, doing kickflips and handstands and forward and reverse 360s, hoping against hope that she'd come outside to watch and maybe even talk a little bit. It had never worked out that way—in fact, Donna and her family up and moved away before the start of the new school year—but McLaughlin still had fond memories of the place.

Unfortunately, Rosewood was *no bueno*—even with him holding his breath until he got light-headed, McLaughlin couldn't make himself small enough to fit. The concrete platforms were just too damn low to the road. He needed at least a couple more inches of wiggle room. And that wasn't gonna happen. Better to just cut his losses—who knew who might be spying on him from the front window (*"What's that loser McLaughlin up to now?"*), run and tell his wife.

His spirits still high, he made his way over to Hornbeam Road—the street he'd grown up on—and *BOOM! ZAP! WHAM!* (wouldn't you know it; McLaughlin was a huge comic book fan), the first drain he tried proved to be an easy-peasy squeeze. He didn't even have to hold his breath or suck in his stomach.

Standing inside the gloom of the storm drain was like going home again for McLaughlin. The damp, earthy smell. The staccato rhythm of dripping water. The pinpricks of sunlight slanting down through the holes in the manhole cover above him. The rough-hewn concrete walls and slime-slick cement floors. He didn't find much of value inside the drain, but that didn't matter. For the first time in years, he felt like a kid again. His initial take included a nickel and two pennies, a cracked plastic horseshoe he hung on to because he thought it might be good luck (better to keep that streak going), and a beat-up Matchbox car he planned to give to the little boy who lived in the house behind him.

The second storm drain, just down the road a bit, was even less productive. McLaughlin caught a whiff of something rotten in the air even as he approached the mouth of the drain but didn't think anything of it. Once inside, strewn across the concrete floor, he found an old comb with most of the teeth missing, a bright green Bic lighter that refused to spark, the top half of a bowling trophy, and a tangled string of faded red balloons that had either been popped or deflated by time. A few feet inside one of the larger drainage pipes, he discovered the source of the bad smell: a dead cat. Its stomach yawned open like a fur-lined serving bowl. Maggots had made a home there, and they were having quite the party. Tiny gray worms wriggled in and out of the cat's hollowed-out eye sockets. Its tongue, black and withered, was poking out.

Horrified, McLaughlin backed up until he couldn't go any farther—and then he gagged and scrambled up through the opening, scraping his elbows and knees on the asphalt. Writhing on his back in the middle of the road, hands flailing, brushing imaginary critters out of his hair and off his face and arms, McLaughlin looked every bit of a junkie on a bad high. If a cop had driven by at that exact moment, he'd be headed to jail for an overnight. No questions asked. As it was—and as he'd feared—an elderly widow watching from her bay window across the street was on her way to call 911, but just as she was reaching for the telephone, the timer in her kitchen went off. The chocolate brownies she was baking for her grandchildren were ready. By the time she took the pan out of the oven, placed it on the counter to cool, and returned to the window, the scraggly-looking druggie in front of her house was gone. *What in heavens is this town coming to?* she thought, clutching the rosary inside the pocket of her apron. *If Joseph were still alive, he'd be fit to be tied.*

Farther down the street, both of his elbows dripping blood and his stomach on the verge of revolting, McLaughlin eyed the next storm drain, now with fire in his rheumy eyes. He wasn't about to let a little run of bad luck ruin his day. When beer money was at stake, Steve McLaughlin was the consummate overachiever.

Wincing in pain, the vision of the disemboweled cat still firmly implanted in his brain, he glanced around to make sure the coast was clear, scuttled inside the drain—and hit the jackpot.

Sitting right there in plain sight on a small makeshift ledge formed by a pair of loose bricks was a monogrammed money clip—*Thank you, G. S., whoever you are!*—with a nice, fat fold of cash. The bills were moist and delicate and covered in a film of yellowish slime and they smelled like rotten fish, but none of that mattered a lick to McLaughlin. He carefully loosened the money from the rusting metal clip and counted it right there in the available light of the storm drain, eight feet under, while cars drove over top of him, unaware.

By the time he'd finished, his hands were shaking.

One hundred and seventy-four dollars.

Jesus jumpin' Christ.

It was like winning the lottery.

Hell, he now had enough money to buy a whole case of beer (the good stuff too!), fill up the gas tank, and buy the missus some flowers from the supermarket. With plenty left over.

In the illumination from street level, he looked up to the heavens and murmured "Thank you," and genuinely meant it. He intended to hold on to that shiny penny he'd found earlier to keep his good fortune humming along.

In the short term, though, it appeared that fishing was back on, as originally planned.

For just a moment, as he was crawling back onto the road, McLaughlin heard a shrill, high-pitched giggle coming from somewhere behind him— coming from somewhere deep within the labyrinth of storm drains—but then he was standing up in bright sunlight again, the weight of the money clip in his pants pocket pressing against his thigh, and he forgot all about it.

He never even noticed the fifty-dollar bill stuck on the bottom of his left shoe. By the time he crossed the street, it was gone.

5

When Kristine Bair pulled into the Willoughby Woods Swim Club parking lot at ten minutes past six and didn't find Peyton waiting for her by the front gate, she wasn't surprised. Knowing her daughter, she was probably still inside the locker room, blabbing away with a couple of her girlfriends.

Mrs. Bair circled around the rows of parked cars and stopped in the unloading zone. She turned on her hazards and waited. Two little boys scampered out of the fenced-in pool area, tossing a bright orange Frisbee back and forth. Both of them had Popsicles in their mouths and their lips were stained blue. Mrs. Bair thought about rolling down her window and telling them it was dangerous to run around with those little wooden sticks hanging out of their mouths, but decided to mind her own business. A moment later, a harried-looking woman with her hair up in a ponytail and dark circles under her eyes rushed out from behind the fence and herded the boys back inside. Even with the window closed, Mrs. Bair could hear the woman's exasperated voice: ". . . didn't know where you'd gotten off to."

Been there, done that, Mrs. Bair thought to herself and smiled. She glanced at her watch.

Six fifteen. Still no Peyton. *What could be keeping her?*

For the past several days, Mrs. Bair had been listening to the new John Sandford novel on her way to and from work—she had a raging crush on Sandford's leading man, Virgil Flowers; she'd even dreamed about him on several occasions, something she'd never admit to anyone, not even her closest girlfriends—and when the latest chapter came to a dramatic conclusion, she hit pause, picked up her cell phone, and called her daughter.

It went straight to voice mail.

6

It was 8:30 p.m., and Steve McLaughlin was drunk.

Or to be more precise, he was drunk, happy, and seeing things.

Drunk, because as of an hour ago, he'd already put away an entire case of Michelob bottles all by his lonesome.

Happy, because he'd not only caught a nice largemouth bass, but also snagged a pair of big-ass snakeheads, which he was dragging on the ground behind him, and they were going to make one helluva tasty dinner if his old lady was still awake when he got home.

And seeing things, because twice now, he could've sworn he'd spotted a pack of chittering monkeys cavorting in the treetops (but then again that might've been on account of him buying a loose joint from Big Leonard at the car wash and smoking it in his now gassed-up car on the way to the creek because, hell, why not live a little?).

Speaking of his car, there it was just ahead, parked right where he remembered in that little gravel parking lot opposite the pump house at the end of Hanson and Perry. Maybe he wasn't that shit-faced after all.

He started across the wobbly wooden bridge that spanned Winters Run, but stumbled to a halt after only a couple of steps. His stomach turned a cartwheel and he tasted sour bile surging in the back of his throat.

Either he was seeing things again, or there was a naked dead girl on the bridge.

7

I was in the shower when the call came in.

"It's Lieutenant McClernan," Kara said, holding up my phone. "Want me to tell her you'll call back?"

"Please."

She walked away, speaking into the phone. I had just enough time to rinse the shampoo out of my hair before Kara was back again. "She says it's important."

I turned off the water, dried my hands on a towel, and took the phone from her. She rolled her eyes at me as I did.

"Hello?"

"They found another girl." I could hear the hustle in the background. McClernan was at the scene.

"When?"

"Forty-five minutes ago. In Edgewood."

I opened my mouth to ask *Anyone we know?*—and stopped myself.

"Who is she?"

"Local girl. Young. She was strangled and posed. Ligature marks on her wrists and ankles. Left ear gone. Bite marks."

I let out a long breath. "Gallagher's M.O."

"There are some inconsistencies."

"Was she . . ."

"I don't know yet. She was naked when she was found and there's some bruising, but Forensics doesn't think so. We'll know for sure in a couple hours."

"Who found her?"

"Local drunk. He was fishing."

"Any chance he's the guy?"

"Not much of one. A bunch of the uniforms know him. The general consensus is that he's too dumb and lazy to do something like this. Harmless."

"You said the guy was fishing . . . where did he find her?"

"There's a creek at the end of Perry Avenue. It runs by an old pumping station and—"

"I know where it is." I wondered how my voice sounded.

"She was found spread-eagle on the bridge."

8

According to detectives, Mrs. Bair waited another five minutes before trying her daughter's cell phone again. When her second attempt also went direct to voice mail, she turned off the car and went inside.

At that point, she was more irritated than she was concerned. Mrs. Bair rarely worried about her daughter. Peyton was a smart girl and very capable. Her mother believed she could take care of herself.

The first person Mrs. Bair spoke with was seventeen-year-old Mike Bradley, who was working the counter at the snack bar. He didn't know where Peyton was; he couldn't remember seeing her since earlier in the afternoon. Next, she talked to sixteen-year-old Carrie Bridgeport, one of Peyton's closest friends. Carrie told Mrs. Bair that she and Peyton had talked for a short time around 5:45 p.m. and then they'd said goodbye. From the perch of her lifeguard stand, she'd watched Peyton walk outside a few minutes later with her knapsack slung over her shoulder. Peyton was listening to music on her headphones and had been alone at the time.

Finally, Mrs. Bair asked to speak with Kevin Frost, the general manager of the Willoughby Woods Swim Club. It was Mr. Frost who was responsible for hiring Peyton and the other lifeguards at the beginning of the summer; he and Mrs. Bair's first husband were old high school friends.

Mr. Frost immediately checked to see if Peyton had clocked out. She had—her time card read 5:53 p.m. Seventeen minutes before Mrs. Bair had arrived at the swim club.

Peyton's mother was no longer irritated. She was now distraught, on the verge of tears.

Mr. Frost then searched both locker rooms for any sign of the girl—of which there was none—before making an announcement over the intercom system. A thirty-one-year-old Abingdon woman, Nancy Fleagle, reported seeing someone matching Peyton's description standing by the front gate at approximately 5:55 p.m. when she'd arrived at the pool with her two children. The girl she'd seen had been wearing a pink tank top and was carrying a knapsack. Mrs. Bair and Mr. Frost immediately checked the parking lot, frantically searching inside each and every car.

At 6:39 p.m., Mrs. Bair called her husband, who had arrived at home from his office in Timonium just minutes earlier. He immediately phoned a number of Peyton's friends to see if any of them knew where she was.

None of them did.

At 6:52 p.m., Mrs. Bair, now officially freaking out, tried her daughter's cell phone one final time. Once again, she reached her voice mail.

At 6:54 p.m., Mrs. Bair called the police to report her daughter missing and was forced to repeat herself several times as the words tumbled out of her mouth in a blind panic.

9

At 8:49 p.m., Charlotte Waters, age forty-one, cashier of the Texaco station located at the corner of Hanson and Edgewood Roads, called 911 on behalf of a distraught Steve McLaughlin to report the discovery of a body.

Police were on the scene approximately six minutes later.

10

After disconnecting with Lieutenant McClernan and getting dressed, I found Kara hiding out on the back porch. She was sitting on the love seat in the dark, her legs tucked underneath her, drinking a mug of hot tea. Cujo and Ripley were curled up next to her.

"They're already doing their live reports," she said, waving a hand toward the front of our property. "You can see all the camera lights."

"I'm sure most of them are headed to Edgewood by now."

She surprised me by reaching for my hand.

"Rich . . . when is this going to end?"

I wanted to lie to her, but I couldn't.

"I-I don't know."

11

I rewound the security footage and watched again.

It was almost midnight. Kara had gone to sleep hours ago without even bothering to say good night. The house was still and quiet.

Right there, I thought, hitting the pause button and leaning closer to the laptop screen.

It looked like the base of the tree had expanded slightly—almost as if someone dressed all in black were hiding behind it and when they shifted just a tiny bit, they inched into view of the camera.

I rewound and watched it one more time.

Hmmm . . . or maybe it was just a shadow from the lamppost?

Shit. It was difficult to tell.

The footage was from 12:38 a.m., a little less than twenty-four hours ago, and most likely the last time this section of Southampton Road would see any peace and quiet for quite a while. With news of a second victim, the field across the street was lit up like a midwestern tent revival, and the street itself resembled a Fourth of July car rally. Lookie-loos from all across the county—cell phone cameras sticking out their windows—cruised by my house for a firsthand glimpse of what they'd been seeing on their TVs and phones and tablets. A constant stream of media vehicles shuttled back and forth in between the crime scene in Edgewood, the Maryland State Police barracks in Fallston, and their designated parking area just beyond the next intersection. Earlier this evening, I'd gone outside to retrieve Kara's glasses from her car in the driveway, and I'd heard the squeal of brakes and the grinding *screech* of metal on metal. I'd hurried back inside and pulled up the security footage. The camera in our front-yard tree captured in vivid detail an MSNBC van and a Harford County Sheriff's Department SUV tangled together in the middle of the road. I watched as the driver exited the van, holding a towel to his bleeding forehead, and all I could think was: *This is just the beginning; it's going to get worse.*

When my cell phone vibrated on the patio table, I wasn't at all surprised.

I picked it up and checked the ID, hoping it was Lieutenant Mc-Clernan calling to bring me up to speed.

It wasn't.

"Hello?"

A loud beep and the automated voice: "*I have a collect call from the Cumberland Penitentiary from inmate . . .*"

"Josh Gallagher."

"*. . . will you accept the charges?*"

"Yes."

A click, then: "*I don't have much time. I had to call in a rather large favor to get an open line this late.*" He sounded tired.

"It could've waited until tomorrow."

"*No, it couldn't. I just wanted to say I'm sorry.*"

"For what?" I asked.

"*For the turmoil you and your family are about to endure.*"

I paused, then said: "You know about the girl?"

"*I do.*"

Suddenly, I was livid. "You know what? Fuck you. Fuck *you*, Josh. Isn't this what people like you want? To inspire others to follow in your foot-steps? To make your mark on the world? To be remembered somehow?"

"*Ahh, Rich. Haven't you learned a thing after all this time?*"

"Thanks to you, I'm not sure I know anything at all anymore."
"You will, though. That day is coming. For all of us."
Before I could say anything else, he was gone.

Peyton Bair before her homecoming dance *(Photo courtesy of Kris Bair)*

Peyton Bair at a music festival in Delaware *(Photo courtesy of Kris Bair)*

The Willoughby Swim Club parking lot on the evening Peyton Bair was abducted *(Photo courtesy of Steve Sines)*

The Winter's Run bridge where Peyton Bair's body was discovered; this photo was taken two months later after repairs were made *(Photo courtesy of the author)*

A storm drain on Hornbeam Road *(Photo courtesy of the author)*

Detectives at the Peyton Bair crime scene *(Photo courtesy of* The Aegis*)*

Excerpt from in-person interview with Anna Garfield Rafferty, age 55, recorded on April 12, 2019:

CHIZMAR: You were difficult to track down.

RAFFERTY: That was intentional.

CHIZMAR: In all these years, you've only participated in one other interview regarding your relationship with Joshua Gallagher. Why did you finally agree to speak with me?

RAFFERTY: I'm not exactly sure. [pause] I've read how close you are to him . . . and I suppose I thought you might have some answers for me as well.

CHIZMAR: Fair enough. Let's get started. You can respond however you feel comfortable. What is your first memory of Joshua Gallagher?

RAFFERTY: The first time I saw Josh was at the student union.

CHIZMAR: Did you speak with him that day?

RAFFERTY: No. It was probably two weeks later at a freshmen cookout on the commons.

CHIZMAR: And what was your first impression of him?

RAFFERTY: I thought he was handsome. Charming. Funny. A little awkward, but that only made me like him more.

CHIZMAR: And soon after you started dating?

RAFFERTY: Yes, pretty much right away.

CHIZMAR: What was the first sign that Joshua Gallagher had issues of some sort?

RAFFERTY: [pause] He talked to himself. I know lots of people do that. I do it myself sometimes. But he did it a lot, and he couldn't seem to stop even if he wanted to. I teased him about it once, but he didn't like that, so I never mentioned it again.

CHIZMAR: What are some of the things he said to himself?

RAFFERTY: Oh, a little bit of everything. That's the thing. It didn't always make sense. Sometimes it was embarrassing. Other times, it was . . . unsettling.

CHIZMAR: Unsettling in what way?

RAFFERTY: [long pause] Almost like he'd become a completely different person.

SEVEN

AFTERMATH

"I was here in 1988 and it wasn't good."

1

"It's all over the news, even in Charlottesville."

Noah was wearing a bright green Birdwood Golf shirt. In the background I could hear the starter on the intercom summoning the next foursome to the tee box.

"It's a zoo and getting worse," I said. "I'm actually glad you're there and not here."

"Don't let Mom hear you say that."

"I won't and don't you tell her." I poked my head into the bathroom. The shower was still running. Both of the mirrors were steamed over. "She's going to be bummed she missed you."

"I'll try to FaceTime again when I get off work. Sometime around six."

"Sounds good. I'll let her know."

"How are the pups?"

"A little jumpy with all the commotion, but they're okay. They miss you."

"I miss them too. Hey, I gotta run. Love you guys."

"Love you too." I started to end the call but hesitated. "Noah?"

"Yeah?"

"Be safe."

2

Peyton Bair's family and friends appeared on all four local news programs the morning after her body was discovered.

Her tearful parents talked about how special she was, how she'd loved spending time with friends and never had a bad word to say about anyone. "She was a ray of sunshine," her mother, Kristine, told the Channel 2 reporter. She was holding a framed photograph of her daughter in her lap. "She woke up every morning so happy and full of energy."

Her three brothers stood side by side in front of their Hemlock Road home and recounted some of their favorite stories about their little sister. "She wasn't afraid of anything," Jason Bair said. The oldest of the three boys, he'd returned home the night before from Bucknell University, where he was attending summer school and studying finance. "My friends and I used to jump off the old steel bridge down at the Rocks when we were in high school. Most of the girls in our class were too scared to even climb up there. But not Peyton. She tagged along with us one day and before we knew it, she was doing backflips off the railing. And she was only in middle school."

Carol Barker, Peyton's high school lacrosse coach, talked about Peyton's work ethic. "It was unparalleled at this level. She set lofty goals and went after them with a passion. She was the kind of player—and person—who made everyone around her better."

Finally, Jenny Stewart, a bespectacled Edgewood High School sophomore with braces on her teeth, sobbed as she spoke in front of the camera. "Peyton was my best friend. We were supposed to go to the carnival this weekend. She was even going to drive. We had our outfits picked out and everything."

Sitting in front of the television, it felt like déjà vu.

It felt like the summer of 1988 all over again.

3

The majority of the morning's news footage featuring Detective Gonzalez had been recorded the previous night. He stood in the center of the flag court in front of the barracks, squinting in the glare of the camera lights, with what looked like a thousand bugs fluttering around his head like a shimmering halo.

". . . at this time, we have no conclusive evidence supporting a connection between the murders of Anne Riggs and Peyton Bair, but our investigation is still in the preliminary stages. We're currently pursuing a number of leads and hopefully more details will soon become available. Anyone with information about these crimes is asked to call the Maryland State Police at . . ."

Lieutenant McClernan had asked me to keep the details of Peyton Bair's missing ear and the numerous bite marks found on her body off the record. The plan was to withhold that information from the press for as long as possible. It made sense, but from past experience, I knew it wouldn't last very long. One of Peyton's brothers would inevitably share the information with a girlfriend or a buddy from school. One of the uniforms would have too much to drink and mention it to his wife. Those people would tell someone else, and right on down the line it would go. And once it hit TikTok, Twitter, and Facebook, it would all be over. I gave it two or three days, tops.

That would be the next domino to fall.

Once the public discovered that the two killings were inextricably linked, it would be 1988 all over again. Hysteria would set in.

Not that many people didn't already have their suspicions. The moment that Annie Riggs was identified as the first victim, the phrase "copycat killer" began to surface in conversations all across town (not to mention the hundreds, maybe thousands, of frenzied posts on Reddit, as well as all the other true crime message boards). I could only imagine what the backyard gossip gang was saying this morning.

As if to reinforce that line of thinking, just before the Channel 13 field reporter threw it back to the anchor desk, an unseen journalist in the crowd shouted, "Detective Gonzalez . . . was it the Boogeyman?"

The anchorman, a longtime Baltimore favorite with his granite chin, spray-tanned face, and silver hair, raised his eyebrows at the camera and said, "Was it the Boogeyman indeed? I think it's safe to say that question is on all of our minds this tragic morning . . ."

4

In some parts of Edgewood, residents were already preparing for the worst.

In Bayberry Court, a man named Michael Deal was installing bars on the lower-level windows of his house. When Carlos Vargas Sr. walked over from next door and asked him why he was doing it, Deal told him, "I have two teenage daughters. The Boogeyman ain't getting his filthy hands on them."

In a housing development off Willoughby Beach Road, an entire street had mobilized. Doorbell cameras were purchased, motion-detector spotlights were attached to rooftops, and heavy-duty dead bolts were installed on doors. Legal and illegal firearms were cleaned, and a printed page of "safety rules" was stapled to telephone poles and taped to road signs and handed out to all the children in the neighborhood. Punishments were threatened for any transgressions. The number one rule on the list: *Day or night, never go anywhere alone.*

Right around the corner from where I'd grown up, a homeowner on Tupelo Drive was hurriedly loading his car. "I'm taking the family away for a while," he told Lottie Noel, who had lived across the street for going on fifty years now. "I was here in '88, just like you, and I'm not dealing with those shenanigans again. We have a cabin at Deep Creek, so we're heading out on an extended vacation until things settle down."

By midafternoon, there had already been a number of alleged sightings of the killer. A group of boys playing basketball at Cedar Drive reported a man walking in the woods across the street. He was carrying a hammer and wearing a mask. A FedEx driver delivering a package to a home on Perry Avenue told police that he'd glanced at one of the windows on his way back to his truck and saw a man trying on a burlap mask in front of a mirror. An elderly man taking his afternoon walk claimed he witnessed a man climbing down out of a tree in Banyan Court. When the old guy asked the man what he was doing, the stranger took off running. A woman who lived alone on Harewood Drive told reporters that she was washing dishes when a masked man suddenly appeared in the window directly in front of her. In a panic, she'd flung a serving bowl at him, shattering both the window and the dish, and then called 911. When the police arrived a short time later, they'd found her on the kitchen floor clutching her chest and gasping for air. An ambulance took her to Upper Chesapeake, where doctors admitted her for further observation.

The press was everywhere, fishing for sound bites—and it wasn't just the news media this time around. TMZ was in town. Jake Paul and *People* magazine. True crime celebrities from TikTok and YouTube posted videos from the parking lot of Edgewood High School and across the street from Annie Riggs's house. Camera crews staked out grocery stores and the post office, banks and playgrounds. Frightened mothers with little kids clinging to their legs made for good television and viral videos.

5

Closer to home, in Bel Air, things were tense.

Norman Barnes, our neighbor from two doors down, was livid. The previous evening, an intern from one of the cable stations had backed into Barnes's daughter's Jeep in their driveway. When his daughter exited the vehicle to survey the damage and exchange insurance information, the intern had made inappropriate comments and asked for her Snapchat. The intern, who was twenty-three and engaged to be married, was very persistent. Barnes's daughter had rushed inside the house in tears.

Barnes made a point of saying that he didn't blame us for the incident, but it was plainly clear that he did. Otherwise, why else had he shown up at our front door, beet red and waggling his fat finger in my face?

By the time he'd finished ranting, I'd wanted to snap his finger in two and punch him in the mouth, but Kara had intervened before things got violent. She'd eased him off the porch, talking in that slow, calm tone of voice she'd usually reserved for the boys when they were young and fighting with each other. A few minutes later, she returned and said, "I saw you clenching your jaw and I knew you were about to lose it."

Kara's response to the chaos enveloping our neighborhood was typical Kara. While continuing to give me the cold shoulder, she baked a triple batch of chocolate chip cookies, attached handwritten apology notes to the tops of the cellophane-wrapped plates, and walked around delivering them to our neighbors. All of them were understanding and sympathetic, even the notoriously prickly Spanglers, who were headed out for a ten-day vacation in Myrtle Beach. "I think it might've been a different story if they were trapped back here with the rest of us," she told me when she got home.

"Of course, Ken Klein had about a million questions. He's absolutely convinced that you're involved with the police investigation. Before I left, he told me that the detectives were *very* interested in Norman Barnes. Apparently, they showed up at Barnes's house on two separate occasions to talk to him. Ever since that leaf-blowing incident, Ken's had it in for that guy.

"Oh, and Penny Schutz gave my arm a nice, patronizing squeeze and told me to come by anytime, day or night, if I needed to talk about . . . *'well, you know.'* She was whispering when she said it, looking around like one of the neighbors might overhear. As if she's not the queen-bee busybody of all of Bel Air. Hell, she probably falls asleep at night thinking about our marital issues . . ."

The words stung me.

Marital issues.

I guess it shouldn't have surprised me that our troubles had become public knowledge—but it did. I knew Kara hadn't said anything to anyone other than her sister and closest friends, so then how the hell did Penny Schutz know? Was it really that obvious?

6

Lieutenant McClernan stopped by the house later that afternoon. I was out back trimming bushes when she waved me down from the gate. "I rang the doorbell, but no one answered."

"Billy's upstairs," I said, stowing the electric trimmer under the back porch. "Probably has his headphones on. Kara's next door."

She glanced at the neighbors' house. I'd expected her to look tired after last night. Instead, she appeared alert and focused. "I won't keep you long. Just had a couple questions."

"Fire away."

She pulled a photograph out of the portfolio she carried with her everywhere. "Do you know a man named Johnathon Russell?" She handed it to me.

The man in the photo looked about thirty or so. Deeply tanned face. Receding hairline. Bad teeth. A complete stranger. "No, never seen him. Why you asking?"

"His mother lives in the neighborhood across the street. He recently stayed with her for about six months until she kicked him out. That happened two weeks ago. He's got a record for some pretty nasty stuff."

I studied the photo again. Shook my head.

"One of the mom's neighbors accused Russell of peeking in his daughter's bedroom window. She's twelve. No police were involved because the family's tight with the mom, but the timing matches up with when Russell was sent packing."

"Where is he now?"

"Shacked up with an old girlfriend in Darlington."

"You think he could be involved?"

"Well, he's not the only one on the list, but he fits the profile. We're checking on his alibis for both nights."

"What's his Edgewood connection?"

"*You* are—that's why I'm here. His mother claims that *Chasing the Boogeyman* is his favorite book. He's seen the movie seven times. He knew you lived right here on Southampton. Supposedly rode his motorcycle by the house all the time."

I shook my head again. "If he did, I never saw him."

She opened her portfolio and glanced inside. "You mentioned someone named Sam English? My notes aren't complete, so we must've gotten sidetracked or maybe we were interrupted."

"Sam's a student at Edgewood High. I mentor him as part of a school program. Mainly via email, but we've met a number of times too."

"Have you ever met with him here at the house?"

"No. At the library, like three or four times, and once at Barnes and Noble, before the Starbucks closed down."

"And always just the two of you?"

I hesitated. Past experience had taught me that it was nearly impossible to have a casual conversation with a homicide detective and not feel like you'd just robbed a string of banks and murdered an entire church full of nuns. I hated feeling guilty when there was nothing to feel guilty about—yet I felt powerless to stop it. "Yes . . . although I met both his mother and father when they dropped him off and picked him up."

"You ever notice anything unusual about him or his parents?"

"Never. From what I can tell, they're good people."

"Would you be able to share with me their contact info?"

"Sure. I'll text you."

"That'd be great, thanks." She glanced inside her portfolio again. "We're looking into any possible connections between Anne Riggs and Peyton Bair, but I doubt we'll find anything other than their zip codes. Riggs was in her fifties, Bair was sixteen. Nowadays, that practically makes them two different species."

"Do you think they both knew the killer?"

"It's possible." She gave me a look. "You're getting good at this, aren't you?"

"Don't tell Kara that, please."

She cracked a smile, but it left her face almost immediately. "The way both of the victims were taken. Daytime. Public areas. Decent number of people around. No prolonged struggles or cries for help. They could've known their assailant, or maybe he's just very good at what he does."

"With Peyton, I guess that means there were no witnesses at the pool?"

"No, she just clocked out and that was it. Gone."

"How about at the crime scene? Plenty of people fish and hike in that area."

"Not late last night. Our only witness arrived after the fact, and he was plastered. There's a trail cam attached to a telephone pole in the parking lot—people like to dump their trash down there—but it stopped recording about a week earlier. Whether that was the killer's doing or not, we're still trying to figure that out."

"I've been thinking about this . . . have you considered the possibility that the man in the mask in front of my house was working with a partner?"

"Interesting. Why do you ask?"

Suddenly, I felt embarrassed and wished I hadn't opened my big mouth. "I don't know . . . it's probably nothing . . . but I keep thinking about logistics. The bag in front of the house was dropped off in the middle of the night . . . but what if a car had driven by at the moment he was carrying it down the street? A driver might've ignored the bag, but not the mask he was wearing. Someone sees that, and my bet is they're slowing down, maybe calling the police. Or at least they definitely are the next morning once they hear the news." I paused and caught my breath. "So . . . what if there was someone else waiting at the other end of Southampton to warn him in case a car came along?"

She stared at me thoughtfully. "Not bad, but we're way ahead of you there. We're looking into that very possibility." And then suddenly the smile was back. "Appreciate your input, Joe Hardy."

Speechless, I watched her saunter away.

The Hardy Boys . . . again . . . straight from the pages of *Chasing the Boogeyman*.

The gate clanged shut behind her.

Sometimes, I hated that fucking book.

7

That evening, Kara and I ate by the pond.

We'd both been craving Mexican food but knew that going out would be next to impossible. So we'd done the next best thing and asked Billy to order DoorDash from La Tolteca, our favorite local place.

We sat on a blanket in the shade and ate our fajitas. A family of geese swam circles around the island. Turtles rose to the surface to say hello, then disappeared underwater again. It was a nice night. Not too hot. Not too many bugs. And no talk of the Boogeyman.

Not long after my visit with Lieutenant McClernan, I'd had a Zoom conference with my literary agent. Kristin had heard about the murder of Peyton Bair and wanted to make sure I was okay. She'd also wanted to let me know that she'd spoken with the marketing and publicity teams at my publisher. All my appearances for the next two weeks had been canceled.

She hadn't said a word about another Boogeyman book, which surprised and pleased me. I could barely keep an organized thought in my head, much less think about sitting down to craft a cohesive narrative.

As I was cleaning up our dinner mess, Noah followed through on his earlier promise and FaceTimed his mother. They spoke for about ten minutes, mostly about his new job and apartment, and after a last-second reminder to wear sunscreen while working on the golf course, Kara hung up.

Seeing Noah's face had put her in about as close to a good mood as I'd seen since all of this madness had begun. Neither of us was in a hurry to go back inside, where the television and iPad awaited us with more bad news, so we took a lazy walk around the orchard. Kara even surprised me by holding my hand. Twice, I almost opened my mouth to tell her about Henry Metheny—and both times, something stopped me.

Later, I told myself it was because I didn't want to ruin Kara's happy mood.

But deep in my heart, I knew it was something else that had prevented me from telling her.

Fear. Plain and simple.

8

That night—most likely in a misguided attempt to make up for my earlier bout of cowardice—I agreed to do a live on-air interview with Tom Forrester for Channel 45's ten o'clock news broadcast.

Forrester had once interviewed Billy when he'd been a student at the St. Paul's School in Timonium. Billy had been honored with a statewide "Unsung Hero" award for his play as an undersized defensive end on the football team. Channel 45 was one of the award sponsors, so Forrester had shown up on campus one afternoon and conducted a very nice Q&A before practice.

Forrester had politely reminded me of all this when he'd made his request.

The crew arranged a pair of straight-backed chairs on the front porch, set up their light poles, and clipped a tiny microphone to my shirt collar. After a quick soundcheck, they were ready to go. The cameraman counted us down: "Three ... two ... one ... rolling."

Forrester stared into the camera. "Good evening. This is Tom Forrester with WBFF Fox45 News, coming to you live from Bel Air, Maryland, where we have bestselling true crime author Richard Chizmar with us tonight." He turned and looked at me. "It's been quite a week for you and your family, hasn't it, Richard?"

"It's been a difficult time for everyone here in Harford County. I'd like to extend my deepest sympathies to both the Riggs and Bair families."

"Two local murders with connections to your most popular book, *Chasing the Boogeyman*. Have you spoken with the star of that book, Joshua Gallagher, about what is happening?"

"No, I haven't," I lied, hoping that the lack of hesitation on my part would add some credence to my response. "I'd also like to point out that the police have yet to determine whether or not Peyton Bair's tragic death is connected in any way to the killings that took place in Edgewood during the summer of 1988."

It was like he hadn't even heard me. His eyes had gone dark. "What do you have to say to those people who believe you're profiting off the deaths of innocent young women by writing books such as *Chasing the Boogeyman*?"

Shit. Okay, this was definitely not going as planned. "I would say . . . I'm sorry that they feel that way. *Chasing the Boogeyman* is as much a tribute to the victims and their families as it is a chronicling of the loss of innocence . . . not just for a young man who called Edgewood home, but for the entire town itself. You have to remember that when the original book first came out in 1990, I was fresh out of college, and it was released by a very small regional publisher. There was never any intention—"

"And yet the expanded edition and the feature film have done very well, have they not?"

I nodded, feeling the crushing weight of defeat settle onto my shoulders. I should never have agreed to do this. I should have listened to Kara, who was probably watching from inside and cringing.

"One final question, Richard." Even my name sounded foul coming out of his mouth. "There are a number of critics who claim that your participation in a series of exclusive interviews with Joshua Gallagher is helping to make life in prison considerably more comfortable for that confessed serial murderer. Any comments?"

I'd had enough. I leaned as far forward as my chair would allow and stared directly into the camera. "My participation, as you call it, was requested by the Maryland State Police in an attempt to gain vital information regarding the current whereabouts of additional unknown victims of Joshua Gallagher. I am not being compensated for this work. I'm doing it with the hopes of bringing some level of closure and peace to the families of the missing. I deserve neither credit nor scorn for this undertaking. I don't have any further comment—thanks for the interview."

9

As soon as Forrester finished ad-libbing his way back to the studio and the little red light on the camera blinked off, I stood up, unclipped my microphone, and left it on the chair. Before I went inside, I asked Forrester and his crew to kindly get the hell off my porch. Forrester started to say something, but I shut the door in his face. Then I turned off the porch light.

Kara was waiting in the foyer. When she didn't say anything and instead just hugged me, I knew the interview had gone even worse than I'd imagined.

A little later, before she went up to bed, I asked her if I had come across as stern and authoritative when I'd leaned into the camera. She frowned and said I'd looked like a madman.

Ain't true love grand?

10

I was eating a snack in the kitchen when my cell phone started to buzz—and didn't stop.

Already knowing what I was going to find, I tapped into my email account.

Google Alerts. One after the other. Rapid firing into my inbox.

I opened one and clicked on the link. It took me to a TMZ post featuring a fifteen-second clip of my interview. Kara was right. I did look like a madman. The video had been posted eighteen minutes ago and already had more than a half-million views.

The next link connected me to a true crime message board called Daggers and Dames. I'd once done an Ask Me Anything Q&A for the moderator and had a pleasant enough time and even sold some books. But clearly those days were long gone.

A pinned thread had been started twenty minutes earlier by someone with the screen name of FriendorFoe.

The title: "RICHARD CHIZMAR EXPLOITS DEATH FOR PROFIT."

Already, there were nearly two hundred messages.

The first post: *"Did you all see the interview?!? What a scumbag!"*

The second: *"Think about it. Every penny he's ever made has been off the blood and tears of innocent victims. How do you think those families feel???"*

Knowing better but unable to stop myself, I doomscrolled further down the board.

"Have you seen Chizmar's house? He turned his back on Edgewood and lives large while those people . . ."

"Men like him are a different breed of vampire."

"I saw Chizmar at the grocery store last month. Guy looked like shit, so maybe he actually does have a conscience . . ."

And on and on it went.

I closed out the link and tapped on the unsubscribe button at the bottom of the email. Yeah, that would show them. Silencing the phone before leaving it on the counter, I went outside with the dogs.

Even in the far reaches of our backyard, in the shadow of the spring-house, I could still hear the sonorous murmurs of the press in the field across the street.

11

"Jesus," Billy said. "You scared the hell out of me."

"Right back atcha." I was sitting in my reading chair in the corner of the family room. The lights were off. My heart felt like it was going to leap out of my chest.

"I thought everyone was asleep. What are you doing down here anyway?"

"Just thinking . . . and catching up on emails." I knew I was busted.

"Emails, huh?" He walked over and took a look at the laptop screen. "You and those security cameras. You're obsessed, you know that?"

I shrugged. "I wouldn't say obsessed."

"I would."

"So, what are *you* doing up so late?"

"Just finished a story. Came down for some water."

"Good story?"

"Dunno. I'll tell you in the morning."

"I know how that goes."

"You okay?" he asked. "Your voice sounds kind of funny."

"Just tired."

"Me too." He yawned as if to prove his point. "I guess I'll head back up." He went into the kitchen and grabbed a water from the refrigerator. On his way back through the family room, he stopped and looked at me. "You sure you're okay? I saw the interview. And some Twitter posts. Pretty rough."

I didn't answer right away. I couldn't decide whether I wanted to show him what I'd found or not. Finally, I gestured at the computer and said, "Here. You want to take a peek at something?"

"Sure." He came over and took a knee by my chair.

I angled the laptop so he could get a better view. "This is from one of the cameras in the backyard." I tapped some buttons on the keyboard and then hit the Space bar. A dark window filled the entire screen, and as the time code began to run forward, a section of our backyard materialized.

"The springhouse," he said.

I traced my finger across the screen. "Springhouse, back gate, Mom's garden." For just a moment, in the glow of the computer, Billy looked so much like my father it made my heart ache. "Hang on—keep watching."

We studied the screen in silence as another minute ticked by.

"What am I supposed to be—" He leaned closer. "Wait, stop! Can you rewind it?"

I tapped some more buttons. The time code paused, then started ticking backward. After a few seconds, I hit the Space bar again.

Billy practically had his face pressed up against the screen. "Yeah. Right there!" he said, pointing.

I froze the footage.

"Jesus, Dad, when was this taken?"

"Last night."

Peering around the corner of the springhouse was a person dressed all in black. He was wearing a mask.

12

I took a screenshot of the image and attached it to an email for Lieutenant McClernan. I typed an all-caps CALL ME IN THE MORNING! in the subject line, clicked on the little red exclamation point for urgency, and hit send.

After double-checking that the doors were locked and the alarm was set, I went upstairs and climbed into bed next to my sleeping wife—and lay awake for a long time.

The "rules" sheet posted by residents *(Photo courtesy of Stephen Smith)*

Screenshot from security footage of a masked figure behind the springhouse *(Photo courtesy of the author)*

Excerpt from Edgewood: Looking Back, *by Richard Chizmar,*
page 271

Sometimes, you just know.

One minute, you're right there in the thick of it, surrounded by your friends, fully in the moment, laughing jumping shouting spinning with the kind of carefree joy only a twelve-year-old boy on a warm summer afternoon can know.

And the next minute . . . everything around you is moving in panoramic slow motion, you can actually count the beads of sweat shimmering on your best pal's sun-kissed forehead, and the wild laughter and cries of happiness, even the birds in the sky and the cars on the distant roadway, are suddenly hushed and blurred around the edges, and the little voice inside your head is very loud and very clear, and it's telling you: *You'll never forget this moment. For the rest of your life, you'll remember what this feels like, you'll remember every last thing about it, and sometimes late at night, when the world is still and quiet, you'll taste its bittersweet memory in the center of your heart, and you'll yearn to travel back . . .*

Moments like this were how I knew.

My destiny was to remember.

To remember everything.

And tell the world.

EIGHT

GRACE SUNDAY

"The police and the media called him the Lipstick Killer..."

1

Yes, Grace Sunday was her real name.

In the spring of 1983—just days after I donned a cap and gown and walked across the stage in Edgewood, Maryland—eighteen-year-old Grace graduated with honors from Trenton High School in rural upstate New York. The next morning, she checked two medium-sized suitcases at the American Airlines baggage counter at Buffalo Niagara International Airport and boarded a cross-country flight to Burbank, California. Like so many other young, attractive small-town girls, Grace Sunday dreamed of one day becoming a star.

2

One of the innate difficulties involved with the chronicling of a true account—especially those featuring a crime or a series of crimes—is resisting the urge to at times embellish and/or streamline the story. True stories rarely behave like novels. True stories are often messy and frustrating and filled with the kind of maddening minutiae that doesn't necessarily lend itself to breathless page turning. Sometimes, true stories are even boring . . . until they're not.

My point, as an occasional author of true crime tales, is that I have received more than my fair share of both criticism and skepticism in regards to my nonfiction work. A number of significant plot points, various characters' behavior patterns, and a handful of revelatory surprises have all come under fire. I've attempted numerous times to explain that I can only tell the story as it actually happened—that truth teller is my primary role and responsibility—but many jaded critics refuse to accept this line of reasoning.

Take *Chasing the Boogeyman*, for example. Despite the online availability of official police photographs proving their existence, for whatever reason many readers refused to believe that the killer left personal messages on each of the four victims' roadside memorials. They claimed it was a sensational and unrealistic plot twist—most likely invented to help sell movie rights—and could've never actually happened that way. And yet, it had.

Still other critics found it difficult to believe that my dear friend Carly Albright—at the time, a lowly cub reporter at the *Aegis*—was able to source so many vital nuggets of inside information regarding the ongoing police investigation. Surely, our claiming so was merely a journalistic shortcut designed to protect my own high-level anonymous source (Detective Lyle Harper was most often cited) or even a clever device put in place to enable us to wholly manufacture critical details that the general public would never be in a position to prove or disprove. In other words, they inferred that we made up a bunch of information to make for a more compelling story—a really insulting claim, to be sure.

And finally, there was a small but vocal group of Canadian true crime fans (now *there's* a designation for you) who went so far as to publicly suggest that Carly Albright was merely a fictional character used to advance the storyline and not a real living, breathing human being at all.

But I digress. Let me be perfectly clear here:

When *Becoming the Boogeyman* is finally published, I fully expect an army of skeptics to crawl out of the woodwork with bullhorns at the ready: "*So you're telling me I'm supposed to believe that this Chizmar guy survived run-ins with not one, but two confessed serial killers? And he just happens to have a new book out in stores right now? C'mon, what are the odds of that actually happening? If you're gullible enough to believe that one, I've got a bridge in Brooklyn to sell you.*"

3

Sometimes lightning does strike twice.

4

Once she arrived in Los Angeles—following in the footsteps of thousands of other fresh-faced, aspiring starlets—Grace Sunday got a waitressing job.

Two, actually.

Several mornings a week, she served the breakfast and lunch crowds at the Shoestring Diner on Sunset Boulevard. Most of the clientele was friendly, the tips were decent, and she loved looking at the palm trees that lined both sides of the street. The panoramic view outside the diner window was a daily reminder of how far she'd come from her backwoods hometown in upstate New York. On her off days, she went to acting classes and auditions. No luck getting hired yet, but it had only been six months and she was still feeling hopeful. She'd gotten lucky right off the plane and found a one-bedroom apartment to share with a complete stranger, Renea Bitner from Pittsburgh. They'd flipped a coin to see who would sleep on the sofa and Grace had lost. But she didn't really mind. Renea was super nice, didn't smoke or do drugs, and was trying to become a singer, so she was hardly ever home.

At night, Grace worked the outdoor patio at Ramones on Hollywood Boulevard. The tips were much better there, but many of the diners were powerful men who drank a lot. These were people who were used to getting what they wanted, so on many late nights after work, Grace watched her back to make sure no one was following her home.

It was at Ramones that she first saw Kirby Bradshaw.

5

It was Sunday, and the crowd was a bit thin. Even Hollywood's wheelers and dealers had to put in a little family time on the weekends.

Grace had never seen the man dining alone at the corner table before. He was short and stocky, and unlike many of the Ramones regulars who spent half of their meals rubbernecking at the other diners, he seemed very interested in his spaghetti Bolognese. His face hovered mere inches above his plate.

When she'd sat the man earlier in the evening, Grace had noticed right away that he was wearing a hairpiece—and not a very good one. It sat crooked atop his head like a wedge of fluffed-up roadkill and immediately reminded her of the mean guy from *The Three Stooges*, the old black-and-white show that had always made her father laugh so much.

The man didn't say much during his meal. He asked for a second order of dinner rolls and two refills on his water. He complimented Grace on her hair—she'd braided it because she'd been running late and hadn't had time to shower before work—and asked where the nearest bookstore was located.

It made sense to Grace that the man was from out of town. He didn't look like he belonged in Los Angeles. She wasn't being judgmental. It wasn't the crummy hairpiece or the lack of a tan or even the inexpensive Timex on his wrist that made her feel that way; it was the way he carried himself. No expansive chest puffing or false bravado, no posturing or posing or speaking in a voice loud enough to be noticed. He was just a normal guy visiting from somewhere far away, enjoying a nice dinner by himself.

When Grace was little, she used to sit by the river and watch the trains go by on the trestle bridge. She'd stare at the people in the windows and imagine what their lives were like. *Who are they? Where are they going? Are they happy or sad?* And then she'd make up her own stories about them. The older gentleman who was going home after a long, successful business trip. He couldn't wait to see his wife again and take her out dancing. The lady with the long red hair who was traveling back to the town she'd grown up in, as her father had died. She was sad, of course, but what she didn't know was that her father had left her a million dollars in his will. The money was going to change her life. She was going to help so many people with it.

Grace suddenly remembered that game from her childhood and

played it that night at Ramones with the man at the corner table. She imagined that he lived somewhere in Iowa with his wife and two sons. He was a sporting-goods salesman, and he was in town for a big convention. He was depressed because he'd missed coaching his sons' Little League playoff game yesterday—they were twins and played on the same team—but he was also elated because he'd made a lot of great connections at the convention and his boss had noticed. He'd already picked up a couple of gifts for his wife (a California shot glass—she had thirty-three of the fifty states displayed in a cabinet in their den—and an I LOVE LA T-shirt he'd spotted at the airport). He hoped to get each of his sons an autographed George Brett bat before he flew home tomorrow evening.

Despite the slow night, Grace never saw the man leave. Around eight o'clock, she'd returned from the kitchen with another party's order and noticed that the corner table was empty. The cloth napkin he'd used had been folded in a neat square and left draped over his chair. He'd left cash on the table and tipped Grace a generous 25 percent.

Grace carried the man's dirty dishes back to the kitchen and promptly forgot all about him until two nights later, when she woke up on her sofa and found him standing over her.

6

His left hand was wrapped around her throat, cutting off her air and pinning her to the cushion; his right hand held a knife. At first, she didn't recognize him; the apartment was dark, and he was wearing pantyhose over his face, flattening all his features. But then he spoke—she'd remember those words for as long as she lived: *"If you scream, I'll kill you"*—and she knew it was the man from the restaurant.

At that moment, Grace had no idea that the person who had broken into her apartment was Kirby Bradshaw, and not only did he live within the city limits of Los Angeles, but he'd also been born and raised there. She also didn't know that he'd been watching her for the past two nights and that since 1980 he'd been responsible for the deaths of eleven young women.

The police and the media called him the Lipstick Killer because all his victims had been found with the bright red cosmetic smeared all over their faces. They'd also had their throats slashed.

Grace didn't know any of this in that moment. What she did know was this: Her roommate, Renea, had gone home to visit family in Pennsylvania, so she was all by herself in the apartment. The man standing over her was going to rape her—she could feel his hardness pressing against her rib cage—and then he was most likely going to kill her.

So when she finally managed to slide her hand underneath the sofa cushion and wrap her fingers around the rubber grip of the .38 special her father had insisted upon buying her, Grace didn't hesitate.

She whipped the revolver out from its hiding place and emptied all six bullets into the chest of the man at the corner table who had tipped her 25 percent.

7

Fast-forward seven years—and countless hours of therapy—and Grace Sunday was still chasing her dreams on the sun-dazzled streets of Los Angeles.

She was no longer waitressing and now lived alone in a studio apartment three blocks from the ocean in her favorite place on earth, Santa Monica. There were several dead bolts on the front door and sturdy locks on each of the four second-story windows. Gold plated crucifixes hung from the curtain rods. She didn't know if there were any vampires floating around LA, but she had recently auditioned for a remake of 'Salem's Lot and had experienced terrible nightmares for nearly a month. She wasn't taking any chances.

For the past eight months, she'd been seeing a handsome surfer named Bradley Love. Bradley owned a bike shop on the beach, and was tall and smart and nice to his mother. He read two or three books a week, loved to cook, and didn't touch a drop of alcohol. For Grace, who had ironically always harbored a secret spiritual side, he was a gift from heaven.

After the incident with Kirby Bradshaw years earlier, she'd almost packed up and went home for good. Her parents had flown out right away and paid for two rooms at a respectable downtown motel so Grace could rest and recover. For the first few days, she was unable to eat or sleep. A steady stream of LAPD detectives visited her room, repeatedly asking the same questions. Her parents never left her side and spoke hopefully of a new start back at home in New York. A desk job at her uncle Bobby's car dealership was waiting for her. Grace went so far as to allow them to purchase a return airline ticket in her name—before abruptly changing her mind.

"I'm not going to let that son of a bitch ruin my life," she announced to her mother. "I came here for a reason. I've dreamt about being an actress ever since I was a little girl. If I do go home one day, it's going to be on my own terms. Not because some psycho liked the way I served his spaghetti Bolognese."

Three months later, she landed a shampoo commercial and a bit part opposite Eddie Murphy in *Beverly Hills Cop*.

And never looked back.

8

If anyone had told Grace Sunday that she would spend most of her twenty-fifth year on this earth making movies with Oliver Stone and Martin Scorsese, she would have laughed them right out of the room.

But that's exactly what happened.

First, she earned a supporting role in Oliver Stone's *The Doors*, playing the role of Pamela Courson's sister. Shooting her scenes took three weeks and went off without a hitch. Even the notoriously prickly Stone had nothing but words of praise for her—which was almost certainly the reason she got her next high-profile supporting role, this one in Martin Scorsese's much-buzzed-about remake of *Cape Fear*. Acting alongside Robert De Niro (her father's favorite actor) and Jessica Lange was a dream come true for Grace, and only added more fuel to her creative fire.

Two months after she wrapped on *Cape Fear*, with only twenty-four hours' advance notice, she auditioned for the role of Evelyn Gardner in director Penny Marshall's *A League of Their Own*—and nailed it. The next week, she hopped a plane to Evansville, Indiana, to participate in a ten-day training camp alongside a stellar cast that included Tom Hanks, Geena Davis, and Madonna. When they weren't taking batting practice or shagging flies or fielding grounders—Grace had played three years of varsity softball at Trenton High, so she'd ended up doing quite a bit of coaching herself—all the women got to know each other better. There were bonfires at night, dance contests and karaoke in their hotel rooms, and even a spa day. It felt more like going away to summer camp than it did an actual job, and with her love life going strong back at home, Grace couldn't ever remember feeling happier.

It was Penny Marshall who knocked on Grace's hotel room door and broke the bad news on the next-to-last day of camp. Something had happened back in California. Something unimaginable.

As soon as she heard Brad's name and that the police were involved, Grace knew that he was gone. That's when she started shaking and wasn't able to stop, not even when the other cast members gathered in her room, hugging her and wiping away her tears. She and Brad had so many big plans for the future. They were going to buy a camper and, in between movies, travel up and down the West Coast. They were going to get dressed up and drink champagne in Paris and hike the cliffs in Ireland. Just before she'd left for Evansville, they'd purchased a brand-new set of dishes for their kitchen. They were talking about putting down a deposit for a puppy.

Grace couldn't imagine a life without Bradley by her side.

But as she soon discovered, it was so much worse than that.

Brad hadn't died in a car accident. He hadn't drowned while surfing the Wedge or ridden his mountain bike over a cliff.

Brad had been shot and killed by a member of the LAPD SWAT team as he'd reached for a weapon in his nightstand. It was Grace's .38 special that he'd died holding in his hand. The SWAT team had gone in after several days of undercover surveillance, during which time they'd gathered enough physical evidence to get a warrant from the judge.

Bradley Love was accused of killing three women over the course of the past six months and disposing of their bodies in the Malibu hills and canyons. Detectives found souvenirs from each of the victims hidden on an upper shelf in Love's garage. In addition, they discovered a videocassette tape containing footage of two of the women begging for their lives in an undisclosed location.

He also left behind a journal.

9

Grace Sunday never returned to Los Angeles, not even to recover her personal belongings. She hired a company out of Burbank to perform that task.

When her agent asked if she'd had any suspicions at all, Grace laughed hysterically and said, "He'd been acting strange for a couple weeks before I left, but you want to know how foolish I am? I thought he'd bought a ring and was going to propose when I got back from the shoot. I thought he was just nervous."

The agent didn't know what to say to that, so she said nothing. But that didn't stop Grace from going on. "It was all in his journal. He knew I was a survivor. He got off on being so close to me, to being trusted by me. It was all a fucking game to him."

After that, her agent made an excuse to get off the phone.

They never spoke again, unless one counted the formal letter from Grace diplomatically severing their relationship.

The role of Evelyn Gardner was filled by the talented actress Bitty Schram, and *A League of Their Own* went on to earn over $100 million at the U.S. box office and received two Golden Globe nominations.

Grace Sunday was rumored to now be living somewhere along the east coast of Florida, where she spent her days writing a series of popular romance novels under a pseudonym.

10

According to Jay Darabont of *True Crime Buzz*, "During the 1970s and 1980s, Los Angeles was a city gripped with fear as more than twenty serial killers were operating simultaneously within a five-mile radius. Murderers such as the Hillside Strangler and the Freeway Killer became household names as their crimes struck panic among Angelenos. As body after body turned up around the city, Los Angeles became known as the 'serial killer capital of America,' and the LAPD's Robbery-Homicide Division embarked on a quest to find and stop these cold-blooded killers."

Harford County, Maryland—with its rolling hills, horse pastures, and low-six-figure population—was a far cry from the bustling, urban streets of Los Angeles.

Yet, for a period of time in the 1980s, not one, but two active serial killers called it home.

And somehow, both of these men—Joshua Gallagher and Henry Metheny—became an integral part of my life.

The question that still haunted my sleepless nights was: *Why?*

11

Perhaps, all that time, the question should have been: *Why Edgewood?*

In Michael Hanlon's "Derry: An Unauthorized Town History"—featured prominently within the pages of Stephen King's magnum opus, *It*—Hanlon poses a fascinating question to readers:

"Can an *entire city* be haunted?"

I believe the answer to be an unequivocal yes.

I also believe that Edgewood, Maryland, may very well be such a place.

While many of the dark and mysterious incidents that have occurred within the town's borders have been noted in public record, dozens of other lesser-known stories exist only in the time-dulled memories of the town's oldest residents.

In *Chasing the Boogeyman*, I wrote about the deadly gunfight that occurred at the Edgewood train station in 1903 and made mention of the suspicious fire that destroyed the ramshackle jazz club known as the Black Hole in the summer of 1920.

I also recounted in great detail my former neighbor Bernard Gentile's front porch tale of three Edgewood children who met their unfortunate fate—two went missing, never to be heard from again; the third was murdered in the woods surrounding Cedar Drive—in the late 1960s and early 1970s, a tale later verified by the *Baltimore Sun* archives.

But what of the other stories I'd learned of over the years?

In the late nineteenth century, the leather-bound journal of a man named Benjamin Lock—a Confederate infantryman from Hawthorne, Virginia—was found hidden in the rafters of an old barn. In an entry dated late July 1864, Lock writes in painstaking detail about a disturbing incident that took place on a grassy piece of land not far from where the Edgewood Library now stands. For going on several weeks, the rebel forces had been coming upon slain soldiers on the battlefield with their throats torn out. They'd assumed it was the handiwork of particularly vicious Union troops, most likely members of the First Maryland Cavalry, who were notorious for such savagery. One summer night, following a brief skirmish with an advance unit of Yankee scouts, Lock snuck to a nearby creek to fill an armful of canteens. On his way back, he became lost in the woods and stumbled upon the edge of a moonlit clearing, which had, from the looks of it, recently been the scene of a formidable battle. A scattering of fresh corpses, as well as a destroyed battery of Union cannon and a score of dead horses, littered the ground. A fog had settled over the land, and from within the mist, Lock could hear "moaning and sucking sounds." Curious, he crept closer—and from the cover of the tree line, he was able to observe "a long-haired Yankee cavalry officer—alas, not from the First, but the Seventh—drop to his knees beside several fallen soldiers and lower his hungry mouth to their still throats." What he saw next was "unholy." A shocked Benjamin Lock fled into the woods and eventually found his way back to camp, where he told no one of the horrors he'd just witnessed. For months afterward, he suffered terrible nightmares in which he heard "wet sucking sounds coming from within the foggy darkness" and "awoke to the blood-smeared, grinning countenance of whatever godforsaken Yankee devil [he'd] crossed paths with."

At the beginning of the twentieth century, a man named Daniel Larson lived in a cabin on the shoreline of the Bush River with his wife and son and daughter. One cold winter night, he left them at the dinner table to retrieve additional wood for the fire. When he returned, no more than ten minutes later, his family was nowhere to be found. His daughter's chair was upturned and there was a single napkin strewn on the floor—otherwise there were no signs of a struggle. The food on their plates was untouched. Their glasses remained full of warm milk. Sitting upon his wife's chair was a circular black rock the size of a marble. There was four inches of fresh snow on the ground surrounding the cabin. Larson searched and could not find a single footprint other than his own. It was as if his wife and children had simply vanished into thin air. They were never found. A month later, a forlorn Daniel Larson leapt to his death from a nearby cliff.

In 1938, at the tail end of the Great Depression, an abandoned fish market located in the heart of Edgewood was struck by lightning and burned to the ground. Once the fire was out, the charred remains of eleven children were discovered among the rubble. None of the unidentified victims appeared to be local and no one knew from where they'd come. Rumors soon spread throughout the town claiming that the majority of the bodies had been missing limbs and that the fish market doors had been chained and locked from the outside. The mystery of the eleven young victims remains unsolved.

In the late 1960s, in response to the emerging war in Vietnam, military officials at the Edgewood Proving Ground announced a series of new weapons testing that required additional restrictions placed on the Bush and Gunpowder Rivers and their respective shorelines. Between June 1968 and September 1969, fourteen civilians were reported missing from the waters of the Bush and Gunpowder. Eight were commercial fishermen or crabbers. Six were experienced pleasure boaters. All gone, as if they'd never existed. It's important to note that in each instance their boats—devoid of any sign of passengers but in perfectly fine working condition—were discovered adrift in unrestricted sections of the two rivers.

At the onset of the Satanic Panic movement—most often credited to have started with the 1980 publication of *Michelle Remembers* by Lawrence Pazder and his wife, Michelle Smith—a makeshift altar was discovered in the woods behind the Edgewood post office. Satanic symbols, including pentagrams and upside-down crosses, were carved into the bark of several nearby trees. Dark stains appeared on both the rough stone surface of the altar and the ground beneath it. Subsequent testing revealed that the stains had been made by significant quantities of human blood. The remains of a bonfire were also found. Within the ashes, police unearthed several small bones later identified as belonging to the left hand of an adult male. Six months later, a similar altar was found in a wooded area off Trimble Road by a group of hikers.

I had several notebooks on a shelf in my office filled with other such tragic oddities—many of them shared with me in the months immediately following the initial publication of *Chasing the Boogeyman*—but what, if anything, did these stories prove?

Perhaps Edgewood was once the site of an unspeakable Indigenous American massacre, and the vast volume of spilled blood had somehow tainted the land;

or maybe the town was the subject of an ancient curse sent forth by a rageful shaman or an accused witch or dark sorcerer hell-bent on eternal vengeance;

or perhaps the ground upon which Edgewood was born—the very soil and rocks and sediment—had been bad from the very beginning.

Evil ground attracts evil doings. Like moths drawn to a flame. Maybe Stephen King was onto something.

Joshua Gallagher greeted life in a Russian orphanage. Through no design of his own, he crossed an ocean to call Edgewood, Maryland, his home. Was it his dark destiny? Or was Gallagher merely one more entry in a lengthy ledger containing the town's ever-growing list of hapless victims?

And what of Henry Metheny, who grew up in backwoods Georgia and never once crossed state lines until the summer after he graduated from high school when he and some friends visited a South Carolina beach resort? What forces summoned him north—at the age of thirty-three—to a dot-on-the-map town in northern Maryland? Was it a laborer's job making $15.50 an hour, and time and a half on weekends? Or was it something else that called to him—something unseen and unnamable?

Can an *entire city* be haunted?
Yes, I believe so.
I lived there.

Grace Sunday shortly before her high school graduation *(Photo courtesy of Aaron Thompson)*

Grace Sunday in Santa Monica, California
(Photo courtesy of Aaron Thompson)

Bradley Love *(Photo courtesy of*
Los Angeles Times*)*

Excerpt from in-person interview with Samantha Gallagher, age 53, Florida, recorded on September 16, 2021:

CHIZMAR: So, just to reassure you, if this interview is ever published, you'll be listed as Samantha Gallagher. Your new identity will never be mentioned publicly nor will the name of the town in which you currently reside.

GALLAGHER: Okay . . . thank you.

CHIZMAR: I know this is difficult.

GALLAGHER: Yes, it is.

CHIZMAR: I'd like to begin with some background information. You were married to Joshua Gallagher for twenty-four years and share two sons. Before that, you dated for eighteen months. At the time of his arrest, the four of you lived together in Hanover, Pennsylvania. Following his 2019 arrest, you filed for divorce a year later.

GALLAGHER: That's correct.

CHIZMAR: At any time during your relationship, did you have any suspicion that something was wrong with Joshua? Was there ever a moment where you believed him capable of committing the kind of acts he's confessed to?

GALLAGHER: No, never. I know some people still don't believe me, but it's a hundred percent true.

CHIZMAR: Was there anything particularly odd or unusual about Joshua? I realize that's a fairly broad question, but what I'm looking for is anything that might be considered beyond typical societal norms.

GALLAGHER: [long pause] There are two things I've never told anyone. I don't know if they mean anything, but for Joshua—and me—they were definitely unusual.

CHIZMAR: Take your time. Tell me what happened.

GALLAGHER: It was the week before Christmas—2007, I believe. I was taking a cup of hot chocolate down to him in the basement. I'd said good night quite a bit earlier, so I'm sure he'd thought I was already upstairs in bed. But I'd gotten sidetracked in the kitchen and thought it would be a nice thing to do. The basement door was closed and locked. That was unusual. I couldn't remember the last time that'd happened. I started to knock but I heard a voice coming from the basement, so I stopped. It was Josh, but his voice sounded different, and he was talking . . . nonsense. None of it made any sense to me. I stood there and listened for a while and then I finally knocked. He came up right away and opened the door. His face was red, like I'd caught him doing something wrong. I asked whom he'd been talking to, and his face got even redder. He told me he'd been watching a movie on his computer and I must have heard one of the characters speaking. I knew for sure he was lying. It bothered me all that night and the next day. I almost brought it up at dinner the next evening but changed my mind. As far as I know, he never locked the basement door again after that.

NINE

THE HANGMAN COMETH

"There will be others."

1

Lieutenant McClernan didn't call the next morning as I'd requested in my email.

Instead, she showed up bright and early at the front door with Detective Gonzalez at her side. They'd driven separately, their unmarked cars parked side by side at the top of the driveway. A dark blue sedan with a bubble light on the roof sat behind them; it was empty. Today was the first time I'd seen Gonzalez in person since the morning I'd discovered Annie Riggs's body, and once again, I found myself staring at his mustache. Something was obviously wrong with me.

Kara was upstairs sleeping, so we stepped outside and talked on the porch. I glanced across the street and thought: *The hell with the press. Let's give them something to talk about.*

"Our people are checking out the springhouse," the lieutenant said. "We'll take a look at the woods next."

"I've been thinking about it," I said. "He could've parked in the neighborhood behind us. All he'd have to do is cut across someone's backyard, jump over the creek, and hop the fence." I pointed toward the pond. "Or he could've cut across the woods from Fountain Green and walked in that way."

"That's a pretty long walk, don't you think?" Gonzalez asked. "Especially in the dark."

I shrugged. "I guess."

"Has anyone else been back there since Monday night?"

"Not that I know of. There's nothing behind that old springhouse except for a pile of firewood."

"So we shouldn't find your prints back there?" He stole a glance at the lieutenant.

I didn't answer right away. The question struck me as rather foolish, and Detective Gonzalez was not a foolish man. Something was going on. "I mean . . . you might. We've lived here for a few years now."

"Do you think the person in your security footage could've been someone playing a prank, Mr. Chizmar?" His voice had gone tight.

"I'd love for it to be a prank. Nothing would make me happier."

"Or even someone participating in a publicity stunt of some kind?"

"Publicity stunt . . . ?" Now it was starting to make sense. "Oh my *God*. You're serious?! You think *I* did this? You think I put on a mask and filmed myself on the security camera?"

"Take it easy, Rich," McClernan said. "That's not what he's trying to say."

"That's exactly what he's trying to say. Why the hell would I do that?!" I could feel my blood pressure rising. "To sell more books? In case you haven't noticed . . ." I gestured across the street. "I'm a pretty popular guy right now."

"And they're probably listening to every word you're saying," McClernan said. "Keep your voice down."

"I'm not accusing you of anything, Mr. Chizmar," he said. "I'm just covering all the bases. That's my job. For all we know, it was one of your sons' friends playing a joke."

Cool mustache or not, I wanted to tell him to get the hell off my porch—but I knew I couldn't do that. "I have no idea who's underneath that mask, Detective. But I can assure you it wasn't me. And my boys and their friends know better."

"Fair enough." He stood and stretched, looked over at Lieutenant McClernan. "See you out back?"

"Give me a few."

He nodded and walked away.

I gave the back of his head the middle finger.

"What's his problem?" I asked as soon as he was out of earshot.

"He has trust issues."

"No shit, Sherlock."

I expected her to at least smile, but she gave me nothing.

"After everything I've done for your department, he still doesn't trust me?"

"He had no idea you were famous when all this started. Now that he does, he's wary. All he knows about celebrities is that most of them love their bank accounts more than their spouses, and they'll do practically anything to remain in the spotlight."

"Oh, for Christ's sake, I'm not a celebrity!" I shot back. "I mow my own grass and pick up dog crap in little plastic bags."

This time she did crack a smile.

"By the way," she said, "for whatever it's worth, we didn't miss the guy on your security footage. The techs are just a couple of nights behind."

"I figured as much."

"Spotting him was pretty impressive on your part."

"Uh-oh. If you're blowing smoke up my ass, you must feel guilty about something."

"Not at all. It was a sincere compliment." She shifted in her chair. "Although . . . there *is* something I need to tell you."

"I knew it."

"Gonzalez originally asked me not to . . ."

"Big surprise there."

". . . but after your email last night, he changed his mind."

"He's still an asshole."

"He's a good detective, and this is technically his case."

"Tell me or don't tell me. I don't care." I knew I sounded like a twelve-year-old, but I couldn't help it.

She opened the clasp on a manila envelope I hadn't even noticed she was holding. She slid out a photograph and handed it to me, positioning it so only I could see. Across the street, an army of cameras *click*ed and *whirr*ed.

The photo was an extreme close-up of an outstretched hand. The fingers were dirty and slightly curled. Light blue nail polish coated a partially visible thumbnail. A silver charm bracelet encircled the victim's slender wrist. In the center of the upturned palm was a small, childlike drawing of a hangman figure. Beneath it, there were eight dashes. The last one had been filled in with a "7". The remaining dashes were blank.

I looked up at the lieutenant. "Peyton Bair?"

She nodded.

I briefly pondered the implications. "Seven . . . seven . . . so . . . Gallagher left behind the number six after he killed Cassidy Burch on Halloween night 1988 . . ." I handed the photograph back. ". . . and now, thirty-four years later, we have number seven."

"We think he's picking up where Gallagher left off."

"Any idea what the missing word is?"

She looked at me. "Seven blanks. C-H-I-Z-M-A-R?"

2

Kara and I discussed the situation over breakfast.

She took the news of the crime scene photo better than I thought she would. Almost as if she'd been expecting it. I told her what Lieutenant McClernan had said about the missing word, but she wasn't convinced. Neither was I, for that matter. Too much of a coincidence. I'd already googled seven-letter words—there were more than thirty-five thousand of them.

The team of detectives poking around our property was an entirely different story. As soon as I explained what I'd seen the night before on our security footage, Kara lost it.

"Nothing about this is okay!" she said, her voice rising as she watched from the kitchen window. The dogs were going crazy running up and down the fence. I secretly hoped that Detective Gonzalez would reach over to pet one of them and get a nice little nip on the hand for his trouble.

"There's a state trooper parked in our driveway twenty-four seven," she continued, "and somehow, we still have a psycho sneaking around our house. And on the same night that girl was killed. Jesus, Rich! When will it be—"

The words were out of my mouth before I could stop them. "Detective Gonzalez thinks it might've been a prank." I obviously had no shame left in me.

"Detective Gonzalez needs to catch whoever the hell is doing this." She sat down next to me with a sigh. "Prank or no prank, this freak's obsessed with you. He's not going to leave us alone."

"McClernan and Gonzalez are good at their jobs. They'll get him."

"But how long is it going to take? How many more girls are going to die?"

"Honey, they're doing the best—"

"We really need to think about packing up and getting out of here." And then she said the words I was most afraid to hear: "Or at least Billy and I do."

And with that she left the room.

3

As if there hadn't already been enough excitement for one morning, a staff photographer from the *Baltimore Sun* was arrested for trespassing shortly after noon. He'd been caught hiding in a tree on our next-door neighbor's property taking photos of the detectives in our backyard.

Our neighbors Mike and Molly had been unsure of whether they wanted to press charges, so they'd left the decision up to me. Initially, I was equally uncertain, but Lieutenant McClernan encouraged me to go forward with it, if only to discourage other members of the media from following suit.

I was standing outside talking to Mike when a pair of uniformed officers escorted the reporter in handcuffs to a squad car at the bottom of the driveway.

"What are the police looking for, Mr. Chizmar?" the reporter shouted when he saw me. "Did they find another body?"

One of the officers opened the back door. His partner shoved the reporter inside and slammed it shut. As they drove away, our mail truck turned into the driveway. A UPS box truck pulled in right behind him and tooted its horn.

"It's a goddamn circus out here today," Mike said, not too kindly.

"I'm sorry." It was all I could think to say.

Carl, our friendly neighborhood UPS man, and the mailman, whose name I still couldn't remember, walked up together, both of them carrying packages. Carl was smiling, as usual. Our mailman was not. He looked hot and sweaty and a little peeved.

"Mr. Chiz, thank you again so much for signing your book," Carl said as he handed over a small cardboard box. "Made my wife's entire summer."

"I was happy to do it."

He looked around and gave a whistle. "All this commotion caused by one bad man. It's hard to believe."

"Yes, it is," I said, taking a package and a stack of letters from the mailman. He surprised me with a smile.

"Does that mean you'd sign a book for me, too?"

"Of course. Anytime." I did my best to look like I meant it.

"That's mighty nice of you," he said. "Good friend of mine delivers the mail down by Edgewood High School, and he says you're the talk of the town."

"I can vouch for that," Carl said. "My aunt Thelma lives in Harford Square, and she was talking about you just last night at dinner."

"Okay. Good things, I hope."

His smile faltered, just for a second, and I immediately regretted keeping the conversation going.

"Of course, Mr. Chiz. All good things. You're a full-fledged celebrity around here." What he said next made my stomach roil: "Heck, you and the Boogeyman put Edgewood on the map."

4

The good folks of Edgewood had their hands full.

By late that Wednesday evening—not quite forty-eight hours since the news of Peyton Bair's murder had gone public—it felt like the town was ready to implode.

The previous night, a thirteen-year-old boy (tall for his age, the starting center on his summer league basketball team) had been escorted home by police after being held at gunpoint by a frightened homeowner. The boy had exercised poor judgment by taking his older brother's Boogeyman mask from a dresser drawer in his bedroom, slipping it over his head, and proceeding to scare half the neighborhood by peering into a number of first-floor windows. Between nine fifteen and ten o'clock, six residents of Larch Drive called 911 to report a masked man outside their homes. The seventh caller, a retired World War II veteran, called to say that he had a man wearing a mask in custody in his backyard. When police arrived and discovered the identity and age of the individual being held, the ninety-one-year-old homeowner had to be helped back inside his house. "I was a split second away," he told his wife in tears. "One more beat of my heart, and as God is my witness, I would've pulled the trigger. He's just a damn kid. I don't know how I would've been able to live with myself."

A two-man crew from Fox News—acting on an anonymous tip—had been foolish enough to venture behind the old Giant shopping center after dark. Once they'd reached the rendezvous point, three armed men wearing ski masks emerged from the trees and beat and robbed them. The cameraman was currently in Upper Chesapeake Medical Center suffering from broken ribs, a punctured lung, and numerous facial injuries that would require surgery. The on-air reporter was still unconscious and listed in critical condition at Shock Trauma in downtown

Baltimore. Both men's wallets, as well as their vehicle and camera equipment, had been stolen. Police officials had yet to publicly comment on the incident, but Fox News was offering a $10,000 reward for any information leading to the arrest of the assailants.

The local police were critically overwhelmed. Calls to 911 were coming in at a record pace. Officers could barely drive down neighborhood streets without one or more of the residents stopping them to report suspicious activity or to provide them with the identity of Peyton Bair's killer. The fact that many of the men—and in two instances, the women—being accused of the girl's murder were former husbands, wives, boyfriends, and girlfriends surprised no one.

Of the dozens of alleged sightings that took place within the town limits, there were a handful that stood out for a variety of reasons. The most credible report may have come from nineteen-year-old James Tasker. James and two friends had been walking home from 7-Eleven at approximately 10:50 p.m. last Monday night. As they'd crossed Edgewood Road not far from the library, they'd noticed a man wearing a mask watching them from the tree line next to the gravel driveway leading up to the Meyers House. One of James's friends called out to the masked man, but he didn't respond. James pulled out his cell phone and snapped a photograph. A moment later, the man disappeared into the shadows. The image James Tasker captured on his phone was a far cry from the high-definition security footage recorded outside our house, but it did show someone standing in the trees wearing what appeared to be a burlap mask. I later learned from Lieutenant McClernan that a woman who lived on Cherry Road, whose backyard abutted the Meyers House property, called police at 10:44 p.m. to report a prowler. She was watching a movie in the den when she heard a thump against the air conditioner outside. A moment later, the dogs started barking. Peyton Bair's body had been discovered just two hours earlier, less than a mile away.

An equally fascinating—albeit considerably less convincing—sighting occurred not far from my parents' old house on Hanson Road. Harold and Jessica Citro, both in their late fifties, had only lived on Tupelo Court for the past three years. Incredibly, neither of them had ever heard of the original Boogeyman murders. But on the night of Sunday, June 5, 2022, Mr. Citro had gone into his backyard, having forgotten to turn off the propane tank to his grill—upon which he'd cooked steaks and baked potatoes for dinner—and come face-to-face with a masked intruder. The man—Mr. Citro described him as at least six-three and solidly built—had been dressed in dark clothing and was in the process of leaping down from the top of his six-foot-tall fence. Mr. Citro picked up a rake that was leaning against the house and shouted for the man to stop, unintentionally drawing Mrs. Citro to the sliding glass door, where she, too, saw the man in the mask. Instead of stopping, the man slowly approached them. He did not appear to be carrying a weapon. Once he came within twelve or fifteen feet of the terrified couple, the man stopped and appeared to study them.

"He cocked his head from one side to the other, real slow like, the way a dog will do when it's deciding whether to attack or turn tail and run, and then he started making a kind of snorting sound," Mr. Citro told the police.

His wife was a bit more explicit. "He was sniffing us. The whole damn time I was yanking my husband into the house, that son of a bitch was watching us with those beady black eyes of his and smelling after us like some kind of wild animal."

According to Mrs. Citro, once they'd backed into the house, her husband slid shut the glass door and locked the dead bolt. While she'd searched for the cordless telephone to call 911, he remained on guard at the door. By the time she'd returned, less than a minute later, the backyard was empty.

"I never took my eyes off of him," Mr. Citro said. "Not even for a second. When I hollered that my wife was calling the police, I expected him to take off running the way he'd come. Back over the fence. But instead, he took two or three big steps and leapt right up onto the roof. I know that's not possible, but I saw what I saw. I heard his footsteps over top of me, and then nothing. He was just gone."

5

The memorial for Annie Riggs, the only survivor of Joshua Gallagher's original reign of terror, had spread from a small circular patch of grass surrounding the fire hydrant to an expanse of lawn stretching all the way back to the fence line. Each day more stuffed animals, balloons, candles, and flowers were added to the display. I'd watched a news story the previous afternoon about a group of Harford Day School eighth graders who'd drawn homemade sympathy cards in art class and walked the not-quite-a-mile route to our house. Once they'd finished placing their cards at the memorial, the students linked hands and sang a surprisingly touching rendition of "Amazing Grace." Then, they'd walked back to the school together.

Overnight, someone had Scotch-taped a poster-sized photograph of Annie Riggs to the fence. In the photo, high school Annie was wearing a red bandana in her hair and holding a field hockey stick. A big smile was plastered on her face. Lieutenant McClernan made a point of telling us that we were within our rights to take the poster down—the entire makeshift memorial, for that matter—but we wanted nothing to do with that idea. The way we saw it, the memorial wasn't hurting anyone, and in some small way, it was probably helping people to grieve. Besides, the last thing I needed was *Live at Five* news footage of me, the damnable scourge of Edgewood, tearing down such a heartfelt and personal tribute.

I picked up an empty beer can from the shoulder of Southampton Road and did my best to ignore the half dozen or so photographers snapping my picture from across the street. I could see the reporters' mouths moving as they shouted their questions, but thanks to the Air-Pods I was wearing, all I could hear was the gritty, melancholy strains of Bruce Springsteen's "Blood Brothers."

There had been an influx of younger faces amid the crowd. Most of these newcomers were attractive and tanned and clearly from out of town. I didn't know their names, but I recognized a handful of them from their frequent posts on TikTok and Instagram. Making my way back to the house, I didn't bother looking over my shoulder to see if they were following me. I knew they were. Like hungry vultures surrounding fresh roadkill.

The song suddenly cut off in midchorus and there was a beeping sound in my ears. I pulled out my cell phone. An Edgewood number. I hit accept.

"Hello?"

Silence.

"Hel-loooo?"

Rhythmic breathing—in stereo, thanks to my AirPods.

"Guess what, asshole. I'm not playing this game today."

I waited a few more seconds, and when the caller didn't say anything, I hung up and went inside.

6

In the world of publishing, weekly bestseller lists are made available to the public on Thursday morning. However, the majority of industry insiders receive this information on Wednesday evening, usually right around dinnertime.

My agent texted me that night:

Chasing the Boogeyman paperback once again on the lists...
#4 on NY TIMES.
#3 on USA TODAY.
#2 on all of Amazon.
Just wanted to let you know.

There were no congrats or smiley faces. She knew better.

7

The *Bullets and Brains* podcast—arranged by my old friend and true crime writer extraordinaire James Renner—was scheduled for 8:00 to 9:30 p.m. EST, and it was pretty typical fare for the first seventy-five minutes.

Billy and I set up the lights and microphones in my office, and after doing a best two-out-of-three Rock Paper Scissors to decide whose computer we were going to use—Billy won, so we went with his PC; I was a devout Apple guy—we were ready to go.

The host, Warren Lovecraft (he swore it was his real name), was a retired private detective from Pensacola, Florida. He opened with an update on the two recent murders in Edgewood, tied them into Joshua Gallagher's 1988 killing spree, and then launched into an in-depth discussion of *Chasing the Boogeyman*. All of which I had expected. Lovecraft was a fast talker with a buttery-smooth voice and seemed like a straight shooter. He wasn't a huge fan of the *Boogeyman* movie but had plenty of nice things to say about the book.

After the first commercial break, he switched gears and focused on Billy for a while, talking about his writing process, his current work in progress, and what it had been like to grow up in the house of indie book and magazine publisher *Cemetery Dance*. Billy handled all of it with grace and good humor, and provided some terrific insights into what it was like to host a successful Patreon page.

Another quick break and Lovecraft moved on to *Widow's Point*, the haunted-lighthouse novella that Billy and I had written together. The highlight of the night—for me—was listening to my son talk about how much fun he'd had writing alongside his old man and his surprise reveal that we were planning to one day soon pen a sequel to the story.

The trouble started not long after Lovecraft casually announced that he would be accepting live callers for the remainder of the show. That hadn't been part of the original agreement, and I was tempted to end the podcast interview right then and there. The problem with live callers was they were unpredictable. The problem with live callers on podcast shows was they were not only unpredictable, but also uncensored. They could pretty much say anything they wanted and get away with it.

In the end, I stuck around—mostly out of some kind of misguided notion that if I cut and ran, I'd come across as nothing more than a second-rate prima donna.

It started out well—as it often does.

The first man who called into the show gave high praise to both the book and the movie, which he'd claimed to have already seen three times. The second caller, a middle school art teacher from York, Pennsylvania, said that she and her daughter had met me last fall at a Books-A-Million signing and that she'd ordered a half dozen extra copies to give away as Christmas gifts. All safe territory, but I was bracing myself for what I knew was coming.

Next up was an older woman from South Carolina. "I don't mean to be rude," she said, "but you came across as kind of a brat in *Chasing the Boogeyman*. Throwing snowballs at cars, mooning people from the roofs of gas stations, stealing Bigfoot hairs from the library . . . I mean, goodness gracious, your poor parents." Billy had to mute his microphone, as he was laughing so hard.

Caller number four was a strange one right out of the gate. "Hey, Rich, it's David Boyd. From high school?"

"Umm, sure . . . I think so. How are you, David?"

"I'm actually not doing so well these days, but no one wants to hear about me. Let's talk about you."

"Okay, what do you want to—"

"I've been telling folks down here that I knew both you and Josh Gallagher, and how much alike you two used to be."

Lovely, I thought. *Just fucking lovely*. "Is that right?"

"Yes, sir. Both of you was smart, sporty, on the quiet side. I wrestled with Josh for three years. Knew you from senior-year homeroom and Mr. Griffin's business-math class." Now I could picture him. Tall kid, greasy hair, grew up on a farm. Nice guy, but a little out there. "You two were always nice to people, I remember that, too. Never looked down on or bullied anyone."

"Well, thanks, David. I was far from perfect, as our last caller so adroitly pointed out, but I appreciate the kind words."

"Do you 'member that time I got jumped in the parking lot after a school dance and you and Josh were the first ones there to break it up?"

"Can't say I do. Sorry. Anyway, listen, thanks for calling in. I hope you—"

"Tell Josh that David Boyd from Edgewood says hello next time you talk to him."

"It was . . . great catching up, David. Hope you have a good night."

"You too, Richard!"

8

The fifth, and final, call of the night, went like this:

CALLER: She never even cried.

CHIZMAR: I'm sorry? I missed what you just said.

CALLER: She never even cried.

CHIZMAR: Who never cried?

CALLER: Peyton Bair.

CHIZMAR: Who is this?

CALLER: A friend.

CHIZMAR: Okay. If you're a friend . . . then why don't you tell me your name.

CALLER: [laughter] I don't think so.

CHIZMAR: What do you want?

CALLER: I've been a fan of yours for quite some time, Mr. Chizmar. I thought it would be nice to finally chat.

CHIZMAR: The floor's yours. Chat away.

CALLER: Oh, don't get shy on me now. For the past year, you've had plenty to say to anyone who would listen.

CHIZMAR: That's exactly my point. I'm a little tired of the sound of my own voice. Why don't you talk for a while instead?

CALLER: Just long enough for the police to trace this call, right?

CHIZMAR: I seriously doubt that the police are monitoring Mr. Lovecraft's phone line.

CALLER: There will be others.

CHIZMAR: Others? What do you mean?

CALLER: Dead girls.

CHIZMAR: Hasn't there been enough already?

CALLER: No.

CHIZMAR: Why don't you stop hiding behind a mask and tell me who you are? Why are you doing this?

CALLER: There will be others. Soon. Who knows? Maybe even *you*.

[phone call ends]

9

REDDIT THREAD

r/theboogeyman
u/TheElder – 3h
How many of you were listening tonight?!? Holy shitballs! The killer called in!

Hardo – 41m
Sorry but no way was that the real killer. Guy sounded like a stoner.

LarrytheLarge – 39m
Agree to disagree. I think it was the real deal. He was trying to disguise his voice.

Casssandraxo – 27m
why didn't lovecraft shut it down? think they were tracing the call?

Aholelooper – 23m
BULLSHITTTTT. Whole thing's a setup to sell more books. Shit never ends.

RattlesnakeJake – 18m
My bf recognized the voice. It was his old boss at the Burger King where he used to work. I told him to call the police but he's too freaked out.

Lucifer66 – 11m
If you slow down the audio of the phonecall you can hear a woman crying in the background swear to god

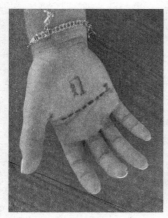

The hangman figure on Peyton Bair's hand *(Photo courtesy of Maryland State Police)*

Billy Chizmar and Richard Chizmar being interviewed on the *Bullets and Brains* podcast *(Photo courtesy of the author)*

The Citros' house in Tupelo Court *(Photo courtesy of the author)*

Excerpt from Edgewood: Looking Back, *by Richard Chizmar, pages 234–235:*

"What do you see?" Brian asked. "Tell us!"

"I can't see anything." I was standing on my tiptoes, straining to reach the window. "I'm not high enough."

There was a pile of old firewood stacked up against the side of the Meyers House. It had been there for as long as any of us could remember. A little while ago, thanks to a heartbreaking, last-minute defeat in a game of three-on-three football, Brian and Jimmy and I had lost a bet to John Schaech and the Baliko brothers. That's why I was perched so precariously atop that wobbly woodpile with my fingers grasping for purchase on the windowsill above me.

"Jimmy, take off your jacket."

Behind me, I heard a pair of zippers go down.

"Okay, Chiz, move over a little bit," Brian said, and I knew from the tone of his voice that something dumb was about to happen. "I'm gonna get down on all fours. Jimmy, fold up our jackets and put them on my back. Chiz, you stand on top of them."

He climbed onto the woodpile, knocking several of the logs to the ground. Backing up against the house, I glanced at Jimmy and raised my eyebrows.

He shrugged his skinny shoulders. "Better you than me."

"Hurry up!" the others shouted from the safety of the apple orchard thirty yards away. "It's getting dark."

Jimmy answered them with a pair of upright middle fingers.

"I'm ready," Brian said. "Make sure you—"

Before I could lose my nerve, I stepped onto his back and slowly straightened up. He grunted under the burden of my weight, and I heard another log tumble to the ground. I began to sway, first in one direction, and then the other. Gripping the windowsill to steady myself, I whispered, "Can you hunch your back a little? I need two or three more inches."

Whatever he did gave me twice that—and suddenly I was looking through the window at someone's bedroom. There was a huge bed centered against the far wall. It was covered with a mound of blankets and a fancy, flowered canopy overhead. Two large dressers, a hulking wardrobe, and a pair of sitting chairs surrounded it. Tucked in the corner was a vanity with an ornately designed mirror.

An old woman was sitting on a stool in front of it brushing her long gray hair.

As I watched, she put down the brush, stood, and walked over to the only other window in the room. She was wearing a nightgown, and the November dusk seeping through the open drapes instantly rendered it transparent. With her back to me, I could see the outline of her naked body underneath. She looked like a skeleton.

"You see anything?" Jimmy asked.

"Shhh."

The woman turned her head in my direction.

I ducked and held my breath.

I'd only had a glimpse of the woman's face, but what I'd seen had shocked me.

Her eyes were the color of emeralds—a deep, sparkling, otherworldly green—and there were no wrinkles anywhere on her face.

I slowly raised up and peered into the window, half expecting the old woman to be standing right in front of me, our faces only separated by dusty panes of glass.

Instead, she was dancing.

I immediately recognized the step, slide, and step from my seventh-grade music class. In the center of the room, the old woman was dancing the waltz with an invisible partner. Her head was tilted back and her eyes were closed. Her nightgown billowed around her bony hips as she moved with the grace of a ballerina.

Looking down, I realized why.

Her bare feet weren't touching the ground.

TEN

BORING . . . UNTIL IT'S NOT

"That's when I found my voice and screamed."

1

At approximately 11:05 a.m. on Saturday, June 11, 2022, forty-three-year-old Wint Singleton walked into Halligan's Furniture Showplace on Route 1 in Fallston and opened fire with an illegally purchased AR-15 rifle, killing three people and critically wounding four others. All of the fatalities were store employees, as was one of the injured. The remaining wounded—a husband, wife, and young daughter—were store customers.

After the shooting, Singleton crossed Bel Air Road on foot and fled into a wooded area adjacent to Amy's Playground. The fourteen-acre park was immediately evacuated. A two-hour standoff with members of the Maryland State Police and the Harford County Sheriff's Department ensued, after which it appeared that Singleton was ready to surrender.

Multiple news footage showed Singleton emerging from the woods with his hands in the air. The AR-15 was nowhere in sight. As tactical-unit officers approached, Singleton pulled his shirt over his head, allegedly to demonstrate that he wasn't hiding any weapons. He then dropped his shirt to the ground in front of him and detonated a hidden fragmentary explosive device. The resulting blast killed Singleton and two police officers, and injured a third.

Singleton, a Forest Hill resident, was a disgruntled former employee at Halligan's Furniture Showplace. He had been fired from his job three weeks earlier for undisclosed reasons.

2

By 11:25 on Saturday morning, the field across the street from my house was empty.

3

Even before the shooting occurred, it had been a quiet couple of days on Southampton Road.

The ominous phone call I'd received during the *Bullets and Brains* podcast had quickly been determined to be a hoax. After consulting with the phone company, police were able to identify the caller as nineteen-year-old Nicky McClane, a second-year student at Howard Community College in Columbia, Maryland. Not only had McClane been foolish enough to make threatening remarks on a public forum, but he'd also been bold enough to make the call from the main business extension of the smoke shop at which he worked. If all that hadn't been bad enough, in-store security cameras had captured the ill-fated phone call from start to finish. Nicky McClane was in a hell of a lot of trouble.

On Thursday morning, Ken Klein from across the street waved me down as I was fetching the newspaper from the driveway. He'd watched the podcast live online and wanted to know if we had any weapons in the house. "You need to be able to protect yourself and your family," he said. "You've become a public target." When I told him that we were in good shape in that regard, he gave me a look like he didn't quite believe me, and went back to washing his car.

Peyton Bair's funeral service was held on Friday afternoon at the Prince of Peace Church on Willoughby Beach Road. Immediately after, there was a graveside gathering at Bel Air Memorial Gardens, which was located within walking distance of my house. Police closed down several roads and posted online travel delays due to the funeral procession. According to local newscasts, as many as five hundred people attended the service, many of them Peyton's classmates from Edgewood High School. I wasn't one of them. Instead, I watched with a heavy heart on television as Peyton's three older brothers helped carry her casket from inside the church to a waiting hearse parked at the curb. Before Channel 11 cut back to the studio, I caught a glimpse of Lieutenant McClernan and Detective Gonzalez in the crowd of mourners.

Other than a brief conversation with the lieutenant—during which she'd confirmed that the trail cam located at the Peyton Bair crime scene had purposely been disabled—I hadn't heard much of anything about the ongoing investigation. I was anxious to find out if they'd discovered anything of interest on my property, but I was determined not to bother them with any more phone calls. I knew they were understaffed and drowning in work. There was also a ticking clock hanging over their heads.

A brief flurry of excitement (for the media) and dread (for the rest of us) erupted later that Saturday afternoon when Edgewood resident Loretta Glover reported her thirteen-year-old daughter, Renee, missing. The girl, who didn't have a cell phone, had gone to the local Rite Aid for her mother and never returned. Ms. Glover, who'd been distracted by one of her television shows, hadn't noticed until more than an hour had passed. Normally, the round trip took no more than twenty or thirty minutes. After driving to Rite Aid and finding no sign of her daughter along the route or inside the store, Ms. Glover asked an employee to call the police. At this point, it had only been an hour and a half since she'd last seen her daughter, but she wasn't taking any chances. Neither were the police; they immediately issued a BOLO for Renee Glover and began searching the surrounding neighborhoods. Programming on several networks was interrupted by special reports featuring a detailed description of the missing girl, as well as a recent school photo—all in conjunction with a major social media push from the precinct. By late afternoon, the news was everywhere.

As I watched Channel 13 report live from the Rite Aid parking lot, memories rushed back to me of staggered lines of police officers and private citizens searching the woods and open fields surrounding the schools. I closed my eyes and offered a silent prayer that today's search would end much differently than the one in the summer of 1988 had ended for Madeline Wilcox.

A short time later, as Kara and I were sitting down for dinner, the news broke that Renee was safe and sound and back at home with her mother. Ms. Glover—who'd collapsed to her knees and sobbed tears of joy when she first saw the police car with her daughter sitting in the front seat turn in to her driveway—had already grounded the thirteen-year-old for the remainder of the summer.

As it turned out, nothing at all nefarious had occurred.

Renee Glover had been walking down the sidewalk en route to the store when something caught her eye. Nestled in the weeds, up against a chain-link fence where the summer winds had blown it, among fast food wrappers and cigarette butts and empty plastic bottles and an assortment of other trash, was a sun-faded, badly wrinkled fifty-dollar bill. At first, she'd thought it was pretend money from a board game like Life or Monopoly—no way was she that lucky; she'd never found so much as a single dollar bill before, much less a fifty—but it didn't take her long to realize otherwise. She'd gotten so excited that she'd run three blocks in flip-flops to her best friend Latisha Warren's house to show her. Once there, Latisha had convinced her to make a detour to La Bella Pizzeria on Edgewood Road, where they'd gorged themselves on a large pepperoni pie and a double order of gravy fries. After that, they'd cut through the woods to 7-Eleven for candy and ice cream sandwiches, stopped back at Latisha's house to change into bathing suits, and gone swimming in Latisha's down-the-street neighbors' pool (the neighbors were vacationing at Rehoboth Beach and had given Latisha permission to use it in their absence). Hours later, nineteen dollars and change in her pocket, suffering from sunburn and a wicked stomachache, and still blissfully unaware of the ongoing search, Renee finally decided that she'd better hightail it to the drugstore to pick up the packet of rubber bands and plastic silverware her mother needed. On her way to Rite Aid, a police officer drove by and spotted her hurrying along the sidewalk. After confirming her identity and notifying dispatch, the officer escorted Renee home. The emotional homecoming was captured by a freelance cameraman. The photos and short video spread like wildfire all over the internet. For the first time in what felt like a long while, there had been a happy ending in Edgewood.

4

After dinner, my somber mood buoyed by news of Renee Glover's safe return, I took the dogs for a swim in the pond. In the rush to grab the dogs' collars, I accidentally left my cell phone behind on the counter in the mudroom. When I returned, I saw that I'd missed a call from Joshua Gallagher, only the second time that had ever happened in the nearly three years since his arrest. I couldn't say I was disappointed.

5

Not to be overshadowed by the girl's dramatic homecoming was Channel 2 reporter Stewart Farris's breaking news announcement that police officials were currently questioning two local men in connection with the murders of Anne Riggs and Peyton Bair.

The initial suspect was identified as Johnathon Russell, the motorcycle-driving man whom Lieutenant McClernan had already asked me about. A video of Russell walking out of the Maryland State Police barracks flashed on the screen. He looked different on television than he did in the headshot the lieutenant had shown me. Older and thinner and not quite as menacing. Nevertheless, I still couldn't place him as anyone I'd ever seen in public, much less driving by my house.

The second suspect was identified as fifty-eight-year-old Stephen Grant, and he wasn't a stranger to me. I hadn't seen his face in over thirty years, but I recognized him the moment they showed his photo. He was a little fleshier around the eyes and chin, and his hair was lighter and shorter, but otherwise, he looked the same. Grant had graduated from Joppatowne High School in 1981, two years before me at Edgewood. At the time, we'd shared a number of mutual friends and often socialized at parties and ball games. But once I'd moved away to college, I'd pretty much forgotten all about him. Just one of those people. Years later, when I was in my early thirties, I'd been shocked to hear from a friend that Grant had been arrested the previous summer for the rape and attempted murder of his coworker's girlfriend. That December, after a jury found him guilty of all charges, Grant began serving a thirteen-and-a-half-year sentence at the Jessup Correctional Institution.

Stephen Grant now resided on Rumsey Island in Joppatowne, not far from where Joshua Gallagher had once rented a town house. Grant had a live-in girlfriend and worked as a laborer for a local construction company. In 2018, he'd been suspected of breaking into a Churchville home and raping a twenty-two-year-old woman, but no charges had been brought due to a lack of evidence. More recently, he'd been questioned in relation to a string of residential break-ins in Joppatowne and Rosedale, but once again no charges were made.

As soon as the news segment was over, I texted Lieutenant McClernan and let her know about the connection. Two minutes later, she wrote back: I know. On my list to talk to you about. His name wasn't supposed to go public.

6

In most active criminal investigations, there is a lull.

Veteran detectives often speak of the ebb and flow of the process. One week they might spend dawn to dusk knocking on doors, manning the phones at their desks, or sifting through box after box of paperwork and receipts—all the while searching for that one nugget of evidence that might help turn the case. The next week, their current leads exhausted and close to losing their minds waiting on results from the lab, they might be resigned to reinterviewing old witnesses or sniffing around past crime scenes, hoping for something—anything—to shake loose.

The general public often views these down periods as a "no news is good news" scenario and embraces them as a sign to be hopeful. Nothing much is happening, so perhaps the bad guy has moved on and the dark days are over.

It usually doesn't work that way.

Earlier, I claimed that many crime investigations reached a point where they were considered "boring . . . until they're not." Credit for that astute bit of phrasing belonged to my old friend Detective Lyle Harper, who, more than any other person I'd ever met, knew his way around a criminal investigation. Three years ago, he'd suffered a stroke while on the job and took his final breaths in a rat-infested Baltimore City alleyway. Even now, I missed him terribly and thought of him often.

Whether anyone recognized it at the time or not, the Thursday, Friday, and Saturday of that second week of June was our lull.

By late Saturday night, all hell would break loose.

7

The state trooper assigned to our house was not to blame.

At approximately ten o'clock on Saturday night, June 11, a major accident occurred at the intersection of Route 543 and Route 22—locals referred to that particular traffic light as "the Gauntlet" because of its dangerous nature—involving a tractor trailer and two passenger cars. One of the vehicles, a late-model Jeep Cherokee, rolled several times, trapping the driver and a lone passenger inside the wreckage. Because the trooper stationed in our driveway was so close to the scene—less than a half mile away—and because it was considered a life-threatening situation, he had no other choice but to respond.

8

The following transcription represents Kara Chizmar's official, unabridged statement—recorded via audio file on her personal cell phone—which she turned over to Detective Tony Gonzalez of the Maryland State Police Department at 12:55 a.m. on Sunday, June 12, 2022. It is reprinted here with her permission.

Billy was spending the weekend with friends at a music festival in Delaware, so Rich and I were alone for the night. We'd just finished watching a movie in the family room. It was Rich's turn to pick this time, and he chose *The Northman*. Too long, too weird, too violent. He loved it. Me, not so much. (The detective asked me to be as specific as possible, so there you go.) The movie ended at around eleven. I dumped the leftover popcorn into the trash can and pulled out the garbage bag because it was full. Rich offered to take it out to the driveway, but I told him I was going out anyway to get the mail. So while Rich loaded the dishwasher, I took the trash outside, dumped it in the can, and proceeded to walk down the driveway to the mailbox. Ever since all of this started, we'd waited until it was dark to go out and get the mail because it was more difficult for the photographers to see us coming. That night, because of the furniture store shooting in Fallston, there were no reporters set up across the street. Southampton Road was quiet. And dark. No cars—that I noticed—drove by while I was outside. By this time, it was pretty late, probably around 11:10 p.m.

Trooper Parker had knocked on the door about an hour earlier and told us that he'd be gone for a short time due to a car accident. He was in a big hurry, so it must've been a bad one. It didn't bother me at all that he was gone. In a way, it felt good to have the house all to ourselves again. No press and no police. Just us.

The walk to the mailbox is fairly long, maybe seventy or eighty yards, and mostly well lit. I don't remember seeing or hearing anything unusual or out of the ordinary. Just lots of crickets and the bullfrogs from the pond. Everything else was still and peaceful. I remember seeing fireflies under the trees and in the road where the light didn't reach. As I took our mail from inside the box, I remember thinking how happy I was that there were no reporters yelling at me from across the street, and wondering if they would be back again by morning.

That's when I noticed that the lamppost by the opposite entrance of the driveway was dark. You can usually see a good portion of the side yard by the pond but not tonight. There was nothing over there but shadows. Standing by the mailbox, I suddenly felt nervous and on guard. I patted my pockets for my cell phone, but it wasn't there. For the first time, I wished that Trooper Parker was back in our driveway. I tried to think of when we'd last changed the light bulb in the lamppost, but my brain wouldn't work fast enough. All of a sudden, all I could see was that awful mask peering out from behind the springhouse.

The mask made me think about the security cameras, and for some reason, that made me feel a little safer and helped me get moving. I started walking back to the house. For a second, I thought about running, but that's all it came to. Just a flash of a thought, it came and went. I've talked to Rich about that scene in *Chasing the Boogeyman*, the one that everyone always brings up at book signings, where he takes out the trash at his parents' house and feels Gallagher's presence lurking in the darkness. I didn't feel like evil was there with me, as Rich described, but I *did* feel like someone was watching me. I can't tell you exactly what it felt like, other than I was suddenly sure I wasn't alone. I scanned the darkness up ahead by the garage; I looked over my shoulder behind me and even high up in the trees.

I was halfway to the house when I saw something move on the other side of the driveway and heard what sounded like someone moaning. I almost took off running. If I hadn't been so frightened, I think I would have, and all of this would've had a completely different ending. But I didn't. Instead, I sucked in my breath and started walking faster, never taking my eyes off the side yard, certain by this point that someone was going to explode out of the darkness and start chasing after me. And then I saw something move again, something tall and pale, and for a moment, as crazy as it sounds, I thought it was a naked person walking toward me.

Then, I realized it wasn't walking. It was swinging in the breeze.

I started to get angry. And a little embarrassed.

Because I had seen something like this before. In the daylight.

It was a mannequin.

That's when I knew someone was playing a prank on us, and I'd fallen for it hook, line, and sinker.

I immediately headed for the side yard, feeling more ticked off with every step.

As I got closer, I saw that there was more than one mannequin hanging from the sycamore tree. There were at least three of them, gently swaying back and forth, and they were all dressed in wigs. The moaning I'd heard was the sound of the ropes looped around their necks rubbing against the branches they were tied to.

I reached up and was about to give one of the mannequins a good yank when I suddenly froze. The sensation of being watched was back. Much stronger this time. I could feel goose bumps rise all over my legs and arms. My skin went cold. The crickets and frogs had gone silent. The only sound was the ropes scraping against the tree.

I backed up and prepared to run. I wasn't going to freeze this time. I heard a branch snap somewhere in the darkness. I slowly backed up another step. And suddenly, I knew. The Boogeyman was hiding in the tree above me. I was going to look up and he would be right there, squatting on one of the lower branches, face hidden beneath that awful mask, and he was going to pounce out of the tree and take me to the ground, where he would choke the life out of me and sink his teeth into my flesh over and over again.

Suddenly, the night got brighter.

"Kara? You okay?" The front door was standing open, the light spilling out from inside the foyer, and Rich was standing on the porch. "Kara?"

Becoming the Boogeyman

I tried to answer, but no words would come.

I heard that moaning sound again. Louder this time.

It was the mannequins dancing in a sudden gust of wind.

Seizing my courage, I stepped forward and looked up into the tree—and Annie Riggs was staring back at me.

Her severed head had been attached to the mannequin's body. The flesh was rotting from her skull, her limp hair falling out in tangled clumps. Something small and dark skittered across her sunken cheek.

That's when I finally found my voice and screamed.

Wint Singleton *(Photo courtesy of* The Aegis*)*

The sycamore tree in Chizmar's front yard where the mannequins were hung *(Photo courtesy of the author)*

211

Excerpt from in-person interview with Joshua Gallagher, age 56, inmate #AC4311920 at Cumberland Penitentiary, recorded on February 10, 2022:

CHIZMAR: Growing up, were you ever mistreated by your parents or any of the other adult figures in your life?

GALLAGHER: No, never.

CHIZMAR: Surely you were reprimanded and punished as a child.

GALLAGHER: Only when I deserved it.

CHIZMAR: Did you ever feel unloved or uncared for?

GALLAGHER: Never.

CHIZMAR: What is your earliest memory?

GALLAGHER: [long pause] I remember walking around the kitchen at our new house in Edgewood. Everything felt so big. I leaned back against one of the cabinets, and it moved. It was just the lazy Susan, but I had no idea it was there. I had no idea such things even existed. It felt like some kind of a secret doorway to me. I was fascinated.

CHIZMAR: Did you like secrets when you were a child?

GALLAGHER: Oh yeah. I loved them.

CHIZMAR: Why do you think you loved them so much?

GALLAGHER: Because my whole life has been a secret.

ELEVEN

THE COPYCAT EFFECT

"The killer had slithered unseen into frame . . ."

1

None of us got any sleep that night.

After getting Kara back inside and calmed down, I called Lieutenant McClernan on her cell phone and woke her up. By the time she arrived at the house—thirty-five minutes later—Detective Gonzalez and his crew were already hard at work. The lieutenant had instructed everyone to avoid using their radios, if at all possible, so as not to alert the press. So far, her plan seemed to be working, and they had the side yard to themselves.

As McClernan interviewed my wife in the family room, Gonzalez and the other detectives worked the crime scene. Lights on tripods were assembled, as was a large screen, blocking the mannequins from view. Men with flashlights searched the grassy meadow surrounding the pond. Even with the windows closed, I could hear the geese honking their displeasure. Back at the station, technicians were poring over tonight's security footage. I was anxious to take a look myself, but that would have to wait.

After a while, Gonzalez came into the house with a notebook full of questions for Kara. McClernan left them to it and joined me in the kitchen. Her hair was arranged in a messy ponytail, and she was wearing gray sweatpants, a gray hoodie, and Adidas sneakers. She looked like one of the moms at the gym.

"She's a tough chick, isn't she?"

My head felt like it was filled with sand. I nodded anyway. "Yes, she is. Always has been."

McClernan sighed. "What a clusterfuck."

"You're telling me."

"On one hand, this guy's a mess. He's all over the damn place."

"And on the other hand?" I asked.

"He's incredibly resourceful. The logistics necessary to make this work . . ." She gestured out the window. ". . . are extremely complicated. Somehow, he had to have eyes on the house. How else did he know there was no one standing guard? Then, there's the light bulb. It was unscrewed. When did he manage to do that without being seen? Not to mention the risk and time involved with hauling in three mannequins—those things aren't light—and hanging them up in your tree. And we won't even get into how the head was attached."

"What bothers me is that he had to be somewhere nearby all this time," I said. "He obviously wasn't responsible for the shooting that got rid of the media, but he was close enough to move in as soon as the trooper left our driveway. That's a seriously narrow time frame. So he either got very lucky with the timing, which I don't believe even for a minute, or he's been watching us and waiting."

"We'll check out every possible sight line in the morning once it's light outside. Your neighbors probably won't be happy, but fuck 'em. We'll also get to work tracking down where the mannequins came from. That's not the kind of item you can pick up at Target or Dollar Tree."

"What about the press?"

"We'll frame it as a prank and send a strong message to the public that if anything like it happens again, there'll be dire consequences."

"Any chance it's one of the suspects I saw on television?"

"Possible, but unlikely. We're still checking them out."

"Stephen Grant . . . how did you find out we knew each other?"

"Grant told us before we even had a chance to ask. He's followed your story over the years. He's quite a fan."

"The Stevie Grant I grew up with barely knew how to read."

"I guess he had plenty of time to learn in prison."

I almost didn't ask, then thought what the hell. After tonight, everything was back on the table. "How about the springhouse? Anything?"

"Not really," she said. "No useable prints. No fibers. Nothing on the ground, except for a couple of snakes."

"They love the woodpile back there."

She paused. "Well . . . there *was* one thing."

"What?"

"It's probably nothing, but based on measurements the techs made, the individual hiding behind your springhouse appeared to be considerably shorter than the man we saw carrying the trash bag on Southampton Road. A lot of factors could be responsible for that. He could've been stooped down. It could've been the angle of the camera. Only a small portion of him is visible on the footage. Or, the most likely scenario in my mind, it was someone playing a prank."

"Pretty risky prank. That's a good way to get yourself shot."

There was a loud knock at the front door. I got up to answer it, but before I was halfway across the kitchen, a uniformed trooper opened it and poked her head inside. "Hey, boss!"

Detective Gonzalez looked over at her. "What's up?"

"We've got press outside."

Behind me, the lieutenant muttered something under her breath.

"If anyone comes on the property, arrest them," Gonzalez said.

"Will do. One more thing . . . you told me to check out the camera on the roof."

"That's right."

"There's no camera up there," she said. "But there *is* a piece of gutter hanging loose on the corner. I think maybe someone took it."

2

The killer approached our house on foot.

He came in from the woods by the pond. Only the geese saw

him pass, a shadow among many. Even they avoided his presence. Once he reached the split-rail fence, he slipped over the top rail, dropped low to the ground, and crawled on his stomach until he reached the lattice panel that disguised the front porch's foundation.

The security cameras captured none of this. It was all merely speculation. The killer had somehow known that there was a blind spot in the system. That meant he knew our property.

What *could* be seen by the camera's watchful eye was this:

A dark figure wearing a mask emerging from a deep pool of darkness at the bottom of the screen. The killer had slithered unseen into frame—and then simply stood up. The first time I watched it on Kara's laptop, it gave me chills. It was as if Death itself were rising from the depths of hell. That awful mask drawing ever closer to the camera.

What happened next was a point of contention among the small group of detectives and technicians who viewed the footage:

The picture momentarily blurred, *rippling* from left to right across the frame, and as the intruder lifted his arms into the air, the screen suddenly went blank.

The majority of the viewers claimed that the man in the mask had thrown something—most likely some type of heavy object that knocked the camera from its perch or even a length of rope designed to lasso the camera and yank it down. Yet neither an object nor any rope was visible in the footage.

Others were convinced that something extraordinary had taken place. Despite the fact that the camera was attached to a corner of the roof some eighteen feet off the ground, they believed that the man in the mask had simply jumped straight up into the air and torn off the camera with his bare hands.

3

"**A**re you sure?"

Kara nodded and pulled the covers up to her chin. She looked very small lying in the bed next to me.

"Just say the word and we can go," I continued. "I mean it this time."

"I know you do, but I'm not going anywhere."

Hearing my wife say those words should've made me feel better, but it didn't. All this time I'd been so afraid of her picking up and leaving, and now that it was probably the right thing to do, she was being stubborn.

It was 6 a.m. and already light outside. The police were still working in the yard—although the mannequins and Annie Riggs's severed head had been taken away hours ago—and once again they had an audience watching their every move from across the street. Despite the radio silence, the media currently outnumbered nosy neighbors by about a five-to-one ratio, but I expected that gap to close as more residents woke up to greet the day. Once word got out about why the police were *really* here, this whole thing was going to turn into a complete and total shitshow. No matter how jaded the world had become, an innocent victim's missing head hanging in a suburban front-yard tree was pretty much the point of no return.

"Do you think you can sleep?" I asked.

"Every time I close my eyes, I see her face."

I didn't say it to her then, but I knew exactly how she felt. Every time a moment of prolonged silence fell over the house, I heard my wife's screams echoing inside my head . . . and then I relived the moment when I'd sprinted off the porch and found her on her knees in the side yard. I looked at the dark circles under her eyes and started to lose it. Turning away, I wiped a tear from my face.

"I'm okay, I promise. I just need to rest for a while."

"Want me to turn on a movie?"

She thought about it. "I'll put my headphones on and listen to some music. Maybe that'll help."

"Think about what I said . . . we can go anywhere you want."

"I told you . . . I'm not letting him drive us out of our own house. Besides, we're probably safer here than anywhere else. At least that's what Clara said."

"Clara, huh."

"The lieutenant was very kind to me today."

I squeezed her hand. "Get some rest. I'll be right here. I love you."

She paused, long enough so that I didn't think she was going to say it.

"I love you too." She started to put in her earbuds, then turned and looked at me. "Are all the doors locked?"

4

ZachWillett @ZachWillett – 1h
Hahahahahaha. Saw the mannequins on the news. I wish I'd thought of it!

Falling Stars and Applejacks @Claywagner
So funny!!! My best friend was the one who hung the mannequins on Chizmar's fence 2 years ago!!!

TJ Suspiria @ThomasReagan
Umm dude you may want to delete that tweet...

5

News of the "mannequin prank" hit the internet with the ferocity of a tornado and made it on the air in time for the Sunday afternoon broadcasts—but still the furniture store shooting remained the lead story.

That would all change later that Sunday evening when Channel 2 interrupted an episode of *Celebrity Wheel of Fortune* to reveal exclusive crime scene photos of the hangman figure on Peyton Bair's palm. A somber anchorwoman explained to viewers that the killer had used a fine-point Sharpie with black ink and made the connection between the number seven written on Peyton Bair's hand and the sequence of numbers Joshua Gallagher had used in 1988 to differentiate his victims. Surprisingly, there was no speculation as to what the missing word could be.

Most likely because they were in such a hurry to get to their next jaw-dropping revelation.

The anchorwoman—who was new to the Baltimore area and looked as if she wanted to go back to wherever it was she'd come from—crossed her hands in front of her and said, "And now we have Reid McNulty with a live report from Edgewood."

"Thanks, Brandy." Reid McNulty was in his early thirties. John Lennon glasses. Carefully tousled blond hair. Chin that could slice an apple. He was standing in front of Winters Run, the wooden bridge where Peyton Bair's body was discovered looming in the spotlit background.

"In what is already a very sad day for the Bair family, and in fact this entire Edgewood community, I'm afraid we have even more tragic news to report. If you have young children present in the room, you may want to ask them to leave." He lowered his eyes from the camera for a moment before continuing. "In this Channel 2 exclusive, we learned a short time ago that Peyton Bair's killer used either a thin-bladed knife or a scalpel to slice off the young girl's left ear. Detectives indicated that this almost certainly occurred postmortem. There was no sign of the severed ear at the crime scene, indicating that the killer took it with him."

He turned and slowly walked across the bridge. "You may remember that Joshua Gallagher, the serial murderer known as the Boogeyman, sliced off the ears of his victims during his infamous 1988 killing spree . . ."

And with that information now public, the dam had officially broken.

6

"*The Boogeyman IS back!*" became the media's rallying cry, and by the time most families were sitting down for dinner that Sunday evening, "Edgewood's Dark History Repeats Itself—A Copycat Killer on the Loose" was the lead story on CNN.

You couldn't scroll for more than a few seconds on Facebook, Twitter, or TikTok without being bombarded with news of the "Edgewood

Boogeyman copycat killer." The close-up image of the hangman on Peyton Bair's lifeless palm was viewed more than two million times in the first hour it appeared online.

The lull was over.

The circus was back in town.

7

I read and reread all the articles I could find about copycat killers until I could practically repeat them verbatim. I watched the documentaries and studied the textbooks and journals.

And each time I finished, I always circled back to the same troubling question:

How much of the responsibility for what was happening was my own?

8

A summer evening on Main Street in historic downtown Bel Air was normally a scene straight out of a Norman Rockwell painting.

Small shops lined both sides of the narrow two-lane street, storefront windows painted gold and red by the rays of the setting sun. There were clothing boutiques, outdoor cafés, coffee shops, florists, and a pair of family-owned bakeries. There was a comic book store, a watch repair shop, and a hardware store that had laid down its roots here at the turn of the twentieth century. Even the handful of banks, law offices, and real estate companies made an effort to fit in, with their forest-green canopies and old-fashioned wooden benches out front. Potted plants and hand-painted signs decorated most of the storefronts. Miniature American flags and bright red ribbons adorned the lampposts. A red-white-and-blue banner advertising the upcoming Fourth of July carnival hung over the busy intersection at Main and Third. On Monday nights, large pizzas were two for one at Buentempo Brothers, and the takeout line usually stretched all the way out the door. Sean Bolan's Pub was the only place in town where you could get a five-dollar pitcher of dark beer and a steaming-hot plate of corned beef and cabbage; every day was St. Paddy's Day at Bolan's.

Most summer nights, the sidewalks were swarming with families on their way to or from dinner, giggling packs of children eating ice cream cones, and hand-holding couples of all ages out for a romantic stroll. Smiling dogs on leashes, double-decker baby strollers, and little kids on scooters were everywhere you looked.

But on the Sunday night that the world learned about the horrific details of Peyton Bair's death, the scene on Main Street was quite a bit different.

The stores and restaurants were open but mostly empty. The sidewalks were strangely bare. There was no music or laughter—just a breathless tension in the air, a foreboding sense of waiting for the other shoe to drop.

At the south end of Main Street, a large crowd had gathered in front of the courthouse, overflowing the sidewalk and spilling out onto the road. A frazzled Bel Air town cop who couldn't have been more than a year or two away from retirement tried his best to corral people back to safety while his partner blew his whistle and directed traffic around them. Car horns blew and tempers flared.

The mood within the crowd wasn't much better. People were scared, and angry.

The media had assembled in a roped-off area at the front of the throng of people—an undulating mass of cameras and microphones and blinding lights.

At the top of the courthouse steps, Lieutenant McClernan stood ramrod straight in front of the podium. Dressed in her uniform, she cut an impressive figure. Detective Gonzalez, who had already given his statement, stood at her side. Either he'd trimmed his mustache for the press conference, or he'd used some kind of shaping gel. I stood a few feet behind them, doing my best not to pass out or vomit.

". . . and I'd just like to reiterate what Detective Gonzalez said a short time ago. In an effort to remain vigilant and safe, we are asking residents to lock their doors and windows at all times, and to avoid walking anywhere alone. Day or night. When we say 'anywhere,' we mean that in a literal sense. An example . . . even if you need to simply walk outside to get something from your car, take someone else with you. Don't take any unnecessary chances. And, finally, if you see something, say something. Anything at all out of the ordinary, please call it in."

The lieutenant picked up the sheet of paper in front of her, folded it, and stuffed it into her pocket. "Now, we'll take a handful of questions."

Everyone began shouting at once. A forest of waving hands shot high into the air.

Lieutenant McClernan searched the crowd for a friendly face. I'd attended a number of these things over the years, and I knew from experience that the first question or two were usually prearranged softballs. She finally settled on a woman with short curly hair and glasses in the second row.

"Kendra," the lieutenant said into the microphone, pointing. The crowd noise dropped to an uneasy murmur.

"Has Joshua Gallagher assisted in any way with this investigation?"

Tough question. Definitely not a plant.

"He has not," the lieutenant answered.

The same lady: "Do you believe he could be involved in the murders of Anne Riggs or Peyton Bair?"

"At this point, we do not believe that is the case. Joshua Gallagher is being held in a maximum security prison. He's only allowed out of his cell for a total of ninety minutes a day. His mail and phone calls are carefully screened."

The cacophony of shouting returned.

Lieutenant McClernan pointed at a man wearing an expensive suit in the front row. I recognized him from the Channel 11 evening news.

"This question is for Richard Chizmar."

I took a deep breath and stepped up to the podium. *This is why you're here, Rich. Let folks see you're as concerned as they are.*

"When you were twenty-two years old and first sat down to write a book about Joshua Gallagher, did you ever think that—"

A booming voice sounded from somewhere in the crowd, drowning out the rest of the question. "IS IT TRUE THAT YOU'VE BEEN EX-PECTING THESE MURDERS FOR SOME TIME NOW?! AND THAT YOU'RE GOING TO WRITE A BOOK ABOUT THEM?!"

My mouth dropped open in surprise. When I saw myself later on television, I immediately knew that the screenshot would become a meme and go viral. It was just too perfect—with the crowd and the lights and my wide, startled eyes, I looked like a bad actor playing an idiot on TV.

"WHAT ABOUT YOUR RECENT VISIT WITH JOSHUA GALLAGHER?!"

"I . . . I don't have any plans to write another true crime book." My mouth was nowhere near the microphone. Other than the lieutenant and Detective Gonzalez, I'm almost certain no one heard me.

"WHAT'S THE REAL REASON THE POLICE WERE AT YOUR HOUSE LAST NIGHT?!"

Lieutenant McClernan stepped in front of me and leaned close to the microphone. "I'm sorry, but that's all for tonight."

She took me by the arm and escorted me inside the courthouse.

9

The following posts were excerpted from a thirty-nine-page thread entitled "Peyton Bair News!" from the *Boogeyman Lives* message board:

Sunday, June 12, 2022 – 10:34 p.m. CST – BEELZEBUB
I was right! He cut off her fucking ear!

Sunday, June 12, 2022 – 10:34 p.m. CST – THE FINAL GIRL
Any guesses on the hangman word? Phantom? Haunted?

Sunday, June 12, 2022 – 10:35 p.m. CST – THE NIGHT STALKER
Chizmar's the one. I'll bet ya anything.

Sunday, June 12, 2022 – 10:37 p.m. CST – DARK ANGEL

It makes me sick how girls keep dying and he keeps making money. Someone should do something about it.

Sunday, June 12, 2022 – 10:39 p.m. CST – LAST CHANCE CHARLIE

Gallagher is innocent! These murders prove it!

Sunday, June 12, 2022 – 10:41 p.m. CST – BUNDY'S BITCH

I saw Chizmar in his front yard the other day. I think him and Gallagher are working together. Just wait and see.

Sunday, June 12, 2022 – 10:42 p.m. CST – RANK AND FILE FLIGHT RISK

There's no way Josh Gallagher's in jail. It's gotta be a body double or something.

Sunday, June 12, 2022 – 10:44 p.m. CST – THE FINAL GIRL

Any guesses on when the next murder will occur???

Sunday, June 12, 2022 – 10:47 p.m. CST – LOUIS CREED

I drove by Chizmar's house last night. Cops fuckin everywhere.

Sunday, June 12, 2022 – 10:49 p.m. CST – JORDAN PEELE ROCKS (AND ROLLS)

Heard that Joshua Gallagher's going to make a public statement soon. Be ready for a bombshell!!

Sunday, June 12, 2022 – 10:51 p.m. CST – FLYING MONKEYS

Was anyone at the press conference tonight? Link's here. Was a shitshow.

Sunday, June 12, 2022 – 10:52 p.m. CST – PREZ OF THE MICHAEL MYERS FAN CLUB

Listen to Chizmar talk for awhile. I'm telling you somethings not right with that guy . . .

Main Street in downtown Bel Air *(Photo courtesy of the author)*

The porch roof bracket where the missing security camera was once attached *(Photo courtesy of the author)*

Excerpt from Edgewood: Looking Back, *by Richard Chizmar, pages 119–120:*

Despite being the youngest of five children and having the best friends a boy could have, I spent a lot of time by myself. Usually, this was by choice. I had library books and comics to keep me company, daydreams to dream, and important things to think about. My family was a loving bunch but far from perfect, and I longed to figure out why. I couldn't understand even basic algebra, not a lick of it, no matter how hard I tried. Some of my friends were changing, and it troubled me. The world, in many ways, troubled me. And then there were girls. They were a complete and total mystery, and all of a sudden, they were everywhere.

So, yes, you could say my twelve-year-old brain was busy.

But there was another reason I so often chose such a solitary existence.

I'd learned that it was easier to find magic when no one else was around.

And when I was a kid, growing up in Edgewood, Maryland, magic was everywhere.

It was shooting stars and four-leaf clovers and bird nests so tiny and delicate you could cradle them in the palm of your hand.

It was rainbows after a thunderstorm and full moons that followed you home and snowflakes melting on your tongue.

It was bottle rockets and fireflies, pocket knives and fishing poles.

It was finding an arrowhead buried in a creek bank and a feather that could tell the future.

It was a bird that came close enough to eat from your hand.

A squirrel that played tag with you at the playground.

Magic was plunging your hands into a swift-moving stream and watching the sunlight dance between your fingertips.

It was catching a fish on your last cast of the day and finding a frog in your window well.

It was discovering a rock buried in your backyard that was so shiny and so perfectly round that it had to have come from another planet.

It was pulling three Baltimore Orioles from a single pack of baseball cards.

Sometimes, magic was a person. The man who looked like Santa Claus in line at the grocery store. The teenage girl buying a snow cone whose hair was the color of an October sunset. A soldier in uniform home on leave hugging his crying mother on a street corner.

These things were easier for me to see—and feel—when I was all by myself.

TWELVE

SURPRISE VISITOR

"I'll be your Hannibal Lecter if you'll be my Clarice Starling."

1

The next morning was pure chaos.

Overnight, the field across the street had transformed into a miniature Woodstock. Tents had been erected, clusters of lawn chairs arranged, and coolers of every imaginable size hauled in. A hammock hung between two trees. A man was shaving and a woman was brushing her hair in front of a lighted vanity mirror that had been set up on top of a folding table. A Lady Gaga song was playing from an unseen stereo speaker while two young men wearing NBC baseball caps tossed a football back and forth. There were even a couple of food vendors in box trucks selling coffee and doughnuts and breakfast sandwiches. Earlier this morning, the police had had no choice but to finally close down Southampton Road from the traffic circle on Moores Mill to the light on Route 543.

After taking in the view from our bedroom window, Kara hadn't said a single word to me all morning. And I couldn't really blame her. It felt as if we were living a nightmare.

Several deputies waved back a surge of photographers as I pulled out of the driveway. I had an appointment in Forest Hill at 8 a.m. and I was already running late. Wasn't that the way it was going? I made a fool of myself on national television the night before and had to wake up early the next morning for a stupid dentist appointment. Should have canceled, but go figure.

Mike and Molly Peele were the reasons I was late. When I'd walked outside to my car, I'd heard voices coming from next door and noticed a flurry of activity in their driveway. Peeking between the neat row of juniper trees that separated our houses, I'd watched as the two of them, along with their daughters, loaded suitcases and backpacks and plastic bags of groceries into two cars parked side by side with their hatchbacks standing open. They were going somewhere in a hurry.

After a minute, the oldest daughter, Maggie, saw me standing there. She nudged her father.

"Hey, Rich," Mike said, a sheepish look on his face. "Look, we're . . . we're bailing out of here. Going to Jersey for a little while."

Molly's family had a place in Avalon. They went every summer, but not like this. It looked like they were fleeing a hurricane—and maybe they were.

"I'm really sorry . . . about everything," I said. "Are you taking the dogs?"

"Oh yeah. The whole gang's going," Mike said, trying hard to smile.

Molly walked outside with an armful of beach towels. "Please don't be sorry." She placed them in the back seat of one of the cars. "None of this is your fault."

"I'm not so sure about that." I felt awful. Kara was going to feel even worse when I told her.

"Just be safe," Molly said, crossing her arms over her chest. "Take care of yourself and your family."

I nodded, unsure if I could trust my voice, and retreated to my car.

2

The man in the crowd yelling questions had been identified as Jeremy Hollister, Peyton Bair's stepfather. He wasn't in any kind of trouble—technically, he'd done nothing wrong—but Detective Gonzalez had tracked him down just the same and had a chat with him. Trust issues aside, Mr. Mustache was good at his job. Or maybe that's *why* he was good at his job.

Suffice to say, Jeremy Hollister was not a fan of mine. As evidenced by the aggressive nature of his questioning, Hollister was convinced that I was a low-life hustler and charlatan exploiting people's bad fortune and, at the very least, partially responsible for the death of his stepdaughter. Gonzalez assured me that he'd given the man a not-so-subtle warning to stay away from me and my family, and that he didn't believe it would be any further issue. Hollister and his wife had been drinking last night at a Bel Air restaurant and had stumbled upon the press conference by accident. Hearing the detectives talk about their daughter in front of all those strangers had brought a lot of private emotions to the boiling point.

The press conference had been Lieutenant McClernan's idea, and it had gone relatively smooth right up until it'd been my turn at the podium—which was precisely what I'd been afraid of. I'd sensed it from the crowd even before Detective Gonzalez had started talking. I'd *seen* it dancing around the edges of their eyes. In a matter of days, I'd gone from the feel-good success story of "hometown boy makes good" to *what do we really know about this guy, and what kind of monster has he invited into our community?*

If only they'd known that Annie Riggs's missing head had turned up in a tree in my side yard Saturday night, they probably would've shown up at the house with torches and pitchforks and run me out of town.

The detectives had been busy since Saturday night. Every inch of our property had been poked and prodded and meticulously combed over. The woods had been thoroughly searched. The security footage had been viewed numerous times.

All their investigative work pointed to one likely—yet also highly unlikely—scenario: the killer had snuck into our yard by way of a blind spot in the security system (which none of us had known existed); allowed himself to appear on camera for exactly three and a half seconds, just long enough to disable said camera; unscrewed the light bulb in the lamppost; hauled in three mannequins weighing just over thirty pounds each; hung them from a tree using three-foot lengths of three-eighths-of-an-inch manila rope, in clear view of Southampton Road and multiple neighbors; and then disappeared into the night, leaving behind not a trace of physical evidence.

All within a window of approximately fifty-seven minutes.

And with Trooper Parker's imminent return possible at any moment.

The mannequins remained the biggest question mark in a great big pile of question marks. At thirty-one pounds each and awkward as hell to carry, the killer would've most likely had to drag them behind him. Yet, detectives had been unable to find a single drag mark in the grass, dirt, or mud. Plus, even during the driest of months, which this hadn't been, a good portion of the woods were swampy; the killer would've had to carry the mannequins (perhaps one at a time) in order to cross that particular area.

Unless he'd had help, of course. A sobering point that had surely been dancing on the edge of everyone's suspicions for some time now.

And that very real possibility opened up a whole new can of headaches for the detectives.

Two probable hiding spots had been identified as having clear enough sight lines with which to surveil my house and driveway. The first was located in the Stevensons' side yard across the street: a cramped space sandwiched in between a chest-high row of shrubbery and a copse of tall pines. The view was a good one, especially at night, but there was a logistics problem: Unless the person hiding there was relatively short and wearing full-body camouflage, remaining unseen during the daytime hours presented a difficult challenge. The house directly behind them stood at an angle on a moderate hillside and two of the master bedroom windows looked down upon the hideaway with a relatively clear view.

The second spot was in Ken Klein's backyard. Several adult sycamore trees provided a natural border between his property and the residence behind him, as well as ample shade for both of their lawns. The middle tree was the tallest of the three, and approximately twenty-five feet above the ground, detectives discovered a natural perch formed by the juncture of several large branches. Portions of bark on two of the branches were rubbed or worn away by what they believed to be the bottom of someone's shoes. A few smaller twigs higher up in the tree—where the person's handholds might be located—were bent and broken. As expected, Ken Klein was very cooperative with the police. He allowed them to use the extension ladder from his garage, and one of the detectives told Lieutenant McClernan that when he'd stood in the tree, using a quality pair of binoculars, he could see right into our bedroom window. I left that little tidbit out when repeating the story to Kara.

Before the lieutenant dropped me off at the house last night, she'd shared one final piece of interesting news. The techs had almost completed their examination of Joshua Gallagher's fan mail, and it looked as if I would finally be able to visit with him later this week. At the time, numb and embarrassed from my performance at the press conference, I hadn't known what to think or how to feel about the news.

When I woke up this morning, I still didn't.

3

An hour later, teeth still tingling from my annual cleaning, I gave a half-hearted wave to Carl the UPS man as he was pulling away, and turned into the driveway.

There was a black Hummer I'd never seen before parked in my spot in front of the garage. It dwarfed my pickup as I pulled up alongside it. On my way to the house, I stopped and peered into one of the windows. There was a heap of wrinkled clothes piled on the passenger seat. The floor was littered with empty Diet Coke cans.

All of a sudden, I had a feeling I knew who was waiting inside for me.

As the gate clanged shut, the dogs came running and swarmed around my ankles. "We're down here!" Kara yelled from the backyard.

A little excited, despite myself, I took the steps two at a time, almost tripping on the last one. My guess had been a good one. Carly Albright was sitting next to Kara at the edge of the swimming pool, their legs dangling in the water. They both got up as I approached.

"Surprise," Kara said, with a big smile on her face.

"I can't believe it," I said, giving Carly a hug. "How long's it been?"

She squeezed me so hard I could feel my ribs bending. "Wouldn't have been nearly this long if you'd bothered answering my messages."

Uh-oh. I glanced at Kara. She gave me a look that said: *You have some explaining to do, mister.*

"Wow, you look great," I said to Carly, my eyes already stinging from the potency of her perfume.

"Thanks. You look like shit."

Same old Carly. Nothing had changed.

"Nice ride by the way. Good on gas and even better for the environment."

"Shut up and give me another hug," she said, and I happily obliged.

4

We made ourselves comfortable on the back porch.

When I'd complimented her earlier by the pool, I'd merely been trying to change the subject, but I had to hand it to Carly—she really *did* look good. She'd dropped an alarming amount of weight immediately after the funeral and her skin had taken on a sickly pale appearance. Probably because, for weeks after, she'd refused to leave the house.

Since mid-December, the last time I'd seen her in person, she'd gained all the weight back. She looked healthy and fit. Her eyes were clear and sharp, and she was the tannest I'd ever seen her. She'd also opted for a new hairstyle and color. The old ginger tower of power beehive was gone, replaced by a uniformly dark, curled-under bob. I couldn't believe I was saying it, but it made her look years younger and kind of trendy.

"That's because Antonio is a stylist for the stars," she said in a really bad Joan Rivers imitation. "He does Anderson Cooper's and Margot Robbie's hair."

"Who?" I asked.

She dismissed me with a haughty flip of her hand. "As for the weight, I just finally decided to start eating again."

"Well, we're glad you did," Kara said. "We missed you. So much."

"I've missed you too," Carly said, her eyes suddenly glistening. "When you called and left a message last week . . ."

Now it was my turn to give Kara a look.

". . . I was in the Australian Outback with the girls, blissfully unaware of all the drama unfolding back here in Maryland. Hearing your voice was such a wonderful surprise."

"How was Australia?" I asked.

"Beautiful but buggy. Too many spiders and snakes."

"And how's work?"

"I quit," she said.

My mouth dropped open. "You quit the *Post*? Why?"

"The day after Christmas. When the girls went to sleep that night, I sat in my study and typed up my letter of resignation." She shrugged. "I was dying inside. I had to do something."

"You're amazing," Kara said.

"As luck would have it, my boss refused to even look at the letter. He offered me a one-year sabbatical on the spot. That's why there was never a public announcement. The job's still mine if I want it."

I tried to keep the shock out of my voice. "Are . . . you going back?"

"I haven't decided yet. Some days, I miss it like hell. Other days, not even a little bit."

"What have you been doing with yourself since December?"

"Reading books, something I was never able to do while working all the time. Playing a little golf. I started writing a novel, but decided it was too soon, so I put it aside for later. Mostly, I've been spending Walter's pension and traveling around the world." She paused. "Home . . . man, home was too many painful memories for me—especially during the holidays—so I packed my suitcase and left. The girls even took off work and joined me on a couple of trips."

"That sounds like time well spent," I said.

"It has been. You learn a lot about yourself on the road." She looked at me and Kara. "Sorry, I sound like a self-help seminar. So how about you two?"

"Are you kidding?" Kara said.

I spread my arms in front of me. "I mean . . . hey, the Boogeyman's back!"

"That's not funny," Kara said, scolding me.

"It's a little funny," Carly said.

"That's because you don't live with this guy every day."

"He still obsessed with Gallagher?"

"Worse than ever."

"I'm right here, you two."

Carly leaned closer to Kara. "Explain."

"You already know most of it. He's still trying to find answers where there are none to be found, and he just *won't* let it go. The only difference now is Gallagher's practically part of the family."

"Oh my God," I said, sitting up. "That is so not true!"

"I hate it when he calls the house. I hate it when he calls him *Rich*, like they're old friends. Most of all, I hate that people think they *are* old friends."

"I understand," Carly said, nodding.

"Not everyone thinks that." I hated how whiny my voice sounded.

"Even just one person is too many."

Carly turned to me. "Are you still making regular visits to Cumberland to see him in person?"

"I haven't been there since February or March. Too busy promoting the book." I didn't say a word about what the lieutenant had told me last night.

"I mean, I guess some things *have* gotten better," Kara said, glaring at me. "You don't stay up all night staring at those photos anymore. And I haven't heard you listening to the interview tapes nearly as often as you used to."

"What photos?"

I waited for Kara to answer, and when she didn't, I went ahead: "I have a box of old photographs and videotapes of Gallagher. Family cook-outs, vacations, school pictures and graduation, a handful of wrestling matches, a bonfire down by the post office. That sort of thing."

"For a while there, if he wasn't watching videos or looking at pictures," Kara went on, "he was fixated on those ridiculous message boards or sitting there in a trance staring at social media posts twenty-four seven. You wouldn't believe the things some people write for all the world to see."

Twirling her hair between her fingers—something I'd seen her do hundreds of times before—Carly processed everything we'd just told her. "And now . . . all these years later . . . we suddenly have a copycat."

"Looks like it," I said.

"I assume there's more than what I've been seeing out there."

"Lots more," Kara said. "Tell her what happened Satur—"

My phone buzzed in my pocket. I pulled it out and looked. Holding it up for Carly to see, I said, "Looks like you already made the news."

TMZ had tweeted a photo of Carly sitting behind the wheel of her Hummer—and it was already going viral. She was wearing sunglasses and smiling for the camera. Her teeth looked very white. The bright red, triple-decker headline centered above the photograph read:

VETERAN JOURNALIST CARLY ALBRIGHT
VISITS OLD FRIEND IN BEL AIR, MARYLAND—
BACK ON THE HUNT?

"On that note," Kara said, getting to her feet. "I'm running to the store. You're staying for dinner, Carly, and I won't accept no for an answer."

"I was actually kind of hoping I could crash in your guest room for a night or two."

Kara's smile was brighter than the sun. "Are you kidding me? You can stay as long as you want."

"Do you think you might whip up those amazing brownies of yours for dessert?"

"Done!" Kara said, heading for the door. She stopped and looked back. "I don't suppose either of you want to tag along?"

"I have a better idea." I turned to Carly. "You want to go for a ride?"

5

"How long's it been?"

We were sitting in front of Carly's old house on Banyan Road. Much like the split-level I'd grown up in, it looked smaller, faded, diminished somehow.

"Four or five years . . . at least." She glanced at me. "Don't look so surprised. I live in D.C., Rich, not just down the road. Plus, I'm not a hopeless romantic like you."

"What does that have to do with anything?"

"You know you've always romanticized the past. In life and in your books."

"Maybe," I said.

"No maybes about it. And then there's that Catholic side of you, where you believe that if you don't come back and pay tribute every few months, you're dishonoring your childhood and the memory of your parents."

I had forgotten how much I truly hated when Carly Albright was right and I was wrong.

I grunted and pulled away from the curb, checking the rearview mirror to make sure no one was following us. On the way here, I'd noticed a dark SUV a couple of cars behind us on Route 40. It had made the left turn onto Edgewood Road along with us, but I'd lost sight of it after the traffic light and hadn't seen it since. It wouldn't have surprised me if it had been a reporter.

During the fifteen-minute drive to Edgewood, I'd filled Carly in on the investigation. She'd listened in silence and twirled her hair like a madwoman. When I'd told her what had happened to Kara on Saturday night, she'd shook her head and said, "The Boogeyman done pissed off the wrong woman."

"Ain't that the truth."

As we drove down Willoughby Beach Road—I'd promised myself that I wouldn't bitch and moan about the new high school, and I didn't—Carly's questions began.

"So, you've told me what the police think. What do *you* think?"

"I . . . honestly don't know. My head's all screwed up. Every day feels like crisis mode."

"Does it feel that much different than it did back in '88?"

I thought about it. "I was so young then. I was almost more . . . *offended* that someone was killing people in my hometown than I actually was scared. It felt like, I don't know . . . a *movie* I was watching back then. Now, I have a family and a career, and we're right in the goddamn middle of it."

"You scared this time?"

"Hell yes, I'm scared. I can't figure out what my role in all of this is. The guy's obviously a psycho, but is he killing people and playing games with me in order to impress Gallagher? To use your words, to pay *tribute* to him? Or is it all just a shortcut to getting headlines?"

"Maybe it's both."

"Okay, right, maybe both. So then what's the endgame? Am I really in danger? Is my family? Or does this sick fuck just need me around to write *his* version of *The Boogeyman*?"

"His own version of immortality, you mean."

"Exactly. Look at Gallagher. He's practically a celebrity now, and I'm partially to blame." I slowed down and pointed out the passenger window. "That's Annie Riggs's house."

Carly craned her neck for a better look. The gate was closed. The driveway was empty. The shades were drawn in the windows. It had only been a week and a half, but the house already had an abandoned feel to it. "Have you spoken to anyone in her family?"

"Oh, God, no. I've stayed out of that one."

"You think they blame you?"

"Probably. Everyone else seems to."

She gave me the hairy eyeball. "Aww, poor baby Rich, the tortured bestselling author."

I started to protest, but stopped. She was right. Again.

"See, that's the bitch of it, Carly. I feel selfish as hell for saying it, and don't you start with me, but I can't help feeling like a victim in all of this. How can I not? I've got a psycho watching my every move and leaving fucking body parts in my yard. *Body* parts! Everything I've worked so hard to build in my career suddenly feels . . . *wrong*. Oh, they're buying the book like crazy and the movie crushed at the box office, but people are looking at me like I'm just another one of those wacko serial killer groupies. Hell, even my own wife thinks I invited this into our lives. And she's starting to hate me for it."

"She doesn't hate you. She's just worried about you."

"I know she is. I get that. I'm just . . . all twisted up inside. I don't even know what to do anymore, except wait around for something else to hit me from left field."

"I'm pretty sure that's a normal reaction to everything that's happened."

"Maybe . . . but like you said, *boo-hoo-hoo, poor baby Rich.* Two innocent people are dead, a whole community's in mourning, but hey, I'm back on the bestseller lists. And still I can't stop thinking *Why me?* And not in a good way. I know, I'm horrible—I'm sorry."

This time, she didn't have an answer.

We drove past Flying Point Park and the marina in silence. The skies were clear and the temperature was hovering in the mideighties. Summer was finally here. The playground was packed with children. The dock lined with crabbers and fishermen. A fleet of boats motored up and down the river. Our windows were down and I could hear squeals of distant laughter and music playing from somewhere inside the park. Life kept on going when the sun was out, no matter what happened in the shadows.

"Have you done any snooping around yourself?" Carly asked as we turned onto Willoughby and headed back toward the heart of town. "Or you letting the police handle everything like a good boy?"

"You know, I wouldn't even know where to start. It's all been such a whirlwind."

"That doesn't sound like the Joe Hardy I know."

I smiled. "McClernan called me that the other day."

"Aha, so you *were* doing some poking around where you didn't belong."

"Not really. I just gave my opinion on something and she pretty much laughed in my face. I don't even remember what it was."

Carly looked disappointed.

"I mean . . . I've done a couple things, I guess. I kept a file of weird emails and letters I've received since *Boogeyman* came out. I made copies before I handed them over to the detectives, but there really wasn't anything there."

"What else?"

"I've watched most of the security footage."

"I heard that."

"My wife's a blabbermouth."

"Your wife didn't say a word. Your son did. He was on his way out this morning when I pulled in. By the way, he told me he wants a Hummer for Christmas."

"Excellent. You can give him yours."

"Don't tempt me. What else?"

"Nothing really. I check out the memorial in our front yard every day in case the killer decides to leave a message, but I think he's too smart for that."

"Now *that's* one of the things I remember from back in the day."

"What is?"

"You always gave Gallagher too much credit. Remember what I told you that time . . . that because you'd just finished reading *The Silence of the Lambs*, you wanted the Boogeyman to be a genius like Hannibal Lecter?"

"I remember."

"But in the end, he wasn't even close. Gallagher was no genius. He was just the quiet kid who sat in the corner and ended up killing a bunch of girls that reminded him of the one that broke his heart." She looked at me closely, and I knew what she was going to say before she opened her mouth. "You think Gallagher might have the answer to all this, don't you?"

I didn't respond right away, so she kept going.

"You going to see him?"

"Later this week. Don't tell Kara."

"I wouldn't dream of it. That's all on you."

"I don't know if he has any answers. They've searched his cell, his mail, found nothing. But still . . ." I didn't like the way she was staring at me.

"That's something else I remember from back then," she said. "You never really believed Gallagher was a monster like the rest of us did. A part of you always felt sorry for him." She shook her head at me. "I just hope you're being careful, Rich. This could all blow up in your face."

If she only knew.

6

As we drove past the old Santoni's shopping center, I noticed a look of somber contemplation on Carly's face. For the past ten minutes, she'd been staring out the passenger window and not saying much. It wasn't at all like her.

"It's changed," I finally said.

She looked at me. "What, Santoni's?"

"Everything. The whole town."

"Yeah, it has," she said, nodding. "Everything always does."

I stopped at the traffic light on Edgewood Road. There was a hang-man spray-painted on the side of the Texaco station. Someone with a warped sense of humor had filled in the blanks:

B O O G E R M A N

"Sometimes I don't even recognize it anymore."

"It's strange, though," she said, and for a moment, she looked genu-inely perplexed. "With the risk of sounding like a sappy old sentimental fart like you, it still feels like home to me."

"It does? Really?" I didn't even bother trying to hide my surprise.

"My first job was mopping floors at Santoni's. Four bucks an hour. My second job was right across the street at the library." She pointed out the window. "My best friend Val Kellagher lived just down the road." She looked around and I could see tears shimmering in her eyes. "My mother and father have been gone a long time . . . but I feel close to them here. They loved living in Edgewood."

"I didn't mean to make you sad." Despite growing up with three sis-ters, I'd never done well with crying women. They scared me. "Maybe I shouldn't have brought you here. I'm sorry."

"Don't be." She wiped her eyes and gave me a smile that reminded me of the Carly Albright I'd first met nearly thirty-five years ago. "I've traveled all over the world these past six months . . . and honestly, if you can believe it . . . this just might be my favorite place of all. I'd forgotten that until today . . . right now."

I sat up a little taller in the driver's seat. "I guess it does feel like home, doesn't it?"

"I'd like to bring the girls back here sometime. Give them a little tour."

I raised my eyebrows at her.

She gave my shoulder a pat. "Hush up and drive."

Smiling, that's what I did.

7

"Maybe you shouldn't have given those photographers the middle finger."

Carly undid her seatbelt. "Maybe those sonsawhores shouldn't have blocked your driveway."

"McClernan's going to love that."

We got out of the truck and started for the house.

"Can I ask you something before we go inside?" she said.

I stopped and looked at her. "Sure."

"My texts and voice mails . . . why didn't you answer me?"

Frankly, I was surprised she'd waited this long to ask. "From last week, you mean?"

"No. Before that."

I took a deep breath. Let it out. "I, um . . . at the funeral, and even before that . . . I felt like I kept saying the wrong thing. You were so sad and angry and distant, and I was making everything worse."

"I was grieving, you idiot."

"I know you were, but . . ."

"But what?"

"But you're my friend . . . and you were hurting *so* bad . . . and I was the one who was supposed to make everything better." I didn't bother wiping the tears that were suddenly filling my eyes.

"Rich, your job as my friend was to *be* there. To listen. To remind me that there were still good things left in the world. And you did that. You *were* there for me. Every day. Until suddenly you weren't. And that's what I don't understand."

"I felt like I'd . . . I'd failed you."

Now she was crying too. Really crying. Mascara ran down her cheeks in dark rivulets. She looked like a demented clown. "Kara's right. You really are an imbecile."

I nodded. "I know I am."

"She's also right that you have the biggest heart of anyone in this awful, awful world." She pulled me into her arms. My ribs immediately started to ache again. "You didn't fail me, Rich, or anyone else. You need to remember that, no matter what happens going forward, okay? Fuck what anybody else thinks."

I didn't say anything. I just hugged her back—and in the end, goddamn if it wasn't exactly what I needed.

8

"You're right. That's creepy as hell." Carly rewound the surveillance footage and watched it again. "The way he walks by and stares at the house. Jesus. That's big-time Michael Myers vibes."

"I still can't stop thinking about what's inside the bag."

Kara came into the family room. "When you two ghouls are finished, dinner's ready on the back porch."

"I'm starving." I started to close the laptop, but Carly stopped me.

"Wait." She tapped the keyboard, rewinding again—she'd gotten the hang of it a lot quicker than I had—and then she hit the Space bar. Once again, the man in the mask walked slowly across the screen. When he was gone, she looked up at me.

"I know you're gonna think I'm crazy . . . but there's something familiar about this guy. I just can't quite put my finger on what it is."

"Seriously?"

"Yeah . . . I need to think about this."

9

After wolfing down three large servings of lasagna and half a loaf of homemade bread—I'd saved room by skipping the salad—I crashed on the loveseat while Kara and Carly polished off a bottle of wine and blabbed about the new season of *Ozark*. Within minutes, I dozed off to the sound of their happy voices.

I'd left my cell phone next to the pillow on which my head was resting, and when it vibrated a short time later, I startled awake and answered without even bothering to check the caller ID.

"Hello?"

"How was dinner?"

I sat up. Too fast. My head swam. "How . . . how the hell did you get a direct line?"

He chuckled. "Do you know what one of my rudimentary sketches goes for on eBay these days?"

I ignored the question. "You saw the news about the hangman?"

"Talk about rudimentary. Made mine look like a Picasso."

"It appears you have an admirer. He took Peyton Bair's ear."

Kara and Carly had stopped talking. They were staring at me.

"I suspect he's as much of an admirer of yours as he is mine."

"Any idea why he's doing this?"

"Why not?"

Kara got up and started pacing.

"Can you help us find him?"

"Ah. I'll be your Hannibal Lecter if you'll be my Clarice Starling."

I sighed. "Why are you calling me?"

"I've missed you. Do you realize it's been ninety-seven days since we last sat across from each other?"

"I didn't know that."

"And because I heard that you'll be coming to see me soon, I wanted to give you something to think about during that long, tiresome drive."

Kara's cheeks had gone red and not because of the wine. She looked like she wanted to strangle me.

"And what would that be?"

"Tell the lieutenant to run my DNA again. If they do that, I'll give you a fourth name."

"Why would she do that?"

"Just tell her." There was a scraping sound like he'd pushed a chair away and stood up. "Oh, and Rich?"

"Yes?"

"Please give Carly Albright my very best."

The phone went dead.

Carly Albright *(Photo courtesy of the author)*

One of the mannequins left at the Chizmar residence *(Photo courtesy of Maryland State Police)*

Carly Albright's childhood home on Banyan Road *(Photo courtesy of the author)*

Excerpt from in-person interview with Brendan Watts, age 57, Parkersburg, West Virginia, recorded on June 16, 2020:

CHIZMAR: Mr. Watts, you were teammates with Joshua Gallagher on the wrestling team at Penn State University, correct?

WATTS: For one semester, yes.

CHIZMAR: Did you consider Gallagher a friend or merely a teammate?

WATTS: Usually, those two things are one and the same. You spend a lot of time together and you get to know each other really well. But Gallagher didn't even last a year, so it was different with him. I wouldn't say any of the guys were actually friends with him.

CHIZMAR: Any specific memories that you can share? The more detail, the better.

WATTS: Uh, he was a strong wrestler. Even injured, he put other guys on their backs. If he would've stuck it out, he might've made a name for himself . . . in a different way than he did.

CHIZMAR: Do you remember anything about his personality? Sense of humor? Temper? Any particular quirks or habits?

WATTS: He read a lot; I remember that. Some of the guys used to make fun of him. Nothing mean, just being typical jock wise-asses. Bennett Brown—he was one of the captains—used to call Gallagher "the Professor," because he always had a book with him. What else? *[pause]* I don't remember anything about his sense of humor. He was pretty quiet. He was more of a listener than a talker. Sometimes, you'd catch him staring at you, but a lot of freshmen did that. Most of the first-years were scared to death. D1 wrestling is no joke, and being away from home for the first time isn't easy.

CHIZMAR: Did you ever meet his girlfriend, Anna Garfield?

WATTS: Yeah, a few times. Man, she was gorgeous. And nice enough, but kind of controlling. The guys gave him hell for that, too.

CHIZMAR: In what ways was she controlling?

WATTS: Maybe "bossy" would be a better word to describe her. One time, she made him leave a party early just because someone spilled beer on her sweater. I was sitting right next to her when it happened and you could barely see the wet spot on her shoulder. It probably would've dried in like five minutes. But nope, that was it—"take me home," that sort of thing. Another time, back in the dorm, we were all going out and she made him change his shirt because the one he was wearing was all wrinkled and didn't have a collar.

CHIZMAR: How did Gallagher react when these things happened?

WATTS: He didn't say much, but you could tell that he didn't like it. You know, being told what to do?

THIRTEEN

HOW MONSTERS ARE MADE?

"It was also around this time that Henry began stalking humans."

1

The March 1993 issue of *Psychology Journal* featured a nineteen-page article entitled "How Monsters Are Made," written by prominent New York psychiatrist James L. Largent. Published almost a decade after Henry Metheny's arrest, the article was the result of a yearlong series of interviews Largent conducted with Metheny at Ware State Prison in Waycross, Georgia.

Convicted of the first-degree murders of Brennan Lloyd (1978), Carlton Bowers (1978), Patricia Cotter (1982), Noelle Stockton (1983), and Bernadette Palletto (1983), Metheny was extradited to the state of Georgia and sentenced to prison in December 1984 for five consecutive life terms.

As of summer 2022, Henry Metheny was seventy-four years old and in charge of the Ware State Prison library.

2

The following narratives have been culled from James L. Largent's extraordinary account of Henry Metheny's formative years. They are recounted here, summarized in my own words, with the author's written permission.

3

When Henry Metheny was eight years old, he moved to Parsons, Georgia, a small town on the shoreline of the Chattahoochee River, to live with his grandparents. Henry's father, Stuart, had abandoned his family earlier that summer and would never be heard from again. It was later learned that Stuart Metheny was killed by police in 1963 during an armed robbery standoff somewhere in East Texas. Henry's mother, Jean, suffered from a variety of ailments—both physical and mental—and felt she was no longer able to care for her only child, so she asked her parents to take him in until her health improved. Evidently, that improvement occurred a mere six months later, when she ran away with a traveling salesman named John Derry. She, too, was never heard from again.

Henry Metheny's grandparents, Allen and Nancy Opitz, were churchgoing, God-fearing people with a singularly harsh outlook on life. They believed that hard work and fervent prayer were the only ingredients necessary for contentment, and the earlier you got started, the better. Within a week of Henry's arrival, he was laboring in the Opitzes' family butchery, where he was responsible for hosing down blood and viscera matter from the killing stalls. By the time school began in the fall, he was slaughtering chickens.

Allen and Nancy Opitz also believed in severe punishment. When eight-year-old Henry brought home a C grade on a spelling quiz, he was forbidden to eat for two days. When ten-year-old Henry was caught smoking a hand-rolled cigarette with a classmate, he was beaten with a rake. A spiderweb of scars still covers his upper back and shoulders to this day. And when eleven-year-old Henry was found behind the Larsons' shed with his pants down around his ankles and Trudy Larson's dress hiked up around her hips, he was locked in a dark, uncleaned killing stall for seventy-two consecutive hours. When they finally let him out, he was naked and his entire body was smeared with dried blood and gore. He didn't utter a single word for the next two weeks.

By the time Henry Metheny was thirteen, he was killing small animals and runaway pets in the woods for pleasure, usually with a hunting knife he had received for his tenth birthday, but sometimes with a hammer he'd stolen from a neighbor's truck. He kept a collection of their bones in a shoebox hidden at the bottom of his closet.

It was also around this time that Henry began stalking people. Jennifer Hammel was the first. Jenny was fourteen, blonde, and a tomboy who loved fishing and frogging and hiking on the dirt trails that ran alongside the river. Whether she was alone or with friends, Henry watched her partake in all these activities and more on a near-daily basis. He learned where she would be and when she would be there. He found out where she lived, which second-floor window belonged to her bedroom, and at what time she usually showered and returned to her room wearing only a towel to brush her hair in front of the mirror.

Henry never once made his presence known to Jenny Hammel. He never once spoke to her or so much as waved to her in passing. He never caused her a single moment of harm or concern. But for nearly a month, most of his waking moments were spent fantasizing about what it would feel like to repeatedly stab her in the face with his hunting knife, and then slather her naked body with her own blood before having sex with her corpse. He kept a journal containing these thoughts hidden beneath a loose floorboard in the barn. There were also drawings and detailed diagrams. In Henry Metheny's fantasy world, he cooked and ate Jenny Hammel's flesh before disposing of her body in the swamp.

4

There were many others after Jennifer Hammel.

A middle-aged housewife from nearby Rock Mills who'd accidentally bumped fenders with a seventeen-year-old Henry Metheny at a traffic light. She'd had the prettiest smile and wavy auburn hair that reminded Metheny of his mother. They'd exchanged information on the side of the road and gone their separate ways. Metheny watched her from afar for almost two months before finally breaking into her house and masturbating in her bedroom closet while she slept. Her husband was out of town on a business trip. Before he snuck away, Metheny stole an expensive hairbrush from the top drawer of her vanity. For the next two weeks, at dinner each night, he ate strands of the woman's hair and washed it down with beer.

A year later, there was a man who called balls and strikes at a church league baseball game Metheny played in. There was something about the man's deep voice that made Metheny's heart beat a little quicker. For the next two weeks, he followed the man to and from the hardware store he worked at, and even attended Sunday morning worship at the fellow's Baptist church. While attempting to pick the lock on the man's basement door late one night, Metheny was attacked and bitten on the leg by the man's angry German shepherd. He managed to fight off the dog, but as he scrambled over the backyard fence, a series of gunshots rang out behind him. One of the bullets grazed his hip, leaving him with an ugly knot of scar tissue. Metheny never followed the man again after that.

On his eighteenth birthday, Metheny went out with a couple of friends for burgers and beers. Their waitress that night was new. Her name was Jodie and she'd just moved there from Florida with her older sister. Less than two weeks passed before Metheny slipped through her bedroom window while she was at work and stole a pair of dirty pink panties from her hamper. A week later, it was a toothbrush.

And on and on it went.

5

Henry Metheny was twenty-nine years old in 1978 when he committed his first murder—that of his best friend, Brennan Lloyd, in Macon, Georgia. During his confession, six years later, he told detectives that he'd killed Lloyd because of a drunken kiss and an argument about fishing tackle.

The argument came first.

Henry and Brennan got off work that night around six. They both loaded boxes onto tractor trailers for the same warehouse company and carpooled to save gas. After clocking out, they drove to a local bar, drank their dinner, and then went night fishing at a nearby creek. According to Henry, Brennan was in a bad mood right from the start.

"The whole way there, he was griping about my driving. *Slow down. Speed up. You drive like my aunt Sally.* I let him run his mouth because I was tired and drunk, but then once we got to the fishing hole, he started in on the bait."

Henry had brought along a ziplock bag of cheese balls (a five-star delicacy to Georgia catfish), but Brennan preferred to use night crawlers because they didn't stink so much. "I told him that if he wanted to use worms instead of cheese balls, he was welcome to dig some up himself because I wasn't going to. He grumbled about it some more and then proceeded to slide the biggest cheese ball in the bag onto his hook without so much as a thank-you or 'I'm sorry.'

"And wouldn't you know it, he snagged a big one on his first cast. Had to be at least a ten pounder. I saw its tail flapping around in the mud as he hauled it up the bank, and then *snap*, *splash*, it was gone. The line had broken. That's when he called me a jackass and accused me of bringing the wrong fishing rod.

"But the thing was, that was the only rod and reel Brennie had left. He'd lost the Daiwa with the twenty-pound test two weeks earlier in a dice game. I reminded him of that, but by that point he was too far gone to give a hoot, and off he went to sulk and drink some more. He was like that sometimes. A big baby."

Two things happened next that led to Brennan Lloyd's imminent death.

For the next half hour or so, Brennan sat on his ass about twenty yards downstream and pretended to fish. His line was in the water, but his hook was emptier than a church pew on Friday night. What Brennan was really doing was sipping away on a pint of whiskey he'd hidden in his waistband with no intention of sharing. By the time he'd polished off the bottle, he was approaching falling-down-drunk territory and feeling mischievous.

"The next thing I know, a bottle comes flying out of nowhere and conks me on the back of the head. It hurt bad, but the worst of it was it surprised me, and I let out a little squeal, like a piggy on a farm. Well, that got Brennie laughing, and when I cussed him out, he started laughing even harder and called me a pussy.

"The bump on my head made me mad. But being called a pussy? That made me a whole lot madder. So I cussed him out some more and eventually went back to fishing, telling him this was the last time I was bringing him along with me. But even after all that, he wasn't done. He snuck up and tackled me and we started wrestling, something we did a lot of back in those days. Usually, it was a coin flip to see who ended up on top, but not that night. Brennie was piss-drunk and I was just pissed off. It took about thirty seconds for me to pin him.

"That's when things got weird. Brennie was lying underneath me on his back, trying to catch his breath, dirt and spit all over his face, and he had this strange look in his eyes, like he'd just woken up from a dream. Before I knew what was happening, he lifted his head off the ground and kissed me. Right on the lips. I scrambled up as fast as I could, wiping my mouth with my sleeve, but he just laid there with that goofy look on his face."

Henry Metheny then climbed into his truck and drove away, leaving his friend alone at the creek. During one of the interview sessions, he admitted to James L. Largent that he had a "boner the size of a wrench in his pants" and felt sick and angry and confused—both at Brennan Lloyd and himself. Instead of driving home, he went straight to Brennan's garage apartment on Henderson Lane. Once there, he used the spare key from underneath the doormat to unlock the door, hid inside a closet, and waited.

It took Brennan forty-five minutes to walk the nearly three miles home. Once inside, he urinated all over the toilet seat in the bathroom and then collapsed onto the bed. He didn't notice the closet door was ajar. Minutes later, Henry Metheny crept out of the closet, an eight-inch pearl-handle hunting knife clutched in his hand, and stabbed his friend by his own estimation more than fifty times in the face and torso. Then he castrated him. He threw the severed penis in the creek for the catfish

("How's that for a motherfuckin' cheese ball?" he muttered as he did the dirty deed) and buried the body deep in the woods.

It would be six long years before Brennan Lloyd's family learned the truth of what really happened that night.

6

The internet was in its infancy in 1993 when Largent's article was first published in *Psychology Journal*. I didn't stumble upon it until four years later when, on a whim, I did a Google search for Henry Metheny. It was one of only five articles that were listed.

The day I found it, heart racing, I immediately scanned the piece for mentions of Aberdeen Proving Ground, Edgewood Arsenal, and based on completely illogical reasoning, my own name. APG and Edgewood popped up a handful of times, but that was all. The meat of Largent's story focused on Henry Metheny's formative years and the many types of abuse he had suffered.

For years following the incident, I'd feared that I would one day open the door to find a stone-faced detective bearing news that Metheny had confessed to attacking me that long-ago August night and spewing a succession of rapid-fire questions—and condemnations—as to why I had failed to report him. In another nightmare scenario, I opened that same door to find an unshaven veteran reporter who had tracked down a number of Metheny's Aberdeen coworkers and, to a man, they had all named me as Henry Metheny's closest friend.

"*If you were his best friend,*" the reporter conjured by my imagination asked, "*why didn't you stop him?*"

Eventually, I began to realize—not without some relief—that none of these things were going to happen. My actions from back then would never be questioned; my name would never be mentioned—in print or otherwise—in relation to Henry Metheny; my darkest secret would never be revealed.

If the passage of time had taught me anything, it was this:

Henry Metheny had forgotten all about me.

Henry Metheny's second-floor apartment in
Havre de Grace *(Photo courtesy of* The Aegis*)*

Brennan Lloyd, several months before his murder
(Photo courtesy of Julianne Lloyd)

Excerpt from Edgewood: Looking Back, *by Richard Chizmar,*
pages 220–221:

The landmarks of our youth were etched in my memory like sacred words upon a gravestone. The winds of time might smooth their edges, but they would never disappear. At least not in my lifetime.

The house on Hanson Road: the center of my universe.

The weeping willow tree in the side yard: my safe haven.

The half-moon-shaped section of sidewalk at the junction of Hanson and Tupelo: home to my lemonade stand and guardian of my initials.

The bright yellow fire hydrant at the corner of Tupelo and Cherry Court: our official launching point for jumping ramps and our secret rendezvous spot long before cell phones made it easy to find each other.

The witchgrass covered hills of Cedar Drive: while only two blocks away from my house, it might as well have been an ocean's voyage, a kind of no-man's-land where few rules existed and time seemed to stand still on long summer afternoons.

The manhole cover in Bayberry Court: home plate and a monument to glory.

The library: the quiet oasis where I fell in love with words.

Bullen Field: the patch of dirt and rocks where I learned to turn a double play.

The Meyers House: brooding, patient, eternally haunted.

And then there was Water Tower Hill, maybe the most special of them all:

where I'd learned how to sled and hurl snowballs and dream the impossible;

where my father had once slung his strong arm around my shoulders, the December air cold enough to see his breath, and told me to "look around, son, the world is a magical place if only you believe enough to search for it; we are surrounded by miracles," and in that moment, it had felt like we were the only two people alive in the world;

and where, on the verge of making my college decision, I'd once sat upon the tower's rusting metal spokes, legs dangling, sipping a warm beer and staring out at the shrinking town in which I'd grown up as the streetlights blinked on, tired mothers opening and closing screen doors, calling in their children for supper, a melancholy, lonely feeling hanging heavy in the air all around me, thinking: *You'll be okay, Rich. Don't be scared. It's time to go. You'll be okay.*

FOURTEEN

FACE-TO-FACE

"I want the world to see."

1

Traffic was light on Tuesday morning, and the drive to the Cumberland Penitentiary in western Maryland took only two hours and forty-five minutes. Normally, it was a three-hour-plus slog, so I took that as a good sign.

My brain was on overload, and even after having not made the trip in several months, it felt like my truck was steering itself. I ate pistachios to stay awake and listened to an old *Nebraska* CD during the first half of the drive, Springsteen's storyteller's voice soothing my frazzled nerves; the rest of the time I drove in silence. The note card reading *He's wearing a mask underneath his mask* was taped to my dashboard above the radio. From time to time, I found myself mouthing the words.

Lieutenant McClernan had called late last night to tell me that I'd been given the official go-ahead to meet with Joshua Gallagher at eleven this morning. If I couldn't swing that, I would have to wait until Thursday afternoon. No explanation was offered as to why that was the case.

After agreeing to take the meeting—only after Carly offered to stick around the house all day with Kara—I told the lieutenant what Gallagher had said to me on the phone about retesting his DNA, but she didn't seem very interested.

"I once had a guy swear up and down to me that he wasn't human and that if we x-rayed his head, we would see the proof because his skull was shaped differently than any other person on Earth. Gallagher's just playing games with you, like he always does. You really need to understand that about him."

And then she'd asked if I could compile a list of all the people I knew who were experienced hunters. Because of the disabled trail cam and the likely surveillance perch discovered in Ken Klein's backyard tree, they felt it was an avenue worth exploring. I had to admit it was a pretty brilliant deduction, and I mentally kicked myself for not having thought of it earlier.

I made the list as I drove. It was a short one: the McGirks, Todd Simmons, Dave Pruitt, Pat Pollard, Alex Baliko, Bob Martin . . . that was all I could think of off the top of my head. I'd known these people for most of my life. I couldn't imagine anything useful coming from it.

There *had* been some interesting developments, though, in the past couple of days.

A man from Michigan who mailed Gallagher lengthy handwritten letters on a weekly basis had scrawled a hangman figure at the end of one of his fawning missives. It was dated back in May, well before Peyton Bair was killed. When detectives questioned him, he told them it'd been a joke, and that Gallagher and he were pen pals and he was just trying to jump-start a game. The Flint Police Department was giving the guy a closer look.

There was a Connecticut woman who often sent Gallagher half-nude sketches of herself. Six months ago, she'd professed her love for him in a Hallmark greeting card and hinted at seeking revenge in his name. When detectives paid the woman a visit at her home, they'd found two framed photographs on the mantel above her fireplace. The first photo was of NASCAR legend Dale Earnhardt. The second was Joshua Gallagher. In many ways, the woman was an unlikely suspect. She was forty-three years old and widowed. A substitute teacher and respected member of the PTA, she was a mother to two well-behaved teenaged sons. Then again, she was also an accomplished triathlete in peak physical condition, towered over most women and many men at six-one, and had a lengthy arrest record that included charges of breaking and entering, assault and battery, and stalking and harassment. Drawing a direct parallel to Joshua Gallagher, she had once been kicked out of college for behavioral issues involving a former lover.

Closer to home, detectives had discovered that one of the most active and provocative participants on the *Boogeyman Lives* message board was a nineteen-year-old Fallston resident named Tucker Hipson. He lived in his parents' basement and went by the screen name CHIZMAR-SUCKS. Detective Gonzalez had spoken with the young man and his parents on two separate occasions, and although Hipson had said all the right things and appeared to have solid alibis for the nights of Annie Riggs's and Peyton Bair's murders, Gonzalez still felt something wasn't quite right about him. Hipson's arrest record was clean. He did, however, have a valid State of Maryland hunting license. Gonzalez planned to speak with him again in the near future.

2

Cumberland Penitentiary was a federally funded maximum security prison that housed an all-male population of just over 1,200 inmates. More than 90 percent of the prisoners had been convicted of violent crimes. Approximately 22 percent were serving life sentences. Accessing the interview rooms was much like entering a busy airport shortly after 9/11.

I showed my identification and signed the logbook, and the guard at the main entrance—a bearded man I didn't recognize—gave me the customary pat-down. After placing my cell phone and keys in a secure locker and removing my shoes for inspection, another guard—this one I did know; his name was Elgin and he was a hoot with a never-ending supply of dirty jokes—guided me through a full body scanner. I was allowed one small notebook and two felt-tipped pens. The interviews were recorded by prison cameras mounted on the wall in each room. I had instant access to the digital files. Elgin asked if I'd heard the one about the horny nun and the alligator (I hadn't) as he escorted me down a long hallway with yellow-painted walls to Interrogation Room C, where I sat behind a metal desk that was bolted to the floor and waited for the prisoner to be brought in.

3

A short time later, two guards led Joshua Gallagher into the room. I vaguely remembered the tall guard with bad skin. The other man was a stranger. His eyes were wide and his uniform buttons looked brand-new. It could have been his first day, for all I knew.

Joshua Gallagher had changed even more since the last time I'd seen him. I wouldn't call it a transformation—the changes were more subtle than that—but he looked stronger and brighter somehow. There was no red around his startling gray irises and he wasn't squinting. He appeared well rested. His teeth even looked whiter. Maybe it was his aura, if you believed in such things. All I knew was that for a brief moment, as he sat down in the chair opposite of me, I felt like I was looking at Gallagher's younger brother (the one he didn't actually have), and then he spoke and he was the old Josh I knew so well.

"It's good to see you, Rich. I'd shake your hand, but as you can see . . ." He held up his shackled hands. ". . . I'm a little tied up right now."

It was a familiar greeting, Gallagher's way of breaking the ice. A serial killer dad joke.

"It's been a while, Josh. How are you?"

I noticed he wasn't wearing aftershave. That odd, earthy scent caressed me from across the table. There was nothing else like it.

"I'd say the more important question is . . . how are *you*?"

4

The following is an abridged conversation between Richard Chizmar and Joshua Gallagher, inmate #AC4311920. It took place at the Cumberland Penitentiary on Tuesday, June 14, 2022.

CHIZMAR: I've been better, but we're not here to talk about me.

GALLAGHER: Ahh, but that's not entirely true now, is it? We've always shared the intricacies of our lives with each other.

CHIZMAR: I guess so.

GALLAGHER: So, then, why would we stop now?

CHIZMAR: Because someone you've inspired is killing innocent women.

GALLAGHER: Based on the mannequins your wife found in the yard the other night, I'd wager that we each bear some measure of responsibility. After all, the mannequins came straight from your *New York Times* bestselling imagination. Not mine.

CHIZMAR: We're not going to get anywhere until I tell you everything, are we?

GALLAGHER: [chuckles] Probably not.

CHIZMAR: Okay, here goes. I'm a fucking mess. The guy knows where we live. He's watching us. He left Anne Riggs's body—what was left of it—in my front yard. The house is surrounded by press 24/7. And everyone's acting as if I'm the one who's responsible.

GALLAGHER: Where does the investigation stand?

CHIZMAR: [pause] The guy's been very careful. They don't have much to work with. That's all I really know.

GALLAGHER: Or is that all you're willing to share with me?

CHIZMAR: Look, I came here for your help . . . whatever that might be. I can tell you anything you want to know to the best of my knowledge, but I don't have access to the case file.

GALLAGHER: The police asked me their questions already. I answered truthfully. So, how can I help *you*?

CHIZMAR: What did they ask you?

GALLAGHER: If I knew who the killer was.

CHIZMAR: Do you?

GALLAGHER: No. I do not.

CHIZMAR: Would you tell me if you did?

GALLAGHER: [sigh] I'm honestly offended you would ask me that.

CHIZMAR: Okay then . . . what else?

GALLAGHER: They wanted to know if the killer had contacted me in any way.

CHIZMAR: And?

GALLAGHER: He has not. Although, they stopped my mail, so I have no way of knowing as of now.

CHIZMAR: What else did they ask you?

GALLAGHER: If there was anyone in my past who I believed capable of killing these women. Again, I told them no. Then they asked if there was anyone I had corresponded with during my time here who I believed was capable. I gave them one name, but I think he's already been cleared.

CHIZMAR: What was the name?

GALLAGHER: [pause] Benjamin Thacker.

CHIZMAR: Interesting. Why him?

GALLAGHER: He writes long letters that, on the surface, say very little. But something about the cadence of his prose is off. It's unsettled, and some of the words he chooses to describe certain things are very telling. His letters remind me of my old journal entries. Like there are two different people writing them, wrestling for control.

CHIZMAR: Can I read his letters?

GALLAGHER: You would have to ask the lieutenant. I no longer have them.

CHIZMAR: Did they ask you anything else?

GALLAGHER: They asked if I thought *you* could be involved in any way.

CHIZMAR: [voice raised] What?! Who?! Who asked that?!

GALLAGHER: One of the detectives. I don't remember his name.

CHIZMAR: Gonzalez? Short. Mustache.

GALLAGHER: Hmmm. I don't believe so.

CHIZMAR: And what did you tell them?

GALLAGHER: That you are certainly clever enough, but have no reason to do such a thing.

CHIZMAR: What did they say to that?

GALLAGHER: Nothing.

CHIZMAR: [pause] Why do you think the killer dismembered Anne Riggs's body and then decided to pose Peyton Bair after removing her ear?

GALLAGHER: I think he was angry at Riggs.

CHIZMAR: Because she'd escaped from you all those years ago?

GALLAGHER: Presumably. What else is there?

CHIZMAR: Do you believe I'm in any danger? My family?

GALLAGHER: Probably not Kara and the boys.

CHIZMAR: So just me, in other words?

GALLAGHER: I'm really not sure. If I had to wager a guess, I'd say no. I think this is as much about you as it is me. But I'm a machinist—or rather, I *was* a machinist—not a psychiatrist, so what do I know. This isn't the movies, Rich. [pause] Unless . . .

CHIZMAR: Unless?

GALLAGHER: It just dawned on me. Unless he's *jealous* in some way?

CHIZMAR: Of what?

GALLAGHER: Jealous of you for sharing such a close relationship with me. Jealous of me for having someone of your stature to tell my story.

CHIZMAR: I have to say, that's an angle I hadn't really thought of. [pause] Do you have any thoughts about the hangman figure the killer left on Peyton Bair's hand?

GALLAGHER: I thought it was amusing. And interesting.

CHIZMAR: How so?

GALLAGHER: That's another reason I thought about Benjamin Thacker. He's a man of words. Whoever drew the hangman game on that girl's hand is someone with a passion for words.

CHIZMAR: Any thoughts on the seven blank letters?

GALLAGHER: I've actually given that a lot of consideration.

CHIZMAR: And?

GALLAGHER: I assume someone has brought it to your attention that both your first and last names contain seven letters?

CHIZMAR: Of course.

GALLAGHER: I don't think that's the winner, though. Too easy.

CHIZMAR: One of the detectives suggested C-O-P-Y-C-A-T.

GALLAGHER: Ridiculous.

CHIZMAR: I agree.

GALLAGHER: Whoever is doing this is much more than a mere imitator. The compulsion is real. And it's getting stronger.

CHIZMAR: You think he'll do it again?

GALLAGHER: [nods] Soon.

CHIZMAR: How did you know Carly Albright was at my house when you called?

GALLAGHER: How do you think?

CHIZMAR: I think you saw her on the news.

GALLAGHER: That's certainly the most likely explanation. So, did you tell Lieutenant McClernan what I asked you to tell her?

CHIZMAR: I did.

GALLAGHER: And her response?

CHIZMAR: [pause] She said she would consider it.

GALLAGHER: Did she really?

CHIZMAR: She thinks you're playing games.

GALLAGHER: Of course she does.

CHIZMAR: Are you?

GALLAGHER: Games keep us young at heart, Rich. They keep us sharp.

CHIZMAR: Games get old and tiresome.

GALLAGHER: Sometimes . . . and sometimes new rules are required to freshen things up a bit.

CHIZMAR: Speaking of fresh, I have to say you look good. Well rested. They must have improved your diet.

GALLAGHER: It's almost time.

CHIZMAR: Time for what?

GALLAGHER: I'm changing, Rich.

CHIZMAR: I can see that.

GALLAGHER: Oh, but I want the whole world to see . . .

Cumberland Penitentiary *(Photo courtesy of* The Cumberland Times*)*

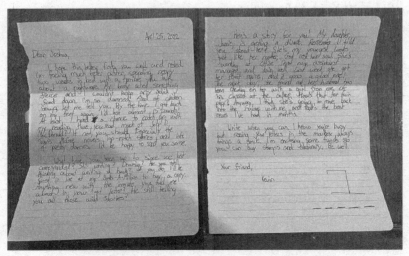

Joshua Gallagher fan mail featuring a hangman figure *(Photo courtesy of Maryland State Police)*

Note card reminder on the dashboard of Chizmar's truck *(Photo courtesy of the author)*

Excerpt from telephone interview with James L. Largent, retired psychiatrist, state of New York, recorded October 14, 2019:

LARGENT: Atkinson was a lot like Bundy in that regard. A frenzy killer. Multiple victims within a short period of time, often during the same night. Extreme sexual compulsion and loss of control. Atkinson was a hunter. Always searching for his next victim. Had he not made the mistake that led to his arrest, he would have gone on killing for decades, I'm sure of it.

CHIZMAR: I was surprised by how little you've written about Joshua Gallagher. How familiar were you with the Edgewood murders when they occurred in 1988?

LARGENT: The Boogeyman murders captivated the entire country that summer, and I was no exception. But as luck would have it, someone beat me to the punch and wrote a real insider's view of the case. [laughs] All kidding aside, Richard, you did a terrific job with your book. I'm anxious to read the follow-up once you've completed it. I assume that's the reason for your email. Research for the sequel?

CHIZMAR: [pause] Yes, exactly. What are your current thoughts regarding Gallagher?

LARGENT: Joshua Gallagher is what I call an atypical visionary serial murderer. He believed—through his visions—that he was being instructed to kill. He most likely suffers from some form of psychosis that alters his perception of reality. Where Gallagher differs from other killers in this category—the Son of Sam, for example—is the fact that he went to great lengths to cover up his crimes and elude capture. Gallagher was a great many things, but a disorganized killer was not one of them. This is all textbook analysis, of course. I imagine you could teach me a thing or two about Mr. Gallagher.

CHIZMAR: I read an article you wrote about a man named Henry Metheny. This was years ago and I don't recall many of the details, but I've always been curious because Metheny lived in Maryland for a number of years. What can you tell me about him?

LARGENT: Metheny was a fascinating subject. Much more controlled than, say, Atkinson. Horribly abused as a child: physically, mentally, sexually. Beginning as a teenager, he experienced lengthy, extremely detailed fantasies that involved taking control over strangers. Somewhat surprisingly, it took him years to finally act upon these fantasies.

CHIZMAR: It's my understanding that you interviewed Henry Metheny face-to-face on numerous occasions. What kind of impression did he make on you?

LARGENT: Metheny was often talkative and could speak on a variety of subjects when he wanted to. He was also rather moody. [pause] Other than that, in person, I found him rather . . . ordinary, I suppose. He'd killed five people that the authorities knew of, yet he couldn't even begin to articulate why he'd done it. His facial expressions rarely changed. His voice was monotone. He had absolutely no remorse for his victims. No guilt whatsoever for his actions. Even after all those hours of research, Henry Metheny remained very much a mystery to me . . .

FIFTEEN

CHIZAPALOOZA

"A dark shadow fell upon me."

1

The drive home that afternoon felt endless.

I kept replaying my conversation with Joshua Gallagher inside my head. As usual, I was left with the nagging suspicion that he had tiptoed around something of vital importance—all while saying nothing at all. It was like that with him. He was a puzzle. Some days, the pieces fit. Other times, no matter how much you twisted and turned them, it was like trying to fit a square peg into a round hole. He liked to dance around things, answer questions with questions of his own. It was maddening. You had to keep pushing and prodding, but at the same time, you had to remain patient and not show weakness—the one thing he craved, even now.

I was barely out of the correctional facility's parking lot when Lieutenant McClernan called to ask how the meeting had gone. I didn't know what to tell her, so I pulled a Gallagher and encouraged her to watch the interview video and get back to me with what *she* thought. McClernan promised she would and hurried off the phone before I could ask the two questions that were weighing the most heavily on my mind:

Who was the detective that had asked Gallagher if he thought I was involved with the murders?

And why in the hell would he ask such a thing?

I almost called her back once I got on the freeway but decided against it. She had more important things to deal with today.

The three mannequins that had been hung from the sycamore tree in my side yard had been traced back to a flea market superstore in Hanover, Pennsylvania, called the Black Rose. The cashier who had rung up the purchase was seventy years old and remembered very little of the person who had bought them. He was male, Caucasian, somewhere between twenty-five and forty, and unshaven. That was about it, narrowing it down to countless individuals. McClernan didn't believe it was a coincidence—nor did I, for that matter—that the mannequins had been obtained in the same town where Joshua Gallagher and his family had lived at the time of his arrest. The Black Rose was a sprawling two-hundred-thousand-square-foot maze of independently leased booths and display lots, most of which were not under any type of video surveillance. There were, however, security cameras positioned outside in the parking lot. Detectives were currently in the process of tracking down the appropriate footage—after all, those mannequins weren't transported out to the lot in little gift bags meant for artisanal soap.

Detective Gonzalez called a short time later—I have to admit I almost didn't answer the call—but he never once mentioned my meeting with Gallagher. "What can you tell me about your neighbor Ken Klein?" He was on speakerphone in his car. There was an annoying echo.

"Not much. Seems like a nice enough guy. He's a talker."

"That he is. Anything about him strike you as . . . unusual?"

I thought about it. "I mean . . . no more than the next guy. Like I said, he's a talker. He tends to show up when I'm outside doing yard work. Bends my ear for a while and goes back home again. Kara thinks he's lonely."

"You think he watches for you?"

I shrugged my shoulders even though Gonzalez couldn't see me. "I don't know if he's watching, but he sure knows when I'm out there. I wouldn't be surprised if his other neighbors say the same thing." I hesitated for a moment, then said, "He asked the other day if we had a gun in the house."

"Why did he ask that?"

"He said I needed to protect my family."

"When was this?"

"A few days ago, I think."

"What did you tell him?"

"That we were good. I didn't go into any details."

Gonzalez was quiet for a moment. I was about to ask if I'd lost him when he spoke again. "Klein was in the crowd videos we took on the day you discovered Anne Riggs's body. People came and went, but not Klein. The guy never left. He's also a regular visitor at the memorial in your front yard. My detectives tell me he hasn't missed a single day."

"That doesn't surprise me." I wondered what his detectives said about my daily visits to Annie Riggs's memorial.

"He also has quite the library in his home. A whole row of shelves devoted to true crime and serial killer books. Appears to be a special interest of his."

"Is he . . . do you consider him a suspect?"

"I consider him a person of interest," Gonzalez said without hesitation. "I can't see him climbing that tree in his backyard and spying on your house, much less murdering two people. Then again, stranger things have happened. I will say he definitely has an unhealthy interest in the case . . . and you, in particular."

"Me?"

Another pause. "You should know that he practically has a shrine set up in the corner of his library. Copies of all of your books with those little 'autographed' stickers on the covers and what looks like a bunch of promotional items. He even has a stack of magazines and some photographs."

"Of me?"

"A couple from a book signing. I asked and he said they were taken at the Bel Air Barnes and Noble. There was another one from what looked like a movie premiere."

"I guess he's a big fan . . . I had no idea." My voice sounded calm enough, but just the thought of what Gonzalez was saying gave me the creeps. "So . . . what happens next?"

"Not much. We'll keep eyes on him for a while. If he comes over again and chats you up, let me know."

"Will do," I said, and we ended the call.

2

After saying goodbye to the detective, I connected to Bluetooth and listened to a podcast for a while to pass the time. Bad idea. Fifteen minutes in, a guy I'd barely known in high school was interviewed. He claimed I was a loner and obsessed with horror even back then. And then he told a story about me bringing a Jason Voorhees hockey mask to school one day and scaring my classmates. What he failed to mention was that it was Halloween and all the kids in my homeroom had dressed up for a class photo. Shortly after, when the podcast host started referring to me as "Creepy Chiz," I turned it off.

And called my wife.

All this time, I'd been stalling, but I knew I couldn't put it off any longer.

She answered on the first ring. "Hey. How did it go?"

"Okay, I guess. Glad it's over."

"Me too," she said. "Even gladder if you hadn't gone in the first place."

"Well . . . hopefully, I won't need to go back for a while."

She sighed. "I wish I could believe you mean that."

"I do," I said. "The whole thing was . . . exhausting."

"It's *always* exhausting, Rich! And then you come home a different person. Distant. Distracted. Quiet. I hate it."

Trying to change the subject: "Anyway . . . I'm on 70 around Frederick, so I should be there in less than an hour and a half. Unless I run into traffic."

There was a long pause. Then: "Did he say anything? Anything at all that might help the police?"

I wanted to lie to her, to claim that my visit had been helpful to the investigation—that by talking to Gallagher today, I had uncovered crucial information that would help catch a killer and save innocent lives.

But in the end, I simply told her the truth. I didn't really know anything.

3

For the second evening in a row, we ate dinner on the screened-in back porch. Spicy fish tacos, fresh salsa and guacamole, and a frosty pitcher of margaritas. Suffice to say, there were no leftovers.

Billy was playing poker at a friend's house and wouldn't be home until late, so it was just the three of us again. Kara and Carly were sunburned and chatty. Mostly, we talked about their day—they'd binge-watched the first few episodes of a series called *Hightown* and lounged by the pool catching up on gossip—but eventually, the conversation turned to the big event scheduled for tomorrow night.

In the spring of 2017, when *Gwendy's Button Box*, a novella I'd cowritten with my friend Stephen King, became a surprise bestseller, I'd celebrated by inviting over a handful of good friends for a bonfire. Beers were consumed, stories were told, car keys were hidden, and the bonfire soon became a sleepover in the grassy field beside our pond. The next June we did it all over again—this time with tents and food and a few more guests—and it was promptly christened (not by me) Chizapalooza.

Tomorrow night would mark our five-year anniversary—we'd skipped 2020 due to COVID—and the confirmed guest list included such beloved childhood friends as Jimmy and Jeffrey Cavanaugh, Brian Anderson, Steve Sines, Bill Caughron, and Bob Eiring. Sadly, regular attendees the Pruitts and the Crawfords were out of town on family vacations.

I'd initially argued—for the better part of the past week—that this year's soiree should be canceled because of everything that was going on.

Wouldn't it be in seriously bad taste to host a party when two people were dead and the local community was in such turmoil? But Kara had disagreed and made repeated arguments that this year, more than ever, the show needed to go on. It wasn't hard to figure out her reasoning. Anything that might distract me from Joshua Gallagher and the recent murders—even for just one night—was a good thing.

"You know how much everyone looks forward to this," she said. "The Cavanaughs can't cancel their airline tickets this late. And besides, Brian's already on his way from West Virginia. He's staying at his parents' tonight."

"I'm really not in the mood," I said.

"All the more reason to do it."

"If the press finds out, they'll crucify me."

"They won't find out," Carly said. "I'll pick up all the goodies you need. We can have the guys park at the school, and I'll taxi them right up to your gate. No one will even know they're here."

"You need to do something fun for a change," Kara said. "It's like you're being held hostage in your own house."

I slouched in my chair and let out a deep breath. As usual, when Kara and Carly teamed up against me, I didn't stand a fighting chance.

4

I was in the garage looking for camping gear when my phone buzzed.

I slid it out of my pocket and checked the screen, figuring it was one of the guys letting me know their travel plans.

It wasn't.

It was an Edgewood number that looked familiar.

"Hello?"

Someone breathing on the other end.

"Okay, I'm hanging up."

"Mr. Chizmar?"

He sounded different, but I recognized the voice of my mentee right away.

"Sam? Hey . . . what's up? Are you okay?"

"I'm sorry to have to tell you this . . . but my parents don't want me to see you for a while, so I can't come to lunch next week."

I could tell he was upset. We'd both been looking forward to the next writing session. "What did they say exactly?"

"That it was best if we took a break until things calmed down." He lowered his voice. "I think it's because of those stupid cops."

"What stupid cops?"

"The ones who came to my house. They were here twice."

I already knew that Detective Gonzalez had spoken with Sam's parents, but I hadn't heard anything about a repeat visit. "It's okay. You can still email me your stories, Sam."

"It's not okay." He coughed into the phone, and I could tell he was trying not to cry. "I finished the first chapter of what I think could be a novel. I really wanted to show you."

"So send it right over. I'll read it tonight."

"I appreciate that, but it's not the same." I heard someone talking in the background, and then: "I have to go now, Mr. Chizmar."

"Okay. Thanks for calling to—"

But he was already gone.

5

That night in bed, the television playing, my laptop open in front of me:

"I'm glad you changed your mind about the bonfire."

"Did I have a choice?"

"Of course," Kara said. "You always have a choice."

"If you say so."

"It was nice of Carly to offer to stay and help."

"Europe. Alaska. Australia. Our guest room. She's really making the rounds."

"She seems to have found some peace."

"I hope so. I hope she still feels it when she goes home again."

"I think that's what she's working toward. Finding her place in the world again. At least, that's how I see it." Kara shuddered and hugged herself. "I can't even imagine what I would do if I lost you."

"No need to. You're stuck with me for a long time."

"I better be."

I closed the laptop and placed it on the nightstand.

"Any sign of the Boogeyman?"

I looked at her in the glow of the TV screen. "Did you really just say that?"

"It was a serious question. Kind of."

"Uh-huh. No sign of him on the security cameras, if that's what you mean. I'm sure he's far away from here by now."

"That's what you said last time." She rolled onto her side, facing me. "What was it like today?"

"Seeing Gallagher?"

"Yes."

"Pretty much the same as it always is. Frustrating."

"Were you scared?"

"No."

"Why not?"

"He's all chained up. The guards are there. You know that."

"If he wasn't chained, would you be scared?"

I gave it some thought. "I don't know. Probably."

"Sometimes . . . when I think about you being so close to him, I worry that you might catch something . . . some kind of germ that'll make you turn into someone like him." Her eyes were closing. "I have . . . nightmares about it . . . sometimes."

Five seconds later, she was asleep.

6

Carly caught up with me the next morning after breakfast.

"I was dying to ask about it during dinner, but I knew better than to bring it up." She was sitting outside in the breezeway, drinking coffee and reading the newspaper.

"I figured as much." I sat down across from her.

"Well, tell me how it *really* went. And not the Kara version."

"It . . . went." I rubbed the sleep out of my eyes. "I really need to watch the video. Sometimes it's like that. A blur."

"Can I watch it with you?"

"Sure."

"Would he approve of that?"

"Gallagher? I honestly don't know. Might depend on his mood."

"What kind of mood was he in yesterday?"

I thought about it. "Playful."

She made a face. "'Playful' sounds like such a dirty word when you use it to describe someone like Joshua Gallagher."

"You asked."

"Okay . . . playful how?"

"Just some of the things he said. The way he said them. He was try-ing to keep me off-balance."

"Was he any help at all?"

"I don't think so. I don't think he knows anything." I shrugged. "I could be wrong, though. I really need to watch the tape."

"Today?"

"Tomorrow, probably. I have phone calls with Sales and Marketing and the publicity folks at Simon and Schuster. They want to talk about new dates for the appearances we postponed. I have a feeling it's going to take most of the afternoon."

"They're not wasting any time, huh?"

"They've actually been pretty great. They're looking at dates in Au-gust and September now, so it's not like they're rushing me."

"Well, that's good to hear." She took a sip of coffee. "I was surprised Kara asked about Gallagher when you called yesterday. She told me she hasn't done that in a long time."

"She used to in the beginning." JJ burst out of the doggy door and waddled over to be petted. "But that initial curiosity is long gone. She says he's poison. Most of the time, she doesn't even want to hear his name."

"You know that day will come, right?"

"What do you mean?"

"The day when it's not just Kara but pretty much the whole world who isn't interested in hearing his name anymore. And then he'll just fade away into history like all the others. Have you thought about what you're going to do when that happens?"

I didn't even try to disguise my irritation. "I've written two books about the guy. That's it."

"Do you remember a long time ago when you told me that a fiction writer is always writing, even when they're not? That you might spend five or six months writing a book, but that didn't account for the other two or three months you walked around with the story forming itself inside your head?"

"I remember."

"All these years . . . ever since you were twenty-two and living with your folks . . . all this time, you've never stopped writing the Boogeyman's story inside your head."

7

The gang started showing up at around four that afternoon.

One by one, they texted to say that they were pulling into the parking lot at Southampton Middle School, a mile down the road. Each time they did, Carly hopped into her Hummer and played shuttle driver, the guys taking turns lying down in the back seat to avoid being seen by any press.

Brian Anderson brought a box of bright pink T-shirts with CHIZAPALOOZA 2022 printed on the back. Bob Eiring carried with him a Tupperware container full of homemade Cajun smoked sausage. Bill Caughron showed up with three fishing poles and a telescope. Having arrived at the school just minutes apart, Steve Sines and Jeff Cavanaugh shared a ride to the house. While ducking down in Carly's back seat, they accidentally knocked heads together. Hard. Steve had a bump the size of a walnut on his forehead. Jeff's left eye was swollen halfway shut and was already turning an ugly shade of black and blue. True to form, Jimmy Cavanaugh was the last to arrive, rolling in at just past six o'clock. He'd gotten lost coming from the airport. Again. It had become a yearly occurrence, so none of us were worried.

Once we were all gathered together in the family room, beers were passed around and the conversation quickly turned to the murders.

"I think it's someone you know," Steve said.

Brian rolled his eyes. "See, that's why you're a fireman and not a cop."

"I'd be a great cop."

"You'd be Barney fucking Fife."

"Hey," I said. "I love Barney Fife."

"Are they any closer to catching someone?" Jimmy asked.

"I honestly have no idea."

"I think Steve's right," Bill said. "It's definitely someone you know. That would fit the pattern from the last time this happened."

Bill Caughron had two nicknames growing up. The first was Cliffie, inspired by the obnoxious know-it-all mailman from the 1980s sitcom *Cheers*. Like Cliff Clavin, Bill Caughron was a self-proclaimed expert on pretty much everything and anything, and he wasn't shy about letting folks know it. When someone asked him how he knew so much about rare birds or forensic science or the mating habits of South American reptiles, the answer was always the same: "I read about it somewhere." Over the years, we'd learned to take everything he said with a grain of salt.

But the nickname that had stuck with Bill Caughron from the early days of middle school and which would probably be etched upon his gravestone was the supremely indelicate "Fat Bill." As kids, he earned this rather unkind moniker by simply being taller and bigger than the rest of us. It wasn't until we were all together at this same event last summer that the nickname finally received its proper scrutiny. When Bill announced that he had to "take a leak" and headed for the woods, I watched him make his way over to the tree line and said to the others, "You know what, guys . . . I hate to say it, but I'm not sure Bill ever was fat." Jimmy nodded thoughtfully and said, "I've often thought the same thing. I'm pretty sure he's just big-boned." Bob agreed and asked, "Should we stop calling him Fat Bill?" Brian answered for all of us with typical Brian Anderson grace: "Fuck no." And that was that. Discussion over.

"The killer could even be one of us." We all turned and looked at Bob Eiring. The expression on his face was deadpan; I couldn't tell if he was serious or not.

"Now *that* would be a helluva plot twist," Billy said.

"My vote goes to Brian," Jeff said. "He tried to drown me when we were kids."

"How many times do I have to tell you? That was an accident. I had a cramp."

"I'm thinking Chiz." Bob started pacing back and forth in front of me. "It's always the quiet ones you have to worry about."

I laughed, but inside I was cringing. Bob's comment hit a little too close to home.

"What if he shows up tonight?" Bill said.

"Who?" I asked. "The killer?"

"Yeah."

"Let's hope he doesn't."

Jimmy flexed a flabby bicep. "He shows up, he's all mine."

"Twenty bucks you run and hide in the house," Brian said, and belched.

"I'll take it," Jimmy said. "Twenty bucks is all it costs to bang your mom these days."

"That's funny," Brian said, not missing a beat. "I heard twenty bucks is all it costs to bang your mom *and* your sister."

Back and forth they went—sisters, wives, even grandmothers entering the mix—until the front door suddenly swung wide open and the dogs erupted in a cacophony of frenzied barking.

The banter halted midsentence and all heads turned in time to watch my son Noah stroll into the foyer, a knapsack slung over his shoulder and a big goofy grin on his face. "I see you started the party without me."

8

While Billy and Noah drove off in the Ranger to set up the tents, the rest of us headed to the swimming pool. A spirited game of knockout commenced, but it didn't last very long. After two near fights and the second black eye of the day (this time it was Bob Eiring, who caught a flying elbow while going up for a rebound), we gave up and moved on to a diving contest. Kara and Carly volunteered to be judges, and in between bouts of hysterical laughter, they held up our scores on dry-erase boards. Bill Caughron won the opening round with a pair of 9.5s for a spectacular front flip into a belly flop that hurt just to watch it. A short time later, Steve Sines emerged from behind the pool house and performed a naked swan dive, and that was the end of the contest, as both Kara and Carly retreated to the house in disgust. As a result, Bill was crowned winner by default. We then tried to get a game of pool volleyball going, but it quickly turned into full-contact dodgeball. After the third or fourth time the ball landed outside the pool, everyone was too tired to get out and retrieve it, so we just floated around for a while, talking about our kids and our jobs and how much improved the Orioles' pitching staff was this year. Eventually, Brian Anderson announced that he'd just peed in the pool, and we all made a mass exodus.

By the time we toweled off and changed into dry clothes, dusk had fallen over the land. Walking side by side, our shadows chasing us in the moonlight, we made our way to the grassy field beyond the pond. We didn't say much because, at that moment, not much of anything needed to be said. Most of us hadn't seen each other in close to a year, but that didn't matter.

By coming here today, we had stepped into a time machine. For one night, we were kids again. And we were all together. The Hanson Road boys.

9

"This is the life," Jimmy said, poking the fire with a stick. "Next year, we should do this for a long weekend instead of just one night."

"We'd end up killing each other," Steve said to murmurs of agreement.

The nine of us were sitting in a circle around the fire. It had taken nearly an hour for us to be able to get this close. When we'd first lit it, using balls of crumpled newspaper soaked in gasoline, the fire had reached as high as twenty feet into the sky, sparks and ashes swirling everywhere in fiery tornadoes.

I took another bite of Cajun sausage and chased it with a swallow of beer. My stomach protested, but I ignored it. The sausage was from Bob's late mother's secret recipe—she'd always cooked it for us at sleepovers when we were kids—and it tasted like a slice of heaven wrapped in a toasted bun. Bob had already polished off three of them and been rewarded with a desperate sprint to the woods. Luckily, he'd planned ahead and stolen a roll of toilet paper from our foyer bathroom.

"I've been trying to figure it out all night," Brian said, staring at Steve. "And I finally got it. With that bump on your head, you look like a fucking unicorn."

"Don't make me come over there," Steve threatened, never taking his eyes off the fire.

Brian stood up and began spraying bug repellent all over his arms and legs and neck. After using what appeared to be half the can, he sat down again, now enveloped in a thick gray mist.

"Christ," Steve said, waving his hands in the air. "That stuff stinks."

Before Brian could manage a response, Jimmy lifted his leg and farted—for at least five seconds. It sounded like a machine gun firing underwater. When he was finished, half the guys groaned in disgust and the other half applauded. Brian sprayed Jimmy with mosquito repellant. Jeff crumpled a beer can and hurled it at his older brother. It hit him on the back of the head and knocked off his baseball cap. Jimmy threatened to fart on both of them in retaliation.

And that's pretty much how the next couple of hours passed.

Bob wolfed down two more sausages and made a return trip to the woods.

Steve showed Noah how to shotgun a beer.

Billy showed Steve how to light a fart.

Brian accidentally lit his own shoes on fire.

Brian purposely lit my shoes on fire.

Steve took a kayak out on the pond.

Billy and Noah and I bombarded Steve with rocks.

Jimmy lit his brother's pants on fire.

Steve gave Noah a wedgie and ripped his underwear.

Fat Bill caught a catfish and slapped Brian in the face with it.

Brian tackled Fat Bill and shoved the catfish down his pants.

Billy pulled a banjo out of his tent and played a few songs.

Noah stole Billy's banjo and hid it in the woods.

Bob swam out to the island to win a thirty-dollar bet.

Fat Bill chased a deer, tripped, and did a somersault.

Brian and Steve climbed a tree.

Steve pushed Brian out of the tree.

Marshmallows were roasted. And eaten. And thrown. Jimmy learned the hard way that a red-hot marshmallow sticks to chest hair like Elmer's glue.

A four-on-four football game broke out with a full can of beer filling in as the ball. Billy picked teams and was all-time quarterback. I twisted my ankle on the first play. Steve tackled Jeff into the pond on the second play. Jimmy leg-whipped Brian on the third. Noah scored the only touchdown. Game was called early due to numerous injuries, including a chipped tooth.

Jimmy summoned his brother to the edge of the pond to look at a humongous bullfrog, and when he leaned over, Jimmy planted a foot on his brother's backside and pushed him in face-first. Jeff seemed to be the only person there who didn't know this was going to happen. A fifteen-minute wrestling match resulted. Testicles were smashed, hair was pulled, and eyes were poked. It was like watching a fight scene from *Gangs of New York*. A fragile peace was finally restored when Jimmy apologized and promised to jump in the pond the next morning as reparation. It was a promise, I knew, he had no intention of keeping.

Eventually, we all got tired.

10

"What do you think your parents would've said about all of this?" Brian asked.

It was past midnight. A bloated moon hung high in the sky. The beer was gone and the fire was down to glowing embers. Bob Eiring and Jeff Cavanaugh had already retreated to the sleeping bags inside their tents. Someone had used red Magic Marker to draw penises on each of their foreheads. Billy was slumped in a lawn chair, his hat pulled down over his eyes. The rest of us were spread out around the dying fire, none of us quite ready to call it a night.

"The murders?"

"No. Your book. The bestseller list. The movie."

"They would've loved every minute of it." I'd thought about it a lot, actually. I'd even gone to the cemetery to talk with them about it. "They wouldn't have understood half of what was going on—especially my mom—but man, they would've loved it."

No one spoke for a while after that, each of us lost in our own private thoughts. Brian bent down and stoked the fire. It snapped and hissed and threw pinwheeling spirals of sparks into the darkness. I watched them flare and flutter and drift away like distant fireworks on the Fourth of July.

"They were really proud of you," Steve said, finally breaking the silence. "We all are."

"I'm proud of *all* of us," I said, looking around. "We did good."

"Who would've guessed it?" Bill said. "Bunch of Edgewood degenerates."

"We took a lot of shit for being from the Wood, didn't we?" Brian asked.

"Still do," I said. "Some things never change."

Steve got up and stretched. The bump on his head looked enormous in the silhouette of the moon. He actually did look a little bit like a unicorn. "I'll tell you what, I wouldn't trade it for anything in the world.

Growing up in Edgewood taught us how to put our heads down and do the work. That and the example our parents set for us. We were damn lucky."

Brian nodded his head. "Yes, we were."

"Still are lucky," I said. "You know how many people are still tight with the guys they grew up with?" I shook my head. "Not many."

"That's a fact." Steve cleared his throat. "You might all be idiots, but you're my idiots. I'd give every damn one of you a kidney if you needed it."

"Don't need a kidney," Brian said, "but you sure could use some ice for that bump, you Quasimodo-looking motherfucker."

We all cracked up laughing.

And as another wrestling match broke out, I made my way to the woods to pee.

11

Stephen King once wrote: "I never had any friends later on like the ones I had when I was twelve. Jesus, did you?"

Sometimes, in life, you got very lucky.

The Hanson Road boys were proof of that.

12

I almost peed on Billy's banjo.

Noah had stashed it underneath a tangle of thornbushes just off the path—maybe fifteen or twenty yards inside the tree line—and I'd spotted it just in the nick of time. Two or three more seconds, and it would've gotten soaked. Instead, I spun around and did my business in the opposite direction. After zipping up, I freed the banjo and gave it a good look. There were several deep scratches in the wood and one of the strings was broken. Noah was going to be in a heap of trouble tomorrow morning when Billy found out.

I'd just started making my way back to camp when I heard something move in the nearby brush. A chill touched me. My first instinct was to run, but I knew I'd never hear the end of it if the guys saw me booking it from a rabbit or a squirrel.

I stopped and listened.

The woods around me were silent and still.

Bill's voice crept, uninvited, into my head: *What if he shows up tonight?*

Then he's a dumbass, I thought. *There's a small army gathered out there around the fire, not to mention a trooper parked in the driveway.*

Maybe, another voice whispered in my ear. *But they're not here right now, are they? No one is. You're all alone. In the woods. In the dark.*

The wind sighed through the trees.

I started walking, holding the banjo out in front of me like a shield.

The noise came again.

Closer this time and on the opposite side of the path.

I thought, *I should've brought the flashlight*—and picked up my pace.

I could see a break in the trees ahead.

I broke into a jog.

Suddenly, from behind me: "Is that you, Chizmar?"

Relief flooding my body, I stopped and spun around. "Jesus, you scared the hell out—"

There was no one there.

As the words left my mouth, I realized that I hadn't recognized the voice that'd called out to me—and besides, none of these guys ever called me by my last name . . .

I raised the banjo and ducked—but it was too late.

A dark shadow fell upon me.

My head exploded in pain and the ground rushed up to meet me. I landed on my face with a *thud.*

Heavy footsteps approached in the darkness. I felt a steel-tipped boot nudge me in the ribs. I opened my mouth to speak, but no words came out. I could taste blood and dirt in the back of my throat.

Grunting in pain, I rolled over onto my back and slowly opened my eyes. Through a veil of blood, I recognized the monster standing over me.

I tried to speak, but whatever words I managed—I have no memory of them now—were drowned out by the drunken battle cries of my friends coming to the rescue.

A swarm of bodies took down my attacker.

13

Voices in the darkness:

"All that blood on his face, I thought for sure Chiz was a goner."

"Hide that beer before a nurse sees it."

"That son of a bitch is lucky we took it easy on him."

"Bastard kicked me in the balls. I think they're still swollen."

"Billy and Noah got there first. They're the real heroes."

"Keep your voices down. Before we get thrown out again."

"Good thing I woke up and had to take another shit or we never would've known."

I recognized the last voice as Bob Eiring's.

Thank God for his mother's Cajun sausage, I thought in a haze of pain-killers.

It was a few minutes past seven o'clock on Thursday morning, and I was lying in a hospital bed at Upper Chesapeake with my eyes closed and an ice pack on my head. Kara was sitting beside me, holding my hand. Billy and Noah stood by themselves in the corner of the room, while the rest of the guys gathered at the foot of the bed. They were trying their best to be quiet, but most of them were still drunk. An emergency room nurse named Rolanda had already kicked them out twice. Lieutenant McClernan had gone outside to talk to the press. Before she'd left, she'd promised not to mention the word "Chizapalooza" in any part of her statement.

The man who attacked me in the woods was Peyton Bair's step-father, Jeremy Hollister. When the police shoved him into the back of a squad car at 2:30 a.m., cameras clicking away across the street, Hollister reeked of alcohol and could barely walk. He was bleeding from the nose and mouth. The boys had done a real number on him.

Initially, I'd told Detective Gonzalez that I didn't want to press charges, but he'd encouraged me to reconsider. Hollister had hit me on the side of my head with an axe handle. It was a good thing I still had decent reflexes and had managed to duck. A few inches to the left or right, and he may have killed me. As it was, I had a concussion and needed thirty-three stitches to close the gash on my scalp. My head felt like someone had used it as a golf ball. Ironically, the police had located Hollister's pickup truck in the Southampton Middle School parking lot. Inside the glove compartment, they'd found a legally registered semiautomatic handgun, as well as two hunting knives. Under the driver's seat were two empty whiskey bottles.

"Think about it," Gonzalez told me. "If there'd been a third empty bottle under that seat, he may have decided to bring the gun with him instead of the axe handle."

In the end, I went ahead with the charges.

No reward for bad behavior, right?

14

Later that morning on Twitter:

Dreadhead @TimothyDowl - 1h
You guys see the newz?!? CHIZMAR GOT JUMPED!
HE'S IN THE HOSPITAL!

Keith Jennings @keithjennings414 - 1h
Whoever did it should never have to buy a drink again!

SlasherChick @LucyLuckkk6 - 1h
I call bullshit... Chizmar probably set the whole thing up
to get sympathy.

TheBluntMan @michelrobinson09 - 1h
Or he's trying to throw the police off his trail...

Larry Jones @Jonesyboy3 - 1h
Anyone know who did it? I heard it was a cop!

Bonfire preparation *(Photo courtesy of the author)*

The woods where Richard Chizmar was attacked by Jeremy Hollister *(Photo courtesy of the author)*

The scene of the Jeremy Hollister attack *(Photo courtesy of the author)*

Excerpt from Edgewood: Looking Back, *by Richard Chizmar, pages 311–312:*

Sometimes, I dream about the future.

All of us Hanson Road boys, old and wise and gray.

Still kicking. Still friends.

We get together for the weekend or a long dinner or perhaps a golf trip. There are handshakes and hugs and tears. We laugh at who got fat, who got skinny, who got bald, and who got their ears pierced (after all these years, the midlife crisis sufferer). We talk about wives and sons and daughters. We remember mothers and fathers and friends we lost too soon. Mostly, we relive the stories of our childhood as each of us remembers them. I am amazed at how those memories differ, what time and wishful thinking have done to our youth. Once again, I'm reminded that the past is a tricky beast and not to be trusted.

In one of these dreams, we sit around a great fire. Our faces bathed in a flickering orange glow that brings whispers in the wind of front porch jack-o'-lanterns and the scent of woodsmoke. Much time has passed. There have been weddings and divorces, funerals and births, cancers, goodbyes, and journeys to faraway places.

Yet, on this night, we are in the here and now.

And we are all together again.

I study my friends' faces in the firelight.

Steadfast.

Loyal.

Wrinkled and worn by time and experience.

And I see myself in each of them.

SIXTEEN

MALLORY

"His eyes were the color of hell."

1

Seventeen-year-old Mallory Tucker knew the rules, but she was in love.

Ricky Ford was handsome, funny, and successful. Three months shy of his twentieth birthday, he already ran his own landscaping business and lived by himself in a second-floor apartment in downtown Bel Air. In addition to a fleet of riding mowers, he owned two work trucks and a convertible BMW that he'd bought used and had repainted candy apple red. He was also the lead guitarist for Dragon Tears, a popular local band.

Two weeks earlier, Ricky and Mallory had met at a backyard party where the band was playing in Joppatowne. Mallory had known about Ricky, of course, and had seen him before at a number of parties, but they'd never actually spoken until that night. During one of the band's breaks, they'd bumped into each other in the crowd and Mallory's Budweiser had gone all over the front of Ricky's Tom Petty and the Heartbreakers T-shirt. Instead of freaking out or getting pissed, he made a joke about it and cut the keg line to get her a refill. After he was finished playing for the night, they'd sat on the party host's pier and talked until after midnight—which also happened to be Mallory's curfew.

Her father punished her for being late and smelling like beer—two weeks with no car—but it was worth it. After exchanging phone numbers on the pier, Ricky had walked Mallory to her car and given her the most amazing good night kiss of her entire life. For days afterward, her knees went weak and her stomach swam with butterflies every time she thought about it.

The morning after the party, Mallory woke to find a text waiting for her. Ricky saying that he couldn't stop thinking about her. Unable to stop smiling, she spent the next ten minutes trying to come up with the perfect response. She finally just typed I was thinking of u 2! and, after a moment's hesitation, added a heart emoji at the end. That afternoon, they met at the playground down the street from Mallory's house and held hands on the swings. Afterward, they walked to the Edgewood Creamery for milkshakes. The next day, Ricky picked up Mallory at the playground and they drove to Flying Point Park and had a picnic on the beach.

Mallory's parents were strict and old-fashioned, so she couldn't tell them about the whirlwind romance with her new boyfriend. First, they would want to meet him. And second, they would want to know how old he was. And third, Ricky Ford would then be history.

So she kept him a secret.

Only a week after meeting at the party, while making out at the drive-in, Mallory slipped and told Ricky that she loved him. The moment the words left her mouth, she regretted it. Guys like Ricky Ford didn't fall in love with girls like Mallory Tucker. Sure, she was blonde and sort of pretty and the high school boys liked her just fine, but she wasn't very exciting or interesting or fun. She got As and Bs and played the clarinet in the Edgewood High School band. She took piano lessons and went to church on Sunday. She didn't dress like other girls her age, preferring a kind of hippie chic that she'd picked up from her older cousin. She was also a vegetarian. And while she downed the occasional beer or two—and sometimes got busted for it, like last weekend—she would never be mistaken for a party girl.

When Ricky kissed her on the side of her neck—something that sent tingles down her entire body every time he did it—and told her that he loved her too, Mallory almost fainted in the front seat of his BMW. If she could've run away and been with him forever after that night, she would have happily done so.

Which was why—at 8 p.m. on Friday, June 17—Mallory Tucker came downstairs and told her parents that she was going out for pizza and a movie with her best friend, Yvonne Marino.

The plan was for Yvonne to pick up Mallory in front of her house so that Mallory's parents would see her getting into her friend's car and driving away. Yvonne would then drop Mallory off at the playground, where Ricky would be waiting to take her to a party in Fallston at which Dragon Tears was scheduled to play. Mallory had already imagined—at least a hundred times, if she was being honest with herself—what it would feel like to walk into the party on the arm of Ricky Ford. Every girl there would be green-eyed with envy. She couldn't wait.

2

B ut Ricky wasn't waiting for her at the playground.

As they pulled up to the curb, her cell phone pinged. She looked at the text message: running 5-10 mins late sorry babe

"I can wait," Yvonne said, checking the time.

"No, you can't." Mallory opened the door. "Jason's waiting for you. Go. It's not even dark out yet."

Yvonne stared doubtfully at her friend. "I don't know . . ."

"I do." She got out of the car. "Go! Have fun! And thank you for doing this. I owe you big."

"If you say so. You guys have fun too."

Mallory closed the door and waved goodbye to her friend.

The car remained idling at the curb. The passenger window slid down.

"I really don't mind waiting," Yvonne said.

"I really don't need you to." Mallory pointed down the road. "Go, girl!"

"Fine," she huffed. "Don't be late getting home. It's your last night without a car—don't blow it, Mal."

"Thanks, Mom!"

"Whateverrrr."

The window went back up and Yvonne drove away.

Mallory checked the time on her phone. 8:14. Not dark yet, but the streetlights were already winking on. So were the lights inside the two houses she could see from where she was standing. Speaking of which, she needed to get away from the road before one of her parents' nosy friends drove by and saw her. That would be just her luck.

She walked over to the playground and sat on a swing. She'd always loved the swings—they made her feel like a little girl again. She pushed off with her feet. The chains squealed against the brackets that held them, startling her. If her father had been there, he would've remarked, *Those chains need some oilin'* and then he probably would've driven straight home to get a ladder and a can of WD-40 to do it himself.

Glancing over her shoulder, Mallory felt a sudden shiver of unease. Here in the playground, she was much closer to the trees—and the pockets of gloomy darkness hidden within—than she had been standing beside the road.

She tapped on Ricky's name and typed: "please hurry I'm here by myself" and hit send.

When she looked up from her phone, the breath caught in her throat.

There was a man walking toward her.

She immediately swiped the screen of her phone, the emergency 911 icon coming up. She poised her finger.

The man was coming fast from the direction of the road. She glanced at the houses in the distance. They were too far away. Her only escape route was the trees behind her.

"Hey, there," the man said, raising his hand in a half-hearted wave and slowing his pace. "I didn't mean to frighten you."

He was tall and broad across the shoulders. She couldn't quite make out his face in the dimming light.

"You didn't," she said, and instantly hated how young she sounded.

"Just taking a shortcut through the woods. I live right behind there."

He was wearing jeans and a dark T-shirt. His arms were tan and muscular.

She knew if she tapped the screen, her night would be over. There would be no party. No Ricky. And her parents would find out everything.

She flexed her legs, preparing to run.

She opened her mouth, ready to scream louder than she'd ever screamed before.

And then he was striding right past her, barely even giving her a sideways glance.

"Have yourself a good night," he said, and she turned and watched the man disappear into the woods.

"You too!" she called after him, heart thrumming in her chest. She giggled to herself, feeling equal measures giddy and foolish. He hadn't been dangerous after all. He hadn't even really been a stranger—after seeing him up close, Mallory was certain she'd seen the man somewhere before around town.

She glanced down at her phone. 8:20.

Where in the heck are you, Ricky?

Suddenly, Mallory was sure that the man who'd passed her had circled back and was standing right behind her. She could hear his heavy breathing and feel the weight of his—

She jumped off the swing and spun around.

The field behind her was empty. Fireflies sparkled in the deepening darkness. Moonlight silvered the top of the trees.

"Get ahold of yourself, girl." She took a deep, wavering breath and started walking toward the road—and her phone slipped out of her hand. "Shit."

Bending over to pick it up, she heard the unmistakable sound of stealthy footfalls coming closer in the grass.

As she slowly rose—already knowing somewhere deep in the basement of her brain that she was never going to see Ricky again—the man was revealed from the ground up.

Dark boots.

Jeans.

A Grateful Dead belt buckle.

Black T-shirt.

Muscular arms.

His face . . .

. . . now concealed behind a burlap mask.

His eyes were the color of hell.

3

After examining the wound on my head and administering a cognitive test, the emergency room doctor on duty at Upper Chesapeake Medical Center admitted me for a twenty-four-hour observation period. Shortly after noon on Thursday, two nurses slid me onto a gurney and wheeled me to a private room on the third floor. I was only allowed to sleep for short periods of time, so I mostly lay around in the dark with the television volume on low, watching news reports about the Jeremy Hollister assault and talking to Kara and the boys. I also ate about a half dozen ice cream sandwiches from a nearby vending machine. Carly had stayed back at the house to take care of the dogs, and once my friends had been reassured that I was going to be okay, they'd said their goodbyes and returned to their own families. I'm pretty sure every last one of them walked a little taller to their cars in the parking lot, knowing that they had probably just saved my life.

Lieutenant McClernan stopped by, as did Detective Gonzalez, which really surprised me. Gonzalez himself told me how terrible he felt because he'd misread Jeremy Hollister's intentions—and then he actually apologized for it. I told him not to bother. It was no one's fault but Hollister's. Who would've guessed that the man would become so unhinged?

By the time Gonzalez left the hospital, my fascination with his facial hair had returned. I blamed it on the concussion.

McClernan told me that Hollister had expressed remorse for the attack when she'd spoken with him earlier that morning but that he'd also been sober at the time. An intoxicated Hollister would most likely be a whole different story. Fortunately, the judge had jacked up Hollister's bail, so he wasn't going anywhere for the foreseeable future.

Before she went back to work, McClernan also told me that she'd finally watched the digital footage of my interview with Joshua Gallagher. She promised to discuss it with me later, once I was back on my feet, but the gist I got from our brief conversation was that she didn't think much of importance had been shared. *Typical Gallagher*, she complained on her way out the door. *Playing stupid games.* Even in my fuzzy condition, I was inclined to agree.

4

Shortly after lunch on Friday afternoon, my discharge papers showed up and Kara signed me out and drove us home.

McClernan had texted the troopers at our house ahead of time, so they were ready for our arrival. So was the media. I lowered my head and closed my eyes as we pulled into the driveway. Even with the windows closed, I could hear the swarm of cameras invading our privacy.

The dogs greeted me at the gate like I'd been gone for a month instead of a single day. I was instantly reminded of a meme I'd recently seen that read: WE DON'T DESERVE DOGS. Billy and Noah met us in the breezeway with hugs and kisses. Noah would be heading back to school first thing in the morning. Carly was waiting in the kitchen. She stared with dismay at the bandage on my head and gave me the most delicate of embraces—more of a wraparound two-handed pat on the back—as though she were afraid I might break apart in her arms. Coming from her, I found the gesture oddly touching.

A blanket and pillow awaited me on the arm of my recliner. The television remote and a glass of ice water rested on the end table. The overhead lights were dimmed. Once I was settled in, Cujo and Ripley assumed their normal positions on either side of me, and Kara asked if I wanted a snack. When she brought me a bowl of vanilla ice cream topped with a freshly baked brownie and whipped cream and tucked the blanket underneath my feet, I decided the gash on the side of my head was definitely worth it.

Fifteen minutes later—my ice cream bowl licked clean by JJ and a baseball game in extra innings on TV—I fell sound asleep.

5

While I was snoring in my recliner, the next wave of articles about the Jeremy Hollister attack appeared online. Most of the reports were accompanied by a wide-angle photograph of me exiting the car in our driveway—my head wrapped in bright white bandages like a wounded Civil War soldier—as well as Jeremy Hollister's official mug shot. Additional details of the attack—including the weapon used and the extent of my injuries—were revealed. Social media exploded with the news. The message boards went into a frenzy. I immediately began trending on both Twitter and Instagram, as did Peyton Bair and Jeremy Hollister. And, of course, Joshua Gallagher.

It had finally happened.

The circus had become a spectacle.

6

Deputy George Fonda—"no relation to Henry or Peter" as he liked to tell people—shone the spotlight into a cluster of bushes by the entrance to Cedar Drive Elementary School. Nothing stirred, not even a whisper of a breeze. After a moment, he drove on.

The missing girl lived three blocks away on Boxelder Drive. If a man wearing a mask really had dragged her into the woods—as the witness who'd just happened to drive by the playground the moment the abduction took place had claimed—then it was Deputy Fonda's professional opinion that the girl was in a shitload of trouble right about now and no-where near Cedar Drive.

But none of that mattered. An order was an order. Besides, if there really was a copycat killer on the loose—and he had his serious doubts about that—Cedar Drive might very well hold a special attraction for the sick bastard. Even though Deputy Fonda hadn't yet been born in 1988, he'd heard plenty of stories about the Boogeyman's grisly killing spree and the dead girl they'd found on the playground sliding board.

There were only a handful of cars in the Boys and Girls Club parking lot. He pulled over and used his flashlight to check inside each of the vehi-cles. On the way back to his cruiser, he noticed that the club's front door was propped open with a traffic cone, a sword of bright light stabbing the dark-ness. He thought about going in and telling the workers that they should close and lock the door, but then he remembered the last time he'd dropped by. One of the women who worked the front desk had given him all kinds of hell for sneaking a soda out of the break-room fridge. One measly can of Coke. He hadn't even swiped a bag of pretzels like he usually did. The whole thing had been terribly embarrassing, and he felt his cheeks grow warm just thinking about it. He got in his car, slammed the door, and drove away.

Using the spotlight attached to the car's roof, he searched the edge of the woods across the street. At the bottom of the hill, something shiny caught the light. The deputy tapped his brakes and readjusted the beam. There was a hubcap hanging from a branch in a tree. From the looks of it, some kids with a pellet gun had been using it for target practice. He was about to pull away when a family of deer emerged from the trees and crossed the road in front of him. The largest, a broad-chested buck with an impressive rack, stopped and stared at him, issuing a timeless chal-lenge. The deputy leaned on the horn and the deer sauntered away, as if it couldn't be bothered, disappearing into the darkness.

Suddenly in a foul mood, and not entirely sure why, Deputy Fonda gunned the engine and laid rubber. The speedometer jumped from zero to fifty in the blink of an eye.

Fifty-five.

Sixty.

Sixty-five . . .

Thoughts of his last performance review flooding his head, he eased off the gas and dropped back down to forty. As he rounded the corner where the old kindergarten building once stood, he noticed a flicker of light coming from high on the hill across the street. *There it is again!*

He braked to a stop and quickly switched off his headlights. After maneuvering a blind three-point turn, he pulled into the grass and turned off the engine. The deputy knew the spotlight couldn't reach to the top of the ridge, so he radioed in and let dispatch know that he was exiting the vehicle. With his flashlight—still dark—in one hand and his other hand resting on the butt of his sidearm, Deputy Fonda started up the hill.

Ever since the initial glimmer of light—he knew a flashlight beam when he saw one—the hill had remained cloaked in a blanket of darkness. If someone had been messing around up there, they'd most likely seen him coming, and either took off . . . or were lying in wait.

Fonda stopped walking. Holding his breath, he listened.

Nothing.

He looked down at his hand holding the flashlight.

Again, nothing.

The darkness—like the silence—was complete.

Moving ahead at a slower pace, careful to step as quietly as possible, the deputy made his way up the hill. In his heart, he didn't expect to find anything. He rarely did on nights like this. Instead, he felt like an actor playing a scene in a cop movie, the kind his father used to watch on television before the lung cancer killed him. Only the director would need a hell of a lot more light than this, and Fonda was a-okay with that, because he couldn't see a fucking thing in front of him.

That's when he smelled it.

Deputy Fonda stopped and pulled his weapon.

In his five and a half years with the sheriff's department, he'd only been on the scene of two murders. In both cases, the victim had vacated his bowels. That inimitable stench of blood, body fluids, and shit had plagued his memory for months afterward.

It's what he was smelling now.

Somewhere up ahead, close by, someone was dead.

Steeling himself, Fonda lifted the hand holding the flashlight. With his other hand, he leveled his sidearm.

His finger brushed against the trigger.

He turned on the flashlight.

What he saw would haunt him for the rest of his days.

7

When Kara shook me awake, the first thought that surfaced in my mind was:

Why am I in my recliner and not in a hospital bed?

Then I remembered that I'd been discharged and had returned home.

I glanced at the time in the corner of the television screen: 10:32 p.m.

And evidently slept all day.

"Jesus," I mumbled. My mouth felt like a desert. "Why'd you let me sleep so long?"

"The doctor said you needed to catch up." She held up my cell phone. "It's Lieutenant McClernan. Something's happened."

I reached for the phone. She held it just out of my reach. "She gets five minutes. You need to eat and go to bed."

"I just slept like eight or nine hours."

"I didn't say you had to sleep." Her voice had an edge to it; I knew better than to push it. "You need to rest." She handed me the phone. "This isn't good for you."

"Hello?"

"He got another one."

"What? When?"

"A witness saw a man wearing a mask dragging someone into the woods off Trimble Road. She called 911 at 8:22 p.m. Police flooded the area. Found drag marks in the pine needles and a scrap of torn clothing on a tree branch." I could hear someone at the crime scene ask the lieutenant a question. She answered and continued. "Half hour later, another 911 came in from a Michael Tucker. Boxelder Drive. His seventeen-year-old daughter Mallory told him and his wife that she was going to a movie with a girl-friend. The friend picked her up and dropped her off at a playground on Trimble to meet her boyfriend. The boyfriend showed up late and found Mallory's cell phone in the grass. He panicked and went to see the parents."

I looked at the clock again. 10:35 p.m. "It's only been two hours. She might still be alive if we—"

"They already found her."

"Ah, shit." Kara squeezed my shoulder. "Where?"

"Cedar Drive. The killer staked her up like a scarecrow."

"What do you mean?"

"Just what I said. He mounted her with rope on a cross made by a couple of long two-by-fours and staked her into the ground."

"My God."

"Strangled. Left ear gone. Ligature and bite marks. And this was dif-ferent . . . he cut off a clump of her hair." Someone interrupted again. "Hang on, I'll be right there. Sorry. She also has defensive wounds. She put up a hell of a fight."

"I hope she gouged that fucker's eye out."

"Both eyes."

"Sexually assaulted?"

"It doesn't look like it."

"Another hangman?" I asked.

"The number eight written on both of her cheeks. That's all we could find. He was in a hurry."

"So it's a repeat of what happened with Peyton Bair. Take her, kill her, dump her—all within a narrow window of time." Goddammit. I couldn't figure it out. For most serial murderers, it was about spending time with their victims—*possessing* them. "Why is this guy in such a rush?"

"I'm starting to believe it's not about the killing with him, or even domination. It's all about the performance."

"For the record, that's not what Gallagher thinks," I said. "He says the compulsion is real."

"Fuck what Gallagher thinks. Let's just say *I* have my doubts."

"Where in Cedar Drive did they find her?"

"At the top of a hill. I can see your old house from where I'm standing. One of the sheriffs told me there used to be a water tower . . ."

Whatever strength I had left drained out of me. I slumped in the recliner. "Oh Jesus."

"That's it," Kara said, putting her hand out for the phone. "Five minutes are up."

"Stop," I snapped, leaning away from her. "Lieutenant?"

"I'm here."

"I'm going to email you a file. There's something you need to see."

8

t's all about the performance . . .

An hour later, as I lay in bed staring at the ceiling, the lieutenant's words were still rattling around inside my head.

She'd been incredulous when I'd told her. "Rich, what the hell is going on here? How could he possibly have a copy of your book when it hasn't even been published yet?"

"Forget about being published," I'd said. "It hasn't even gone anywhere yet. I just finished writing it a month ago. The only person I've sent it to is my literary agent. That's it. No one else. Other than that, it exists only on my hard drive and inside my head."

"And you wrote about both the bridge and the water tower?"

"I wrote about a handful of places that I consider to be the sacred landmarks of my youth in Edgewood. Both the bridge and that hill are discussed in great detail."

"Have you ever written or talked about them publicly before?"

"The bridge . . . never. I mentioned the water tower in *Chasing the Boogeyman*, but it was just a passing reference. Two sentences, maybe—no real significance."

The lieutenant was quiet for a moment—letting the gravity of what I'd just told her sink in. Finally:

"Email the file. I'll come by your house first thing in the morning."

Mallory Tucker *(Photo courtesy of Robert Tucker)*

Mallory Tucker *(Photo courtesy of Robert Tucker)*

The Trimble Road playground where Mallory Tucker was abducted *(Photo courtesy of the author)*

Peyton Bair's stepfather, Jeremy Hollister
(Photo courtesy of Marryland State Police)

The Mallory Tucker crime scene atop Water Tower Hill *(Photo courtesy of Harford County Sheriff's Department)*

Excerpt from telephone interview with James L. Largent, retired psychiatrist, state of New York, recorded October 14, 2019:

CHIZMAR: The lack of remorse for Metheny's actions . . . wouldn't that make him a sociopath?

LARGENT: Oh, he was most certainly a sociopath. Make no bones about it, he was an extremely dangerous individual. You asked me what kind of impression he made in person . . . and to be honest, he didn't make much of one. He had a rather sedate personality. On the other hand, I was only with him for two hours at a time, so I'm certain I didn't get the full picture. I remember our initial meeting had to be postponed because he was suffering from terrible migraines. Henry Metheny's brain scans were notable. There was considerable damage present, which is a common trait among modern-day serial murderers. [pause] Now that I'm thinking about it, I do recall one rather odd incident.

CHIZMAR: What was that?

LARGENT: When one of our final sessions was over and he was being escorted out of the room, he began to speak gibberish.

CHIZMAR: What did he say?

LARGENT: In my younger days, I used to be somewhat of a *Star Trek* fan, and for a moment, I'd thought he was speaking some form of Klingon. I know how absolutely ridiculous that sounds.

CHIZMAR: Was he talking to one of the guards?

LARGENT: I'm not entirely sure. I imagine either one of the guards or perhaps he was just talking to himself.

CHIZMAR: Did he seem distressed? Happy? Sad?

LARGENT: It was a long time ago, but as best as I can remember . . . he sounded excited. Almost childlike.

SEVENTEEN

THE MEYERS HOUSE

"The house loomed above us like a sleeping giant."

1

I was sitting in the kitchen watching Mallory Tucker's parents, Michael and Cynthia, read from a prepared statement on my iPad screen when the doorbell rang.

Carly called out from the family room. "I'll get it!"

The Tuckers were standing in front of their home on Boxelder Drive. A priest stood solemnly beside them. Mrs. Tucker went first, or at least she tried to. Before she was able to get out even a single word, she looked up at the crowd of reporters assembled in front of her and broke down in tears. She turned away from the microphone and buried her face in her husband's shoulder. The sound of her muffled sobs was heartrending. After a moment, the husband gently handed her off to the priest and stepped up to the podium.

"I want to thank everyone for coming," he said in a surprisingly strong voice as he stared down at the sheet of paper in his hand. Mr. Tucker was a delicate-looking man in his early forties. Slender, bespectacled, with a receding hairline, he looked like an accountant in an H&R Block commercial. "Our daughter, Mallory Marie Tucker, was a very special girl. We will miss her every day for the rest of our lives. Only seventeen, she had already made a significant impact on this world. For the past two years, she volunteered at the Bright Oaks Nursing Home and the humane society in Fallston. She also tutored students at Edgewood High School in mathematics and Spanish.

"Mallory loved to play the piano and ride horses. She was an avid reader and liked to write poetry. Mallory had a sweet tooth. She especially loved her mother's homemade apple pie and ice cream cake from Cold Stone Creamery. She was constantly singing around the house. I'll miss hearing her voice while I'm reading the morning paper or watching television. Mallory had the sweetest voice . . . and the biggest heart."

He looked up from the paper he was holding. His eyes had gone flinty. His jaw tightened.

"To whoever took away our daughter . . . if you're watching this, the police are going to hunt you down and they *will* find you. May God have mercy on your sorry soul.

"To everyone else watching . . . my employer for the past fifteen years, Stanley Black and Decker, has kindly offered a reward of fifty thousand dollars for any information leading to the arrest of the person responsible for our daughter's death. A hotline phone number has been set up and can be accessed by calling . . ."

2

Carly walked into the kitchen with Lieutenant McClernan and a man and woman I'd never seen before trailing behind her.

The lieutenant had been up all night. Dark circles hung heavy beneath her eyes and her normally confident stride was gone. She looked like she couldn't wait to get off her feet. A moment later, with a groan of relief, she settled onto the stool beside me. Gesturing to the man and woman, she said, "Richard Chizmar, this is Officer Tim Bakewell and Officer Elise Hoffman from the Maryland State Police Cyber Crime Unit."

They both gave a polite nod. I'm not sure what I imagined computer cops would look like, but this wasn't it. Both officers were young and attractive and impeccably dressed. Their shoes probably cost more than the nicest suit hanging in my closet.

"The lieutenant explained the situation, Mr. Chizmar." Officer Hoffman stepped forward and placed her briefcase on the island. "May I?"

"Of course."

She opened it and pulled out a sheaf of paperwork. "What we'd like to do today, with you and your wife's permission, is examine your electronic devices. Desktop. Laptop. iPads. Phones. The works."

"You think we were hacked? For real?"

"There's no way to tell until we run some diagnostic tests, but if you and your literary agent are the only two people with direct access to your manuscript, then we believe it's likely."

"How would someone go about doing that?"

"A number of ways. Lieutenant McClernan tells us you've had a large group of workers both inside and outside of your home during the past year. It would only take a moment for someone with experience to install tracking software on one of your devices, especially if it was vulnerable."

"I guess that's possible," I said. "You get used to having people around and you eventually lower your guard."

"Or it could've been done remotely. For example, a phishing campaign where you're encouraged to click on a link or a file. It could also be handled via a vulnerable RDP—that's a remote desktop protocol."

My head was aching, and it wasn't the concussion. "My wife's outside with the dogs. I'll give her a shout, but I'm sure she'll be fine with whatever you need to do."

Officer Hoffman gave her partner a nod, and he headed for the front door, presumably to retrieve their equipment.

"We would usually do this at the lab, but the lieutenant asked us to fast-track our analysis."

I glanced at McClernan.

"We don't have much time, Rich," she said. "Gallagher killed four girls before he was caught. This guy has three. He's still hunting."

3

When the news hit late last night that a girl had been abducted, the town of Edgewood—long simmering in a stew of unease and suspicion—finally boiled over. A couple hours later, when word got out that the girl's mutilated body had been discovered at Cedar Drive, my hometown exploded.

In Wingleaf Court, just down the street from Mallory Tucker's house, a father and son got into a fistfight right in their front yard. The father lost a tooth. The son's nose was broken, as were two of the fingers on his right hand. Several of their neighbors called the police, and when the responding officer asked the father what in the hell was going on, he told the officer that he suspected his twenty-one-year-old son of being the Boogeyman copycat killer. The son had dropped out of college and had been living at home for the past six months. He'd become increasingly withdrawn and secretive. On the night of Peyton Bair's murder, and again last night, the son had been acting strangely before disappearing for a period of several hours. The father had confronted his son when he'd gotten home shortly after midnight, but the young man—who had fresh scratches on his arm and smelled strongly of alcohol—refused to reveal his whereabouts. The father continued to press the issue, and a blowout fight ensued. When the officer questioned the son in private, the young man finally admitted that he was having an affair with a married woman who lived two blocks away on Larch Drive. Under the circumstances, both father and son declined to press charges and the officer let them go with a stern warning.

At the Quickie-Mart on Edgewood Road, a woman named Bertha Barnhart was working the night shift. Shortly after midnight, two young males entered the store and proceeded to the fountain soda machine in the rear aisle. When they approached the register a few minutes later, one of the boys was wearing a burlap mask. He raised his arms at Ms. Barnhart in a threatening manner. She screamed; hit the panic button next to the register, summoning the police; and then pointed a stun gun at the boy in the mask. Before he could tell her it was all a joke, she blasted him. Twice. He dropped to the ground, twitching and drooling, and urinated in his jeans. The other boy with him ran away.

Claude Remy, the assistant manager of the Sunoco station, and his good buddy, Owen LaSalle, simply grabbed their deer rifles and went looking for the killer. A longtime viewer of *America's Most Wanted*, Remy conducted the search using a complicated grid-pattern strategy he'd learned from one of the reenactments he'd seen on the show. First, they covered a ten-block area behind the library moving from east to west with overlapping rotations. Then they moved on to the other side of Edgewood Meadows and worked their way west to east utilizing the same method until they reached the outskirts of the Courts of Harford Square. When that didn't turn up anything, they cut down Trimble and hopped onto Willoughby Beach Road to cover the numerous developments its windy route bisected. Again, they spotted nothing suspicious. Although stone-cold sober and highly motivated, with Johnny Cash blaring from the cassette deck in Remy's classic Chevy Chevelle, by 1:15 a.m., both men were having a hard time keeping their eyes open. They decided to call it a night. Remy dropped LaSalle off at home on Bayberry Drive and continued on his way to his rancher on Rosewood. As he was making a left off Hornbeam, he spotted a man dressed in dark clothing disappear in between two houses. He slammed on the brakes and grabbed his rifle from the back seat—and promptly shot himself in the foot. In terrible pain and bleeding profusely, Remy managed to drive himself to the emergency room at Upper Chesapeake, sideswiping two parked cars and running down a mailbox on the way. Doctors were able to save two of the toes on his left foot.

The numbers were staggering. Over a ten-hour period, there were ninety-seven calls to 911. Residents reported hearing everything from screams in the distance to footsteps on rooftops. There were numerous panicked calls regarding the sudden appearance of mysterious footprints in flower beds located beneath windows, as well as broken fence posts and wide-open backyard gates that were always kept closed. One woman swore that the family photos in her living room had been moved and a set of steak knives was missing from her kitchen counter. Two homeowners, who lived miles apart, claimed that the light bulbs in their porch lights had been unscrewed and sliding glass doors had been tampered with. A teacher from the middle school told police that she'd been awakened by a noise. When she sat up in bed, she saw a flashlight beam probing her bedroom window.

In all, nineteen arrests were made for crimes ranging from assault and battery and trespassing to possession of illegal firearms and breaking and entering. The Edgewood Fire Company answered nearly a dozen emergencies, including three fires—one in a dumpster behind the Dunkin' Donuts on Route 40, another in an abandoned building on Edgewood Road, and a garage fire in Perry Court that spread to the main structure before the blaze was extinguished.

In addition, someone vandalized Joshua Gallagher's former home on Hawthorne Drive. Bricks were thrown through several windows, the windshield of a vehicle parked in the driveway was smashed, and FUCK YOU BOOGEYMAN was spray-painted on the street in front of the house. Home security footage revealed that there were three assailants. They were all wearing burlap masks.

4

When Kara came in from the backyard, she took one look at Lieutenant McClernan and immediately started a pot of coffee. Ten minutes later, the lieutenant was already working on her second cup. While the cyber crew examined our laptops in the quiet of my office, she filled me in on the madness of the previous night.

"They're testing the rope," McClernan said, "to see if it's a match for what was used on the mannequins in your tree. My hunch is it will be."

I shook my head, unable to stop thinking about the crime scene as the lieutenant had described it. "We used to sled on that hill every winter."

"I'm pretty sure we got her down before anyone in the media saw. Otherwise, we would have seen pictures by now. Trust me, it was a spectacle—as intended."

"And the water tower . . . I used to have dreams about it."

"He's claiming your special spots for himself."

"Gallagher told me he thought the killer was just as much a fan of mine as he was of his . . . but it sure doesn't feel that way. It feels like the guy's pissed off—and wants to hurt me."

"Speaking of Gallagher, we received an anonymous tip that one of the guards has been pulling special favors for him. A convicted serial killer phoning you directly with no monitoring did not sit well with a lot of people on my end. The person who called it in didn't give up a name, but we're looking closely at two guards, both longtimers, which is a real shame. Hopefully, Gonzalez will have some answers soon."

My stomach roiled and for a moment I thought I might get sick. I took a sip of water and did my best to play it off. "How much trouble are they in?"

"Depends on what they've done."

"I'm guessing it was another guard that reported it?"

She glanced over her shoulder. "Listen, I've been thinking about this all morning." Lowering her voice: "If I was to get clearance, would you be willing to take a look at some of Gallagher's correspondence?"

"Haven't your people already done that?"

"They have, but they didn't have much luck. I'm hoping you might be able to spot something they missed. Especially since you and Gallagher are so . . . since you're so familiar with him."

Especially since you and Gallagher are so close, she was about to say.

I was prepared to come back with *I'm only close to him because of you*—but I stopped myself. As much as I wanted it to be true, it wasn't. Even now, my stomach in knots after what the lieutenant had just told me about the rogue prison guards, I had to admit that I was intrigued by the idea of poking around in Gallagher's personal mail. Intrigued? Who was I kidding? I couldn't wait to get my hands on it. And I was almost certain that meant something was very wrong with me.

"Sure, I could do that," I told her.

"I'll make a call. See if I can have it brought here to the house."

"Today?"

She nodded. "As soon as possible. It's only a matter of time until he kills again."

5

As soon as Lieutenant McClernan left, I stepped outside and made a call. It went right to voice mail. I waited for the beep and left a message: "Delete everything. Get rid of your burner phone. Right away." I hung up, erased the number from my contacts, and went back inside.

6

Shortly before noon, two plainclothes detectives pulled up by the gate and took turns lugging in Joshua Gallagher's mail. I asked them to stack the cartons on the kitchen floor and began emptying their contents onto the island. Kara walked by and gave me the stink eye but didn't say anything. She knew how important this was.

Neither detective was particularly friendly—in fact, one of them refused to even make eye contact with me—and it didn't take long to figure out why. They were both members of the unit that had spent the past seven days going over Gallagher's mail with a fine-tooth comb. Having to hand-deliver their work to someone I'm certain they viewed as a wannabe cop—or even worse—so *he* could look it over in order to spot something they might've missed was a major case of adding insult to injury. It had to be at least a little bit humiliating.

As soon as the grumpy detectives left, Carly joined me in the kitchen. The lieutenant hadn't said anything about Carly helping—and she certainly hadn't been granted clearance—but I wasn't too worried about that. With my head the way it was, I needed a second pair of eyes, and whether she wanted to admit it or not, Carly knew her stuff when it came to Joshua Gallagher.

Lieutenant McClernan hadn't been exaggerating. Today's delivery was only a partial sampling of Gallagher's mail, but it was overwhelming to look at. There were piles upon piles of postcards and letters, greeting cards marking every imaginable occasion. Stacks of photographs featuring an eclectic range of subjects—people of all ages, many of them in various stages of undress, along with cats and dogs, gardens and mountains, sunsets and birthday cakes. There were books and magazines and newspapers from all over the country. Two cartons stuffed entirely with Bibles, some of them family heirlooms, many with personalized messages scrawled inside.

And they all had a distinctive smell to them. The cloying aroma of closed, locked-away spaces with not enough fresh air. Not necessarily musty, like when you first walk into a small-town antique shop, the little bell over the door tinkling your arrival. At least that odor came with a comforting familiarity that embraced you and immediately made you feel welcome. This smell was something different. Somber and filled with echoes of loneliness and regret. It was a *forgotten* smell, the kind you experienced when you stumbled upon a shoebox filled with old love letters at the bottom of your closet. The handwriting might still be a bit familiar, but the person who wrote those once meaningful words was a stranger to you now.

The first couple hours of work was fascinating and much more entertaining than I ever would've imagined. Joshua Gallagher was currently one of the country's most infamous figures and we were getting an unfiltered peek at the collective mindset of his legion of followers. These weren't comments on a public message board or a series of vicious tweets or anonymous ravings on a podcast hotline. These were passionate, private thoughts and emotions laid bare. These were secret missives from hearts and souls, intended exclusively for Gallagher's eyes.

Supportive—often downright fawning—letters outnumbered the hate mail by a ten-to-one ratio. I read several marriage proposals out loud. Carly read twice as many letters expressing undying love and admiration, some rather explicit. Kara popped into the kitchen just long enough to grab a container of yogurt and solidify our reputation as ghouls after Carly recited a poem about seashells that an eighteen-year-old girl from Long Beach, California, had mailed to the prison.

The rest of the afternoon passed a bit slower and without as much fanfare. We were already beginning to notice a repetitiveness in the letters, especially those written by women. Most of them wanted to heal Gallagher by showering him with the love they felt he'd been denied. There were also a number of long-winded attempts at religious conversion. Baptists mostly, with Methodists and Catholics as close runners-up, can you say an amen.

The photographs, though, were the worst of it, at least for me. So many young people, dazed and unsmiling. The same with the dozens of self-taken portraits of lonely and forlorn men and women, the majority appearing to be in their thirties, forties, and fifties. No one looked happy, and it wasn't difficult to figure out why. For one tantalizing moment, I thought that Mr. Schatz, my third-grade teacher, was part of the Gallagher fanbase, but then I realized that he'd have to be in his late seventies these days, and it was merely a much younger lookalike. There were also missives scrawled on the backs of menus, church bulletins, promotional flyers, and junk mail envelopes. Carly and I took an especially close look at these to determine if there was any hidden messaging on the reverse sides, but failed to come up with anything even remotely usable.

By five thirty, my stomach was growling and my head was beginning to throb. I told myself just one more carton and then I'd take a break. As luck would have it, that's when I came across a large stack of letters bound together with thick rubber bands. They were all from Benjamin Thacker, the man Josh Gallagher had told me about.

I explained to Carly what Gallagher had said to me about Thacker—how the cadence was off in his writing. As I finished reading each handwritten page, I passed them across the island for her to review. When we were done with the letters, we made shrimp salad sandwiches and discussed our thoughts.

"I don't know," Carly said in between bites. "I see what he means about the cadence, but it feels more like sloppy writing than anything else."

"Maybe," I said, cramming a handful of barbecue chips into my mouth. "But there's definitely some kind of weird rhythm going on too.

It's like he's one person when he's writing about things that are happy or exciting, and he's completely different when he's writing about things that make him angry or sad." I picked up one of the letters and pointed at a paragraph break. "Even the handwriting is slightly off."

Carly leaned closer for a better look. "Huh. You're right. Wow. I didn't notice that."

"That's because I'm an ace investigator and you're not."

"How about you're an ace moron and I'm not?"

7

"Hey, I think I might've found something."

I looked up at Carly and my eyes had trouble focusing. It was almost eight o'clock, and we were spent. Only a carton and a half of mail remained on the kitchen island. "What is it?"

"It might be nothing." She picked up a handful of letters and passed them over to me. "Look at these in the order that I have them. Tell me if you notice anything interesting."

I read them one after the other. When I was finished, I read them again.

The first letter was from a woman who lived in Crisfield, a tiny town located on the eastern shore of Maryland. It was handwritten in flawless script. The second, from a female college student in Reading, Pennsylvania, was generated by an old dot-matrix printer. The words were blurry around the edges but still readable. The final letter was laser-printed on textured paper stock. The author was from my current home of Bel Air, although I didn't recognize the street name.

"You see it yet?"

"Um . . ." I looked up at Carly. ". . . they all seem to mention the name Meyers? Meyers Road. Meyers Park. This one, Meyers Manufacturing."

"Very good. What else?"

I looked down at the unfolded sheet of paper in my hand. "This is the third mention in as many letters about window wells. This one too. Why do they all bring up window wells at some point?"

"Not normally such a popular topic, is it?"

"I wrote in *Chasing the Boogeyman* about how we used to catch toads in window wells when we were kids."

"I remember."

"Do me a favor," I said, my brain suddenly switching gears. "Google 'Meyers Road' in Crisfield. See if it actually exists." I picked up my phone. "I'll look for 'Meyers Park' in Reading."

It took less than ninety seconds.

"No Meyers Road anywhere near Crisfield," she reported.

I put my phone down. "Three parks in Reading. None of them Meyers."

"So they made it up? But why?"

I picked up the letters and examined the envelopes in which they'd been delivered. "They're all postmarked the third or fourth week of May. Right before the murders began."

"You think it's worth passing on to McClernan?"

"I think so." I hesitated, something else hovering at the edge of my fried brain. "Wait a minute . . ." I flipped through the pages again. "The first lady . . . she mentions that she's left-handed. The second one writes that she broke the thumb on her left hand when she was a little girl."

"And the third?"

I scanned the letter again. "There it is! His nickname in the navy was Lefty."

"So are you going to tell me what it all means?"

I got up and stretched. "It means we're going to the Meyers House to look in a window well."

8

I did my best to drive the speed limit, but it wasn't easy.

"I'm still not sure I get it," Carly said. "If you think there's something hidden in the window well, why would these people be giving clues to Gallagher? It's not like he can jump in a car and go look for himself."

"I think *I* was meant to find those clues. Or at least the police were, but they missed it."

"How in the . . . why would Gallagher do that?"

"You've been saying it yourself for years. So has McClernan. Gallagher's all about playing games. He's all about proving that he's smarter than the rest of us."

She started twirling her hair. "So you're saying Gallagher set all this up weeks before Anne Riggs was killed?"

"Based on the postmarks on those letters . . . yes."

"And how did he get these people to play along?"

"I can't figure that part out."

"Wait a minute . . . doesn't that mean he knows who the killer is?"

"Maybe. Probably."

"What if we check the window wells and don't find anything?"

"I guess it means I'm full of shit and wrong about all of this." I thought for a moment. "Or someone else beat us to it."

My cell phone buzzed. It was Lieutenant McClernan.

"Hey, you're on speakerphone."

"Kara said you two went somewhere in a hurry, but she didn't know where you were headed. I'm pretty sure she was lying. Anything I should be worried about?"

"Not at all. Just taking a drive to clear our heads. It's been a long day."

"You find anything?"

"Maybe. We're not sure. We might have something to show you later tonight."

"We, huh?" She made that *tsk*ing sound in the back of her throat. "So, Joe Hardy and Nancy Drew are back on the case?"

"Remind me to flip you the bird next time I see you."

"I'm actually on my way to your house right now."

I glanced at Carly. "Did something else happen?"

"I just got off the phone with Officer Hoffman. Someone definitely infiltrated both of your laptops. Looks like it was done remotely. Whoever did it had access to your email accounts, your personal files, even the security system." She took a deep breath. "Not good, Rich."

9

The walk up the long gravel driveway in front of the Meyers House felt like it took an eternity, but in reality, it was probably less than five minutes. My head was still spinning over Lieutenant McClernan's revelation that all my personal information had been compromised by a bad actor. One who wanted to do me serious harm.

We'd just gotten started when Carly asked, "What if it's a trap and someone's waiting up there in the dark to strangle us and cut off our ears?"

"He won't get both of us. We'll be fine."

"So what you're saying is the slowest runner is screwed." She giggled nervously.

"No one's going to be running. Now keep quiet."

We walked for the next few minutes in silence, the only sounds the crunching of gravel beneath our shoes and the occasional passing car.

Other than the scattering of trees that had grown so tall around it, shading windows that had once seen nothing but sunlight, the Meyers House looked like a faded snapshot from our youth. Built in the mid-1800s, it was a massive Victorian structure with a wide, deeply shadowed front porch, twin gabled peaks, and dozens of windows that watched over the town with a foreboding intensity. We'd grown up believing that the house had once been home to a coven of nineteenth-century witches, but no one could remember if we'd made that story up or if it was true. Of course, we could've easily googled it to find out, but none of us were really interested in that. I knew what I believed, and that's all that really mattered. It was only 8:50 p.m., but all the windows were dark and the porch light was off. Crickets chirped in the tall grass. The house loomed above us like a sleeping giant.

"Is it the left side when we're facing the house?" Carly whispered. "Or when we're standing on the porch looking out?"

Shit. Good question. "We're the visitors here, so I pick facing the house."

The closer we got, the slower we walked, but eventually we made it to the end of the driveway. With me taking the lead, we tiptoed into the uncut grass until we reached the edge of the porch, and then we dropped down onto our bellies, clothes be damned, and crawled the rest of the way in. I should have felt foolish, but I didn't. Not even a little bit. I was too nervous—and excited.

Without using the flashlight on my cell phone, it was impossible to see where the window wells were located on this side of the house. I tried to remember from when I was a kid, but I couldn't and that ticked me off more than it should have. Small rocks and twigs nipped at my hands and knees. The grass itched my face and arms, and made me want to sneeze. I caught a strong whiff of dog crap somewhere close by. I prayed whoever lived here didn't have a big dog—or any dog at all, for that matter.

A moment later, a bed of mulch replaced the grassy lawn upon which we were crawling, and my outstretched hand brushed against the curved metal frame of a window well. I motioned for Carly to ease up alongside me—and with my heart pounding in my chest, I blindly reached down into the well. My fingers touched wet rocks, muddy earth, and a scattering of weeds. Holding my breath, I braced myself for the mottled slick skin of a fat toad or even a whole family of toads. Squirming and hopping and spraying pee everywhere. A toad pissing all over my hand was one thing, but if a snake of any size so much as slithered against my fingers, I was going to scream like a child with skinned knees on a playground. I didn't care who the hell I woke up or how many guard dogs they had. Gritting my teeth, I dug around for another minute or so, but didn't find anything.

I began crawling again, working my way further up the side of the house. The smell of dog shit grew stronger. Pausing momentarily to wipe the sweat out of my eyes, I accidentally kicked Carly in the side of her head. Behind me, I heard her hiss, "Ow! Watch it, you cocksucker."

God, it was good to have her back. "Sorry."

"Idiot."

The next window well was filled with tiny pebbles. I dug deep, using both hands, and felt something with the tips of my fingers, maybe five or six inches down. I widened my hands and burrowed underneath the object until I felt it come loose. Finally, I scooped it out, a waterfall of pebbles raining down between my fingers into the well.

"Shhh," Carly whispered.

It was too dark to see any details, but I could plainly feel *two* objects resting in the palms of my hands. The first was a baseball. I could tell by the raised stitches—and the memory of my father teaching me how to throw a curveball in the backyard after dinner rushed out of the darkness and filled my head. I pushed it away as quickly as I could.

The second object was a pair of eyeglasses. Just the frames, really. Both of the lenses were missing.

A thought suddenly came to me.

Three letters containing clues . . . three buried treasures . . . it makes sense, I decided, handing off the ball and glasses to Carly. Leaning forward again, I dug deeper this time, almost to my elbows. I wiggled my fingers and made contact with something almost immediately. From the shape and feel of it, I had no idea what I'd found.

Carly suddenly poked me hard in the ribs.

"What the—"

"Someone's coming!"

I listened and heard the distant crunch of car tires on gravel. A split-second later, headlights emerged from the darkness halfway up the driveway.

"What do we do?" Carly whispered.

I looked around. It was too late to run. Any direction we fled, we would be seen.

"Lay down flat," I said. "I'm going to bury you."

"You're going to *what?*"

"Shut up and lie down." She did and I began covering her in mulch. If whoever was driving that car parked in front, we might be okay. But if

they parked out back, they'd almost certainly get an up close and personal view of our hiding spot on their way by—and we'd be toast.

"Don't get it in my eyes. I'm wearing contacts."

"Be quiet and don't move."

"Rich, it's going to look like someone buried a body in their garden.
Not exactly the right vibe these days."

"For God's sake, please shut the fuck up!"

I crab-walked to the nearest window well and slid my legs inside. I
used to hide in window wells all the time when I was a kid, but I wasn't
twelve anymore. Nor was I skinny. The entire top half of my body was
exposed. Feeling like a total jackass, I pulled my T-shirt up to my eyes
and lowered my head, trying to will myself to disappear.

Headlights washed over us and then abruptly swung toward the
front of the porch, leaving us in darkness again. We were in luck.
So far.

The engine turned off. I heard the chirring of crickets and Carly's
heavy breathing. Jesus. It sounded like she was hyperventilating.

A car door slammed shut.

Keys jangled.

Noisy footfalls went silent as the driver stepped into the grass.

And coughed.

A man.

And then he began humming.

The air around me suddenly went ice-cold. Gooseflesh rose on my
arms and legs.

It was the same somber tune Joshua Gallagher always hummed
when he was trying to remember something. The man out there in the
dark was a little off-key, but I was sure of it.

Heavy footsteps crossed the front porch.

A key was inserted into a doorknob.

A door opened and closed.

Silence.

I held my breath and waited for a light to come on inside the house—but it never did.

I silently counted to twenty and shimmied out of the window well.

"Let's go," I whispered, feeling around for Carly. "Try not to make any noise."

She shrugged off a blanket of mulch—like a corpse erupting from a grave—and followed close behind me.

Retracing our path, we crawled on our elbows to the corner of the porch. Then, we got to our feet and ran as fast as we could back to the car, which was parked across the street in front of the bank. By the time we got there, we were both gasping for breath. The front of our shorts and T-shirts were stained and filthy. Carly's hair was a tangled mess of dirt and bits of mulch. One—or both—of us smelled like dog shit. An older couple coming out of the Chinese restaurant next door took one look at us, glaring with daggers of suspicion, and hurried to their car.

Before we pulled out of the parking lot, I turned on the interior light and examined the objects we'd found.

A baseball signed by Stephen King and dated on my birthday. It was smudged with dirt and the autograph was barely visible. It normally sat on an overcrowded bookshelf in my office.

A pair of Ray-Ban sunglasses belonging to my wife. They'd been missing now for weeks.

And a small hand-carved ashtray my father had brought home from Italy after World War II. The last place I'd seen it was on the mantel of the fireplace in our living room.

10

Lieutenant McClernan's unmarked sedan was sitting in the driveway when we pulled in. As I steered around it, I glanced at the front of the house and did a double-take. The lieutenant was standing on the porch with Detective Gonzalez at her side. In front of them was a uniformed trooper; my wife, Kara; and Ken Klein.

Uh-oh, I thought, getting out and hurrying over. Behind me, camera flashes transformed night into day. Jagged shadows danced all around me.

"What's going on?" I asked, looking at Kara. "Everything okay?"

"We just had a bit of excitement," the lieutenant answered, "but everything's fine."

Carly bounded onto the porch. "What happened?"

"I thought he was trying to sneak into the backyard," Ken Klein sputtered. "That's the only reason I tackled him."

I looked at McClernan for an explanation.

"About forty minutes ago, Mr. Klein noticed a young male standing around Anne Riggs's memorial. The boy eventually drifted closer to the house and took a seat on the split-rail fence by your driveway. Mr. Klein approached him in an admittedly aggressive manner and asked him what he was doing. The boy fled over the fence into your side yard and was eventually tackled by Mr. Klein."

Ken's face flushed a deep crimson. He stared down at the ground. I waited for the rest of the story.

"Mr. Klein took the boy over to Trooper Parker, who was sitting inside his cruiser on the opposite side of the driveway. The boy identified himself as one of your writing students."

"Students?" I asked. "I don't . . . *oh*, wait a minute, is his name Sam?"

Detective Gonzalez consulted his notebook. "Samuel English, yep. Fifteen years old."

"Jesus," I said, looking around. "Is he still here? Is he okay?"

"He's fine," the lieutenant said. "His parents picked him up about ten minutes ago. They seemed very upset . . . about all of this."

"No fucking wonder. The poor kid called a few days ago to tell me he wasn't allowed to meet with me anymore about his writing."

"You didn't tell me that," Kara said.

"I forgot. Too much stuff crammed inside my head."

"He told us he was spending the night with a friend a couple of blocks away from here," Gonzalez said. "He came by to make sure you were okay after your hospital visit."

I glared at my neighbor. "And you decided to beat him up."

"I didn't mean to . . . I was just trying to help."

"For fuck's sake, Ken! Next time, leave the helping to the police, will you?"

I stormed past him into the house.

11

"You were kind of rough on Ken tonight," Kara said once we were settled in bed.

"Ken's an idiot. And you can quote me on that."

She smiled and turned off the light. "What did Sam's father have to say when you called?"

"Not much. I'm persona non grata in the English household right now."

"They'll come around."

"Ehhh, I don't know about that. Maybe."

"If I ask you something, do you promise you'll tell the truth? Even if it doesn't make me feel good?"

Uh-oh. "Yes, of course."

"Do you really think they're going to catch this guy? I've been thinking about it . . . Rich, it took almost thirty years to arrest Gallagher."

"Police investigations are a lot more sophisticated now than they were in the eighties. He'll make a mistake and they'll catch him."

"Before or after he kills another girl?"

"That part I don't know."

She sighed and put her hand on my chest. "Today was really . . . *really* bad."

"I know. I'm sorry."

"Do you think our computers are safe now?"

"To the best of my knowledge. At least that's what McClernan says. Officer Hoffman and her partner made sure of it."

"I still can't believe we were hacked. You read about it happening to other people and you see it on television all the time . . . but it feels different when it happens to you." She shuddered. "And it's not like he even did it to steal money or our identities. He used it to *spy* on us. All this time we've been talking about this guy, he was right here with us . . . hiding in plain sight."

"I'm sorry I didn't tell you about the Meyers House. I didn't want you to worry." I cleared my throat. "Or get mad."

"Oh, I'm plenty mad," she said, and pinched my nipple.

"Oww! What the hell?"

"That's what you get for sneaking around that old house in the dark on some kind of ridiculous scavenger hunt."

"I had no choice."

"Did you ever think that it could've been a trick just to get you there?"

"As a matter of fact, Carly and I both thought of that."

"Don't even say her name. She's just as bad as you are—and she can make her own damn breakfast tomorrow morning."

"This is exactly why I didn't want to tell you."

"McClernan was plenty pissed too, in case you didn't notice."

"I noticed."

We lay in silence for a while. When Kara spoke again, her voice sounded very small.

"If I think about it long enough . . . someone sneaking around inside our house . . . in your office . . . taking those things . . . I just want to scream and break something."

I rolled onto my side and hugged her close in the dark of our bedroom. It should've felt like the safest place in the world—but I knew better.

A small sampling of Joshua Gallagher's mail *(Photo courtesy of Carly Albright)*

The Meyers House *(Photo courtesy of Alex Baliko)*

Excerpt from "unsupervised" phone interview with Joshua Gallagher, age 55, inmate #AC4311920 at Cumberland Penitentiary, recorded on June 1, 2020:

CHIZMAR: Besides Anne Riggs, were there any other women who got away from you after you'd targeted them?

GALLAGHER: Yes.

CHIZMAR: What can you tell me about them?

GALLAGHER: There were only two, and I will always remember their faces.

CHIZMAR: If you were set free tomorrow, would you try to find them? Would you kill again?

GALLAGHER: I don't know.

CHIZMAR: I think you do know. Just be honest with me, Josh. If you were set free in the world tomorrow, no strings attached, would you kill again?

GALLAGHER: [pause] I don't know.

EIGHTEEN

A CULT OF PERSONALITY

"I really am the Darkness."

1

My phone buzzed on the nightstand, pulling me up from the murky depths of a fragile sleep.

I reached over and tried to silence it, thinking it was the alarm, but then I saw the notice for a front yard motion alert. I tapped the little arrow and watched Lieutenant McClernan climb out of her car. It was 7:15 a.m. Something was up. I slipped out of bed and padded quietly downstairs, hoping to reach her before she rang the bell.

Sidestepping several of JJ's dog toys, I crossed the foyer and pulled open the door, offering the lieutenant a sleepy smile. "We have to stop meeting like this."

"We need to talk. Now." Her face was granite.

Uh-oh. My stomach sank as I suddenly realized why she was here. Dressed in my pajamas, I stepped onto the porch and closed the door behind me.

"You didn't think we'd find out?" she asked, with barely contained rage. Her eyes were a forest fire. The veins in her neck were bulging. "Do you know what the hell you've done?"

I struggled to look at her. "I fucked up. I'm sorry."

She glanced at the handful of photographers standing across the street. "I just got off the phone with Gonzalez. Do you know how badly he wants to press charges? And not just against Ridgely and Runk. He wants you, too."

"Runk? He had nothing to do with this."

"I know that," she hissed, straining to keep her voice low. "He got caught up in your tail-wash. He's been selling Gallagher's drawings for five hundred bucks a pop. In exchange for a regular supply, he smuggled Gallagher a burner phone. We took it out of his cell an hour ago, but there was no SIM card. We think he flushed it. Or swallowed it."

"Jesus." Gallagher in possession of a phone changed everything. "How long did he have it?"

"That's what we're trying to figure out. At least two weeks. Runk took it back when word got out that we were going to search Gallagher's cell."

"And gave it back to him again?"

"Sure did," she said, shaking her head in disgust. "Carl Runk's life is about to change. A whole pile of shit is coming his way."

"What about Sharon? Will she lose her job because of this?"

"Gee, you think, Rich? These are serious security breaches." She looked across the street again. "When those guys over there get wind of this, I'm not sure we can keep your name out of it."

I hadn't even thought about that. "I deserve whatever I get."

"One thing has been swirling around inside my head: Was it worth it? All of this mess—*all* of it—for a stupid book?"

I looked up at her in surprise. "It was never about a book."

She laughed, and it was an ugly sound. "I trusted you, Rich. All this time. And you threw it away for what, fortune and glory? The goddamn bestseller list?"

"Listen to me," I said, walking closer to her. "I know I screwed up. Bad. I'll accept full responsibility for that. But you have to believe me . . . this was never about a book or a movie or anything like that."

She looked down her nose at me, like an annoyed teacher studying a disobedient child. "Then what *was* it for, Rich? Why the hell else would you bribe a guard to get Gallagher's medical reports, psychiatrist notes, his family history? Why? Why else did you want to speak to him unsupervised?"

"It was . . . it was all . . . for me." I suddenly realized that I was fighting back tears. "I was trying to *understand*. Why he was the way he was." I cleared my throat. "And trying to understand myself. Why all this happened the way it did. And not just with Gallagher . . ."

"What are you talking about?"

"Can we sit down for a minute?" I wiped my eyes and gestured to the front stoop. "There's something I need to tell you . . ."

2

"I'm still pissed off."

It had taken nearly an hour to tell Lieutenant McClernan the story of Henry Metheny and to come clean about all I had done—just long enough for her to calm down. A little bit, anyway. Kara had poked her head out the door a while back, asked if everything was okay, and disappeared back into the house when we lied and said it was.

"Just wait until I tell my wife everything I just told you, and she finds out I told you first. You'll have to wait in line to kick my ass."

"It'll be worth it." She shouldered me, but not too hard. "You've jeopardized the whole investigation, you realize that. And now Gonzalez is out for blood."

"I can try talking to him."

"Yeah . . . no. You might want to wait a few days for that."

"There should be phone records of all three of the unsupervised calls between me and Gallagher. Gonzalez will be able to see that they occurred over a year ago."

"That's the thing. He's a hell of an investigator, and he'll believe there's more to the story. Because in our experience, there usually is once something like this is uncovered."

"But there's not. Ridgely got me the paperwork piecemeal over an eighteen-month period. Every time something new was added to his file, she made a copy. One other time, she photocopied some pages from his journal. And the three phone calls. That was it."

"And you're telling me it was a coincidence that both Ridgely and Runk just happened to end up with burner phones?"

"Completely. I had nothing to do with Sharon getting a second phone. That was all her. She was trying to be careful."

"Gonzalez is going to want to look at your phone records all the way back to when Gallagher was first arrested."

"He's welcome to. I have nothing . . . else to hide."

"I hope you're telling me the truth this time."

I held up my hand like a Boy Scout. "I swear I am."

"You know, I would've gotten those things for you, if you'd asked—not the unsupervised calls, but the rest of it."

"I did ask. You said no."

Her forehead wrinkled. "When?"

"Back when all this started. Right after the first time I interviewed him."

"We had way too many eyes on us in the beginning, namely the governor and his ass-kissing sycophants. You should have waited a few months and asked again."

"I didn't know."

"Well, you're an idiot."

"That, I do know."

The mailman swung into the driveway and stopped behind the lieutenant's car. He got out and walked over to us. "Sorry to interrupt. I have a package you need to sign for." He reached out with his handheld scanner. I took the stylus dangling from the side and signed my name on the dotted line. He handed me a large envelope and went on his way. "You all have a nice day."

"You too." I glanced at the label. It was from Kristin, my literary agent. I looked up and the lieutenant was staring at me.

"Promise me one more time that it wasn't all for your book."

"I promise," I said.

She took a deep breath. "Gonzalez is going to hate it, but you know what we have to do now?"

3

"I'll have you folks back on the ground in just under an hour, Lieutenant."

If I'd needed a reminder of the urgency with which the Maryland State Police were pursuing this case, I was currently riding in the back of it. I watched out the window as the Forest Hill Airpark grew smaller.

It was 9:55 a.m., and Lieutenant McClernan and I were sitting in the back of an EC135 helicopter en route to the Cumberland Penitentiary. We were both harnessed in and wearing headphones with built-in microphones. Our pilot's name was Ronald. He looked all of twenty years old.

For the first time since all of this started, I felt like the investigation had some sort of forward momentum. I regretted every second of going behind Lieutenant McClernan's back, and I was devastated to learn that Sharon Ridgely was going to lose her job, but I still couldn't help but think that maybe something good might come of it. Because I'd been busted, the police had discovered Gallagher's burner phone and confirmed his involvement. Now, they had somewhere to start. It'd also led to me telling the lieutenant about Henry Metheny. An immense weight had been lifted off my shoulders. I knew it was a selfish thought, but I couldn't help it. Thirty-nine years was a long time to walk around with such a deeply buried secret in your heart.

I looked over at McClernan in the seat next to me. *"You mentioned that Runk did other favors for Gallagher . . . !"*

"You don't have to shout," she replied, giving me that annoyed teacher look again. "The mics are very sensitive."

"Sorry."

"The other perks of their little deal included extra time in the yard, access to online crossword puzzles in the library, girlie magazines, postage stamps, that sort of thing. The burner phone was the main prize."

"And there's no way to track who he was talking to?"

"Not without that SIM card. That's where you come in."

"You really think he'll tell me?"

"You certainly have a better chance than the rest of us."

I stared out the window at the passing countryside. "He had to be talking to whoever's doing this. The timing's too perfect."

"I'd bet on it." She looked at me. "Do you feel like he betrayed you?"

I thought of the note card I kept in my truck.

He's wearing a mask underneath his mask.

"No. I knew what he was capable of." I readjusted the headphones so they'd stop rubbing against my bandage. I no longer had a splitting headache, but the stitches were itching like crazy. "Anything else come in about the people who own the Meyers House?"

"Just what I told you before." She opened the notepad in her lap. "Casey and Eleanor Sherman. Both in their late seventies. They bought the house nineteen years ago. He's a retired judge. She used to be a nurse. Two adult children. Both live out of state. No known connections to Joshua Gallagher or his family. They were living in Cecil County when the original murders occurred."

"I wish you could ask him about the song he was humming."

"Me too. But I can't exactly say you overheard him while you were hiding in his goddamn window well."

"I said I was sorry."

"You're lucky you didn't get the both of you killed."

"It was fine," I said, wishing I hadn't brought it up.

"But you didn't know that then, did you?"

I shook my head.

"How positive are you it was the same song?"

"A hundred percent."

Her eyes remained locked on me. "I'm going to go against Gonzalez's very strong wishes and share two things with you. Don't make me regret it."

"I swear I won't."

"Do you know a man named Sean Phillips?"

I thought about it. "I don't think so."

She held up her cell phone. On the screen, there was a photo of a white male, twenties, with several facial scars and medium-length hair that was almost white. He was missing half an eyebrow.

"Never seen him before. I would've remembered someone who looked like that."

"He worked on your home in April of this year."

"I was on the road for most of April."

"According to the owner of the HVAC company, Sean Phillips was a temporary fill-in for an employee who was hospitalized with a bleeding ulcer. For two days—April 27 and 28—he had access to your house and home office."

"So you think he's the one who took the items we found in the window well?"

"It's starting to look that way," she said. "The owner had forgotten to tell us about Phillips during our initial questioning. We spoke with him again late last night and he brought it up then. We ran Phillips's name right away. He's got an interesting record that he lied about to his employers. Gonzalez said he was definitely hiding something during our questioning this morning."

"What's his connection to Gallagher?"

"We haven't found anything yet, but we're still looking. We're also checking out his alibis for the nights of the murders."

"Is this like . . . some kind of cult?" I asked. "Joshua Gallagher's followers doing his bidding for him?"

"An interesting angle. It wouldn't be the first time it's happened. Charles Manson. Jim Jones. It's a long list."

I watched as a train crossed over a trestle bridge spanning a muddy river thousands of feet below us. It reminded me of the miniature railroad my father and I used to build in our basement during the holidays. If he had known about what I'd done—and all the people I'd lied to—he would've been ashamed of me.

"The second thing I have to tell you," the lieutenant said, "is a bit more sensitive . . . and you cannot repeat it to *anyone*."

"I won't."

"This is strictly confidential, Rich. You understand me? It *cannot* come out."

"Understood."

"Okay . . . we're still figuring this one out. The bite marks we found on Anne Riggs and Peyton Bair were difficult to work with. They were sloppy, tentative. In each instance, the skin was broken and bruised, but there weren't enough precise indentations to measure or compare. We chalked this up to the killer being in a hurry, something you noted as well."

"Right."

"But the marks on Mallory Tucker are different. They're deep, and distinctive. And . . . somehow . . ."

I held my breath, waiting for her to finish.

". . . they're an exact match to Joshua Gallagher."

4

My favorite guard, Elgin, escorted me down the hallway. He was uncharacteristically quiet and didn't hit me with a single joke—dirty or otherwise—which made me wonder if he knew I'd helped cost Sharon Ridgely her job.

He left me alone in the interview room for almost fifteen minutes before the other guards brought in Joshua Gallagher. They'd been instructed to pay special attention today in case the prisoner tried anything.

I'd told the lieutenant that I planned to really push Gallagher, something I'd never done in all these years. Even now, I didn't want to give too much thought as to why that was the case. To ease my mind, McClernan assured me that she would be right next door watching from behind a two-way mirror.

Earlier, the lieutenant had told me that Joshua Gallagher's cell had been thoroughly searched overnight, turning up the burner phone and a handful of other less notable contraband. All his reading and drawing materials had been confiscated, as well as the photographs of his family he kept taped to his wall. I'd expected Gallagher to be furious at this invasion of privacy, or at the very least, seriously annoyed.

But as it turned out, I was wrong.

When I heard the door to the interrogation room open, I put down my notebook and looked up.

Joshua Gallagher was smiling.

5

The following is an unabridged conversation between Richard Chizmar and Joshua Gallagher, inmate #AC4311920. It took place at the Cumberland Penitentiary on Sunday, June 19, 2022.

CHIZMAR: What are you so happy about?

GALLAGHER: I wouldn't say I'm particularly happy. Amused, maybe.

CHIZMAR: I'm not in the mood for games today, Josh.

GALLAGHER: I should think not. Especially with that bandage on your head. That must've been terribly painful.

CHIZMAR: Who's the copycat killer?

GALLAGHER: I already told you, I don't know.

CHIZMAR: You're lying.

GALLAGHER: I absolutely am not.

CHIZMAR: We already know you talked to him on the burner phone, so stop bullshitting me.

GALLAGHER: That doesn't mean I know who he is.

CHIZMAR: You're saying you don't know his actual identity?

GALLAGHER: I do not.

CHIZMAR: Is he local? Where does he live?

GALLAGHER: Well, sure, close by, of course.

CHIZMAR: Edgewood?

GALLAGHER: What do you think?

CHIZMAR: What else do you know about him?

GALLAGHER: Not that much.

CHIZMAR: Why don't you just come out and tell me?

GALLAGHER: [pause] I'm unaware of his actual age. I believe he's neither young or old. He's well spoken and well traveled. A man of letters, so to speak. And *very* devoted to his cause.

CHIZMAR: Which is?

GALLAGHER: You and me, of course. And history.

CHIZMAR: How so?

GALLAGHER: Immortality.

CHIZMAR: How often did you talk to him?

GALLAGHER: I spoke with him on two different occasions. Both times, he called me.

CHIZMAR: How did he manage to do that?

GALLAGHER: Through a friend.

CHIZMAR: [pause] What's this friend's name?

GALLAGHER: I actually don't know. I asked him not to tell me.

CHIZMAR: So it's a *him*. You've spoken with this friend on the phone?

GALLAGHER: [nods] Numerous times.

CHIZMAR: And . . . this friend is working hand-in-hand with the copycat killer. The friend knows who's doing this.

GALLAGHER: No more than I do. You're barking up the wrong tree here, Rich. He was contacted anonymously and was only too happy to pass along my information.

CHIZMAR: I don't understand this at all. How did the copycat killer know this person, this friend, had access to you?

GALLAGHER: I'm afraid that's rather complicated. I don't fully understand all of the details myself.

CHIZMAR: I think you're lying to me again.

GALLAGHER: I think you know better, Rich. I grew up in a different time, as much as you did. There are things I don't understand.

CHIZMAR: Did you speak with anyone else on the phone?

GALLAGHER: Not anyone related to this . . . situation.

CHIZMAR: What the hell does that mean?

GALLAGHER: It means I may have used it to satisfy my own curiosity about . . . certain things and certain people . . . but nothing that had anything to do with what's currently happening in our beloved hometown.

CHIZMAR: Would your friend's name happen to be Sean Phillips?

GALLAGHER: I'm sorry, but I told you already—I don't know.

CHIZMAR: Or maybe Sean Phillips is the copycat killer's real name.

GALLAGHER: [shrugs] If you say so. I have no idea.

CHIZMAR: Was it your friend who stole those things from my house?

GALLAGHER: [smiles] Oh! You found them?

CHIZMAR: [nods] Yesterday.

GALLAGHER: I *told* him you would! I *knew* it! I always knew you were smarter than the police.

CHIZMAR: You told *who* I would?

GALLAGHER: My friend, of course! He thought it was a waste of time. I, however, insisted otherwise. Thank you for proving me right!

CHIZMAR: All this time . . . the police, the public . . . they were right about you. You love all this. You're fucking crazy. It's all about gamesmanship for you. That, and feeding your enormous ego. You're nothing but a cheap carnival barker.

GALLAGHER: Cheap, huh? You might ask Peyton Bair or Mallory Tucker how cheap I am. [smiles] Oh, that's right, you can't.

CHIZMAR: You know . . . I used to feel sorry for you? Everyone warned me not to, but I didn't listen.

GALLAGHER: I never once asked for your pity, Rich.

CHIZMAR: That's not the point. Josh—every time I came here, I tried to find something . . . *redeemable* in you. Something still human. But . . . there's really nothing to find, is there?

GALLAGHER: [mocking voice] Richard Chizmar, renowned author and honorable family man . . . you know, I wonder what people would think if they knew about some of the things we've talked about. I wonder what they'd say if they knew about some of the dreams you have.

CHIZMAR: Fuck you. Go ahead and threaten me all you want. I don't care anymore. I'm ready for the truth to come out.

GALLAGHER: Well, if that is indeed the case, then perhaps it's time for my little media blackout to come to an end.

CHIZMAR: [voice rising] Do you know what the guards say about you?

GALLAGHER: Are you referring to the guards that you've bribed, or the other ones?

CHIZMAR: [unintelligible]

GALLAGHER: Ahh, I see I've touched the proverbial sore spot.

CHIZMAR: They say that you're nothing but a tired old man who naps too much and harasses the other inmates to play cards for nickels.

GALLAGHER: You forgot about chess and backgammon.

CHIZMAR: That's right. And online crossword puzzles—thanks to Runk. Don't forget about that. Although they must not bring you as much joy since you're only competing against yourself.

GALLAGHER: I think you'd be very surprised at how much joy they bring me.

CHIZMAR: I'm going to ask you one more time and then I'm leaving . . . and I won't be coming back after today.

GALLAGHER: [laughs]

CHIZMAR: Do you know who the copycat killer is?

GALLAGHER: I do not.

CHIZMAR: Do you know how to contact the copycat killer?

GALLAGHER: [pause] Maybe my friend could. But you know, I'm not sure I remember the number. Plus, by now, I'm not even certain he'd take my call anyway. [pause] Or if he even exists for that matter.

CHIZMAR: [slams fist down on table] *Enough!*

GUARD #1: Everything okay, Mr. Chizmar?

CHIZMAR: It's fine, everything's fine. I'm sorry. [to Gallagher] You know, I hate that I've allowed you to waste so much of my time.

GALLAGHER: And yet that so-called waste of time . . . has led you to a life of fame and fortune.

CHIZMAR: Only because people don't know the truth about you, no matter how hard I tried to tell them. They think you're what . . . *special*? Mystical. Powerful. So much so that you've started to believe it yourself. [mimicking him] *"I'm changing. Tell McClernan to recheck my DNA. I want the whole world to see. It's time."* Yeah, I've seen that movie too, Josh. It wasn't that good the first time around. You want the whole world to see what? That you've gotten old and fat and—

GALLAGHER: I could've taken you any day, do you realize that? Not just in the summer and fall of '88. Any day before . . . or since. [leans forward] You think you're so smart, huh? You don't think I watched you over the years? Rosedale? Abingdon? That little house with the basketball court out back? Do you remember the tree you always touched when you went jogging? The big oak in the courtyard of that apartment complex on the hill. You tapped it three times and turned around and headed for home. The same route every evening. And when you bought your first house . . . the way you mowed the lawn in a different pattern every time. Or how you taught Billy to shoot free throws. Do you know that Kara rarely locked the doors when you left back then? You think you're better than me? *Please.* I could've taken you any day I wanted. It would've been so *easy*.

CHIZMAR: [quietly] Then why didn't you, you sick fuck?

GALLAGHER: I answered that question thirty-four years ago, the first time you sat down with me. The day we played basketball. H-O-R-S-E. I beat you two games out of three, and when we were finished, you told me to keep the ball.

CHIZMAR: I remember.

GALLAGHER: That was the last time I felt anything resembling

353

normal. The last time I believed that kind of life was possible for me. And it was because of you.

CHIZMAR: Then why [spreads arms] all! Of! *This!* Why are you *punishing* me? Why are you tormenting my family?

GALLAGHER: Who's tormenting? I *adore* your family, Rich. Do you know that I'm one of Billy's original Patreon supporters? He's quite the talent, takes after his father. And Noah—I spoke with him at Birdwood just last week.

CHIZMAR: You *what*?!

GALLAGHER: I used my own name to reserve an afternoon tee time and he didn't even ask me to repeat it. Just wrote it down and asked for my credit card info. He's very good at his job.

CHIZMAR: If you ever fucking hurt them—

GALLAGHER: I would never, ever hurt them, Rich. How could you think that of me? I love you.

CHIZMAR: Oh my God. [pause] Then . . . why do you want to hurt me? Tell me.

GALLAGHER: [stares at something in the opposite corner of the interrogation room] Sometimes, it gets all mixed up, you know? Love and hate. Sometimes, it begins to mean the same thing. [stares directly at Chizmar] I only know what they show me, what they tell me.

CHIZMAR: What *who* shows you, Josh?

GALLAGHER: Them.

CHIZMAR: [glances over his shoulder; there's nothing there]

GALLAGHER: Do you want to know something, Rich?

CHIZMAR: [nods]

GALLAGHER: The stories are *true*. I *am* the Darkness. I *am* the Boogeyman.

CHIZMAR: [shakes head; sighs] No. No, no—you're just plain old Joshua Gallagher. You're a fifty-seven-year old man. Your brain scans show a number of abnormalities. You see visions inside your head and believe them to be true—

GALLAGHER: I love you, Richard Chizmar. Even more than I loved my sister, and my father, and all of the others.

CHIZMAR: [voice rising] Then help us *stop* whoever is doing this!

GALLAGHER: I'm taller now. Stronger. My wisdom teeth have grown back, did you know that? Make McClernan look at my DNA. It's almost time.

CHIZMAR: Josh, for Christ's sake—none of that is real! None of it makes any—

GALLAGHER: I want the whole world to see. Soon.

CHIZMAR: Josh—!

GALLAGHER: Guards? I'm ready now. I'm tired and would like to return to my cell.

CHIZMAR: Talk to me, Josh. Please! Just for a little bit longer.

GALLAGHER: Not today. Another time, perhaps.

CHIZMAR: I told you already—I'm *not* coming back. I mean it.

GALLAGHER: [stands] You always come back.

GUARD #1: Mr. Chizmar?

CHIZMAR: [looks at two-way mirror; sighs] Go ahead—take him. I'm so done.

GUARD #2: [places a hand on Gallagher's shoulder] Okay, let's go.

GALLAGHER: [gets up from table; smiles] Goodbye for now . . . Richie Rich. [shuffles out the door]

6

"Are you going to tell me what's wrong?" the lieutenant asked. "You look like you just saw a ghost."

"Not here." I pushed open the door and started across the parking lot. "I don't trust anyone in that place."

"Slow down, dammit."

I walked a little farther, stopped, and turned around. My chest was burning. I could barely catch my breath. "He called me Richie Rich."

"Okay . . . I heard that."

"Besides the kids in my first-grade class, there's only one other person who has ever called me that."

"Who and why does it matter?"

"Hank Metheny."

Her eyebrows went up. "The guy you told me about this morning?"

I nodded.

"So he . . . wait a minute. What are you trying to tell me?"

"That Gallagher and Metheny have fucking been in contact with each other!" Something invisible stabbed me in the chest. "I don't know when and I don't know how, but it's *both* of them doing this."

"Rich . . . this morning, after you told me what happened . . . I ran a quick check on Metheny. He's been locked up in federal prison in Georgia."

"I know that—"

"Just wait—there's more. Two weeks ago, Metheny slipped into a coma. The doctors have no idea why it happened. He still hasn't regained consciousness."

7

We were back in the air and on our way home when my cell phone buzzed.

I considered not answering it. My brain was still scrambled from what Josh Gallagher had said to me—*Goodbye for now . . . Richie Rich*—not to mention what the lieutenant had just told me about Henry Metheny.

Sliding the phone out of my pants pocket, I checked the caller ID.

It was Carly Albright. She knew where I was and what I was doing, which meant it had to be important. I took my headset off and placed it onto my lap.

"Hello?"

"I finally figured it out!"

I winced and pulled the phone away from my ear. "Figured what out?"

"I've been watching this damn security footage all morning."

"And?"

"And I was right. Something *was* familiar about this guy. He has one leg shorter than the other. Just like my Walter did. He's wearing an insert in his shoe, Rich. If you watch closely, you can just make out a little over-step. I'm telling you—I'm right about this . . ."

Cumberland Penitentiary guard Carl Runk *(Photo courtesy of Stanley Freed)*

Cumberland Penitentiary guard Sharon Ridgely *(Photo courtesy of Larissa Perkins)*

Joshua Gallagher's burner phone *(Photo courtesy of Maryland State Police)*

DETECTIVE GONZALEZ: Can you describe Henry Metheny's current physical state?

STEVEN WISE, MD: Henry Metheny is in a coma at Jefferson United Hospital. He's unconscious and does not respond to light, sound, or stimuli. His brain is functioning at its lowest state of alertness.

DETECTIVE GONZALEZ: I have to ask . . . is there any chance he's faking this condition?

STEVEN WISE, MD: Metheny has been completely unresponsive for twenty-one days. He's not faking.

DETECTIVE GONZALEZ: How did this occur?

STEVEN WISE, MD: On Thursday, June 2, Metheny ate dinner with the other inmates. Nothing unusual was observed. Later that night, at approximately 9:45 p.m., one of the guards spoke with him. According to the guard, Metheny was sitting on his bunk reading a magazine. He sounded and appeared to be fine. Shortly after lights-out, at 11:05 p.m., another guard observed Metheny while doing his rounds. He appeared to be asleep in his bunk. The next morning, Metheny failed to respond to a 6:30 a.m. wake-up for exercise and hygiene. Guards found him in his cell, examined him, and found him to be unresponsive. A short time later, I examined Metheny with the same results. He was immediately moved to the infirmary. Later that afternoon, he was transferred to Jefferson United Hospital, where he has remained under guard ever since.

DETECTIVE GONZALEZ: Any idea why this happened?

STEVEN WISE, MD: Testing, thus far, has been inconclusive. Metheny may have suffered a head injury in younger years. His brain scans exhibit multiple abnormalities. My theory is that these issues contributed to his current condition.

NINETEEN

RECKONING

"It's like a house of cards . . . falling apart all at once."

1

Ronald, our youthful-looking helicopter pilot, had us back on the ground in Forest Hill in just under fifty minutes.

On the way, I told Lieutenant McClernan what Carly had said about the man in the mask—and then I showed her the text I'd just received.

Carly Albright: played the video for kara. twice. she agrees. insert in left shoe. who's the ace investigator nowww?!

Carly's late husband, Walter—following a nine-year career in the NFL—ran a successful physical therapy practice just outside of D.C. for more than two decades. Before she retired five years ago, Kara worked as a full-time physical therapist in a variety of professional settings, including private practice, hospitals, and home health. When it came to things like shoe inserts and walking with a hitch or however Carly had described it, I had full confidence in my wife. She knew her stuff.

The lieutenant was a bit more skeptical. "We looked at the possibility of a limp. We even ran a simulation with one of the detectives. In the end, we decided that the weight of the garbage bag the man was carrying was throwing off his gait." She promised that she would make some calls just in case, but I was doubtful.

Once we landed, it was only a five-minute drive from the airpark to my house. Someone must've tipped off the press that we were coming.

The photographers were waiting for us, crowding the narrow shoulder of Southampton Road like spectators on a parade route. As we hurried inside the house, a reporter shouted, *"Is history repeating itself, Mr. Chizmar?! Do you* know *the copycat killer?! Have you—"*

I slammed the door, cutting him off in midsentence.

An excited Carly was waiting for us in the foyer. "My husband, Walter, was a three-hundred-pound, loud-and-proud Black prince," she told Lieutenant McClernan, "and I knew every inch of that magnificent body. He was a three-time All-Pro and a Super Bowl winner, and all that with his right leg a quarter-inch shorter than his left. I'm telling you—I'd recognize that walk anywhere."

The lieutenant, looking like the proverbial deer caught in the headlights, nodded her head dutifully and mumbled a response. Then, she turned to me:

"They just emailed the file. Where can we watch?"

"Family room. I'll get my laptop." I started up the stairs.

Kara met me on her way down with Cujo and Ripley trailing in her wake. "Your iPad's on the dining room table if you want to use that." She squeezed my arm. "What's going on? Did he tell you anything?"

"That's just it—we don't know what the hell he told us." I turned around and we walked downstairs together. "I'll fill you in on everything after we're finished watching."

I grabbed my iPad and propped it up against some books on the ottoman. The lieutenant and I sat next to each other on the sofa.

Carly walked into the room and stood behind us. McClernan turned and looked at her—and sighed. "Why not? The more, the merrier."

The lieutenant hit the play icon and we watched Joshua Gallagher shuffle into the interrogation room, the shackles around his ankles clanking, and that wicked-looking grin practically dripping off his face.

Over my shoulder, I heard Carly gasp.

2

"Go back again," I said. "To when he says it's complicated."

The lieutenant tapped the screen, waited a few seconds, and tapped it again.

"I'm afraid that's rather complicated. I don't fully understand all of the details myself."

"I think you're lying to me again."

"I think you know better, Rich. I grew up in a different time, as much as you did. There are things I don't understand."

I pointed at the screen. *"There are things I don't understand.* Do you think he's talking about technology? The burner phone?"

"Maybe . . . but it's still just a phone. Nothing really complicated about it."

"No, no, no. There's something there," I said, jiggling my leg with nervous energy. "It's one of the few times I felt like he was telling the truth."

"Even though five minutes later he as much as admits that he made up this friend of his?"

"That's what he does. You know that. He's all about keeping us off-balance."

She lifted her chin toward the screen. "You really got to him with the carnival barker dig. That's the first time I've seen him lash out like that."

"I let myself get angry and react. I don't usually do that."

We watched the next few minutes in silence.

"He's a masterful liar," the lieutenant said, "but I didn't get the impression that he knew who Sean Phillips was."

"At least not by name."

"Does it surprise you that he watched you all those years?"

I glanced over my shoulder to see if Kara was anywhere nearby. "Yes and no," I said, struggling to find the words. "I'm ashamed to admit it after everything that's happened . . . but in a way, he *always* felt close by."

She didn't say anything to that.

On the video, Gallagher, a wistful expression on his face, reminisced about beating me in a game of H-O-R-S-E.

"I asked the lab to retake his DNA."

I looked at the lieutenant in surprise. "You did?"

"I must be getting senile in my old age."

"The stories are true. I am *the Darkness. I* am *the Boogeyman."*

"Holy Mother of Moses," Carly whispered from behind us. "He's batshit crazy."

I slumped back on the sofa and closed my eyes—searching the distant corners of my mind for the missing puzzle piece.

A moment later, from deep within the darkness, I heard his taunting voice:

"Goodbye for now . . . Richie Rich."

3

Lieutenant McClernan asked me to walk her to her car so we could talk in private. The press across the street was still humming with activity. Cameras flashed. Reporters shouted our names repeatedly until we were forced to sit inside her unmarked sedan to finish our conversation.

"I still feel like we missed something in his fan mail," the lieutenant said, starting the engine and turning on the air conditioner. "That *has* to be how initial contact was made."

A short time ago, the same pair of grumpy detectives had picked up the cartons of mail from our house and returned them to the station. According to the lieutenant, they were already back at it, once again combing their way through the stacks.

"It wouldn't surprise me," I said.

"I know you told me that nothing of importance was discussed . . . but what *exactly* did you and Gallagher talk about during those three unsupervised phone calls?"

I'd been waiting for that question since earlier this morning. "It's kind of embarrassing."

She made that *tsk*ing sound in her throat. "You're already in enough hot water as it is. Don't let that stop you."

I cleared my throat. "At first, we just talked the way we always did. I told him how I was doing. He told me the same. And then I eased into the important stuff, or tried to, anyway. Where was he on this date or that date? Did he have anything to do with this missing person or that unidentified body? I thought he might open up more, knowing that he wasn't being recorded."

"And did he?"

"No. It didn't seem to matter to him."

I watched as a car cruised slowly by the house, blowing its horn at a couple of photographers who'd strayed too far into the street. The driver was Ken Klein. He turned onto Runnymede and swung into his driveway.

"About halfway through the second call, I started asking questions . . . about me."

"What kind of questions?"

"That's the embarrassing part." I took a deep breath. "I asked when he'd first noticed me and what he'd thought. I'd known him for years. Gone to school with him, saw him at parties and at church and around the neighborhood." I shrugged. "I guess I wanted to know if I'd always been marked somehow, or if it really was all about us playing basketball that day."

"Did he answer you?"

"He said that I'd always reminded him of himself. I was quiet. I read a lot and kept to myself. I wasn't much of a follower. But at the same time, I was also athletic and popular. He said my parents were always nice to him."

"How did that make you feel?"

"Even more confused, to be honest. I'd been thinking about it for almost thirty-five years, and I felt no closer to getting an answer than I did back when I started."

"So all of this . . . angst was because you felt like lightning had struck for a second time with Gallagher, and you didn't know why, and it was eating you up inside."

"I've always believed in destiny. I remember, back when Kara and I were dating, we were walking down by the water one night, and I told her that I felt like I was meant to do things that no one else had ever done. Good things. Maybe even great things. And because of that, people everywhere were going to know my name." I looked at the lieutenant, half expecting her to be laughing. She wasn't, so I went on.

"I know most kids probably think the same sort of thing and they're just too smart to say it out loud . . . but the thing was, I really believed it. In fact, I never stopped, and I guess, in a way, it kind of came true." I was starting to sweat despite the air-conditioning. I readjusted myself in the seat. "So, yeah, when it came to Gallagher and Metheny . . . I needed to know *why*. I needed to understand."

"Understand what exactly?"

I thought about it, searching for the right words. "Why they were the way they were . . . and why I fell . . . so strongly into their orbit."

"And now?"

I shook my head. Just once. "I'm done looking for answers where there are none."

4

When I walked into the house, Carly was coming out of the guest suite wearing a bathing suit. It was a one-piece. Bright yellow and black with big fluffy fringes. She looked like a bumblebee. I stopped and stared at her in astonishment.

"Loud-and-proud Black prince. Really?"

"I was only speaking the facts, Richie Rich."

I grabbed her arm. "Don't call me that."

Eyes wide, she said, "Hey, ow—that hurts."

I immediately let go and backed away. "I'm sorry. I . . ."

"It's fine," she said.

"I didn't mean to."

"Then we're even. I didn't mean to upset you."

I couldn't believe I'd hurt her. I felt terrible.

"Get that look off your face, Rich. It's fine. You just surprised me, is all."

"I'm sorry."

"You already said that." She gazed into the family room. My iPad was still propped up on the ottoman. "That video . . . was intense. I don't know how you did that." She shook her head. "I know I couldn't."

"That was the last time."

She looked at me. "For real?"

"For real."

"Well, make sure you tell your wife that." She walked past me and gave my shoulder a gentle punch. "It'll be like an early Christmas present."

5

TMZ✓ @TMZ 19m
In a scene straight out of "The Silence of the Lambs," bestselling author Richard Chizmar visits childhood friend and confessed serial murderer Joshua Gallagher in prison to help police track down copycat killer before he claims fourth victim. FULL STORY BELOW.

6

The three of us spent the afternoon decompressing by the pool. Kara made a salad and cut up some watermelon. I cooked chicken and hamburgers on the grill. Billy took a short break from writing and came down to join us. While we ate, Carly entertained us with stories of her overseas adventures, including the first time she'd tried authentic Indian food. I won't go into the sordid details, but suffice to say it involved an overflowing toilet on a crowded cross-country train ride. Billy almost peed his swimsuit laughing.

Normally, I would have been right there with him, but I wasn't in the mood for silly stories. All I could think about was how I'd cost Sharon Ridgely her job at the penitentiary and how the media was going to go ballistic once they learned I'd bribed a prison guard for classified information. The whole thing sounded so scandalous—and let's face it, it was. The press was going to eat me alive.

And then there was Joshua Gallagher—what was he going to think about what I'd done? Would he be angry? Amused? I honestly had no idea.

And finally, like an anvil strapped to the center of my back, there was the almost suffocating reality that I had yet to confess to Kara. She'd already commented earlier this afternoon about my lack of appetite. I'd led her to believe that my visit with Joshua Gallagher was weighing heavily on my mind—which just happened to be the truth.

Goodbye for now . . . Richie Rich.

But if only she knew the complete story—something I couldn't put off telling her for much longer—there would be hell to pay. I dreaded with all my soul the inevitability of that conversation. I wasn't entirely sure that my marriage would survive it.

After lunch, I slipped in my AirPods and found a raft to float on. I closed my eyes, and the warmth of the sun on my skin felt like a lover's embrace. I dipped my hands in the cool water, wiggled my fingers, and tried to will myself to relax. So much had already happened today and it wasn't even three o'clock. I just wanted to lie here and sleep for the rest of the week—or even longer.

I'm not sure how much time passed before I dozed off.

7

"Oh my God," I said, staring at my reflection in the bathroom mirror. "I look like a fucking lobster."

Kara peered over my shoulder—which was approximately the same bright red hue as volcanic lava—and tried not to laugh. "We have sunscreen, you know."

"You told me not to get my bandage wet. I didn't hear a word about sunscreen." I turned away from the sink and carefully slipped on my pajama top. "Ow. Ow. Ow."

"You want me to put on more aloe?"

"No. I just want to lay on my back in the dark and not move a—"

My cell phone buzzed on the nightstand.

I slowly made my way toward it, my arms held out in front of me like the mummy from the Abbott and Costello movie.

"Hello?"

"You okay?" It was Lieutenant McClernan. "Your voice sounds strange."

"I fell asleep on a pool float this afternoon. I'm fried."

"You should've worn sunscreen."

Suddenly, everyone was an expert. "Yeah, well, I forgot."

"What are you . . . twelve?"

I didn't even bother to hide my annoyance. "Why are you calling me at ten o'clock at night?"

"I thought you would want to know that we've already located two individuals with leg issues similar to what Kara and Mrs. Albright described. Both wear inserts, according to insurance paperwork."

"Who?" I looked at Kara and made a face.

"Your mailman, Daniel Kelly, and Scott Peacher, the guy who built your screened-in back porch. Don't get too excited, though. Both of them have squeaky-clean records and detectives already spoke with them after Anne Riggs's remains were found."

My heart sank. I'd known Daniel and Scott for a couple of years now and they'd never been anything less than pleasant and polite. Another dead end. "So what happens now?"

"We'll send someone out to talk to them again. And keep looking. See who else turns up."

I thanked her for the update and ended the call. After relaying the news to Kara, I turned off the lights and eased myself onto the bed. The sheet was pleasingly cool on my back, which did little to offset the fact that the skin on my stomach and chest felt like it was on fire. I closed my eyes and imagined that I could feel blisters forming on the top of my feet. Telling Carly that she was right about the shoe insert—an admission I was certain would result in another *"Who's the ace investigator now?!"*—would just have to wait until tomorrow.

8

THE BOOGEYMAN LIVES MESSAGE BOARD
(June 19, 2022)
Thread: Suspects
Started: June 19, 2022

Jennifer Tuttle
My stepfather knows someone in the Bel Air Police Dept. He told him today that there are two main suspects. One's a teacher. The other one's some kind of artist from the city. The cops are staking out both of their houses and jobs.

TEDlasso
The butler did it. hahahahahahaha

bonnieDarkness
what if it was chizmar's wife all this time? Could u imagine???

Leesa Hyde
I can't even imagine being married to him. Poor woman!

9

The three of us were eating breakfast at the island in the kitchen when I told Carly about Lieutenant McClernan's phone call.

Yesterday's visit with Joshua Gallagher was the lead story on Channel 11's morning broadcast. There was even video of Lieutenant Mc-Clernan and me walking across the tarmac to her car. To make matters worse, true crime mega-celeb Nancy Grace had announced on her show the night before that she believed Gallagher and I were working together to withhold crucial information from the authorities—"In my heart of hearts, I think they're both complicit," she'd spouted with that snooty, head-tilted-to-the-side look of hers—and overnight the clip had gone viral, and then some. A pinned post this morning on the *Boogeyman Lives* message board read: "*GALLAGHER AND CHIZMAR: Partners In Crime???*"

It was due to this particularly egregious assault upon my integrity— at least this was my theory—that Carly didn't gloat when I told her what McClernan had said. In fact, she was downright gracious about the whole thing. Completely unlike her. After giving Kara a high five over a platter of bacon, she'd merely added, "My Walter comes through again"—and then she never mentioned another word about it.

Kara and I were loading the dishwasher when the dogs began barking in the backyard. A moment later, we heard the clank of the gate being opened and closed, and then Lieutenant McClernan was standing at the breezeway door.

I waved her inside.

"Sorry to interrupt," she said, stepping into the mudroom.

"Want some breakfast?" Kara asked. "There are leftovers still warm on the counter."

"Thanks, I grabbed something at the station." She looked at me— and I could tell by the expression on her face that she was excited about something. Unlike Carly—who'd taken to calling me Mr. Tomatohead all morning—she didn't even mention my sunburn.

"Rich, do you know a woman named Alicia Fetterman? She sometimes goes by Alice."

I thought about it. "The name sounds familiar."

"She's from Edgewood. Six or seven years younger than you."

"If it's the same person I'm thinking of, her family used to live on Bayberry. Her brother . . . John or Jake maybe . . . was a few years behind me. I remember he had a little sister."

"That's her."

"Why?"

"Alicia Fetterman is your mailman's girlfriend. She and Daniel Kelly live together in a house in Edgewood that Alicia rents under her name. Do you want to guess where?"

She was talking so fast I was struggling to keep up. "Where?"

"920 Hanson Road."

I dropped the dish towel I was holding.

My old house.

"Holy shit. You're kidding me."

"Nope. And Daniel Kelly might not have a record, but Alicia Fetterman sure does. She lost custody of her kids fifteen years ago, and it's been a steady downhill slide ever since."

"Wait a minute . . . you think Alicia's the copycat killer?"

"We think she and Daniel may be working together. And before you go stomping your feet and hollering about how you were the one who first brought up the possibility of two people working in tandem—yes, I remember."

"And?" I said, unable to stop the shit-eating grin from taking over my face.

The lieutenant sighed. "And I'm sorry I called you Joe Hardy."

10

As soon as Lieutenant McClernan left, I grabbed my iPad from the family room and did a social media search for Daniel Kelly and Alicia Fetterman.

Alicia came up blank, but Daniel had a Facebook page. From what we could gather—by this time, Kara and Carly had joined me on the sofa—Daniel Kelly was quite the bowling enthusiast, twice divorced, and until two or three years ago, lived with his parents in Abingdon. *Mindhunter* was his favorite television show, Van Halen (with Sammy Hagar at the mic) his go-to band, and when he wasn't binge-watching *The Lord of the Rings* or *Star Wars* movies, he was rooting for the Philadelphia Phillies. There were numerous photographs of him wearing his mailman uniform and even more dressed in a black-and-white bowling shirt with a red lightning bolt stitched across the front of it. We only found one photo of him and Alicia together. They were eating steamed crabs and corn on the cob at a picnic table by the water. They made an unlikely couple. Daniel Kelly was tall and athletic looking with a gentle-featured, thoughtful face. He could've passed for a high school guidance counselor. Alicia Fetterman appeared much older and worn down by the world. Her round eyes were a startling deep blue and didn't match the rest of her face, which was as long and lean as a butter knife. Neither of them was smiling in the picture.

Drawn by the sound of our excited voices, Billy came downstairs, JJ trotting at his side, and quickly took over control of the iPad. I watched in amazement as he tapped away on the screen and within minutes was able to access Alicia Fetterman's arrest record from a public website.

Driving while intoxicated, driving without a license, possession of a controlled dangerous substance, breaking and entering, petty theft, felony theft, threat of bodily harm, assault and battery, trespassing, vandalism, solicitation, possession of stolen property, passing bad checks.

Almost all of them multiple offenses.

At a glance, Alicia Fetterman appeared to be Edgewood's own version of Bonnie Parker—or even worse. There was little doubt that the woman was bad news.

A short time later, the mood in the room dramatically shifted when a giggling Billy almost gave me a heart attack by pretending to send Daniel Kelly a friend request from my Facebook account. Exasperated, I chased him off the sofa and into the living room. He scooted around the coffee table, grabbed a steel poker from the fireplace, and attempted to fend me off. I quickly wrestled it out of his hands and whacked him on his backside with the handle. He collapsed to the floor in faux pain, and the dogs immediately mobbed him, smothering his face in sloppy kisses.

The more Billy laughed, the more frenzied their affection became, the dogs pinning him to the floor, tails wagging in tight little circles. And then we were all laughing and it felt like we couldn't stop—and as I stood there watching, it occurred to me what we were experiencing.

Hope.

For the first time in what seemed like forever, there was a feeling in the air that the nightmare might finally be drawing to a close.

The bad guys (and girls) were going to be captured and punished.

The good guys (and girls) were going to win the day.

And in the end we would live happily ever after.

Hope.

11

After a while, Billy lost interest in our snooping and returned upstairs to the story he was writing, Kara loaded the dogs in the back of her car and headed to the McGirks' for a hike, and Carly left to go shopping at the Harford Mall.

In a matter of minutes, I was left alone on the sofa—without even the pups to keep me company—and I couldn't help but feel abandoned.

For the next couple of hours, I did my best to stay busy so that I wouldn't be tempted to call Lieutenant McClernan for an update.

I answered emails on my laptop.

Shot a game of pool in the garage.

Watched the Gallagher interview for the second time.

Fixed the loose doorknob on the mudroom door.

Made myself a ham and cheese sandwich.

Ate the sandwich.

Watched the Gallagher interview for the third time.

Surfed the internet for any leaks regarding Alicia Fetterman and Daniel Kelly.

Read the last few chapters of a Linwood Barclay novel.

Took a walk around the pond.

Did a load of laundry.

And tried to take a nap.

Finally, at a few minutes past 3 p.m., unable to sit still for even one second longer, I grabbed my car keys and drove to Edgewood.

And was shocked by what I found there.

12

Tupelo Road was blocked off, a Harford County Sheriff's cruiser parked diagonally in the middle of the street. A half dozen police cars lined the shoulder in front of 920 Hanson Road, including Lieutenant McClernan's unmarked sedan. A crime lab van was parked in the driveway behind an old Ford pickup.

For just a moment, I felt a stab of anger inside my chest. *What happened to keeping me updated?* I thought, recalling McClernan's parting words from earlier this morning. *I've only been waiting by the phone all goddamn afternoon.* But then just as quickly common sense prevailed and the anger went away. *After all the shit* you *pulled, Chizmar, you're lucky she's even talking to you . . . and not leading you away in handcuffs for all the world to see.*

Across the street, a cluster of neighbors had gathered on the sidewalk, cell phones aimed at Alicia Fetterman's house. Most of them were smiling and laughing. In a nearby driveway, two little girls in pigtails chanted "*Birdie, birdie, in the sky, why'd you do that in my eye?*" as they took turns jumping rope. There didn't appear to be an adult anywhere in sight watching over them. I spotted only a handful of camera crews in the crowd—which meant that the rest of them were on their way. I didn't have much time.

Lowering my baseball cap to hide my face, I pulled away from the curb where I was parked, swung a left into Tupelo Court, and backed my truck in between two other cars. Slouching down in my seat, I watched a Maryland State Police trooper exit the house carrying a stack of Tupperware containers. A minute later, a second officer appeared in the doorway, a pile of what looked like old shoeboxes balanced in his arms.

My cell phone buzzed on the seat beside me.

Glancing at the caller ID, I answered right away.

"Lieutenant?"

"I'm at the house on Hanson," she said. "I only have a minute."

"What's happening?"

"There's a lot of moving pieces right now. We picked up Alicia Fetterman at Winters Run Inn about forty-five minutes ago. Drunk as a skunk and twice as nasty. A short time later, Detective Gonzalez's crew caught up with Daniel Kelly on his mail route. He saw them coming and bolted into the woods. Took them about ten minutes to bring him in."

"He's got to be guilty if he ran."

"Guilty of something," she said. "We also discovered that before he was transferred to Bel Air, Daniel Kelly delivered mail to Edgewood Meadows for almost six years. Both the Bair and Tucker houses were on his route."

"Which meant they probably knew him . . . or at least recognized his face."

"Correct."

"Which could possibly explain the lack of a struggle when Peyton Bair disappeared from outside of the swim club." I was babbling now, but I didn't care. I was too excited to stop. "And hey, that could also explain the—"

Someone banged on the passenger window.

I let out a startled squeal and jumped in my seat, knocking my cell phone to the floor mat.

Heart hammering in my sunburned chest, I peeked out from beneath the brim of my hat and saw Lieutenant McClernan standing there. She motioned for me to lower the window.

With a great deal of reluctance, I did.

"Hello," she said, mock friendly.

"H-hi . . . ?"

"I watched you park from one of the upstairs windows," she said. "You're not nearly as clever as you think you are."

"I'm sorry. I didn't think—"

"You can say that again. Do you have *any* idea what'll happen if the press sees you?"

I forced myself to meet her eyes. "I was bouncing around the house like a crazy person all morning. I swear—I *mean* it—I was just going to drive by and keep going. I didn't know anyone would be here. Never in a million years did I think you'd get a warrant this fast."

"We've been watching them since last night. They've been *very* busy. At 1:35 a.m., they did a drive-by of your house. Between 2:00 and 3:30 a.m., they drove past a duplex on Landers Avenue a total of four times. First thing this morning, we confirmed that a seventeen-year-old girl with long brown hair lives there."

"Wait . . . you knew last night and didn't tell me?"

She ignored the question. "The judge signed the warrant first thing this morning. We waited until we had them both in custody so they couldn't warn each other and get rid of any evidence."

"How long have you been here?"

"Thirty minutes. Maybe less."

"You find anything yet?"

She met my gaze and lowered her voice. "Yeah. It's bad."

Something inside my stomach began to ache. "Can you tell me if—"

"Go home, Rich. *Now.* Before someone recognizes you and it turns into a shitstorm worse than it already is."

I glanced at the crowd on the sidewalk. In the past ten minutes, it had grown nearly a third in size. A half dozen camera crews were set up on the narrow strip of grass bordering the road. A state trooper was trying to move them back. A blonde woman wearing a bright yellow pantsuit and holding a microphone was interviewing a middle-aged couple. Several teenage boys stood behind them, mugging for the camera. I wasn't entirely sure, but the blonde woman looked an awful lot like Nancy Grace.

"You hear me, Rich?" the lieutenant said. "Go home to Kara." And she started to walk away.

I slid the key into the ignition. "Hey, Lieutenant."

She stopped and turned around. "What?"

"Something Gallagher said yesterday is bugging the hell out of me. I just can't figure out what it is."

"Text me when you do."

And she was gone.

13

O n my way home, the news broke.

To my surprise, it wasn't CNN or Fox News or one of the national networks. It was a small, local radio station—WHGM out of Havre de Grace.

As I merged onto Route 24, the afternoon disc jockey cut away from Tim McGraw's latest smash hit and breathlessly announced that "earlier today two longtime Edgewood residents were taken in for questioning by members of the Maryland State Police Department in connection with the murders of Anne Riggs, Peyton Bair, and Mallory Tucker. A search warrant is currently being served at their Hanson Road residence—which in a bizarre turn of events is the exact same house in which acclaimed *Boogeyman* author Richard Chizmar once lived. There's been rampant speculation that Chizmar and ..."

I turned off the radio.

A few miles down the road, while waiting in line at a traffic light, I snuck a peek at Twitter and TikTok. Sure enough, the story was everywhere. TMZ and Radar had already posted photographs of the house. In one of the photos, Lieutenant McClernan could be seen talking to a pair of uniformed officers on the front lawn. Neither of the suspects' names had been released yet, but it was only a matter of time before one of the neighbors spilled the beans. A *Salon* article confirmed that the blonde woman in the bright yellow pantsuit had indeed been Nancy Grace. She was hosting tonight's show from an outdoor set across the street from the courthouse.

Before today, I hadn't believed that the Boogeyman copycat story could possibly gain any more traction. But I was wrong. For the first time, the press sensed that an arrest was imminent, and they were all scrambling to find the best angle from which to cover it. Toss in the absurdity of the Hanson Road connection, and you had a bona fide blockbuster. A media storm, unlike anything I'd ever seen before, was brewing just over the horizon.

And Joshua Gallagher and I were trapped in the eye of the hurricane.

14

"What's wrong?"

"Nothing's wrong," I said. "I just want to talk to you."

Kara was waiting out back with the dogs when I got home—and she was in a mood. The hike had gone well, she told me. She and Juliet Mc-Girk had chatted the entire time, and not once did the Boogeyman (or his protégé) invade their conversation. They walked for nearly two hours in the woods and fields surrounding the farm—the dogs chasing deer and squirrels to the point of exhaustion—and even saw a baby beaver swimming in one of the creeks.

Then, she'd driven home and everything had gone to hell.

As soon as she'd noticed that the field across the street was practically empty, she'd checked her phone to see what was happening. After skimming several articles about the search underway in Edgewood and seeing that my truck was missing from the driveway, she'd immediately put two and two together. She was just about to call and give me a royal ass-chewing when the dogs heard me pull up.

"Talk about what?" she asked. "Did they find something at the house?"

"Just come with me," I said, taking her hand. "Please."

We sat in the shade by the koi pond. The grass itched my sunburned legs and the mosquitoes were out in full force, but I didn't care. I'd made my decision on the drive home from Edgewood. It was time to tell the truth.

"Are you sure you're okay?" she asked.

"I want you to know that I'm done."

She stared at me in surprise. "Just like that? After all this time."

"I mean it. You were right about everything. All these years, I was looking for something that didn't exist."

"That's . . . wonderful." She looked as if she was waiting for the punch line. "But why now?"

"When I met with Gallagher yesterday morning . . . the things we talked about . . . the things he said . . . it's like my eyes suddenly opened and for the first time I saw everything clearly . . . and I realized that I'd been wasting my time. So much damn time." I picked up an acorn from the grass and rolled it between my fingers. "You've always tried to tell me that some things aren't meant to be understood . . . that sometimes you just have to accept things the way they are and move on. Otherwise, you lose the best part of yourself by never allowing yourself to be happy . . . or content . . . or at peace. I think I did that . . . for longer than I'd cared to realize. I lost that part of myself."

"What did Gallagher say to you?"

"It wasn't what he said." I stopped and thought about it. "Later, when all of this is over, I want you to sit with me and watch the video of yesterday's interview. I want you to see and hear and feel for yourself. And then I want to delete the goddamn file and never think about it again."

"Okay . . . we can do that."

"I've done some bad things. Some *truly* foolish things. And when I tell you . . . you're going to be super-angry . . . and disappointed. I know I am." I'd almost reached the point of no return. "But I want you to know something . . . I thought I was trying to help. I really did. I told myself that over and over again until I finally started to believe it. But I should've known better. Years ago. I know that now." I stared down at the ground. "All this time, I was nothing but a pawn in his stupid, pointless games."

She scooted closer. "Honey—tell me what happened."

"I need to start at the beginning . . . which was a long . . ."

Nothing but a pawn in his stupid, pointless games.

"... time ago ..."

A pawn.

It hit me then like a bolt of lightning from a crystal clear summer sky.

A PAWN.

I looked up at my wife. "I'm really sorry to do this. I promise we'll finish this conversation later. But right now I need to call McClernan."

15

My film agent, Ryan Lewis, had been after me for years to play online chess with him. He mentioned it at least every other time we spoke on the phone. One evening, not long after the COVID shutdown, I finally relented—and bombed miserably. The game lasted barely fifteen minutes and he teased me mercilessly the entire time in the comments section that appeared at the bottom of my computer screen, right underneath the digital chessboard. A few days later, as a sort of mea culpa, I received an email invitation from Ryan to sign up for a popular crossword puzzle website. He knew I loved the *New York Times'* crosswords and wanted to partner up to compete against other two-person teams from all around the country. I accepted, and for about a year, we chalked up a pretty impressive win-loss record. We even won a handful of tournaments. But then, as was often the case with computer games, we eventually grew bored with it and gave up. The final puzzle we completed together consisted of very few correct answers. Instead, we'd filled in the squares with a variety of inappropriate language and childish insults. I still had a screenshot of it saved somewhere on my laptop.

All of those memories had rushed back at me the moment I mentioned the word "pawn" to Kara. Something in the back of my brain had been nagging at me since yesterday morning. When I'd met with Gallagher, I'd taunted him about his affinity for online crossword puzzles because Lieutenant McClernan had mentioned them as one of the perks he'd received in his illicit dealings with Carl Runk.

"And online crossword puzzles—thanks to Runk," I'd said. *"Don't forget about that. Although they must not bring you as much joy since you're only competing against yourself."*

"I think you'd be very surprised at how much joy they bring me."

Joshua Gallagher loved playing games.

Pawn . . . chess . . . cards . . . crossword puzzles . . . online crossword puzzles . . .

Hank Metheny worked in the prison library—where he almost certainly had access to computers.

When I explained all this to Lieutenant McClernan, she practically hung up the telephone on me in her hurry to contact the authorities at Ware State Prison.

Forty-five minutes later, she called back.

"That's how they did it!" she said, her voice buzzing with excitement. "I still think we missed the initial contact somewhere in his mail, but this is how they communicated in real time. This is how they traded phone numbers and started the whole damn thing in motion."

While waiting for the lieutenant to call back, I'd explained everything to Kara and Carly. Between the two of them, they'd asked a dozen questions I had no answers for. Now, they were sitting with me on the back porch, listening to our conversation on speakerphone.

"You found their numbers in the crossword puzzles?" I asked.

"Phone numbers . . . and a whole lot more." I heard the engine of her car roar to life. "Including Wint Singleton's email address."

"Who?"

"Wint Singleton . . . the mass shooter from the furniture store."

I felt my mouth drop open. "You've got to be shitting me."

"I wish I was. We're sailing in uncharted waters, Rich."

"What's next?"

She laughed. "Isn't that enough? I can barely keep up."

"It's like a house of cards . . . falling apart all at once."

"Gonzalez is about to sit down with Daniel Kelly and Alicia Fetterman. I'm on my way there now. We're also looking at guards at Ware State Prison in Georgia. Someone's dirty down there. Henry Metheny had to have help."

"Did you talk to his physician?"

Both Kara and Carly were staring at me. Kara mouthed: *Who's Henry Metheny?*

I waved away the question. *Tell you later.*

"Twice. There's been no change in his condition."

"I think I figured something else out."

"Christ, I'm going to be out of a job soon. What now?"

"The hangman on Peyton Bair's hand. Seven letters. M-E-T-H-E-N-Y."

"Like a house of cards," she said, and hung up.

16

Harford County Sheriff's Department; Deputy Lucas Foster; badge ID# AC-417-36; Monday, June 20, 2022; 3:41 p.m.; the following report depicts Deputy Foster's body camera footage upon entering 920 Hanson Road, Edgewood, Maryland, on the noted day and time. It's reprinted here with Deputy Foster's permission:

```
Bright sunlight gives way to a dimly lit interior. Shaky
images emerge of a residential living room.

"Make sure you glove-up, Foster."

A pair of hands covered in latex gloves swim into view.

"Already done."

The hands are lowered out of frame and we get a good
look at the interior of the room. Outdated sofa. Faded
yellow flower pattern. Two upholstered sitting chairs.
Dark green. A pair of dark-wood end tables, a matching
coffee table, and a floor lamp missing the shade. There
are framed photographs of an elderly couple, as well as
ashtrays, on the smaller tables, and a stack of magazines
on the larger table. The room is neat enough. No clutter.
```

From somewhere offscreen, a male voice: "Take a look in the garage. You're not gonna believe it."

The angle immediately shifts as the deputy swings around to face an open doorway. The doorknob has been removed.

The sound of footsteps as the deputy approaches the doorway, and then we are inside a single-car garage, pivoting in a slow circle.

"For fuck's sake."

The garage has been soundproofed. Lime-green egg-crate insulation panels cover every inch of the walls and ceiling. There are two digital video cameras affixed to the ceiling in opposite corners. In the middle of the room is a large stainless steel embalming table. A narrow trough for collecting fluids is centered beneath it.

As Deputy Foster moves closer, we see that thick metal shackles have been affixed to the table. A pair meant for a person's wrists and another pair meant for their ankles. There is also a metal bracket equipped with a thick leather strap designed to hold a person's head in place.

Lined up against the back wall of the garage are four life-sized mannequins. Adult males, Caucasian, and unclothed. They've been placed shoulder to shoulder in the standing position. Each of the mannequins is wearing a burlap mask with the eyeholes cut out.

17

The following interrogation between Detective Anthony Gonzalez and Daniel Kelly, age 37, took place at the Maryland State Police Department's Bel Air Barracks on Monday, June 20, 2022:

DETECTIVE GONZALEZ: Please confirm that your full name is Daniel Ray Kelly and you have already been Mirandized.

DANIEL KELLY: [nods]

DETECTIVE GONZALEZ: We need a verbal confirmation for the audio.

DANIEL KELLY: Yes.

DETECTIVE GONZALEZ: How long have you resided at 920 Hanson Road?

DANIEL KELLY: For about seven months.

DETECTIVE GONZALEZ: And how long has Alicia Fetterman lived there?

DANIEL KELLY: Three or four years . . . I don't really know.

DETECTIVE GONZALEZ: And who does Alicia Fetterman rent the house from?

DANIEL KELLY: An old family friend, I think. His name is Todd. I've only met him once.

DETECTIVE GONZALEZ: And your relationship with Ms. Fetterman is romantic in nature?

DANIEL KELLY: [unintelligible] I wouldn't say romantic.

DETECTIVE GONZALEZ: You're more than just friends?

DANIEL KELLY: Yeah. [clears throat] Yes.

DETECTIVE GONZALEZ: Was the interior of the garage at 920 Hanson Road soundproofed when you moved in?

DANIEL KELLY: No.

DETECTIVE GONZALEZ: Do you know who soundproofed the garage?

DANIEL KELLY: I did.

DETECTIVE GONZALEZ: When was this work completed?

DANIEL KELLY: A couple months after I moved in. Late February, I think, or maybe March.

DETECTIVE GONZALEZ: Did you make any other alterations to the home?

DANIEL KELLY: I installed cameras in the garage. By the ceiling.

DETECTIVE GONZALEZ: For what purpose?

DANIEL KELLY: So she could record whatever it is she does in there.

DETECTIVE GONZALEZ: She, meaning Alicia Fetterman?

DANIEL KELLY: Yes.

DETECTIVE GONZALEZ: What *does* she do in the garage?

DANIEL KELLY: I don't know.

DETECTIVE GONZALEZ: You understand that you're under oath, Mr. Kelly?

DANIEL KELLY: [nods] I don't know what she does. I'm not allowed to go in there anymore.

DETECTIVE GONZALEZ: We found something very troubling in the freezer in the kitchen. Do you know what that is?

DANIEL KELLY: [nods]

DETECTIVE GONZALEZ: Can you tell me?

DANIEL KELLY: [pause] Ears.

DETECTIVE GONZALEZ: We found something else in the basement bathroom sink. Can you tell me what that is?

DANIEL KELLY: Teeth. Fake teeth.

DETECTIVE GONZALEZ: And do the fake teeth belong to you or Ms. Fetterman?

DANIEL KELLY: Both of us, I guess.

DETECTIVE GONZALEZ: Do you know where the fake teeth came from?

DANIEL KELLY: [shakes head] She got them from somewhere. I think she had them made.

DETECTIVE GONZALEZ: She, again, meaning Ms. Fetterman?

DANIEL KELLY: Yes.

DETECTIVE GONZALEZ: Just a couple more questions and we can take a break.

DANIEL KELLY: I'm very tired.

DETECTIVE GONZALEZ: I know you are. Just another minute. Upstairs, in the corner bedroom, all over the walls, we found photographs and newspaper articles and even some drawings related to Joshua Gallagher. Did you do this or was it Ms. Fetterman?

DANIEL KELLY: Both of us . . . but mostly her. She started before I moved in.

DETECTIVE GONZALEZ: Do you know a man named Sean Phillips?

DANIEL KELLY: [pause] Yes.

DETECTIVE GONZALEZ: What is your relationship with Mr. Phillips?

DANIEL KELLY: Relationship? Uhh, he's . . . a friend, I guess. I met him through Alice. They've known each other since they were kids.

DETECTIVE GONZALEZ: Is he a frequent visitor at 920 Hanson Road?

DANIEL KELLY: Yes.

DETECTIVE GONZALEZ: What's a rough estimate on how many times Mr. Phillips has been to 920 Hanson Road?

DANIEL KELLY: A lot . . . at least twenty or thirty times.

DETECTIVE GONZALEZ: Can you recall the last time he was there?

DANIEL KELLY: [pause] Two nights ago maybe.

DETECTIVE GONZALEZ: And when did these visits begin?

DANIEL KELLY: A while ago . . . before I moved in.

DETECTIVE GONZALEZ: Have Anne Riggs, Peyton Bair, or Mallory Tucker ever been inside 920 Hanson Road?

DANIEL KELLY: [starting to get upset; unintelligible]

DETECTIVE GONZALEZ: Were Anne Riggs, Peyton Bair, and Mallory Tucker alive when they were inside 920 Hanson Road?

DANIEL KELLY: Not . . . I don't want to talk anymore right now.

DETECTIVE GONZALEZ: You need to answer that last question, please, and then we can be finished.

DANIEL KELLY: [long pause] Okay.

DETECTIVE GONZALEZ: Were they alive, Mr. Kelly?

DANIEL KELLY: Not all of them.

18

The following interrogation between Detective Anthony Gonzalez and Alicia Fetterman, age 49, took place at the Maryland State Police Department's Bel Air Barracks on Monday, June 20, 2022:

DETECTIVE GONZALEZ: Please confirm that your full name is Alicia Marie Fetterman and you have already been Mirandized.

ALICIA FETTERMAN: Fuck you, cunt. I want a lawyer.

19

I was sitting in my office above the garage, trying to summon the courage to go back inside and finish my conversation with Kara, when Lieutenant McClernan called to fill me in on how the interrogations went.

Hearing firsthand the atrocities that Alicia Fetterman and Daniel Kelly had committed inside my childhood home was almost more than I could bear. As soon as we hung up, I crossed my hands atop my desk, lowered my head, and said a silent prayer for the victims and their families. And once again, I felt an overwhelming sense of relief that my parents weren't here to learn of any of the details. They would have been devastated.

Alicia Fetterman's and Daniel Kelly's identities had finally been released to the public, and as expected, the media was in a state of hysteria. Family members, old friends, and acquaintances were dragged in front of cameras and interviewed. Jacob Fetterman, Alicia's older brother, had been located in Sarasota, Florida, where he was living with his second wife and working as a carpenter. Ambushed by reporters at a job site, he looked like a deer caught in the headlights while explaining that he hadn't seen his sister in almost twenty years, not since their father's funeral. Shirley Dierdorf, Daniel Kelly's elderly aunt, who lived in a double-wide trailer on the outskirts of Joppatowne, invited a camera crew from Fox News into her living room, where she showed them several photo albums dating back to the mid-1970s. In one of the photos, a faded black-and-white, Mrs. Dierdorf's young son Andy is standing on a porch dressed in a Zorro costume and holding a plastic pumpkin. Right next to him, an eight-year-old Daniel Kelly is wearing a long black cape and a pillowcase mask with the eyeholes cut out. Margaret and Jacob Inderleid, the suspects' next-door neighbors on Tupelo Drive, swore that it was all a big mistake; both Alicia and Daniel were kind and giving people; they'd even dog-sat for the Inderleids on several occasions. Marty Higgins, one of the weekend bartenders at Winters Run Inn, claimed that Alicia Fetterman had slashed two of the tires on his truck not long ago. And all because he'd cut her off a month earlier for getting too rowdy on the dance floor. Higgins claimed he would've pressed charges, but he didn't have any real proof. A veteran reporter from CNN surprised one of the members of Daniel Kelly's bowling team in the parking lot outside his Abingdon real estate office. Tom McConvey offered several curt "No comment!"s before almost running over the cameraman with his car as he sped away.

And of course there were already a number of distasteful memes making the rounds. The most popular—with almost a half million views—was a cartoon mailman featuring Daniel Kelly's photoshopped face. He was skipping down the sidewalk, carrying a blue mailbag over his shoulder. Someone had added rivulets of blood dripping from the bag into a large puddle on the ground. The caption read: RAIN OR SHINE . . . THE MAILMAN ALWAYS DELIVERS . . . DEAD BODIES!

Disgusted, I swiped out of Twitter and put my phone down.

I knew that Kara was waiting for me inside the house.

I knew what needed to be done.

It was now or never.

Before I walked downstairs, I did something I'd never done before: I turned off my phone and left it in the desk drawer.

20

"**S**o let me get this straight," Kara said, following me into the bathroom. "You worked with Harold Metheny at APG back in high school—"

"*Henry* Metheny and it was right *after* high school," I said. "The summer of '83."

"So . . . he remembers you after all these years and contacts Gallagher and they set this whole thing up with some of Gallagher's . . . I don't even know what to call them . . . groupies? And they kill those girls and torment us why?"

I could tell she was getting angry again. "Because they're sick and they idolize Joshua Gallagher and want to be just like him—and because if enough people hear about their story, they'll achieve a kind of immortality."

She stared at me in disbelief. "It's all so . . . twisted and sad."

"McClernan thinks that Daniel Kelly most likely killed the girls, but it was Alicia Fetterman who was pulling the strings. If there was no Alicia, then Daniel Kelly would still be walking around just fantasizing about hurting people."

"And Annie Riggs, Peyton Bair, and Mallory Tucker would still be alive."

I nodded. "And everyone in that furniture store and the two police officers who died in the explosion afterward."

Letting that sink in, she began brushing her teeth in front of the mirror. She looked exhausted. We both did. It had been a long and eventful couple of days, and for the past hour and a half, we'd sat in the dark on the front stoop—exactly where Lieutenant McClernan and I had sat and talked yesterday morning—and I'd held her hand and told her about Henry Metheny and Sharon Ridgely and why I'd done the things I'd done.

She'd cried.

I'd cried.

She'd gotten angry.

I'd apologized.

And then we'd both cried some more.

In the end, she'd hugged me tight and told me that she loved me and Billy and Noah more than anything else in the world and made me promise to never keep secrets from her again.

I'd crossed my heart and promised—and purposely left out the "hope to die" part.

Kara started the water and stepped into the shower.

I stood there for a while, watching the mirrors fog over, thinking about life and death and the ghosts that haunted us all. For a moment, I considered joining my wife but decided to give her space to process everything we'd just talked about.

Instead, I locked the dogs in the bedroom and headed downstairs for a bottle of water.

The family room and kitchen were dark. Carly had gone to bed early. During dinner, she'd told us that she planned to head back to D.C. first thing in the morning. She was thinking about stopping by the *Post* to talk to her boss. Maybe start with a couple of feature articles to get her feet wet. I was thrilled for her, but I had to admit I was going to miss having her around. Go figure.

After grabbing a water from the fridge, I checked the breezeway door to make sure it was locked and punched in the code to engage the alarm system. I was halfway to the stairs when I saw the mannequin sitting in my recliner.

The water bottle dropped from my hand and rolled away into the foyer. Suddenly, I could hear my heart beating inside my chest. I thought of Kara in the shower and sprinted for the staircase.

I never made it.

Out of the darkness, hands of amazing strength gripped my shoulders. They yanked me backward and slammed my head against the wall. A fireball of pain engulfed me as my stitches ripped open. My legs wobbled, then stopped working and I felt myself slumping to the floor.

Before I could reach up and wipe away the blood from my face, I was jerked to my feet and pinned against the wall. Sean Phillips's dead eyes swam into view, piercing my soul, his mottled skin and long white hair greasy with sweat, his hands closing around my neck, dirty fingers squeezing, crushing my windpipe, squeezing harder, choking the life out of me.

"*The Boogeyman is real,*" he whispered, and I could taste his fetid breath.

Darkness swirled and closed in around me.

My body went cold and my head no longer ached.

My eyes began to close—

I'm sorry, Kara. I'm so damn sorry. For everything.

—and then the hands around my throat were suddenly gone and I could breathe again and I realized I was sitting up on the floor with my back against the wall.

I slowly raised my head and opened my eyes.

Kara was standing in front of me, looking ten feet tall. Her hair was wet and she was wearing a bathrobe—the fluffy pink one I'd given her for Christmas last year.

Sean Phillips, the wannabe Boogeyman, was sprawled on the floor at her feet in a widening puddle of blood. The fireplace poker protruded from the back of his misshapen head, his lifeless eyes staring back at me.

21

"You must have a guardian angel watching over you."

I was sitting in the back of an ambulance with Lieutenant McClernan at my side. A physician's assistant was leaning over me, repairing the stitches in my head. Thanks to the lieutenant's intervention, there would be no hospital visit for me tonight. We'd both agreed that my injury—which was relatively mild—wasn't reason enough to turn Upper Chesapeake into a media zoo. Sew me up, slap on a clean bandage, and I'd be as good as new. Almost.

"If you say so," I said, wincing as she snipped another suture.

I didn't know much of anything about guardian angels. All I knew was that for the second time in less than a week, someone I loved— someone I'd sworn to protect—had swooped in at the last minute and saved my life. I didn't know whether to feel grateful or embarrassed. Truthfully, I felt a whole lot of both.

"There you go, Mr. Chizmar," the PA said, giving my shoulder a pat. "You're all finished."

"Thanks, Doc." I started to get up, but she stopped me.

"Not so fast. You need to sit here for another ten or fifteen minutes so we can keep an eye on you." She pushed open the back door of the ambulance. A sea of camera flashes blinded me. The mass of reporters across the street all began shouting at once.

"Oh my God, I'm so sorry," she said as the lieutenant scrambled to close the door. "I thought the fresh air would be good for you. I didn't think—"

"It's okay," I said. "You can leave it open."

Lieutenant McClernan gave me a surprised look. "You sure?"

"I just want to get this over with and get back to my wife."

The lieutenant stood at the rear of the ambulance, blocking the photographers' view. "Kara's inside with Detective Gonzalez and one of our counselors. Billy and Mrs. Albright are there too. They're all taking good care of her."

"Thank you." My shoulders sagged with relief. "I can't even imagine what she's feeling right now."

"You need to make sure she gets all the help she needs." The lieutenant rubbed her eyes and looked around. "It's going to take a very long time to clean this up."

I knew she wasn't just talking about the crime scene. "What happens next?"

"I'll do my best to keep you out of it . . . but no promises. We have a lot of eyes on us now."

"That's not what I meant. I was asking about the investigation."

"Daniel Kelly's a talker. He's our best hope. Alicia Fetterman lawyered up from the get-go. And Gallagher's not saying a word, of course."

"Fuck him." I tried to sit up, but my head suddenly felt like it was made of concrete. "I'm done with Joshua Gallagher."

"Mr. Chizmar, I need you to calm down." The PA was staring at the monitor I was hooked up to. From the look on her face, I could tell she didn't like what she was seeing. "Please just try to relax."

I sat back and closed my eyes, slowly steadying my breathing. When I opened them again, Lieutenant McClernan was kneeling beside me.

"Rich, listen to me . . . you've done enough." She reached out and put her hand on my knee. "Take care of your family now—and yourself. We'll handle the rest."

"I'm sorry . . . I can't do it anymore."

She shook her head. "You don't have to."

22

Later, after Lieutenant McClernan and Detective Gonzalez and the coroner and the ambulance all left, and Carly and Billy returned to their bedrooms, Kara and I sat in the dark on the back porch. Neither of us said anything for a long time—until finally, she broke the silence.

"I've never seen so many fireflies before."

"When I was a kid, I used to believe they were magic."

She squeezed my hand. "Maybe they are."

"We could use some magic right about now." Tears stung the corners of my eyes. "Are we going to be okay?"

"It'll take time . . . but yeah . . . we'll be okay."

"The world doesn't make much sense right now, does it?"

"No, it doesn't," she said. "But we do." She snuggled her head against my shoulder. "Me and you make perfect sense."

After a while, with the crickets and the bullfrogs serenading us, and the dogs curled up at our feet, we fell asleep in each other's arms.

Alice Fetterman *(Photo courtesy of* The Baltimore Sun*)*

Daniel Kelly *(Photo courtesy of* The Aegis*)*

Daniel Kelly *(Photo courtesy of* The Aegis*)*

Alice Fetterman's rented house on Hanson Road; previously Richard Chizmar's childhood home *(Photo courtesy of the author)*

The fake teeth found in Alice Fetterman's basement sink *(Photo courtesy of Maryland State Police)*

Excerpt from telephone interview with Cole Roberts, age 38, correctional officer at Ware State Prison, conducted by Detective Anthony Gonzalez, recorded on June 23, 2022:

DETECTIVE GONZALEZ: According to Dr. Wise, you spoke with Henry Metheny on the night of Thursday, June 2, at approximately 9:45 p.m.

COLE ROBERTS: Yes, sir. I sure did.

DETECTIVE GONZALEZ: And he appeared to be fine?

COLE ROBERTS: He was in a good mood that night. Real chatty. Hank the Tank—that's what some of us called him on account of him being such a big dude—could be real moody. He'd go days without saying so much as a peep, and then wham bam thank you ma'am, he'd talk your ear off the whole next day.

DETECTIVE GONZALEZ: When that happened, what did he usually talk about?

COLE ROBERTS: Oh, with Hank, it could be anything. Old cars, fishing, a bird he saw flying around in the yard. He wasn't real particular on the subject matter. One day, he told me all about the secret treehouse he'd built at his grandparents' house when he was a kid.

DETECTIVE GONZALEZ: Did he ever discuss the crimes he committed? Or his victims?

COLE ROBERTS: Not to me. Maybe some of the other guards, but I doubt it. Most prisoners don't talk about that stuff with us.

DETECTIVE GONZALEZ: What was your overall impression of Henry Metheny?

COLE ROBERTS: [pause] Hank was a weirdo, but he never gave me any trouble. He mostly kept to himself and did his own thing. None of the other prisoners bothered with him.

DETECTIVE GONZALEZ: How exactly was he weird?

COLE ROBERTS: [pause] He just wasn't all there, if you know what I mean. At first, I thought he was slow or something, but then once he started talking, I realized he was actually pretty smart. He was always drawing weird symbols and stuff in the dirt or on colored paper he got from arts and crafts. They looked like kid drawings, but he didn't care. He hung some of them up in his cell. He also said weird stuff sometimes. He'd be right in the middle of talking about how much he missed New York–style pizza or something normal like that, and then all of a sudden, it was like a switch got thrown and he would start talking nonsense.

DETECTIVE GONZALEZ: Did you ever feel that he was dangerous?

COLE ROBERTS: Not right on the surface or in the moment . . . but underneath, oh yeah. Some of the inmates have a kind of . . . vibration about them. It almost feels like when you stand too close to a transformer and your little hairs start tingling? There's a buzz there, a nasty one. Metheny was like that.

AFTER

JULY 2022

1

It's a postcard-perfect summer afternoon and I'm cutting the grass on my riding mower, breathing in the sweet, tropical scent of suntan lotion and singing along with Bruce Robison on my AirPods, when my cell phone buzzes in my pocket. I pull it out and check the caller ID: LIEUTENANT MCCLERNAN.

I turn off the mower and immediately hear laughter and shouting coming from the swimming pool, where Noah and his friends are playing volleyball and talking about girls. Billy's upstairs writing a story. I can see his bedroom window from where I'm sitting. Kara's working in her vegetable garden by the backyard fence. She looks over at me and smiles and gives me a wave. I blow her a kiss.

I haven't spoken to Lieutenant McClernan in nearly a week. Not since the joint press conference we held in front of the barracks. Other than my family and Carly Albright and a few of the Hanson Road boys, I haven't spoken to much of anyone lately. Not even my literary agent or my publisher. It's been a much-needed break amid the chaotic aftermath of what the media is hyping as "one of the most diabolical killing sprees in modern history."

I answer the phone. "Hello?"

"I'm afraid I have some bad news."

The reception is weak. The lieutenant sounds far away. I climb down off the mower and walk to the edge of the pond. A baby turtle, frightened by my shadow, disappears beneath the sun-gilded surface.

"Josh Gallagher . . ."

"He's dead, isn't he?"

"Rich . . . he escaped."

The ground tilts beneath my feet. I lean back against the picnic table, praying that I misheard but knowing I didn't.

"What?! When?"

"This morning. We don't know how yet."

"He was locked up in a maximum security prison under twenty-four-hour guard. What do you mean you don't know how?!" There's fury in my voice. "What *do* you know?"

"We know he left his cellblock with the other inmates at 6:45 a.m. After exercise and cleanup, we have him on security footage at 8:05 entering the corridor that leads to the cafeteria . . . but he never got there. Somewhere between 8:05 and 8:10, he disappeared."

"Into thin air," I say.

Kara is standing at the fence now, staring at me.

"If he disappeared into thin air, then so did a guard named Elgin Matthews. He signed in for his shift at 5 a.m. and hasn't been seen since. He's either dead and stuffed in a closet somewhere or he helped Gallagher escape."

Elgin. My favorite guard with the big smile and the dirty jokes.

"He's not dead," I say. "They're together."

"How do you know that?"

"Call it a Joe Hardy hunch."

"A couple of troopers are on their way to your house. I'll be back in touch as soon as I—"

I disconnect the call, cutting off the lieutenant, and hurl the phone across the lawn in disgust. After a moment, I begin walking toward my family.

2

A carefully drawn hangman figure had been left on the wall of Joshua Gallagher's cell. Underneath, there are seven blank spaces. They are broken up to signify that the correct answer is composed of two words.

— — —   — — — —

3

Later that afternoon, when Lieutenant McClernan hands me the photograph, I barely bother to give it a glance. I already know the answer:

I̲T̲S̲ T̲I̲M̲E̲

author's note

When I turned in the final draft of *Chasing the Boogeyman* to my publisher in early 2021, I had no intention of writing a sequel. In my mind, the story was complete. Joshua Gallagher had finally been captured and was locked up in prison where he belonged. The families of the victims were traveling the long and twisting road to healing their broken hearts. And the rest of my hometown of Edgewood had moved on with their lives. As had I.

Or so I thought . . .

Fast forward to the summer of 2022. It's a gorgeous afternoon, and I'm outside mowing the lawn. For the curious among you . . . yes, we really do have a pond in our side yard. And yes, I've really driven my riding mower into the pond on more than one occasion. But I digress.

Anyway, I remember it like it was yesterday. I was mowing the tall grass by the edge of the woods, listening to Bob Seger on my headphones, when it hit me like a thunderbolt: *Thirty-five years after Joshua Gallagher's Edgewood killing spree, a monster emerges from the shadows to take care of Gallagher's unfinished business—beginning with his sole survivor, Annie Riggs.*

Right away, I knew that the idea was a novel and the Annie Riggs reveal would serve as the opening chapter's gut-punch conclusion.

Almost as quickly, I knew something else—just as I'd done with *Chasing the Boogeyman*, I wanted to play it straight.

As though the entire story had actually happened—and once again I'd been caught right in the middle of it. Only this time the stakes were much higher. I was no longer a fresh-faced college graduate living in my old bedroom on the second floor of my parents' house.

I had my own home now, and a wife and a family and a successful career.

How far would I go to chase the story?

How much was I willing to risk?

Something pretty wonderful and unexpected began to happen once *Chasing the Boogeyman* hit bookstore shelves.

I started hearing from readers all around the world. There were emails. Facebook, Instagram, and Twitter messages. Social media posts. Even a handful of letters in my mailbox.

The vast majority of these readers were kind and generous. Many of them mentioned that they'd grown up in small suburban towns very similar to Edgewood, Maryland. Others claimed that they'd forgotten much of their youth and that the book had brought back a number of precious memories (at the top of the list: popping tar bubbles on the road, jumping ramps on bikes, and hurling dirt clods at passing cars). Some charitable readers even praised *Chasing the Boogeyman* as the scariest book they'd ever read.

But above and beyond all of these amazing comments, there was a single common theme running through most of the letters and posts: Because of the personal nature of the story, as well as the true-crime format and the series of photographs that appeared at the end of each chapter, many readers believed that *Chasing the Boogeyman* was based on actual events.

A large percentage of these readers were downright shocked when they stumbled upon the "Author's Note" at the end of the book and discovered that while the town of Edgewood really did exist and a twenty-two-year-old Richard Chizmar really had moved there in the summer of 1988 with the hope of launching a writing career, Joshua Gallagher and his grisly murder spree were nothing more than figments of a particularly twisted imagination.

Perhaps even more astounding: A number of readers admitted to knowing that *Chasing the Boogeyman* was a work of fiction when they first started turning the pages only to eventually find themselves taking a break in order to Google names and places and incidents to verify their actual existence.

For the kid who'd grown up obsessing over Orson Welles's 1938 radio broadcast of *The War of the Worlds* and watched *The Blair Witch Project* a half dozen times at the movie theater, this kind of reader reaction was a dream come true.

Now that I've invited you behind the curtain, allow me to tell you a few secrets before I go.

As was the case with *Chasing the Boogeyman*, much of what you've just read was taken from my actual life. My wife and sons. Our friends and neighbors. Our dogs and house with the two front doors and the sleepy neighborhoods that surround us. They all exist, and in most cases, very closely resemble the manner in which they've been portrayed within these pages.

The nostalgia-filled passages from *Edgewood: Looking Back* that appear between many of the chapters—almost all of them are the truth as I remember it.

The house I grew up in on Hanson Road; the water tower at the top of Cedar Drive hill; the old wooden bridge at Winter's Run with Kara's and my initials carved into the handrail—all cherished landmarks from the roadmap of my youth.

And finally the Meyers House, with its twin gabled peaks and dozens of windows that watch over the town—it still stands proudly today and lingers in my dreams.

After that . . . well, that's when things start to get a little blurry—and it becomes increasingly difficult to decipher memory from imagination, fact from fiction.

I *can* tell you this without a glimmer of doubt:

My wife, Kara, is every bit as smart and as tough as she's portrayed in this story. And then some.

Is Carly Albright a real person? Sadly, she is not. Carly is an amalgam of several spirited women in my life.

Where in the hell did all the photographs come from? My oldest son, Billy, and I took most of them using friends and neighbors and a handful of local actors as our subjects. Annie Riggs is played by our next-door neighbor, Molly Keele. Peyton Bair and Mallory Tucker are portrayed by the teenage daughters of some longtime friends. The man in the mask captured on security footage walking along the shoulder of Southampton Road is none other than Bill Caughron, my childhood friend and former college roommate, who I wrote about in great detail in the chapter "Chizapalooza." Billy handed over the camera and filled in for the man in the mask behind the springhouse because he was the only one of us who was agile enough to balance on a jumbled pile of rotting firewood. And then there was Mallory Tucker's dead body, staked up beneath a white sheet on a hillside . . . actually, that was me under there. A six-foot-long fence post duct-taped across my shoulders, sweating like crazy and cursing the entire time for Billy to hurry his ass up and take the picture before I passed out.

I could go on. I could tell you about the time I tried to reenact my childhood by crawling into a storm drain on Hanson Road and almost got stuck. Or I could talk about the Hanson Road boys and how much of their immature behavior I detailed in "Chizapalooza" was based on reality or fantasy. Or I could even reveal what was really inside the black garbage bag we photographed by the fire hydrant.

But listen, I don't want to give away *all* of my secrets. Not yet.

After all, as you just recently discovered, there are more stories to tell.

The Boogeyman isn't finished.

I hope you'll join me for the rest of the journey when that happens.

acknowledgments

As is always the case, I had a lot of help writing this book. I would like to express my heartfelt gratitude to:

Kara and Billy and Noah, my *ka-tet*, for giving me so much to live for.

The Hanson Road Boys, for never forgetting where they came from and always having my back.

Brian Anderson, Bill Caughron, Chris and Julie Lepp, Megan Martin, Caitlin McLaughlin, Kara Tyree, Molly Keele, Mike Buckley, Peyton Hagy, Steve Sines, Brian Walker, Jeff Pruitt, John Ruckman, Ryan Parncutt, Annie Keele, Danielle Marie, Tracy Anderson, Andy Sharretts, Buddy Young, Kait Bischoff, Andrew Agner-Nichols, Jerry Larew, Brooklyn Ewing, and Allie Baliko, for lending their talent and trust to these pages.

Gail Cross of Desert Isle Design, for never-ending technical and design assistance.

Paul Michael Kane, for marketing expertise.

Steve King, Bev Vincent, and Brian Freeman, for friendship, advice, and continued support.

Several unnamed members of the Federal Bureau of Investigation, Maryland State Police, and the Harford County Sheriff's Department, for invaluable information.

The *Becoming the Boogeyman* "Street Team," for their hard work and dedication.

Kristin Nelson, for wisdom, guidance, and kindness.

Ed Schlesinger, for his immense talent and generosity.

And last but certainly not least, to all the good folks of Edgewood—for continuing to give me a place I can always call "home."